THE FAVOR

THE FAVOR

NORA MURPHY

MINOTAUR BOOKS
NEW YORK

First published in the United States by Minotaur Books, an imprint of St. Martin's Publishing Group

THE FAVOR. Copyright © 2022 by Nora Murphy. All rights reserved. Printed in the United States of America. For information, address St. Martin's Publishing Group, 120 Broadway, New York, NY 10271.

www.minotaurbooks.com

Designed by Gabriel Guma

The Library of Congress Cataloging-in-Publication Data is available upon request.

ISBN 978-1-250-82242-0 (hardcover
ISBN 978-1-250-82243-7 (ebook)

33614082922559

Our books may be purchased in bulk for promotional, educational, or business use. Please contact your local bookseller or the Macmillan Corporate and Premium Sales Department at 1-800-221-7945, extension 5442, or by email at MacmillanSpecialMarkets@macmillan.com.

First Edition: 2022

10 9 8 7 6 5 4 3 2 1

For my family. And for the survivors, for those who are stuck, for those we have lost.

THE FAVOR

I thought it would make more noise.

Afterward, I ran quickly, but not too quickly, back to the car, my eyes down, trained on the wet darkness of the tall grass, taking each step carefully. I couldn't afford to fall. I couldn't afford to drop the gun. It was too dark, and I wouldn't be able to locate it if I did. When I reached the car, I peeled off a rubber glove to open the door, then slid the gun beneath the driver's seat before removing the other glove. I felt eerily calm. I felt, strangely, nothing. It had to be done. It was simple.

I pulled away from the curb and rolled the driver's-side window down, letting the cool night air whip around me. It felt restorative, cleansing, even though I knew it would do nothing for the gunshot residue on my clothes. The rain that had soaked me as I ran might have helped with that, but I'd read enough crime fiction to know that I would have to clean everything, to dispose of what I could, when I got home.

I gripped the wheel at ten and two, and drove home carefully, like the law-abiding citizen I no longer was.

NOW
FRIDAY, MAY 3

Leah

The key is to go to a few different stores. I used to always go to Jerry's Liquors on Bonifant Avenue. I was a regular. Too regular. Jerry's mouth started to form a thin line when I'd come in. I could see the conflict on his face. He was glad for the business, but judgmental about the frequency of my visits.

Don't make this hard on me, his face seemed to say. *Don't make me feel bad for you.*

Jerry, like so many others, didn't want to be bothered with sympathy.

Now, I don't go to Jerry's anymore. I have five other stores I frequent, all within a fifteen-mile radius of my house. They all think I'm a regular. A devoted and loyal customer.

They're all right.

Typically, I stop by each one once a week. One store per day, Monday through Friday. I like to go in the early afternoon. Always after three, but usually before four.

My favorite store is Pine View Liquors on Main Street. My Friday store. It's a little bit bougie, amid the boutiques selling clothing of the type I used to wear in my former life, and restaurants serving tapas and crepes, and houseware shops displaying accent chairs to be admired but not sat upon, and teakettles to be visible in the background of Instagram posts but never used, and candles to be sniffed but not lit on fire.

In addition to beer and wine and liquor, Pine View sells bags of kettle chips that shimmer with oil, colorful artisanal sodas, and specialty chocolates stuffed with PB&J, salted caramel, and cookie butter. I always load a few such items into my basket to distract the cashier from the fact that I'm a five-foot-four woman purchasing seven hundred and fifty milliliters of Grey Goose vodka, just as I do nearly every Friday.

It was in Pine View Liquors that I first saw her.

It was like looking at myself, nine months ago.

Her jeans were neither light nor dark, just blue. They grazed her ankles and the hems were frayed purposefully, rather than from wear. I knew, because I have the same ones. A flowing white blouse rested at the level of her narrow hips. She was wearing taupe espadrille wedges— closed toe, it was only May, not quite open-toe shoe season in Maryland. But her fingernails were a shiny coral hue and I could only assume her toenails matched. Her deliberately golden blond hair was loosely wavy, as if she had braided it when wet the night before.

This morning, she woke up, undid the braid, sprayed dry shampoo at the roots and hair spray at the ends and tousled them, for a beachy-looking effect. I could almost see her doing it. She may have wound a few sections around a curling iron for several seconds to enhance the definition of the waves, for a more polished look.

That's what I used to do.

Her mouth was twisted in concentration as she inspected the wall of white wine. The sunlight filtered in through the abundant windows on the front wall of the store, reflecting off the silky-looking yellow liquid filling the bottles, and casting a warm glow across her pretty face. The shelves of wine are in the front of the store, near the windows, while the bottles of liquor and the people who buy them, people like me, are relegated to the back.

Finally, she selected two bottles—one Riesling and one sauvignon blanc—and carefully placed them into her red plastic basket, which already held a six-pack of beer. An option for those who like something sweet, and an option for those who don't. But what about everyone in between?

I stood frozen at the edge of the aisle, watching her, but she paid me no mind until she turned away from the shelves. She moved out of the aisle, smiling slightly at me as she passed, the way strangers in close proximity do when they don't feel threatened by the presence of the other person.

I took her place in the aisle, still fragrant from her presence, and added the same two bottles of wine to my own red plastic basket, even though I'm not usually a wine drinker. Not anymore.

The bottles clattered against each other and the Grey Goose as I followed her to the checkout line. I pictured the bottles shattering from the force of being knocked together, the liquid gushing to the floor in a waterfall, soaking my yoga pants and sneakers, the woman turning to look at me as I melted to the floor in embarrassment.

That didn't happen, and I didn't know whether I wanted it to, or not.

But I had become the sort of person to whom something so shameful might happen. Not like her. Her bottles would never shatter. Mine wouldn't have, either, back then.

On my way to the checkout line, I tossed a bag of chips and two chocolate bars into my basket. I didn't notice which flavors I selected, and that's because it didn't matter. I wouldn't taste them anyway.

I stood in line behind the woman, approximately two feet away. I imagined that I was her. I wished that I was.

And I almost laughed. Because I used to be.

I could see a single gray hair sprouting from the back of her head. It must have been missed when she last had her highlights done. I resisted the urge to reach out and pluck it for her.

I have started to notice a few gray hairs on my own head as well, even though I'm not quite thirty. They're mostly underneath the top layers of hair, around my ears. I, too, used to sit in a black leather swivel chair for three hours every few months while a woman whom I knew very superficially would paint odorous dye onto my head and fold sections of hair into the same aluminum foil used to roast potatoes or salmon. It's been a long time since I've done that, and I don't plan on resuming the dreaded ritual any time soon. I have no need for dyed hair, for multifaceted tresses, for covering grays. Not anymore.

Last Wednesday, when I awoke in the basement guest room, my head pounding and pulsing like a car full of teenagers, my mouth bone dry, I pawed at the nightstand, feeling for my cell phone so that I could check the time. Instead, I'd located a small cardboard box. I'd held it inches from my face trying to make out the words.

Permanent hair color. Ash blonde.

I hadn't purchased it, and I hadn't put it there. I'd thrown the box across the room with strength I hadn't known I possessed.

My only thought: *I wish I could lock him out.*

Abruptly, the woman turned. My mouth fell open in surprise and I almost gasped. Almost, but I didn't. I swallowed it down like a shot of vodka.

"Sorry," the woman said. She smiled slightly at me again before moving out of her place in the line and ducking past me.

That's okay, I wanted to say.

I wanted to, but I didn't. Instead, I stepped forward and assumed what had been her place in the line. I glanced over my shoulder to see her standing in front of the rack holding bags of kettle chips. She selected two and put them in her basket. I turned away, focusing on the bald head of the man in front of me, watching as he stepped forward to pay for his six-pack of beer.

I sensed, rather than saw, the woman standing behind me.

Would she, I wondered, rip open one of the bags of chips before backing out of her parking spot, and eat one after the other on her way home, wiping jalapeño flecks and sea salt and black pepper onto her thighs, like I do? Would she open one of the bottles of wine and pour a few fingers into a stainless steel water bottle, waiting patiently openmouthed in her cup holder? Does she have a wine opener on her keychain, along with keys to her car and her house? I do. Even though I'm not usually a wine drinker—not anymore—I do. Would she sip from the cup as she made her way home, feeling the warm blush of relief burgeoning in her belly?

I felt the buzz of attention. I felt an oddly pleasant glow of affection toward this woman standing behind me. I didn't know for certain whether she was looking at me, but I felt like she was. I wondered whether she was taking her turn, taking stock of my gray hairs.

Was she examining my once black but since faded to charcoal gray yoga pants? Was she seeing the way they stretched, with great difficulty, over my thighs and backside, which had, in the not-too-distant past, been as small and taut as hers? Was she looking at my oversized Georgetown Law sweatshirt—one of the few items I possessed that could still be considered oversized? Was she thinking that I looked sloppy and pathetic? Was she a person who had time for sympathy?

When the bald man spun away from the checkout counter, his cardboard carton of beer in one hand, his other tucking his wallet into unflatteringly too-tight jeans, I stepped forward and heaved my basket up and onto the counter.

"How are you?" said the cashier. It was a new cashier, which was strange. Usually Simran works on Friday afternoons. This cashier had a heavy brow and thick, dark eyelashes. He was very young and hopeful looking. He shouldn't be working in a place like this.

"Great," I lied. "How are you?"

"Great," he echoed. He was lying, too.

Why bother asking, I wondered, when we never told the truth?

I looked at his name tag. It said EVAN. I wanted to ask if he had taken over the Friday afternoon shift. I wanted to know what happened to Simran, and why she wasn't working.

I didn't ask about any of these things because, although I wanted to know the answers, I also wanted to enjoy this modicum of anonymity. Evan does not see me as a regular. He does not realize that I'll be back next Friday, around the same time, purchasing another bottle of vodka the approximate height of my calf.

He tucked each bottle, three this time—I was splurging today—into a brown paper sleeve with exaggerated care, before placing them into a cardboard box. He arranged the bag of chips and chocolate bars in the opposite end of the box after swiping them across the scanner.

He looked up at me, something not unlike surprise registering on his face. It was as if he had become so subsumed in packing up my purchases that he forgot I was there.

"May I," his voice cracked, "see your identification?"

I smiled and reached into my wallet. I slid my driver's license out and handed it to him.

"Thanks," he said, holding it in front of his eyes, making a show out of inspecting it, though I doubted he was even looking at my birth year or performing the requisite calculation.

"No problem. And thank you," I said. "I'm flattered."

It was a stupid thing to say, a shockingly unoriginal excuse for a joke, usually reserved for people much older than twenty-nine.

He laughed anyway, then handed my license back to me.

My total came to $93.40—much more than I usually spent—and I handed over five twenties. He accepted them like I had just handed him Monopoly money, froze for a few seconds, then sprang into action, punching at the keyboard, tucking the bills into their compartments in the money tray and pulling others out. He dropped some coins into my hand and I promptly let them fall into the *Take a penny, leave a penny* tray on the counter. I despise coins. I always have. Dirty and slimy and covered in germs and memories.

I feel the same way about cash, but I've no choice but to use it.

I can use the credit cards at my stores, and sometimes I do. But the credit cards provided too much information. Information I didn't want my husband to have.

I slid the bills into my wallet and wrapped my arms around the cardboard box. I pulled it off the counter.

"Thank you," I told Evan, and he smiled at me. I tried to smile back, but my lips wouldn't obey. My heart was thudding in my chest. I could practically hear it, pounding, echoing, like someone dribbling a basketball in an empty gym. I turned away from the counter and my eyes were dragged toward the woman waiting in line behind me, as though compelled by a magnetic force.

Her eyes met mine, for just a second, before she flashed a small smile, identical to the one she had displayed when we had passed in the wine aisle, and stepped forward to load her items onto the counter.

I felt a faint blush creep across the back of my neck. I didn't want her to think I was strange. I didn't want to be caught watching her. And yet, I couldn't seem to stop. It felt like looking into a mirror, to an earlier time. A simpler time. A happier, and more hopeful time. A time before I'd begun to drown in shame, to attempt to push myself to the surface and gasp for air.

I hurried toward the front door and burst out of the store, my last few seconds of quickness, of vigor, before the lethargy and inertia would set in.

I walked to my Lexus SUV and placed my box on the front passenger seat, before climbing into the driver's seat. I had purposely parked far from the doors to the store. It was my usual spot, by the hedges around the side. I park where I'm less likely to be seen. I reached into the box and lifted the paper bag concealing the bottle of vodka. I twisted the top loose, before pouring a few shots into the empty water bottle resting in my cup holder. I took a sip, feeling the lukewarm liquid run down my throat. It began to burn as it reached my empty stomach. I tore into my bag of chips, and crunched down on a handful, crumbs falling onto my lap.

"You are such a slob," I said. "Disgusting slob," I added as I watched her exit the store. "So sloppy," I threw out. That one he'd said just the other day. I laughed as the woman loaded her brown paper bag into a navy Lexus SUV, a model or two older than mine.

I wiped my salty hands across my yoga pants and turned on my car. When the woman backed her SUV out of her parking spot, I did, too. I could have pulled out of the parking lot right behind her, but I waited for a car to pass first, so that there was a buffer.

I hadn't made a conscious decision to follow her, but that was clearly what was happening, and it felt as if I were powerless to stop. Anyway, she was headed along the same route I take to get home. It could have just been a coincidence that I was one car behind her.

It wasn't, but it could have been. I didn't know her, but I wanted to. Know about her, at least.

It wasn't a recognition. Not quite. It wasn't that we'd ever met before. It was more like I'd seen her in a dream, even though I no longer dreamt.

There was something about this woman.

She looked the way I used to look. She drove a car just like mine. Did she live in a house like my house? What went on inside? Did things look idyllic from the outside? Was there hate and fear behind the pristinely painted front door? Or, was there love? Was there perfection? Was there everything I used to have? Everything I'd thought I had?

I needed to know more.

When we reached River Road, we passed the street leading to my neighborhood, continuing for another mile, before her turn signal began to blink. I slowed until she had made the left turn onto Orchard Grove, and then I followed.

The neighborhood appeared to be identical to my own—single-family, Colonial-style homes between three to four thousand square feet, two-car garages, close-clipped green lawns, professional landscaping, and luxury cars. I could tell that, like in my own neighborhood, paved walking paths were woven amongst the houses, connecting the streets together. There weren't many people out. The younger kids weren't yet out of school, and the nannies and au pairs hadn't yet emerged from the houses to retrieve them. The homeowners weren't home. Still hard at work, earning the money that allowed them to afford a neighborhood like this.

After hanging a right onto Apple Blossom Lane—all of the street names seemed to reference some type of fruit—I saw the woman's navy SUV turn into a driveway up ahead. I kept driving, but I glanced toward the house, committing it to memory, as I sped past. It was light brick with green shutters and a side load garage. Several large terra-cotta pots exploding with pansies decorated the front steps.

I turned onto Pear Tree Circle planning to find a cul-de-sac in which to turn around, but in looking around me, I realized that Pear Tree Circle ran behind Apple Blossom Lane, and I recognized the light brick of the woman's house. I cruised a little farther down the road to a spot that wasn't directly in front of any houses, but also wasn't too far from one, such that my car could still possibly belong to someone's guest. The back of the woman's house, glass doors, a patio, were visible from my parking place.

Anyway, I wasn't worried. There'd be no complaints about my Lexus parked on the street. No complaints about a thirtyish blond woman sitting inside.

Besides, it wasn't unusual, at least in my neighborhood, for nonresidents to arrive by car, park on the street, and stroll along the walking paths, pretending that they belonged, wondering what life would be like if they did. The residents didn't like these outsiders who enjoyed the perfection of the neighborhood without paying upward of $4,000 a month on a mortgage, but there wasn't much they could do about it besides cast disapproving glances as they went out for walks of their own.

I could simply be parked here, typing out a work email, before heading out for a walk. It wasn't a bad cover story.

I drained the rest of my drink and turned my attention to the back of the woman's house. I could see a flagstone patio with a built-in firepit, around which several Adirondack-style chairs were arranged, and a wicker sofa and armchairs with white cushions, which seemed highly impractical for outdoor furniture. I wondered whether she brought them inside every night, to protect them from the elements, as if they were her little children. I wondered whether she had any children.

I covertly poured a few more fingers of vodka into my water bottle and took a sip while I waited. For what, I was not sure.

Finally, I saw a car park on Apple Blossom Lane outside the woman's house. It was a silver sedan, and through the trees lining the street, I caught glimpses of a woman approaching the house. She was petite and had a sleek black bob. Seconds later, another car pulled up. A door slammed, and the woman who had been approaching the house stopped, waiting for her friend to catch up. This woman was blond and very tall. They disappeared from my view, and again, I waited.

I drained my water bottle that wasn't used for water and wondered whether I should just leave. I had no idea what I was doing or why. I was steeling myself to pull away from the curb and make the short drive home—I was confident I could manage the trip even after several drinks—when I caught a glimpse of movement on the patio. The trees were sparse. There was nothing to obscure my view, but for the distance between my car and the woman's back door, across her backyard and the county land abutting it.

Three women, the blonde from the store and her two friends, had emerged from the French doors at the back of the house. The dark-haired woman was carrying two bottles of wine, the tall blonde had three wineglasses tucked between her fingers, and the other blonde, the host, was holding a basket full of kettle chips.

I watched as they settled down onto the outdoor seating. The woman from the store perched on the edge of an armchair while her friends sat down on the sofa across from her. They poured themselves healthy servings of wine and deferentially reached into the basket for chips.

I wanted something sweet to balance the salt and spice from my own chips, so I used my keychain to uncork my bottle of Riesling and poured a helping into my water bottle. The taste of the vodka lingered, but it still satiated my craving. I continued my reconnaissance of the women. After fifteen minutes, they had all sunk deeper into the furniture, becoming loose and heavy from the wine. The chips lay forgotten in the middle of the table. When the tall one threw her head back and laughed, I found myself smiling along with them, wishing I was one of them. I wished I was the sort of person who could spend a Friday afternoon sipping wine and chatting with her friends. I wished that I still had friends. The other armchair was empty, almost as if it were waiting for me.

The French doors opened again, and the blond woman from the store jumped. I did, too. I hadn't seen any other cars approaching. I'd been so engrossed in the little party to which I hadn't been invited.

This time, it was a man who emerged from the house. He was tall and fair haired. He wore a navy blazer over a Kelly-green crew-neck sweater.

The woman from the store popped up from her seat like she'd been burned by it. The man strode toward her, bent his head downward, and they kissed so briefly it was almost lost in a blink. My eyes were becoming heavy from the liquor and wine, but I could swear that she didn't want to kiss him. The man stepped toward the friends and bent again to bestow a superficial cheek-kiss upon each of them. Everyone was all smiles and polite conversation, but there was something quite spurious about the whole scene. A cloud of tension hung over the little group, and when the man turned and went back inside, it only dissipated slightly.

The women continued to sip their wine and chat. A dog began to bark. A rumbling in the distance jolted me, and I was no longer sitting on the patio with them. The fantasy had slipped through my fingers and was replaced with reality. The wine was mingling with the Grey Goose and stomach acid. It felt like a corrosive combination, and I swallowed the urge to vomit. For once, I wished that my water bottle actually held water. I looked up to see a school bus rolling down the street, toward my car. I turned on the engine and checked the time on the dashboard. 4:02.

The fun was over anyway.

I put my cardboard box on the floor of the car, hoping it would be less visible there, and that it wouldn't spill. I did not want to spend the rest of my afternoon cleaning wine off the floor. It would be a nightmare to get the smell out. Not that the smell would bother me, but I expect it would get me arrested on the spot if I ever got pulled over, and that could not happen.

Drinking was an approved activity when at home, behind closed doors. But drinking in the car? Drinking while driving?

That could get me killed.

Although, not in the manner one might expect.

I glanced at the women one last time before I pulled away from the curb. The blonde from the store was perched at the very edge of her chair again. Her shoulders were hiked upward, toward her ears. The light, the vivacity, had left her face.

I was no longer sure whether I wished I was her.

McKenna

It was my fault. As always, it was my fault.

I never should have told my friends that we'd had a new patio installed at the back of the house. But I'd used that as an excuse last time they had suggested we get together.

Alyssa had asked me if I wanted to grab lunch at one of the little cafés on Main Street. "I already talked to Mina," she'd said on the phone that morning. "She's free, too. Daniel is going to watch the baby."

"Oh, I'd love to," I had told her, "but we have workers at the house, finishing up our new patio. I can't leave them unattended."

It had been a long time since I'd seen my friends. I had successfully made excuses week after week, but I was running out of material. I prayed they weren't onto me. I prayed they wouldn't drive by my house to see that there weren't in fact any workers there or that the patio was already finished.

"Why do you have to be there?" Alyssa had asked. "They're not inside the house. Why can't Zack stay home?"

"He's working," I had told her, which was another lie. I had ignored her first question, and she didn't press.

"Okay," she said. "Next time."

And this was next time. In our group text message thread, Mina had suggested a Friday afternoon get-together. Daniel's parents were in town and she needed a break from them. Alyssa had taken the afternoon off work.

It was easier for me to avoid them when they suggested weekend activities. I could claim plans with Zack. Special dinners downtown. Shopping trips at City Center. Weekend getaways. Sometimes it was true. Sometimes it wasn't. Then, I would have to hide for the weekend, fearful that if I went anywhere, I might run into one of my friends or someone else with whom we associated and who might casually mention seeing me out and about. Zack was aware of everything, of course, and he gamely played along. Almost too enthusiastically. He would order food to be delivered or run out for takeout. He would suggest movies we could rent from our family room.

My friends had proposed a happy hour at someone's house, and I'd had no choice but to agree. Mina's wasn't an option. The whole point was for her to escape her guests. Alyssa's one-year-old would be at her house with the nanny. There'd be no avoiding her. She was going through a phase where she was glued to her mother whenever Alyssa was home. I had suggested we go out to a restaurant, but Alyssa had suggested my house instead.

We want to check out your new patio! It's supposed to be a nice day. We can sit outside, she had texted.

What was I supposed to say to that?

I had no choice but to agree. That's what I told Zack.

"Of course," he had replied. "You should invite them over to enjoy the patio." He had chuckled. "That's why we had it put in. To entertain."

But we both knew that wasn't the truth.

I'd made my usual Friday trip to Pine View Liquors. In addition to Zack's six-pack of beer, I had purchased two bottles of wine: Riesling for Alyssa and sauvignon blanc for Mina. I'd send whatever remained in the bottles home with them. The chips had been an afterthought. An impulse purchase. Every good host, every perfect wife, knew that when serving alcohol, one should also serve something on which to snack.

I'd been making my Friday afternoon pilgrimage to Pine View Liquors every week since January. Zack was a regimented person. He drank only on the weekends—Friday evening, Saturday afternoon, into the evening, and Sunday afternoon. One six-pack of beer per week. He used to stop at the liquor store on his way home from work on Fridays, but once I stopped working, that became my responsibility. What else did I have to do? He would send me a text message during the day, or give me a call, to check in, and to tell me what he wanted me to buy for him.

My friends arrived at the same time, precisely three o'clock, just when they said they would be there. They were on their best behavior, having essentially forced themselves into my home.

We carried our provisions out to the patio.

"Be careful of that loose stone," I said, as we moved toward the furniture. "I tripped on it the other day. I'll have to call the company that installed the patio to come back out to fix it."

Perhaps that could serve as an excuse in the future, to avoid plans.

Mina and Alyssa sank onto the sofa, and I perched on a chair across from them. I was embarrassed when I realized that the wine wasn't chilled. I should have thought of that. I should have purchased the bottles the day before, as soon as Zack had given his approval for our plans. But a Thursday trip to Pine View Liquors would have been a deviation from routine, and Zack wouldn't have made his beer selection by Thursday, so I would've had to return to the store on Friday, too.

Mina and Alyssa had waved my apologies away like stray gnats floating in their faces.

"Are you kidding?" Mina asked. "I could not care any less about the temperature of this wine. Do you know how long it's been since I've had a drink?" To prove her point, she moaned as she took a sip. "I pumped two bottles of milk for William this morning just so I could do this.

I'll probably have to pump and dump when I get home, too, but I don't care. It's worth it."

Alyssa topped off her glass and pointed the bottle at me. I shook my head. I shouldn't be drinking at all. I knew that. But Zack was at work. I would wash and dry my glass before he got home.

"How are you doing with that?" Alyssa asked. "The breastfeeding."

They both looked at me. *Is this okay?* asked their eyes. *Is it okay to talk about this?*

I nodded bravely. *It's okay.*

"It's fucking hard," Mina said. She leaned back against the white cushions of my outdoor sofa and closed her eyes.

I had wanted the navy cushions. The white ones would be too hard to maintain, I'd told Zack. *I like a challenge,* he had said. But, of course, it was my challenge, not his.

"I went to see a lactation consultant again this week," Mina continued. "She should be solely credited with my persistence. There is no way I would still be nursing if it weren't for her. Her and the intense guilt I feel every time I think about stopping."

"I know what you mean," Alyssa said. She swirled her wine around in her glass. We all watched the yellow liquid spin until it crashed down in tiny waves. "The guilt was the only thing that kept me going as long as I did. I was certain that if anything ever went wrong with Layla, it would be all my fault because I didn't nurse her until her first birthday. I would go down as the worst mother in history. My face would be plastered all over the internet."

Mina groaned. "Don't say that. There is no way I can keep this up until he's one. I know that's what doctors recommend, but I just don't think that is realistic. I mean, hello? We have jobs."

They fell silent. I could tell that they were thinking about the fact that I had neither a child nor a job.

"It was definitely hard," Alyssa said. "My company was really flexible with me. I still don't think I've worked an eight-hour day since Layla was born. Anyway"—she cleared her throat—"how are you doing, McKenna?"

I ate a chip. "Great," I said.

I could see her mind working behind her hazel eyes. How to ask what she wanted to know without just coming out and saying it? She tried again. "Are you, um, still trying?" she asked.

I ate another chip. It went down as easily as sawdust. "Mmhmm," I lied.

"I know it's hard," said Mina. But she was lying, too. She had gotten pregnant on the first try, and that pregnancy had resulted in the birth of William, who was now almost three months old. No miscarriages for her. No struggles with fertility.

"Good luck," Alyssa said. She leaned forward and squeezed my forearm. "I know it will happen for you."

"Thanks," I said. I smiled bravely again. I hoped she was wrong.

The French doors clicked as one side opened. My stomach felt like it had dropped straight out of me. I put my wineglass down on the wicker coffee table in front of me, pushed it toward the middle. But it didn't matter. There were three people and three glasses. It could only be mine. He would smell it on my breath. He would taste it on my lips when he kissed me, with the salt of the chips, which he stepped forward to do.

"Hi, honey," he said. My husband turned and bent down to kiss Alyssa and Mina on their cheeks. "Please, don't get up," he said. "And don't let me interrupt. I won't bother you ladies."

He asked Mina about William and Daniel, and he asked Alyssa about Layla and Kent. He smiled his dazzling white smile.

I looked at the faces of my friends as they smiled back at him. I knew they saw a tall and handsome man, well-dressed and polished and successful. But when I looked at him, all I saw was danger.

"I'll be no bother," he said again. "I'll just be in my office, working on my notes from my sessions today." He flashed one last brilliant smile before disappearing through the French doors through which he'd come.

My friends waved to him, and then continued chatting. I tried to focus on them, to hear their words, to see their faces, but I couldn't. Their stories felt inane and superficial. Their presence was unwelcome. I wanted them to leave, but at the same time I wanted them to stay forever. I sat immobilized, perched on the edge of my chair, waiting for time to pass.

Clearly, he had come home early to try to catch me. Clearly, he had done just that.

Abruptly, Mina pushed the basket of chips away from her. "Ugh, please get these out of here," she said. "I'm trying to lose the rest of my pregnancy weight."

Grateful for a distraction, a reason to move, I snatched the basket off the table. "Sure," I said. "I'll just put it in the house."

I realized belatedly that I'd done the wrong thing. I should have said, *You don't need to lose a single pound. You look great.* I should have considered that perhaps Mina hadn't *actually* wanted me to take the chips away. But I was becoming desperate for something to happen. I now wanted this get-together to be over. I welcomed the inevitable.

I tossed the basket onto the kitchen island. The house was silent, but not in a peaceful way. It was like the stillness in the air before a thunderstorm rolled in. Zack was nowhere to be seen.

When I returned to the patio, Alyssa and Mina were standing up, brushing off their jeans, and draining their wineglasses.

"We should get going," Alyssa said. "Thanks for having us over." She was smiling, but I could tell she was wondering why she had worked so hard to make plans with me.

Maybe next time she wouldn't try so hard. It was probably for the best.

We carried our wineglasses inside and I loaded them into the dishwasher. I insisted that they each take the remnants of the bottles of wine. "Please," I said. "I'm not drinking much these days. Trying to be careful." I smiled meaningfully.

I walked them to the front door and embraced each of them facetiously, the way one might hug a person with foul body odor, although they both smelled lovely. "We will have to get together again soon," I said, and they agreed heartily. That time, we were all lying.

I closed the door behind them, flipped the lock, and returned to the kitchen. Zack joined me there seconds later. He stood at the kitchen island, gripping it with both hands. His knuckles were turning white.

"Wine, huh?" he asked. "How much did you drink?"

"I only had one glass," I said. My eyes flitted around the room, looking for something with which I could busy myself, but there was nothing. It was immaculate, everything in its place. "Just a little glass."

His knuckles turned even whiter. "Like how earlier this year you had 'just a little stomach virus'?"

I should have known that was what he would say. I should have seen it coming. I should have been prepared. I never should have had the wine. I never should have had my friends here.

I looked down, inspecting the swirls in the marble countertops. "I'm sorry," I said. "You're right. I don't know what I was thinking."

"And chips?" he asked. He nodded toward the basket resting in the middle of the island.

"Oh," I said. It was another mistake. I knew that it was. "I just wanted something for my friends to snack on. I grabbed them from the store when I bought the wine."

"But you ate them," he said. It wasn't a question.

"Just a couple." I winced. *Just a couple chips. Just one glass of wine. Just a little stomach virus.*

"I don't want my perfect wife gaining weight," he said. "Not until she's pregnant."

"I know," I said. I wrapped my arms around myself. "I'm sorry," I said again.

He moved toward me, and my heart pounded. But he wasn't going to hit me. He didn't hit me. Not my husband. When he got close enough, he bent to plant a kiss on my forehead. "Good," he said.

He walked away, but first he reached for the basket of chips on the table. I thought, for a second, he was going to take one and pop it into his mouth. But then I felt silly, because he grabbed the basket and threw it against the wall. The chips scattered and skittered across our dark, hand-scraped hardwood floorboards. The basket spun in a tight circle before finally coming to a rest. We both stared at the mess for a few seconds.

Zack turned away. "Clean that up, would you?" he asked as he headed down the hall toward his office. "I need to finish my work."

And the saddest part is that I was just happy to have something to do.

MONDAY, MAY 6

Leah

The weekend had oozed slowly by like molasses from a tipped-over jar, just like it always did. All I could think about was when I could next watch her. I was desperate to understand what I'd seen. What I thought I'd seen.

Surely, the tension had been real, not imagined—a false premise induced by vodka and wine, by my own circumstances.

I was alone for the week, and for that I was eternally grateful. It was the only thing that got me through the weekend. I couldn't watch her with Liam home, but knew I'd be free to go as much as I wanted come Monday.

More importantly, I'd be free of him. It would just be me in the house. Most people would be disappointed if their spouse was out of town for the week, visiting their mother in honor of Mother's Day.

Most people don't have a spouse like mine.

He had asked me to go with him. In a brief moment of courage, or stupidity, I wasn't sure which, I'd told him he'd need to come up with an excuse for my absence because there wasn't a chance in hell I was going. That had made him angry, but he had agreed. He was still trying to behave.

For now.

I awoke to a pounding head, which was typical. I couldn't remember the last time I awakened feeling refreshed and pain free. I reached for the bottle of Excedrin I keep on my nightstand for just that reason, but my hand didn't lay purchase. I cracked an eye. The bottle was gone. In its place was a note.

Didn't want to wake you. Will text when I land. See you Friday p.m. Be good. Love, Liam

I ripped the note in half, stacked the pieces on top of each other and ripped them in half again, then again and again, until the shreds formed confetti that rained down onto the bed.

I closed my eyes so that I could focus, and I listened. Despite the note, I wanted to be certain.

The house was silent. He was gone, and I hated that he'd been in my room at all.

Be good, which meant, *Stay here. Don't leave.* It meant that if I left, it might be the last thing I ever did.

It meant that if I left, my mom would be in danger, too.

I climbed out of bed and moved toward the door, my heart in my throat. I breathed out a sigh as the knob turned.

I showered in the basement guest bathroom, my bathroom. I spun the dial, turning the water to its coldest setting, and let it pound onto my skin while I counted to ten—the number of months I've been married to Liam. It was punishing, but I felt like I deserved it. I dressed in a clean pair of yoga pants and a long-sleeved T-shirt I'd collected at the finish line of a half-marathon I had run a year ago, trying not to think about how I'd fare if I attempted the same feat now, nor of the racks packed with sleek navy and black suits and silky blouses hanging in my closet two floors up.

Upstairs, I brewed myself a cup of coffee and peered into the liquor cabinet, parked against the back wall of the dining room. I located a bottle of Kahlúa and tipped it over my mug, adding a healthy pour to my coffee, before returning to my basement bedroom. Strangely, the room had become both my jail and my safe place, within the house that no longer felt like a home.

I sat down on the edge of the bed and switched on the flat-screen television hanging on the wall across from me, then flipped through the channels, settling on a news program. The anchors' voices melded and swirled in my head. They may as well have been speaking a foreign language I couldn't understand.

When I had finished my coffee, I rinsed the mug in the bathroom sink, then stood at the vanity, filling the mug with water and drinking it down, cup after cup. I stared at my reflection. It looked the way I felt— tired, gray, and cadaverous. My head was still pounding. I still needed Excedrin.

I pulled my hair back into a ponytail, tugged a baseball cap over my head, and placed my cell phone on the island in the kitchen before heading into the garage. Liam's silver BMW was still there. He must have taken an Uber or Lyft to the airport. I slid past it and climbed into my SUV.

I drove to the nearest CVS where I purchased a bottle of extra-strength Excedrin and a bottle of water. I paid with a debit card, requesting forty dollars of cash back when I made the purchase. It was all I could afford to do. Any more might raise alarm. Any more, and he might ask to see the receipt, which I crumpled and dropped into a trash can as I left the store.

If he happened to ask, I'd apologize. *Sorry,* I'd say. *I accidentally tossed it.*

When I returned home, I'd hide the cash in my bedroom. My Escape Fund. Except, it was difficult for my Escape Fund to grow into anything meaningful. Usually, it was diminished on alcohol purchases.

Back in the car, I swallowed three pills. I stopped at a gas station to fill up my car. And then, what? I felt like a kid with an English class assignment to write an essay, and the day was a blank page. I didn't know how to fill it.

Before I lost my job, the days felt too short. They never seemed to have enough hours to accomplish everything I wanted to do. There were my morning runs, my client meetings, hours spent drafting contracts and agreements, conference calls with opposing counsel, lunches with colleagues. In the evenings there were networking happy hours and bar association events with judges. Now, the days felt far too long. If I could, I would trim off a few hours as if they were the ragged split ends of my hair.

With no other ideas about how to pass the time, I drove to her neighborhood. I cruised by her house first, but I didn't see any action, so I returned to the approximation of my parking spot from Friday afternoon. I looked out at the flagstone patio and impractical white cushions. But that's all there was to see. The woman didn't emerge, and with sunlight reflecting off the windows, I wasn't able to see inside the house.

After fifteen minutes, I pulled away from the curb and drove to my Monday store, Normandy Heights Liquor, in a strip mall ten minutes away. I was earlier than usual, and I didn't recognize the cashier working at the counter, which was just fine with me. I returned to my car with my bottle of vodka concealed within a brown paper sleeve and drove home. I'd finished Friday's bottle over the weekend. The wine, I had poured down the drain in the bathroom. I'd concealed the empty bottles beneath my mattress, and I'd drop them in our next-door neighbor's recycling bin late at night or early in the morning, before collection. The wine had made me feel sick Friday night, and I hadn't wanted to drink any more of it.

There was abundant alcohol in the house, but Liam kept tabs on that alcohol. He could watch the levels in the bottles dip down each day. He could use that information against me. It was better for me to have my own stash, some of which was purchased with cash, about which he didn't know.

Back at home, I filled a glass with ice and vodka, adding a splash of Perrier. Due to Liam's absence, I enjoyed the luxury of sliding the bottle into the fridge. I'd have to remember to take it out before he got home. It was a ridiculous thought, because there was no way it would last until Friday. I'd probably be making a trip to my Wednesday store in a couple days.

I carried my drink to bed and climbed in. I sipped it slowly, letting the warmth wash over me. It brought a modicum of comfort, but far less than it once did. I was having to consume more to achieve the feeling I used to get from a couple of shots' worth. But by the time I finished my glass, my eyes were becoming heavy, and I drifted off into a light but mercifully thought-silencing sleep.

When I awoke, the room was far darker. I had slept the afternoon away, sunset was approaching, and that was as close as I came to accomplishing anything worthwhile these days.

Pulled by a desire to see the woman, hoping that with the darkening sky I'd be able to catch a glimpse of her moving about inside the house,

I pulled my baseball cap back over my head and went upstairs. In the kitchen, I stood in front of the counter and shoveled granola into my mouth straight from the bag and drank two glasses of water. My head still felt foggy, so I brewed a cup of coffee, poured it into a travel cup, and went into the garage.

Automatically, I moved toward my SUV, but I paused. I'd already parked it in the woman's neighborhood twice over the past few days, and I didn't want that to be noticed by anyone. Instead, I climbed into Liam's car and turned it on.

Abruptly, I wanted very badly to plug the address for my mom's house in Stamford, Connecticut, into the GPS and drive straight there. I wanted to let her wrap her arms around me and fix the mess I'd made. But I couldn't. I couldn't let her see me like this. I couldn't tell her the truth. The truth would hurt her, and I'd hurt her enough.

I parked on Pear Tree Circle, from which I could see the back of the woman's house. Darkness had fallen, and the windows were illuminated with movement and light. There was a wall of windows lining the rear of the house, along with the French doors, and no curtains as far as I could see. Perhaps they thought that their house was private, as there was no other house directly behind it, but they hadn't considered that it could be seen from the road or the county property abutting their yard. Or, perhaps they liked the idea of being watched. I might have been doing them a favor.

I could see her shimmering blond hair as she moved around the kitchen. She was wearing a long-sleeved black top that clung to her slender frame. It looked like she was preparing dinner.

Headlights flashed as a car pulled down the street and swung into her driveway. I slunk down farther in my seat. Liam's BMW was much lower to the ground than my car, and my view of the house wasn't as clear, but I still felt safer borrowing his.

The woman's husband entered the kitchen. She turned to greet him. She smiled, he approached her, and they kissed. He moved out of view, and her shoulders slumped just a hair, as if in relief.

Something caught my eye straight ahead and I looked up. A glowing orb was swinging back and forth on the street ahead of me. I stared at it, trying to comprehend what it was. I panicked, turned on the car, and pulled away from the curb. As I got closer, I realized it was a man walking his dog, carrying a flashlight to illuminate his path. He didn't even glance toward my car when I passed.

I drove through the neighborhood for a few minutes before returning to my spot. By now, the woman and her husband were seated at their kitchen table. He had ditched his blazer and was wearing a plain white short-sleeved undershirt. It was all very stereotypical, 1950s-esque, the pretty housewife having dinner ready for her husband when he got home from work. It looked like a scene from a movie, and there was an air of fictitiousness, of fraudulence about all of it. It was like they were playing roles.

Although, I had no idea whether this woman was, in fact, a housewife. She could have been at work all day, for all I knew. When I saw her at the store on Friday, she could have been stopping on her way home. She could have taken the day, or afternoon, off to host her friends.

If I knew her name, I could find out more. I could type it into Google and locate a professional profile, or LinkedIn page, if she had one. But I didn't know her name. All I knew about her was that she drove a dark blue Lexus SUV, she lived at 3224 Apple Blossom Lane, and that when her husband swept into the house, he brought with him a sense of unease.

Except, property records were public information. The State Department of Assessments and Taxation had a website, in which a person could type an address to pull up the complete ownership history and tax assessments for that property. I had used the site countless times for work, back when I was working. I felt stupid for not thinking of it before.

I'd left my phone at home—I had to. I knew Liam was tracking its location and I didn't want him knowing my whereabouts, asking what I was doing. I'd search for their address when I got back.

I returned my gaze to the windows of the house. Dinner was over and the woman was clearing their plates from the table while the man remained seated. He was looking downward, maybe at his cell phone. Absentmindedly, I reached for my drink, before realizing that I didn't have one. Not in this car. All I had was my coffee, which I finished even though I no longer cared to feel alert.

I watched as the couple continued to talk in the kitchen. At first, they were just chatting. Then, tension seemed to rise, like lava threatening to bubble over. The woman was leaning against the counter. The man was out of sight for a few seconds, and then he returned. He moved toward her and my breath caught in my throat. He was angry. I couldn't see their facial features, but it was in his body language. I could feel it. There were ripples of heat steaming from him as if from asphalt on a hot day. I flinched. I knew what was going to happen next. I could feel the sting, the sharp pain.

But then, stillness. Surprise. The anger was gone. One of them had said something to defuse the situation, to suck the anger out of the room. The sense of fictitiousness and fraudulence was back. He stepped toward her. He embraced her, pulling her body against his.

They were still like that when I turned on the car and drove away—touching, as if with love and care. I didn't understand.

In a way, I felt betrayed.

I'd thought she was like me.

McKenna

I opened the oven to check on the salmon. There was liquid sizzling in the baking tray, and the fish had turned the telltale pink. I'd have to pull it out within the next minute or so, or else it would be overcooked. If the salmon was overcooked, it would start things off on the wrong track. Zack would not be happy if the salmon was overcooked.

He'd called from his car when he was leaving his office downtown. He'd told me he would be home by eight. He had sighed as he'd said it.

"Is traffic bad?" I'd asked.

"Looks pretty bad," he had said.

"We should move closer," I had suggested. "We could live closer to your office."

We had chosen this suburb because it was close to my office. He had fallen on his sword. He had wanted me to have a short commute. He didn't mind commuting if it meant I could get to work and back in less than twenty minutes.

That was what he said, but really it was just something to hold over my head. It was Exhibit A, or slide number two in a presentation entitled, "Look What a Wonderful Husband I Am."

And then, just under two years after we'd bought the house, I was no longer working. It didn't make sense for us to live here. We should have been closer to his office, not to an office to which I no longer drove every day.

That had been the wrong thing for me to say. The air had sparked with electricity. "Don't you like our house?" he'd asked. "You don't enjoy our neighborhood?"

"I love it," I'd said. "It's perfect. I just feel awful about you sitting on the beltway every day."

That had been the right thing to say.

"As long as you're happy, McKenna. I'll see you at eight."

I'd timed it perfectly. If he arrived at eight, he would greet me and then he would go upstairs to use the bathroom and change. That would take five minutes. I'd remove the salad from the fridge, the salmon from the oven, at 8:02. I'd plate everything and have it on the table as he was walking down the stairs at 8:05.

Except, here it was, 8:05, and he was not yet home.

The only question was why. Had he hit an unexpected snare of traffic, or had he told me the wrong time on purpose?

I turned the oven off, hoping to keep the fish warm but to not cook it any further. I heard the garage door rising, and I exhaled. But the relief was soon washed away by dread. I wanted him to get home. At the same time, I never wanted him to get home. Could he not be killed in an accident on the highway one day? Could police not show up at my door, and tell me the news? I'd collapse in what appeared to them to be grief. Only I would know that it was relief. I often fantasized about exactly that situation in morbid detail. It was usually what I was thinking about when I fell asleep at night. My own macabre bedtime story. I imagined the accident itself. I pictured his head being crushed from the impact. His handsome face slamming into the airbags. His straight nose breaking. Blood, filling the car, crimson and gruesome. He would be pronounced dead at the scene.

That way, I could be free, without actually leaving. Without packing up my things and driving to my brother's house. Without hiring an attorney and filing for divorce. Without telling everyone about what it was really like being married to Zackary Hawkins. Without watching the disbelief, the questions flicker across their faces.

Is she lying?

She must be lying.

If I did manage to leave him, Zack would make it difficult. He would fight the divorce. He would deny everything I said and refuse to settle. I knew that he would.

We'd end up in a contentious divorce trial. I'd have to sit in the witness box and tell a judge—likely a man—what I'd been through, what my relationship was like, and why I no longer wanted to be married to the charming and successful doctor sitting at the trial table beside his lawyer, not ten feet away from me.

Now, all of it was behind closed doors. It was my dirty little secret. It was shameful enough that way. But after I aired my secret? I could not fathom how shameful that would feel.

The only thing more humiliating, more onerous than staying, was leaving.

I was an intelligent and educated woman. How could I let this happen?

Assuming I could manage all of it anyway, assuming I was capable of it, then it would be Zack's turn.

The psychiatrist would take the witness stand. *She's crazy,* he'd say. *She's making all of it up.*

Whom do you think they would believe?

There were no bruises. No marks on my body. There was no proof of any of it. Nothing but my own memories.

And that was why I was paralyzed. I could do nothing but fantasize about his demise.

But my fantasy was not going to come true today. Not this time. I heard the door leading to the garage swing open with a squeak. My husband strode down the hall, his briefcase in his hand.

My heartbeat quickened, as it always did when I saw him, ever since we first met. It used to speed up with anticipation. He was so handsome. So charming. Now, it sped up in fear.

"Hi," I said as he approached. "How was your day?"

He bent to kiss me. "It was fine," he said. "I'll just go change." He took his cell phone and wallet out of his pocket and placed them on the edge of the counter with his car keys, before heading upstairs.

I spun toward the oven and removed the salmon, sliding a piece onto each plate. I pulled the salad bowl from the fridge, added the dressing and croutons and used the wooden serving tongs to stir everything together. I was carrying the food to the table when he reentered the kitchen.

He'd been good all weekend, after the incident with the chips on Friday afternoon. That's always how it was. That was the only good thing about an "incident." There'd be a period afterward during which he'd be on his best behavior. There'd be a reprieve.

He had apologized that night, as he'd climbed into bed. "I'm sorry I lost my temper," he'd told me. He had reached for me in the bed, tugging my body closer to his. I had almost cried out in revulsion at the feeling of his hands on me. "I just want what's best for you," he'd said. "For us. I want us to have a baby so badly."

He wanted a baby as desperately as I did not. I used to want one desperately, too. Not anymore. Not with him.

Imagine bringing a baby into this environment, I'd tell myself. Imagine having a girl. What would she learn about relationships and marriage, from being our daughter? And what if we had a son? What would he learn about how to treat his spouse?

It wasn't that he wanted to raise a baby, or that he wanted to be a father. It was just that a baby was the next step. It was the missing piece of our picture-perfect life. We had this big, beautiful house. I was thirty-two. He was thirty-six. We were financially stable, healthy, attractive people in prime procreative years. It was time.

When he returned to the kitchen, something had shifted. He was no longer contrite. He was no longer apologetic and sweet. He had re-gained the upper hand. I had done something.

My mind whirred. I felt like a hamster on a wheel, running to no-where. I didn't know what I'd done wrong, and that was the worst part. I couldn't plan. He would set a trap, and I'd walk right into it.

"How did your day go?" I asked, trying again. If only I could keep him talking, I could avoid him bringing up whatever mistake I had made.

But his answers were clipped. He kept his eyes cast down toward his plate as he ate.

"How's the fish?" I asked.

"A little overcooked," he said.

That's your fault, I wanted to say. *You told me you would be home at eight.*

I shuddered to think of what would happen if I said all the things I wanted to say.

I cleared our plates away while Zack remained at the table. He looked down at his phone, probably reading an email. I felt like there was a timer ticking down.

Three, two, one.

"What did you do today?" he finally asked.

I had finished clearing the dishes and loading them into the dish-washer. I knew I was about to be ambushed. I leaned against the counter.

"I worked out downstairs," I said. "I went for a walk around the paths. I did some reading."

I used to belong to a gym in our neighborhood. I would take group classes like spin on Monday nights, my friends Mina and Alyssa on the bikes to either side of me, or Body Pump on Wednesday evenings, or barre Saturday mornings, when the gym was so crowded that rushing to get a spot in front of the mirror was practically a workout itself. I would run into other friends or parents of my patients there, too. In February, Zack installed a home gym in our basement, outfitted with a wall of mirrors, flat-screen televisions, treadmills, spin bikes, free weights, and extra thick floor mats. He had canceled my gym membership. I hadn't found out until I had swiped my card in the reader. A representative from member services had then informed me that my membership had been canceled, effective immediately, the previous day.

"That's right," I'd told him. "I totally forgot. I guess I came here on autopilot." I'd laughed and he had looked at me with such pity that I'd almost cried.

Help me, I had wanted to say.

When confronted, Zack was emphatic. "If you're going to continue going to a gym, you might as well keep working. You are getting exposed to so many germs and people there. Besides, you have everything you need in your home."

Which was, of course, why he had set up the home gym. Never mind that I didn't just go to the gym for exercise. Since leaving my job, it represented one of my only opportunities for socialization and interaction with humans other than my husband. Which was, of course, the other reason he had set up the gym. He was chipping away at my independence. He was encasing me in a bubble of isolation. It was quite methodical and comprehensive.

Zack nodded at me. He stood up from the table. He moved into the family room, disappearing from view. I could tell he was becoming angry. He walked away, as if he was trying to calm himself down. He wasn't. He was reveling in it. He was enjoying this.

"What *didn't* you do today, that I asked you to do?" he asked when he returned.

Shit.

I opened my mouth to speak, but he continued before I could get a word out. "I asked you to get my dry cleaning, McKenna."

He had been waiting for this moment ever since he had gone upstairs to change and had seen the absence of the clear plastic dry cleaning bags that should have been hanging in his closet.

"I'm so sorry," I said. It was best to just apologize. I couldn't very well claim to be too busy. And he'd already asked me what I did today, for just that reason. "I totally forgot. I'm sorry."

He moved toward me. "You being sorry doesn't really help, though. It doesn't, for instance, provide me with something to wear to work tomorrow."

Which was absurd, because he had so many clothes hanging in his half of our walk-in closet. He probably had twenty outfit options for tomorrow, even without the dry cleaning. But I knew I couldn't say that.

The edge of the counter was digging into my back. I tried to think of an excuse. I was desperate.

"I'm sorry," I said again. "I was just a little distracted today. I have some news, actually."

He froze. "What news?"

"I—I'm pregnant," I said.

His eyes widened. "You are?" he asked.

"I took a test this afternoon," I said. "I know you're supposed to take it first thing in the morning. But I was feeling nauseous and so tired, just like last time. I couldn't wait."

He stared at me for what felt like decades. His face was unreadable. He stepped forward, closing the gap between us, paused, and then hugged me to him. "I can't believe it," he said softly. "This is so exciting."

I wondered if he could feel my heart pounding.

He held me for a long time. Finally, he released me, and I felt wobbly, like I could tumble to the floor. I leaned against the counter again.

"This time will be different," he said. "Because you aren't working. You won't get sick."

"Right," I said. "This time we will have a baby."

I could see it in his eyes. He was playing along, but he didn't believe me. What had I done?

I had avoided his ire for now. But what would happen to me when he found out I was lying? I'd be in for far worse than whatever it was he had planned for me tonight.

I turned and began to wipe down the counters. I just wanted to look at something besides his knowing eyes. I wanted something to do.

He knew that my catching that stomach virus hadn't been the reason for my miscarriage. It had been a scapegoat. A way to blame something I had done, rather than accepting that it was something inherent to my biology that had caused that tiny bundle of cells to fail to have a heartbeat at my eight-week doctor's appointment.

I had taken the test on a Tuesday morning. According to the app on my phone, with which I had been studiously tracking my period for months, I was five weeks pregnant. I had taken another test the following day, before telling Zack. The strangest part, looking back on that time, was that I'd been happy. Things were different then. I had still wanted a baby. There'd been glimpses of anger. But ninety percent of the time, he was still the charming man I had married. He was the handsome doctor I had met toward the end of my residency at Georgetown University Medical Center. I was a brand-new doctor then, holding lives in my hands. It was a time when I was experiencing a feeling that didn't seem to be shared by my male counterparts—an overwhelming insecurity—and he made me feel worthy and special.

I had called my obstetrician's office and scheduled an appointment for three weeks later.

"Shouldn't I come in sooner?" I asked. I wanted proof, more than could be offered by two faint and tiny blue lines, soggy with urine. I wanted to see my baby.

"It's standard to schedule the first appointment at eight weeks," said the receptionist.

Zack had attended the appointment with me. It was a cold January morning. We had walked into the medical building with our hands stuffed into our coat pockets.

I'd had no indication that anything was wrong until I'd seen the ultrasound technician's face.

At that point in the pregnancy, it was too early for the type of ultrasound I had always envisioned—running a sensor through the warm gel on my belly, still flat, the not-yet-a-baby just the size of a raspberry. I'd had an internal sonogram instead. The technician stared at the screen in front of her, which was tilted toward her, so that only she could see it. Zack sat on the little bench beside me. We waited, but the screen hanging on the wall in front of us remained black. We waited for it to come to life, to be filled with images of black-and-white swirls and the tiny flicker of a heartbeat. We waited, but it didn't happen.

"Is everything okay?" I asked.

"I'm not allowed to go over the results with you," the technician said.

Her tone was defensive, but she smiled in an exaggeratedly kindly manner. "The doctor will be right in. You can get dressed." She left the room.

I stared at my husband, feeling my eyes filling with tears, watching his fill with anger.

I used a tissue to wipe the excess gel away before stepping into my underwear and then my jeans. I balled up the paper drape that had been spread across my lap and stuffed it into the trash can.

The doctor entered only seconds later. What we had suspected was confirmed. There was no heartbeat. I'd suffered a miscarriage without ever knowing it. I was scheduled for a dilation and curettage procedure the following morning, during which the lining in my uterus would be cleaned.

"Why did this happen?" I asked.

I was a doctor, but I still didn't have any of the answers I wanted.

My obstetrician said there could have been a chromosomal issue, but there was no way of knowing. I was young and healthy. Further testing was not recommended after a first miscarriage. Typically, they waited until a woman had suffered three pregnancy losses before testing was recommended. She assured me that it was nothing I had done, or not done, that had caused this loss.

My husband wouldn't look at me.

"She got sick a couple weeks ago," he told the doctor. "She's a pediatrician. She picked up a stomach virus at work. She was throwing up for days. She couldn't keep anything down. Could that have caused it?"

"It's highly doubtful," the doctor explained. "The body takes care of the fetus first. It is highly doubtful that a stomach virus would cause a miscarriage."

Zack hadn't pushed her, but I could tell he wasn't satisfied with her response. He wanted it to be my fault, and so it would be my fault. What she said, our medical training, and logic—none of that mattered.

We had walked to the car in silence. He didn't speak until we had each slammed our doors closed. I looked down at my lap.

"You will quit your job," he had said. It was not a question. It was not even a suggestion. It was a command.

I stared at him in shocked silence. He turned on the car and slowly backed out of the parking spot.

"No," I finally said. "That wasn't what caused it."

I liked my job. I had attended four years of college, followed by four years of medical school. I had completed a three-year residency program, during which I had worked shifts ranging from twelve to twenty-four hours. That was when I met Zack. He knew how badly I had wanted to be a doctor. I had finished my residency two and a half years earlier and had found a job working for a private practice in a Maryland suburb between DC and Baltimore. We had purchased a house nearby six months after that. Was that not evidence that, in some ways, we were building our lives around my job? How could I quit when I had only been working for two and a half years, but had spent more than seven years preparing?

Zack had turned the car out of the parking lot, and we were gaining speed, creeping toward fifty miles an hour, as we headed to the highway.

He slammed on the brakes. With no warning, no opportunity to prepare my body, I was jolted forward. My seat belt dug into my chest. My neck snapped forward. I was as astonished as if he'd slapped me across the face.

He jerked the wheel. The car screeched to a stop on the shoulder. A horn blared and a truck flew past us.

"You will quit," he said again.

That was the first time I'd felt afraid of my husband. It was the first time I'd felt my heart thudding, my hands shaking, as I wondered what he would do next.

"Fine," I said, because I didn't know what else to do. I was not willing to accept what was happening. This wasn't my charming, accommodating husband. I was desperate for him to transform back into the person I thought he was, the person I thought I knew.

He was just scared, I told myself. He was devastated about the loss of what could have been. The loss of hope. He was desperate to prevent it from happening again.

That was the first time I made excuses for the inexcusable.

Maybe he was right. Maybe my stomach virus had affected the pregnancy. The week I was six weeks pregnant, I had seen several kids with a stomach virus, and I'd been hit with waves of nausea when I returned home that Friday night. Saturday, I had been unable to keep anything down. Even sips of water had sent me sprinting to the toilet. Sunday, I had managed some ginger ale and crackers. Zack had suggested I call my doctor. He had told me to go to the hospital to get intravenous fluids.

"Don't be ridiculous," I'd said. We were doctors. No need to be alarmist. It was just a minor stomach bug. I would be fine. The baby would be fine.

I had been wrong.

Maybe not, but maybe. And wasn't that enough? Why take any chances? We didn't need the money. Zack's practice, based out of a row-home office in Georgetown, had taken off. We had more income than any young couple needed.

I could take a sabbatical. I could claim health reasons, and I could leave my position. I would return to work once we had a healthy baby, and he or she was a few months old.

Once I had agreed, he had softened. The man I knew returned.

"I'm sorry," he had said, and there were tears in his eyes. "I just want this to happen for us so badly. I want to do everything right and be careful."

"I know," I'd said. "It's okay."

He had eased onto the gas and driven us home almost gingerly.

"How are you feeling?" Zack asked me now. "How far along are you?"

"I should be five weeks," I said. I rinsed out the sponge and tucked it behind the faucet. "I'm feeling fine. So far."

I had all the answers, but also none of them. I washed my hands and dried them on a dish towel. We stood there, smiling at each other.

Zack grinned widely. "I'm so happy," he said, and I grinned back.

"Me, too," I told him.

But I could tell that his mind was calculating. And so was mine. I'd won the battle. Or, more accurately, I'd postponed it. Unless I figured something out, when it finally went down, it would be worse than ever before.

NINE MONTHS EARLIER
WEDNESDAY, AUGUST 1

Leah

I shifted my car into park and leaned back against the stiff headrest. I wanted just a minute to myself. A minute to breathe, to think, to be alone, between the frenzy that was my workday, the hell that was my commute, and the frantic activity of my time at home, as I attempted to decompress and unpack, literally, from the day, while preparing for the next one, which would, I knew, be starting in what felt like the blink of an eye.

But my husband—I was still turning the word over, shivering with its novelty—would have heard my car pulling into the garage—he was home already, which was unusual—and he would be wondering what I was doing if I lingered too long. So, I pressed the button on the remote on my visor, directing the garage door to close, and climbed out of my car. I unloaded my purse and lunch bag, before bumping the door closed with my hip as I moved into the house.

When I entered the kitchen, I immediately felt like I was missing something. Liam was standing at the stove, stirring a sizzling pan. There were candles on the kitchen table, casting flickering gold reflections across the wall of windows at the back of the room. The air was thick with garlic and the promise of an evening that was going to be memorable.

I ran through a list in my head. It wasn't my birthday. Not our wedding anniversary, obviously. We just got married last month. We had returned from the Ritz-Carlton in Maui three weeks ago, where we swam and hiked and relaxed in the sun and ate better than any person should.

It wasn't the anniversary of the day we met or officially started dating. It wasn't my husband's birthday.

What else could we be celebrating? Good news I had somehow missed? Something job related? But as far as I knew, there was nothing new happening on that front. I had been working at my law firm in Baltimore for almost nine months, having made the jump from my previous, even smaller firm, for a generous salary bump, albeit a worse commute and longer hours.

It was almost eight now. I'd left the office at seven, after scrawling a note on the legal pad perched on my standing desk to remind myself that I had left off on paragraph five of the form-based contract I was drafting.

I had expanded my practice areas, too, by joining the new firm. I was mostly performing a variety of transactional work, drafting agreements for businesses, marital settlement agreements for divorcing people, and wills, trusts, and medical directives for individuals wanting to plan for the future.

I wasn't going to court, litigating cases, or handling hearings, and I liked it that way. Unlike Liam, I didn't get a rush from trying a case, from standing before a judge and making an argument. I got anxiety, which was often accompanied by diarrhea and profusely sweating underarms, both of which were exceedingly unwelcome in a crowded, public courthouse.

Liam enjoyed the showmanship of litigation. He was a comfortable public speaker. He had focused on trial work as soon as he had graduated from law school, joining a large firm in DC and litigating a wide variety of cases—commercial disputes, medical malpractice cases, and divorces. After a few years, he started to focus only on divorce cases and child custody disputes. Perhaps he was inspired to help single parents due to his own experience being raised by a single mother.

Upon my own graduation from Georgetown, I had joined the same large firm as Liam, and it was there that we met. He was five years older—which gave me pause, but not discomfort—and it wasn't appropriate for the senior associate to be dating the newbie, fresh out of law school. I'd said as much when Liam had invited me out for drinks after work one day.

"I'm not asking you out on a date," he had said, laughing gently, and I had been mortified.

"Jesus," I had told him. "Well, this is embarrassing."

"Drown your embarrassment in a drink with me," he'd said.

So we had walked a block to a bustling and expensive restaurant where he had purchased each of us a sixteen-dollar cocktail.

"I lied," he had said, after I took my first sip.

"Did you? About what?"

I was basking in the warm glow of his undivided attention. He was a superstar at the firm. He was notorious, for his billable hours and for his business generation, despite that he had only been practicing for a few years. And he was so handsome, with his sleek dark hair and amber-flecked green eyes. It was politician hair—shiny and parted to the side, undoubtedly with the assistance of some sort of wax or gel or spray—but it worked for him.

"This is a date," he had said.

"Oh." Our knees were touching beneath the bar.

"But it's okay, and I'll tell you why, but you're sworn to secrecy."

I held up my right hand and swore as if I were a witness preparing to testify in court.

"I'm leaving the firm soon," he said conspiratorially.

"Really?" I had been shocked, but I shouldn't have felt that way.

He was leaving the firm to start his own practice, where, assuming he could draw in enough clients, he could earn much more money than he was making as an associate and, more importantly, he could achieve the title and status of "partner" far sooner than he would at our firm. Partnership track was approximately eight years after graduation, and Liam wasn't willing to wait that long.

So he had launched his law firm, rented an office on the ground floor of an old Victorian house in the suburbs midway between Baltimore and DC, and hired an assistant. He negotiated an outrageous settlement for a DC socialite who praised him across her well-followed social media accounts and won a highly contested custody case for a local politician. By the time he turned thirty-two, he had become one of the most sought-after domestic law attorneys in the Baltimore to DC corridor.

Along the way, there had been more dates, a shared condo, and, finally, a round-cut diamond on a sapphire-studded band—it was unique and beautiful and designed by Liam especially for me and I thought I was the luckiest woman alive.

Liam had purposefully chosen the location of his office, set amidst wealthy communities and approximately midway between the two nearest major cities, and we had elected to purchase our home nearby. Liam's argument was that it allowed me the opportunity to work in either DC or Baltimore, enjoying a mediocre commute to either, rather than living closer to one of the cities and therefore being tied to it. In reality, our house afforded me a horrendous commute to both DC and Baltimore. But my hours were usually long enough that I was already or still at work during the morning and evening rush hours.

Except tonight, staying at work until seven meant that I should have hit little to no traffic on my way home, but there'd been a rush-hour accident on I-95, cleanup from which had not yet been completed, and everyone slowed to stare at the police cars and wreckage. What should have taken forty minutes had taken almost an hour.

Liam turned away from the pot on the stove and I approached him. "What is all this for?" I asked.

He abandoned his wooden spatula and bent to kiss me. "Happy one-month wedding anniversary," he said.

"Oh my God," I told him. "Are we going to celebrate our wedding anniversary every single month, twelve times a year?"

I was squeezing past him, moving around the kitchen, unloading the dirty dishes from my lunch bag.

His face fell and I glanced at it just in time to see a flash of irritation pass through.

I tried to recover. "I'm kidding," I said quickly. "This is so sweet."

And it was. I certainly wasn't trying to discourage having dinner made for myself. Usually, I got home before Liam, and that responsibility had been falling on me, almost by unspoken rule.

I peeked over his shoulder into the pan. He was swirling pasta, spinach leaves, and crushed baby tomatoes, dispatching odors of butter and garlic and Parmesan cheese.

"Looks good," I said.

While Liam switched the burner off and served food onto our plates, I finished loading the containers from the lunch I'd brought to work into the dishwasher. He carried the plates to the table, and I hesitated in the doorway. I wanted to change out of my pencil skirt, blouse, and pumps, but I didn't want to upset him by allowing the dinner he had prepared to grow cold. I settled down in my usual seat at the table and kicked my heels off, letting them fall to the floor with twin thuds.

Liam placed our plates down and went to the fridge to remove a bottle of Chianti. He poured us each a glass. We didn't usually drink on weeknights, but I supposed this was a special occasion. Liam had, at least, turned it into one.

I took a sip of my wine, feeling the coolness run down to my stomach, where it burned gently and pleasantly, like the candles on our table, and I felt, for a minute, that I was very happy and very lucky. *This is my husband,* I thought, as I watched him twirl his fork in his plate of pasta.

"How was your day?" I asked. I speared a cherry tomato with my fork and popped it into my mouth.

"It was really busy," he said. "I wanted to get everything done so I could beat you home to surprise you."

"I was very surprised," I told him.

"One month," he said. "Can you believe it's been a month already?"

I shook my head. I couldn't. The time leading up to and after the wedding had flown by in a blur. We had moved out of our condo in Baltimore and purchased a large suburban colonial in a neighborhood with tree-lined streets and walking paths. It was far more space than the two of us needed, but we agreed that we wanted a family home in which to start our married life. Eventually, we might add a child to the mix. Not yet—we were too focused on our careers. But maybe in a few years. We had time to decide. And if we so chose, we had plenty of space.

After the move, we had been finalizing the preparations for our wedding, which was an intimate ceremony the weekend before the Fourth of July, in front of twenty guests at Liam's mother's lake house in North Carolina. From Charlotte, we had flown to Maui for our ten-day honeymoon. From there, we had returned home, to take care of mounds of laundry, unpack wedding gifts, write thank-you cards, and, most importantly, return to work to get caught up on everything on which we had fallen behind over the previous few weeks.

"How's your food?" Liam asked. He seemed to want to talk about little else but the evening he had put together in celebration of our one-month wedding anniversary. He was clearly very proud of himself.

"It's so good. I fear you have set a precedent," I told him. "I'll come to expect this every month now," I said teasingly.

"Well," he replied, "maybe next month it will be your turn."

I laughed, but seeing the look on his face when I did, I questioned whether he had been joking.

"Definitely," I said, and I smiled up at him, my husband, as handsome and charming as the day our knees had bumped together beneath the swanky DC bar.

"I love you," I told him, tilting my legs toward him until I could feel the solid warmth of his own.

"I love you, too," he replied.

Although I'd heard him say it more than a hundred times before, it still sent a jolt of surprise and pleasure down my spine. And, it seemed, in that moment, like that feeling would last forever.

As it turned out, I'd never been so wrong about anything.

NOW
WEDNESDAY, MAY 8

Leah

This week was a missed opportunity. It was so rare that Liam spent any nights away from our home. I should have taken this time to make my escape.

I sat on the lounge chair, staring out at the woods behind our house, inspecting them, as if a solution might emerge from between the trees.

The problem was money. No one could make an escape without money. I had no job, and no prospects for being able to find one. I didn't have my own bank account. He could see every purchase I made with a credit card or debit card. He could monitor any cash withdrawals. He could check the value of any purchases I made.

After I left, I'd have to buy gas, food. Those were purchases for which I was allowed to use the cards, but he would be able to determine my location. Also permitted were clothing stores, hair or nail salons, spas—places I no longer frequented. He wished I did, and that was why I stopped.

For the most part, the small amount of cash I was able to amass with cash-back withdrawals when making purchases at approved locations, was squandered on alcohol. I wanted to save it up. It would take a long time, but I wanted to hide it in an air vent or beneath my mattress. To take it out and count it and stare into its eyes, imagining the possibilities. I wanted to use it to escape him, but I needed the alcohol until I could.

Money wasn't the only problem. If he arrived home one day to find me gone, he would know where I went. He would go after me, and my mom. He'd made that clear, that night in the closet.

Even if I didn't go to my mom's house, he could still punish her for my departure.

I ran my hands across the canvas cushion of the lounge chair, flicked away a stray dandelion seed. The cushions were navy, far more reasonable for outdoor furniture, unlike McKenna's bright white.

That was her name, the woman I'd been watching. McKenna Hawkins, married to Zackary Hawkins. They had purchased their home two years earlier for $825,000. I had typed her name into Google, but she didn't seem to have any social media accounts. I thought that was strange for a woman of her age. Then again, I was no longer a user of social media, either. None of the results seemed to pertain to her.

When I'd typed in *Zackary Hawkins,* my screen was flooded with hits. Articles he had written. Studies he had led. His LinkedIn page. The first result took me to the website for his business—Zackary Hawkins, MD, LLC. He was a psychiatrist with a private practice in downtown DC. He had graduated from Harvard Medical School, completed his residency at Georgetown University Medical Center, continued to work there for several years, and then opened his own practice in the same area.

I found this information interesting, but I had no real use for any of it.

I wondered what she was doing. Was she, too, sitting outside, admiring her yard? Was she thinking about how pretty it all looked? Did it look pretty, but feel like hell?

I'd missed her yesterday. I had cruised through the neighborhood three times, but I hadn't seen them at all, not even in the evening. Maybe they had gone out.

The sun was beginning to dip, and the trees were casting shadows across the yard. I stood up and walked toward our pool. The dark green cover was still stretched across it. We had not yet had the company come to remove the cover and get the pool ready for the season. Not that it would get much use. Not this year.

I walked across it, bouncing gently, feeling it sink beneath my weight, feeling the frigid water seep through and swirl around my bare feet. For a brief moment, I thought about detaching the cover and climbing beneath it, into the water. That would be one way to escape.

But I couldn't do that. I thought of my mother, and I knew that I couldn't do that.

At this point, though, she might be the only one who cared. With Liam's subtle discouragement, a disinterest whenever I brought them up, grumbles and bad moods when plans were made, I'd lost touch with almost everyone with whom I'd previously been close. It had been easy, alarmingly so, to drift apart from my high school and college friends. Even Tess, my best friend, my freshman-year roommate. We had continued to live together until the summer after graduation, when I had moved down to DC to start law school and she had moved to New York to work for a public relations firm. I'd not made any close or lasting bonds in law school. I'd been too consumed, too stressed. Those relationships had fizzled easily like the flame at the end of a blackened match.

Tess had come to visit us over the summer, after we'd moved into the new house. Liam had been distant, unpleasant, during her visit. Displeased that she was there at all, but too concerned with appearances to flat-out tell me she couldn't come. At the wedding, she was subdued and stony faced, questions, suspicions swirling behind her gray eyes. I'd not wanted to hear them. I was so ashamed, so fearful of what Tess might say when we spoke, I'd been avoiding her. It was probably exactly what he'd wanted.

I'd only had one drink today, even though it was past seven. That was something of a record for me of late. My hands were shaking slightly. Although my body was still craving it, my mind was less so. With Liam out of town, I didn't need it quite as much.

I turned and climbed off the pool cover, shaking the wetness from my feet. My bright, turquoise toenails wiggled back at me. I'd snuck into the master bathroom, as if Liam might be lurking around, and rustled through the bins of discarded toiletries and makeup he had left there. All of it had turned out to be superfluous. I hadn't needed any of it in a month. I'd located my little basket of nail polish and carried it to the deck where I had sat on an outdoor dining chair, propped my feet on the edge of the table, and slicked the color across my toenails. I don't know why. Maybe I was just grasping for something small from my old life. I used to love to paint my nails. I'd started doing it religiously when I was in law school. It afforded a minibreak from my reading, color-coded highlighting, case briefing, and study group meetings.

I slipped on my shoes and went back into the house. It was nice to be free to move around inside of it, without first taking stock of where he was and what he was doing. Was it safe to go into the kitchen? Could I go out back to sit outside? When he was home, though, if he wanted to find me, he always could.

I browsed through the pantry, fridge, and freezer, but nothing called to me. I used to love trying new recipes, preparing food, and dining out. Not on a work night when I was exhausted and just wanted to down something quick and go to bed, but on nights when I left the office a little earlier than usual, on weekends when the weather was so rainy or cold that going out was unappealing.

Not anymore. These days, I ate when I could. Mostly when Liam was at work. Mostly processed foods that I could grab and run away with, like a child sneaking a midnight snack. I no longer enjoyed cooking or baking. I no longer enjoyed much of anything.

I cracked two eggs into a bowl and whisked them together with a dash of milk, then poured them into a sizzling pan with a handful each of shredded cheddar and baby spinach, a sprinkle of salt and pepper. I stirred the mixture with a wooden spatula, then slid it onto a plate. I sat down at the kitchen table to eat. The eggs had browned slightly, and the spinach was slimy. I ate it anyway, but I felt tears begin to seep from my eyes and drip down my cheeks because how had I become such a failure that I could no longer even make scrambled eggs?

I rinsed my plate and washed it by hand. There was no need for the dishwasher. The items would just end up sitting inside all week until it became full enough to justify running it.

I had waited all day to see her, and I could wait no more. What was she doing? Was she okay? I had to know.

I needed to limit my trips to her neighborhood, though. People would begin to notice my car parked in the same spot. There seemed to be little point to going during the day. I hadn't seen her leave her house since I'd first come across her at Pine View Liquors on Friday. And during the day, I wasn't able to see inside.

As I pulled a navy sweatshirt over my head, I heard my phone vibrating on top of the dresser. It was another text message from Liam.

If you don't respond and let me know you're okay, I am sending the police to do a wellness check on you.

He didn't care how I was. I knew that. All that mattered was how things looked. If I had, for example, decided to off myself in the house shortly after he left, and my body wasn't discovered until he returned home, he'd have questions to answer. A good husband would be in frequent contact with his wife while out of town. A good husband would check on her every day, multiple times a day. So that was what he'd done, and I had not responded to a single text or call.

Besides, he needed to make sure I was behaving, even in his absence.

But I didn't want the police to show up. I was afraid of what I might tell them.

I'm fine, I typed. I pressed Send and tucked my phone into my sweatshirt pocket before bending down to lace up my sneakers.

I took my car this time since I had used Liam's most recently. I thought it was helpful to alternate between the two cars. But that would no longer be an option once Liam returned home. I probably would not be continuing to watch her anyway. Not while he was around. He would ask me what I was doing. I wouldn't know what to say. Not when I didn't know myself.

As I turned out of the driveway, I saw Sylvia, my neighbor across the street, waving to me. She was sitting in a lawn chair in her driveway while one child rode his bike in tight circles around her. A toddler was drawing with chalk on the walkway, and she was holding a baby in her arms. She'd told me their names at least once, but I could no longer recall what they were.

Sylvia was a pleasant woman with a round face and long, curly auburn hair that she almost always wore in a drooping bun. She was not employed, but as far as I could tell, she worked much harder than I ever had in my entire life, caring for three children under the age of five, as well as a four-thousand-square-foot house, and a husband who never seemed to be home. He was a consultant of some sort—this was another fact I could not recall—and he traveled with some regularity. I often noticed his absence for days at a time, and I'd seen him rolling a suitcase to and from his car, which apparently did not fit in the garage, due to the children's various and abundant paraphernalia.

I forced my face into a smile, hoped it didn't make me look crazed, and waved back to her.

Sylvia had been so excited when we had moved in. She had two young kids then and was pregnant with the third. I'm sure she'd been hopeful that we would pop out a few children to play with her offspring.

That was never going to happen.

I drove to Apple Blossom Lane and cruised past the front of the house. There was no action, so I traveled to what had become my usual spot on Pear Tree Circle. The lights in the kitchen were on, casting blossoms of gold across the patio and backyard. I marveled again at McKenna and Zackary's apparent allergy to curtains, blinds, and privacy.

I shifted my SUV into park and focused on the scene. It was after eight, but McKenna appeared to be alone. She was moving around the kitchen, possibly making a home-cooked meal for her husband once again, awaiting his return from work.

But then, she carried a bowl of something to the kitchen table, sat down, and began to eat alone as she stared straight ahead. Suddenly, she bent her head, placing her face in her hands. Her shoulders shook.

She was crying.

I felt like I was watching myself.

It lasted for a few minutes, until she lifted her face, wiped her cheeks with the backs of her hands, and gazed at nothing. Finally, she stood up from the table and carried her bowl out of my view.

I couldn't see where she had gone, nor what she was doing, but I desperately wanted to. I wanted to understand why she, like I, had cried as she ate her dinner alone.

The front pocket of my sweatshirt vibrated, and my stomach dropped. I was getting careless. I had accidentally brought it with me, leaving it in my pocket, instead of placing it on top of my dresser before departing the house. I slid the phone out and checked the message.

I hope you're being good.

It was too late. He knew where I was, and he would want to know what I was doing here. If I didn't respond, he might do something drastic, like fly home early. I didn't want that.

Just out for a walk, I wrote back.

While I knew that he kept track of my location using my cell phone, I wasn't sure how detailed the information was. Did it show me stationary in one place, in this neighborhood close to ours and to which we had no connection? Or was the data vaguer than that? Was my excuse plausible? I could only hope that it was.

I turned off the phone and dropped it into the cup holder.

The sky had gone from a deep gray-blue to black. It was a cloudy evening, with no light provided by the stars or the moon. I looked around me, ensuring there were no passersby, dog walkers, or cars approaching me, before I climbed out of my SUV. I picked my way down the hill of the county property abutting the road, which backed to the Hawkinses' yard, weaving my way between the trees. There was a jagged stump, remaining from where a tree had crashed to the ground. I perched on it, tucking my car keys into my pocket. I could see part of the family room from my closer position, as well as more of the kitchen. McKenna had returned and was moving between the rooms.

Her body language made clear that he was home. I could tell before I saw him enter the room, just like the night before last, his briefcase swinging from his hand. This time, he was wearing a crisp navy suit and a green patterned tie. I leaned forward and squinted at it. I had purchased the exact one for a birthday gift for Liam, prior to our marriage.

Get out, I wanted to tell her. *You need to get out.*

But who was I to say anything to her, when I couldn't take my own advice?

He greeted her just as he had earlier in the week, bending to give her a kiss. My stomach churned, as if I could feel her revulsion.

Again, he disappeared for a few minutes, while McKenna moved around the kitchen, doing nothing aside from staying in motion, like she was a great white shark that would die if it stopped swimming. When he returned, they began to talk, and I could feel the tension rising. He was confronting her about something. He was angry. Anxiety and enmity crackled in the air.

The stump was begging to dig into my flesh. I slid to the ground. Cool dampness soaked through my leggings and prickled my skin. I couldn't move, couldn't look away.

They continued to talk, as McKenna backed away from her husband. I didn't know if she realized what she was doing, or if it was a subconscious reaction. Her back hit the wall, and she could go no farther. I could feel its solid flatness against my own back. His warm and acrid breath skimmed my face. My heart was pulsing wildly. Blood was rushing in my ears.

He was going to hit her. I could feel it, because I'd felt it before, the sharp bite of a hand against my cheek. The surge of shock and terror.

I had seen enough.

I reached into my sweatshirt pocket, feeling for my cell phone, but finding only my car keys. I had left it in the cup holder. I pushed to my feet and ran back to the car. I paused behind a tree several feet from the road to look around. There were no people or cars approaching, so I hurtled into my car and grabbed my phone. My mind was racing. Something was happening in the Hawkinses' house, and I had to stop it. I had to stop it for her because no one had ever stopped it for me.

I turned on the phone and my fingers hovered over the keypad. I wanted to call the police, but I didn't want to be tied to the call. I didn't want to have to explain to them why I had been in the neighborhood, or why I'd been watching the Hawkinses. I didn't want to be hit with questions to which I did not have the answers.

There was a way to block one's phone number when making a call. I knew that. I'd done it countless times when I was working and had to call clients from my personal cell phone. I may have been a workaholic, but I had never handed out my personal phone number like candy.

Was it *67 or *69? I couldn't remember.

I opened my browser and searched for the right numbers to use, aware that I was losing precious time to help McKenna.

My fingers shook as I dialed.

*-6-7-9-1-1

I switched the phone to speaker mode and turned on my car. An operator answered after two rings. "Nine-one-one. What is your emergency?"

"I think my neighbors are fighting," I said hurriedly as I pulled away from the curb. "I can hear them. Three-two-two-four Apple Blossom Lane in Clarkstown. It sounds like it's escalating and I'm afraid the woman is in danger." I rushed through my spiel so I wouldn't be interrupted.

"Okay, ma'am," the operator replied. "And what is your name and location?"

I hung up the phone and pressed my foot onto the gas pedal.

McKenna

I'd been trying to find a way out ever since I said those two words Monday night.

I'm pregnant.

It had been a solution to Monday night's problem. But I'd gotten myself into an even worse situation.

Yesterday had been quiet. He'd been sweet and passive. He'd taken me out for a celebratory dinner at my favorite Italian restaurant. I'd eaten bread dredged in olive oil and pasta swirled in cheese—foods I wasn't usually permitted. But, I was supposedly pregnant now. Weight gain was expected and appropriate, to a certain extent.

Tonight, Zack was at a networking event and would be home later than usual. He'd told me to eat without him. I was grateful for the extra time alone. I had to focus on the little things for which I could be grateful. It was the only way I could make myself continue.

Another thing for which I was grateful was not having to prepare a healthy and nutritious dinner. I didn't have to roast meat or fish, sauté vegetables, or toss a salad. I could eat a bowl of cereal if I wanted to, and that was exactly what I wanted to do. I didn't have the energy for anything more complex.

I thought about eating in front of the television, but there wasn't anything I wanted to watch. Not that I wanted to eat alone at the table. Not that I wanted to eat with Zack.

I settled onto a kitchen chair with my granola and almond milk. With each bite, I tried to refocus my mind. I was a doctor. I was intelligent, educated, and sophisticated. Why couldn't I come up with a way to escape this personal version of hell in which I'd been living all year? Why did it feel so overwhelming?

I felt knocked down by sadness, by a sense of helplessness, and, mostly, by shame. It was like a thrashing ocean wave had picked me up and slammed me onto the firm sand, thrusting the air out of my lungs. I let myself cry. It was like a little gift. I so rarely acknowledged or felt permitted to express my emotions.

After a few minutes, I stopped, because I knew that Zack could walk in any second and I didn't want him to ask why I was upset. I didn't want him to draw me close and make me feel like he was my friend, or trick me into admitting that I was crying because I had lied about being pregnant.

I wiped the wetness from my face and stood up. As I washed my dinner dishes, I heard my cell phone ringing from where I'd left it on the coffee table in the family room and I rushed toward it. I'd assumed it was Zack, calling to provide an update as to his progress getting home. My heart lifted when I saw the caller ID.

"Hey, Aiden," I said.

"Mac," said my brother—he was the only one who called me that and it sent a jolt of affection through my core—"where have you been?"

"What do you mean?" I asked, even though I knew what he meant. I moved into the living room as I spoke and looked out the window, waiting for Zack's car. I'd wrap up my conversation when I saw him pulling into the driveway.

"I called you yesterday," he said. "I didn't hear back. It feels like it's been ages since we've seen you."

"I know," I told him. "I'm sorry." Because what else could I say? That

I'd been busy? Aiden knew I wasn't busy. He had been as shocked and disappointed as I was when I quit my job in January. My parents had been less so. They'd had children later in life and had sold our childhood home in Silver Spring and moved down to a condo in West Palm Beach when I was twenty-eight and Aiden was twenty-five. They were anxiously awaiting grandchildren from their condo complex, where they played tennis and joined book clubs and went for walks on the beach where the sand supported their arthritic knees. They approved of any course of action that might expedite their becoming grandparents. Besides, my mother, like me, was the wife of a doctor. She had worked as a nurse until a few months before I was born and hadn't worked since. My years of expensive education notwithstanding, she didn't find it at all strange that I might put my career on hold or abandon it entirely in favor of starting a family.

I'd confided in Aiden about the miscarriage, but not my parents. "It's just temporary," I had told him. "We just really want to focus on having a baby. I will go back to work after that."

He'd been skeptical. "I don't know, Mac. Is you sitting at home all day going to help you have a baby? And then what happens if you want another one, and you stay home longer? All of a sudden, you've been out of the workforce for years. Makes it harder to go back."

"We might not have a second child," I had told him. Already, I had been doubting whether I truly wanted to procreate with my husband. I was even making covert plans, at that point, to ensure there wouldn't be a first child, let alone a second.

"You should come up to the house this weekend," Aiden said. "We could take you out to lunch. Or grab some takeout and eat outside if the weather is nice. Zack, too," he added, somewhat reluctantly. He had never been a fan of my husband. Perhaps it was something in his training, something that made him better than the average person at reading people. Perhaps he had seen at their very first meeting what I had only just begun to notice.

Aiden was a law enforcement agent for a federal agency, and his wife taught seventh grade in Baltimore City. They lived in a small cottage in northern Baltimore County, located on five sprawling acres of wooded land. Aiden had always longed to reside in a rural setting. I think it provided a peaceful and restorative retreat for him and Monica, a reprieve from the intense and stressful nature of their jobs.

When they had first purchased the property, they had invited Zack and me over often, but the more we declined their invitations, claiming other plans, sometimes truthfully and sometimes not, the less we were invited.

It wasn't just that my brother didn't like my husband. The feeling was mutual. Zack exhibited a strange sort of jealousy over our relationship. I found it ridiculous, but I soon noticed that he acted the same way about anyone with whom I was close—Mina, Alyssa, and Aiden. Friends from college and medical school, with whom I eventually lost touch, as his presence grew in my life and I became busier with work and there was little room for anyone else. By the time I had left my job, the only friends with whom I was still in touch were my newest friends—those I had met at my gym—Mina and Alyssa. Now that I had more time for other relationships, I no longer had enough relationships to fill the time. I had time for more activities, but no one with whom to share them.

"Sure," I told Aiden. "I'll talk to him."

While I wanted to see my brother, his invitation only increased my anxiety. This would be yet another problem for which I would need a solution. Zack would not want to go to their house. He would complain, make comments about how I was too close with my brother, that it was abnormal, and suggest other plans which he would pretend he'd been making all along but which he had in fact made up on the spot, until I agreed that it was best that we just not go.

"Okay," said Aiden. He sounded dejected. We both knew we would not be seeing each other this weekend.

"How's Monica?" I asked.

"She's good," he said. "Ready for the school year to be over. She needs a break."

"I'm sure." I paced back and forth between the two living room windows, my eyes trained on the driveway and road beyond.

"How's work going?" I asked him.

"Fine," he said. "Busy."

We both fell silent. He didn't know what to ask me. He couldn't ask me about work. I didn't have any hobbies. My life had become so empty.

I saw Zack's black Audi SUV roll down Apple Blossom Lane. His turn signal blinked as he swung the car into the driveway.

"Hey, Aiden, I have to go," I said. "I'll talk to you later."

"All right. Let me know about this weekend. We're free either day." He sounded relieved to be getting off the phone with me.

I hung up and returned to the kitchen. I waited there for Zack.

As he swept into the house, he brought with him a wave of tension. Something had happened to make him angry. And here I was, an available target to bear the brunt of it.

"Hi," I said, watching him deposit his keys, wallet, and phone onto the kitchen counter. "How was your event?"

"Fine," he said tersely. He didn't elaborate. He stepped toward me and bent to give me a kiss, but his lips stopped just shy of mine. He backed away.

"Did you eat?" I asked.

"I ate," he replied. "I'm going to change out of this suit." He left the room.

I swiped a towel over the dishes resting in the drying rack and put them away while I waited for him to return.

When he stepped into the kitchen, it was as if a dark cloud were hanging over his head, lightning threatening to lash out at any second.

"Is something wrong?" I asked.

He stood in front of the counter, looking down at his cell phone. He squinted at it, as though reading an email. "A patient told me today she is discontinuing treatment with me," he finally said. "She's moving on to work with someone else. Probably another doctor who will be easier on her."

"I'm sorry," I said.

He shrugged, pushed his phone away, and directed his attention to me. I wilted.

"It happens," he said. "How are you feeling?" He took a step toward me and smiled slightly, like he was trying to look caring. The perfect husband, putting his work stress aside to devote his full attention to his wife.

I wished he wouldn't.

"I feel fine," I lied. "It's still early." Which was sort of true. It was so early that I wasn't even pregnant.

"I couldn't help but notice," he said, taking another step toward me, "there wasn't any pregnancy test in our bathroom trash can. Did you save the test?"

My mind raced faster than my heartbeat. He knew.

If I told him I threw it away, he would want to know where. If I told him I'd saved it, he would ask me to produce it.

"I actually took the test at the store, in the bathroom," I said. "I was so eager, and I had to go. I didn't even want to wait until I got home."

"I see," he said. "And you didn't save the test?"

I shook my head. "It was wet. I didn't want to get pee in my purse." I tried to laugh, but it died in my throat.

"I would have thought that would have been something you might have wanted to save. As a memento."

"I saved the test last time," I said. "It was painful when I had to throw it away, after we lost the baby. I don't want to get my hopes up this time."

"I see," he said again.

"What's wrong?" I inquired innocently. "Why are you asking me about the test?"

"I just would have liked to see it," he said. "I can't believe you would have thrown it away." His voice was rising.

"I'm sorry," I told him.

"Your being sorry doesn't really help, though, does it?"

It was one of his favorite lines.

I felt my back hit the wall. He had continued to step toward me, and without realizing it, I had continued to back away. He wasn't going to hit me. He had never hit me—that might create evidence, something tangible, and he knew that could not happen. But I had backed away from him nevertheless.

"This is off to the wrong start," he said. "This doesn't feel right. You're being secretive. I don't like this."

"I can take another test," I said, my voice pleading. "I can buy one tomorrow. I can take it with you."

Could it be that easy? Why hadn't I thought of that sooner? I could take a test and it would, of course, be negative. I would be shocked and upset. I'd make an appointment with my doctor for further tests. The only question was whether I'd be able to pull it off. I'd never been much of an actress, hadn't been a good liar. But I was getting better. Out of necessity, I was getting better.

I felt tension releasing from the room like air from a deflating balloon. The cloud was clearing. The situation was diffused. For now.

"Fine," he said. "You can take one tomorrow night. We'll take it together."

He was still looming over me.

"Okay. I'm just going to go to the bathroom," I said. I placed a hand over my stomach. "I'll be right back."

I ducked around him and he let me go. I climbed the stairs, wanting to put more distance between us, and locked myself in the guest bathroom.

I turned on the sink so he wouldn't hear me crying and sank to the floor. Twice in one day. I couldn't make this a habit.

I needed some time to myself. I needed to think. Was he going to sit beside me tomorrow night and watch me take a test? Could I somehow fake a positive result, or should I pretend to be perplexed by a negative one?

Feeling guilty for being wasteful, I turned off the water and began to pace back and forth across the ivory tiled floor. This bathroom was supposed to be used by our future children. Children I had once desperately wanted. Children I was now desperate to prevent.

I realized that I had left my cell phone downstairs with him. There was no doubt that he'd look through it. He'd see my phone call with Aiden. He'd ask me about what we had discussed, and he'd tell me, in no uncertain terms, that we would not be visiting my brother's home this weekend.

A car door slammed, then another. Seconds later, the doorbell rang. I jumped. I wasn't expecting visitors, and I feared that another unpleasant situation for which I would be blamed was impending.

I pushed the curtains aside and pressed the blinds apart so that I could peek out. The bathroom was one of the few windows in which we had installed blinds and curtains. I'd wanted to install them in every room after we had moved into the new house, but Zack had insisted that only rooms in which we did private things required window coverings—bedrooms and bathrooms. We had compromised by covering the windows in all rooms in the front of the house as well, but the windows in the back were left bare, even though there was a road running behind it. Zack had insisted that the county property behind our yard and the distance from the road afforded sufficient privacy.

I could see that a police car was parked in our driveway and two uniformed officers were standing on the front step. I flipped the locks on the window and pushed it open a fraction, wincing as the paint cracked and the seam squeaked as if the window had never been opened before.

I crouched down so that I could hear, frantically blotting at the tears on my face in case I needed to make an appearance.

"We received a call asking us to perform a check on your residence," said one of the officers. He looked strangely similar to my husband, with his quarterback build and sandy blond hair. His partner was short and squat with dark hair. I half expected to catch a glimpse of a stereotypical donut in his hand.

"Really?" said Zack. "How odd."

"Someone reported an argument," said the partner. "Are you here alone, sir?"

How could that be? I wondered. Had he been that loud, that a neighbor had heard Zack's raised voice? I supposed it was possible someone walking down the sidewalk or on the road behind our house could have heard something, but it didn't seem likely. The argument, if it could even be called that, hadn't lasted very long. And, there'd been far worse. No one had ever called the police before.

"My wife is here," said Zack. "She's upstairs. But we weren't arguing."

"No?" said Sandy Hair. "We got a report that you were."

A flash of movement across the street. I looked up to see my neighbor's minivan pulling into her garage. She had probably gone out to run an errand after putting the kids to bed.

Zack would be livid that our home was a spectacle.

"No," said Zack. "We may have had raised voices, but we weren't arguing."

I couldn't see him from my position, but it was as if I could. He would be smiling sheepishly and running a hand through his hair. "My wife was having a bit of an episode. But, I'm a psychiatrist. I got it under control. That might have been what someone heard. She's upstairs resting now."

"An episode, huh?" said the shorter, dark-haired officer.

Zack laughed. "You know how it is."

The officer laughed, too. "I think my wife had an episode last night."

They were all laughing now.

"Dispatch told us it was a strange call, anyway. The person gave your address, then hung up right away."

"Well, I sure appreciate you checking it out nevertheless," Zack said.

I pulled the window closed. I no longer wanted to bear witness to the demonstration of the exact reason I could never report my husband's behavior. This was exactly how he would be received every time.

And that was exactly how he would portray me. His crazy wife. No one would believe anything I said.

I sat down on the closed toilet seat. I was staring straight ahead of me, but I was seeing nothing.

I heard footsteps ascending the stairs.

"McKenna," said Zack. He tapped on the bathroom door. "It's okay."

His voice was so gentle, so sweet, like he was cooing at a frightened kitten.

"It's okay, McKenna," he said. "I'm sorry."

I took a deep breath, and I closed my eyes. Because he was so convincing. Because I knew I couldn't turn to him, but I also knew I had no one else to turn to. Because I wanted him to be right. I wanted it to be okay.

"Everything's going to be fine," he whispered again. "The police are here to check on things. You just need to come downstairs. Tell the officers that you're okay."

Which would be a lie. But, like I said, I was getting better at lying.

I smoothed my hair and tucked it behind my ears, then stood up and straightened my shirt. I took another deep breath, and let it out slowly, before opening the door. I didn't look at my husband as I walked past and made my way downstairs. I didn't need to see the knowing look in his eyes.

He was so sure I would do exactly what he had asked me to do.

And he was right. Until I discovered a way to get out, to prove who he really was, and to be believed, he was right.

SEVEN MONTHS EARLIER
MONDAY, OCTOBER 1

Leah

My fingers pounded at the keyboard and the words filled the screen. Usually, if I was not in the office, I would respond to work emails on my phone, but when the email from Meredith Daly had come through during my drive home—I knew I shouldn't have checked it, but I'd been sitting in stop-and-go traffic on I-95—it was clear that responding would be a laptop-worthy affair.

I had spent several hours on the phone with Meredith the previous Friday, discussing the terms she wanted to request of her husband in a marital settlement agreement she had hired my firm to draft. We had discussed that to which she was entitled under the law—half of the equity in the family home, a portion of her husband's pension and IRA, half of the money in the bank accounts, even the ones titled to her husband alone, and alimony—likely several years of substantial payments.

We had reached an understanding of everything she would be asking for by way of the proposed agreement, and I'd spent the day drafting it, before firing it off to her late afternoon. Several hours later, she replied to my email, during my drive home, advising that she had changed her mind. She wanted to waive alimony, her interest in her husband's retirement accounts, and her interest in the bank accounts titled in his name only. I knew that he'd gotten to her over the weekend—perhaps he had threatened her—and it was imperative that I talk her out of her decision to walk away from hundreds of thousands of dollars.

While I might have preferred a phone call, my boss, Claudia Granderson, a woman of impressive stature and even more impressive presence, had taught me the importance of creating paper trails and documentation of important client communications. It was a different aspect to lawyering. A practical aspect that couldn't be learned in law school.

You have to protect yourself, Claudia would say. I needed to send something in writing to Meredith Daly, letting her know that I was vehemently opposed to her suggested course of action. That way, if she insisted on waiving her interest in a great deal of marital assets and in alimony, and later regretted her decision, she would not be able to sue me or the firm, alleging that she'd received bad advice. There'd be evidence, the email I was working on at my kitchen table while my high heels rested on the floor beneath the chair, that I had cautioned her against it.

I had just sent the message when I heard Liam's car pulling into the garage, and I startled. I glanced at the time in the corner of my computer screen. It was nearly eight o'clock, and I hadn't started dinner.

I shut my laptop down and tucked it back into my purse as Liam strode into the house.

"Hey," I said, approaching him. I stepped forward to kiss him, but he jerked away from me as if I had bad breath.

"What?" I asked.

His brows wrinkled, as he looked around the room. "You haven't started our dinner?" he asked.

"Something came up," I said. "I had to do something for work when I got home." I moved toward the fridge and opened it, browsing our options.

Liam was still frozen in place.

"What?" I asked again, glancing over my shoulder at him.

"Leah," he said slowly, as if he were trying to explain a difficult concept to a small child, "do you know what day it is?"

I blinked at him. "October first," I said. "It's Monday, October first. Why?"

"Today is our three-month wedding anniversary," he said, with exaggerated patience.

I laughed. "Are we still doing that every month?" I asked.

For our first month, Liam had surprised me. For our second month,

I had planned a special dinner for him, featuring a homemade lasagna I had assembled in the morning before leaving for work and another bottle of Chianti. By the third month, I had assumed we would move on and not acknowledge our anniversary until July 1 the following year.

But it wasn't just that. I had genuinely forgotten. With everything going on at work, with the busyness of the Monday, I hadn't remembered the significance—if there truly was any significance—of October 1.

"Well," Liam said icily, "if it's not that important to you, I guess not."

I slumped. "It's not that it's not important to me. It's just—I didn't know we were going to keep doing that every month."

Liam didn't reply. He turned away from me without a word.

"Okay," I said, "you can go change, and I will make us a nice anniversary dinner."

I spun away from him and began to move around the kitchen. I set a pot of water to boil, emptied a jar of tomato sauce into a pot with a tray of premade meatballs from Wegmans, and threw together a Caesar salad using a packaged kit. A two-thirds-full bottle of pinot grigio, left over from the weekend, was chilling in the door of the refrigerator. I filled two glasses and arranged them on the kitchen table with a single candle.

By the time Liam returned to the room, I had grudgingly, and somewhat resentfully, finished arranging the spurious anniversary meal.

"So, how does your week look?" I asked, trying to inject interest into my voice, to conceal the burbling irritation, as we settled down at the table with our plates of food. "Any court hearings?"

"I have a motion hearing on Wednesday," Liam replied, still cold. "Nothing too major."

"I have a new client meeting Thursday evening," I said, even though he hadn't asked. "She works around here, so I am meeting her in her office after work, as a favor. I will be home a little later than usual. Other than that, I just have a usual week of drafting."

"Sounds boring," Liam said. He leaned back in his chair and yawned, as if the very thought of my work were putting him to sleep.

I bristled. "I like drafting," I said defensively. "Litigation gives me angina."

"I know," he said, but his tone was patronizing.

My phone vibrated on the table nearby. I reached for it and checked the notification.

When I had first started at my current firm, Claudia advised me that the firm didn't pay for employee cell phones.

"Things that are perceived by clients to be emergencies often are not. I caution you against connecting your work email to your cell phone. If you do, don't enable notifications. And you should never give a client your cell phone number."

I had followed her advice about the phone number, but not the email. I soon realized that not having my email pop up on my phone made me feel more stressed than having it there.

The message was from Meredith Daly. *I know,* she'd written in response to the email I had sent her from my laptop after arriving home, *I just want this to be over.*

I sighed, pushed my plate away, and typed a response. *Please call my direct line first thing tomorrow morning.*

When I looked up, it was to see Liam watching me.

"What was so important?" he asked.

"Nothing," I said, sliding my phone to the side of my plate. "Just a client email."

Liam speared a meatball, his fork clanging aggressively against his plate.

"What?" I asked, for what felt like the hundredth time since my husband had arrived home from work, feeling like I was treading on eggshells, cracking with my every breath. "Now what's wrong?"

He took an inordinate amount of time to chew and swallow before responding. "You're writing work emails during our dinner," he said, "even though you were just at work all day."

"We both check and respond to work emails at home all the time," I said. "What is the big deal?"

Liam placed his fork down on the edge of his plate with exaggerated care. "Leah, this is supposed to be our three-month anniversary celebration," he said.

I laughed, but he didn't appear to be kidding.

"Look," I said, "it was cute for the first two months, but I don't really want to be preparing a special anniversary dinner every single month for the rest of our lives. Especially after a long day at work. If you want to do that, at least we could take turns. This month should have been your turn."

Liam remained silent. His eyes had hardened. We'd had disagreements before, of course, but I'd never quite seen him look like this. It was like he'd slid a mask over his familiar face, and I was dining with a stranger.

"Why should I be doing it?" he asked. "Why shouldn't you do that for me every month? I give you everything. You don't even need to work."

"I don't need to work? Liam, what are you talking about? Why wouldn't I work?"

This was a new suggestion. I had attended seven years of higher education. We didn't have any children. The suggestion that work was optional simply did not make sense.

"I'm just saying," he replied, "that I don't work so hard for you to be responding to emails at the dinner table at eight thirty at night. I don't work so hard for you to feel so stressed out that the thought of preparing a special dinner for me once a month is just too much for you to handle."

When he put it like that, it didn't sound as strange, but we both knew that he'd been extremely ambitious, and something of a workaholic, long before he'd met me. I didn't quite agree that I was the reason for his hard work.

"All right," I told him, "but I like my job. I like to work. You know that. Me not working is not a scenario we have ever discussed."

I looked down at my own plate. The remnants of the tomato sauce looked like bloody wounds.

"I know," Liam said. He pushed his plate away. "But we're married now. I just want to make sure you understand that you can do whatever you want. If you were to decide you didn't feel like working anymore, that would be okay."

It was the first time I didn't know what to say to this man who had transformed from my coworker to boyfriend to fiancé to husband over the course of four years.

And, suddenly, I felt rage bubbling inside of me, like the rolling boil of the water that had cooked the pasta on our plates. I felt like my very identity was being threatened. I felt like a cornered animal.

"Well," I said, "I want to work." My voice was shaking, just as it had the one time I had, early in my career, appeared in court. "I am going to work, and if you have a problem with that, then we are going to have a big problem in our marriage."

Liam stood up from the table, soaring and commanding. He reached toward my plate of food, and I thought he was going to pick it up, carry it to the sink, and wash the dishes. To extract himself from the argument, to cool down. But, with the flick of his wrist, he tipped it onto my lap. Pasta and sauce dribbled down my blouse and skirt and onto the floor. A meatball rolled down my front and along the ground, leaving a trail of red behind it. The plate fell with a clatter.

He left the room, as I stared down at the mess, paralyzed by shock.

I heard him climbing the stairs, to our bedroom. I sat, still astounded and immobilized, as he descended the stairs a few minutes later, wearing shorts, a T-shirt, and sneakers. He went down to the basement, where I presumed he planned to exercise, going about his usual evening routine as if nothing strange had happened. He didn't even look at me.

He had left his empty wineglass, his plate, on the kitchen table. I stood, blew out the candle, and collected the dirty dishes.

I wiped the food from my blouse, skirt, and the floor. I put our plates in the sink and began to clean the dishes from our three-month anniversary dinner. What else could I do? My thoughts were racing. Shock and hurt were trembling my lower lip. I didn't understand what had just happened, or why.

I looked down at my clothes as I worked. Greasy round blotches of oil and butter remained. Smears of sauce, as red as fresh blood, adorned my front. I'd send them to the dry cleaner's, but I knew that the stains would never come out.

NOW
THURSDAY, MAY 9

Leah

I was awakened by my ringing cell phone, pulled from a deep and dreamless sleep. It was alcohol induced, and therefore not natural or particularly restful, but it killed some time nevertheless. I reached for the nightstand and grabbed my phone. I thought for a second about not answering, but that would only make her worry.

"Hi, Mom," I said. My mouth felt sticky and dry as flytrap paper.

"Hi, sweetie. How are you?"

"I'm fine," I said. I remembered when I had hated to lie to my mom. It caused a literal stab of pain in my gut. Now, it would pain me not to. "How are you doing?"

I threw the covers off myself and climbed out of bed.

"I'm good. Just finished dinner," she said.

I could picture her alone in her condo, holding the phone to her ear with her shoulder, washing her dishes in the sink.

I checked the clock above the stove. "It's almost nine," I said. "Late dinner."

"Well, it's just me, so I eat when I'm hungry, you know. I don't follow a schedule."

"I know," I told her. "What did you have? Anything good?" I knew her answer would fill me with guilt, but I was very limited as to what I could speak to her about these days.

"I just had some yogurt and a bit of toast," she said hesitantly.

"Mom." I opened my own fridge, removed the pitcher of filtered water, and poured some into a glass. "Yogurt isn't dinner. Yogurt is a snack."

"Well, maybe so, but I don't like to go to a great effort cooking for just myself."

I gulped down the glass of water and poured another. "I know," I told her again. Because what else could I say? That she had no idea how badly I wished I was there with her, instead of here?

"Anyway," she continued, "how was your day today?"

"Um, it was fine. Busy." The lies flowed so easily now.

"You work so hard," my mom said, her voice tinged with concern but also pride.

And that was why I couldn't tell her what had happened with my job.

"Not really," I said, which was a drop of truth in a bucket of false-hoods. "How was your day?" I asked, trying to change the subject.

"It was fine," she said. I could hear water running in the background. She was probably rinsing her yogurt-covered spoon and dropping it in the drying rack. "Pretty uneventful. The school year is winding down, but it's not so close to the end that the kids are unmanageable yet. I still have a couple more weeks before they become uncontrollable."

My mother was a saintly person who taught fifth grade. For as long as I could remember, it had always just been the two of us. I had grown up in a town house in Stamford, Connecticut. She and my dad had divorced sometime before my third birthday, and my dad had disappeared into the sunset, never to be seen again. When I got older, and had aged out of the questions like, "Why don't I have a dad?" or "Why did my dad leave us?" I'd had the sense to ask what was probably the more pertinent question—"Is he paying you any money to contribute to my care?" The answer was "no."

Somehow, though, my mom had made it on her own. We might not have lived in a single-family house like my friends and she might have always driven used cars and dressed me in secondhand clothes until I was old enough to protest, but she made my life comfortable and happy enough that I shouldn't have had any reason to complain. I did complain in the way that only the evil that was teenage girls could manage, but I shouldn't have.

It wasn't until I grew older and had gained more independence that I began to appreciate her as much as I should have. That was why I was so determined to become successful. I had attended the University of Connecticut on a full scholarship and had decided to become a lawyer, operating under the false impression that *lawyer* was a job that would make me undeniably and objectively successful. I had wanted to study law at Yale or Harvard or another top-ten school that was relatively close to home. But I hadn't gotten in, which made me feel like I was a failure.

Georgetown had offered me an acceptance and a partial scholarship, and DC didn't feel *too* far from my mother. Besides, who wouldn't want to attend law school in the nation's capital?

Except, attending law school in DC had led to my first job in DC. And my first job in DC had led me to Liam.

If I could go back in time and do all of it over again, I would.

"What about the weekend?" I asked. I opened the fridge to return the pitcher and to rummage around for something to eat, if for no other reason than to soak up some of the alcohol I could still feel churning inside my stomach and coursing through my veins. "Any plans?"

"Well, I have my book club meeting on Saturday," my mom replied. "Other than that, probably just enjoy some time outside, walk on the beach with Daphne. The weather is starting to warm up here."

My mother had sold the town house in which I had grown up and moved into a two-bedroom condo close to the water shortly after I had graduated from law school, and it became clear that I wasn't going to return to live with her. It was just her and her slightly overweight Lab mix named Daphne. The existence of the second bedroom was another fact that made me sad. That bedroom was supposed to be for me, for when I visited. But I almost never visited.

"That sounds nice," I said. "I miss the water."

"You should come up," she replied. "I know you're busy with work. But whenever you get a chance, come up to visit. Even for a weekend."

"Okay," I said. "That would be good."

We made small talk and said that we loved each other before hanging up. We both knew that I wouldn't be visiting anytime soon. My mother had no idea why I had been tugged further and further away from her, as though pulled by the tide. She didn't know why it was happening, but she did know it was happening. Yet, she didn't ask. She didn't put pressure on me to explain.

Sometimes, I wished she would.

I pulled a loaf of bread from the fridge and made myself a peanut butter sandwich. I had a jar of Jif concealed in the back of the cabinet beneath the sink, behind a row of cleaning products. Liam despised processed foods. He forever seemed to be dieting. He always used to tell me that he was a closeted fat kid. Fighting off an overweight physique was a constant battle. Ice cream, kettle chips, chocolate bars, Jif— all of my favorite foods—were verboten in our house. That was why I concealed Jif behind Clorox spray and dish soap and shoved chips and chocolate into my mouth on my way home from Pine View Liquors on Friday afternoons. It was one reason he'd taken it so personally when I had stopped exercising and started adding pounds to my frame.

I brewed a mug of French vanilla coffee and sipped it slowly, letting the hot liquid clear the peanut butter from my mouth and throat. I still felt like I was surrounded by a gray cloud of fog, but I also believed I was within the legal limit.

I could drive.

I had already cruised by her house, and behind it, twice earlier in the day, and I hadn't seen any action whatsoever. I was hopeful that tonight would present more excitement. I felt a rush of anticipatory nerves. I wanted to get eyes on her, to check in. I was struck by a rush of affection for her. It was like she was my friend. My ally. My avatar in the game of life. I was rooting for her.

I was willing to do more than just that. Yesterday, I had proven that I was willing to breach the divide, to step in and help her if she needed it. It felt good to be helpful and needed. How far would I go?

My limbs were buzzing with anticipation as I returned to my basement bedroom to pull a black sweatshirt over my head and slide my sneakers onto my feet.

I gathered what I needed for an evening of reconnaissance, but left my phone behind in the house before stepping into the garage.

I climbed into Liam's car, since I had used mine to drive through the neighborhood earlier in the day, and backed out of the garage. It was dark already, the latest I had visited her house thus far, and I was hoping I would see something different. Perhaps the second-floor windows above the kitchen belonged to their master bedroom. Perhaps those would be alight with activity.

I parked along Pear Tree Circle and peered at the house. The kitchen was bright, but I couldn't see either of them in it. The lights, though, gave me hope that they would return to the room. Maybe they went out to dinner. An apology dinner, for the events of the previous evening, which started with overpriced flowers that would die before the charge hit the credit card and ended with thirty-five-dollar entrées lit by flickering candles. I was all too familiar with such meals.

So, while they weren't there now, I was confident that they would return. I would wait.

After a while, I started the car and drove a few loops through the neighborhood, not wanting to be observed sitting in one place for too long. But there was no activity at all. Not on the streets, and not in the house.

On my third trip past the front of the house, headlights approached me. The turn signal flashed, and the car swung into their driveway.

They were home.

I continued past the house and returned to my parking spot on Pear Tree Circle, from which the back of their home was visible. Now, she was in the kitchen, leaning forward over the counter. He was nowhere to be seen. She was wearing pajamas. Her long blond hair was loose around her shoulders. They hadn't been out to dinner after all.

I climbed out of the car and began to pick my way through the trees, closer to the house. There was a caustic energy buzzing in the air. It felt like a poisonous cloud. I pushed through it, to the same stump on which I had rested the previous night.

Zackary emerged into the kitchen, and they began to talk. A raindrop splattered against my forehead, and then another. I tugged my hood over my head, then glanced over my shoulder, considering whether I should head back to Liam's car to grab the umbrella I knew he stored inside the trunk. But I didn't want to miss anything.

They were still talking in the kitchen, but McKenna was backing away from him. I pushed myself up from the stump and took a step closer. I could almost smell McKenna's fear, like it was perfume wafting from her pressure points.

Zackary reached for her, the motion quick and sharp and emphatic. He pushed her to the floor. I stepped closer.

There'd been no apology dinner. Not tonight. They hadn't yet reached that part of the cycle. Maybe they never would.

The rain had penetrated the hood of my sweatshirt and was running into my eyes. The umbrella. I needed to get the umbrella.

McKenna stood up slowly. Her expression—it was undeniable. She was shocked.

Zackary pushed her to the floor again. He was standing over her, looking down. I couldn't see her, from where I stood, but I could tell that she was beneath him. I could feel her fear and helplessness as if it was my own. And it was.

I could feel pain radiating from my hips, as I knew it was radiating from hers. I felt hot food running down my front and falling into my lap. I felt the burn of a slap as my cheek tingled and turned red. I thought about the gun, the first time I'd seen it, the swell of fear. Its shininess and power.

That was what I needed. Not the umbrella.

Because tonight might be the first time that he hit her. But it wouldn't be the last.

I turned, and I ran back to the car. I opened the driver's-side door and reached into my purse to remove the thing I had somehow known I would need tonight. The thing that McKenna would need. I pushed the door closed, careful not to make a sound, and I ran back through the woods. I ran closer and closer, until I reached the patio at the back of the house. It had been so long since I'd run anywhere.

I planted my feet on the flagstone. It looked expensive, and recently installed. It was slick with rain. My hood was soaked, and water was still trickling down my forehead. I tugged it off my head and wiped my face with the inside of my sweatshirt.

Zackary's back was to me. Suddenly, his body jolted with movement, as if he had kicked his wife.

I stepped into the warm yellow glow, cast across the stones from the light in the kitchen. All the windows lining the back of the house were open. McKenna had probably pushed them up earlier in the day, to cool the house and invite the fresh air inside.

McKenna rolled to her side, like she was trying to get up from the floor. I could tell that she was in pain.

Zackary had other ideas. His foot shot out, catching her in the stomach.

In that moment, he was not Zackary, a veritable stranger, standing over McKenna. He was Liam, standing over me. I knew exactly what McKenna was feeling. But it wasn't just that.

I'd been there. I knew what would happen next.

Unless I stopped him.

McKenna

When I heard his car pull into the garage, I was ready. I had practiced earlier in the day. I had decided it was best to pretend to be horrified by a negative test result. I didn't know how to orchestrate a false positive, and doing so would only postpone the inevitable. Eventually, I'd have to figure out a way to no longer be pregnant.

It was late, and I was tired. Last night, after being directed to go downstairs, I'd had to step onto the porch and feign surprise by the presence of the officers. With Zack by my side, I'd told them that everything was fine. I had no idea why someone would have called the police.

Once they left, once we were back in the house, it was like a switch had flipped.

"You called them," he said.

"I didn't," I'd told him.

"Why would they have come here?"

"I don't know. My phone was downstairs," I said.

His mouth had tightened, because he knew I was right.

"You used the landline," he said.

"No, I swear. Press Redial."

I had followed him into the kitchen, while he had lifted the cordless phone and done just that. A few seconds later, he lowered it from his ear and hung up. I didn't know what number the phone had called, but I knew it wasn't the police. I knew I didn't call them, and I had no idea who did.

I was off the hook, for the moment.

I didn't have the energy for another charade tonight, but I also didn't have a choice.

Zack always had evening appointments on Thursdays, seeing patients as late as eight or nine at night. By the time he finished his notes and made the commute home, it was often ten or eleven. It was the one night a week I wasn't expected to have dinner with him. He would grab something to eat on his way home, or he would make something easy when he returned. I could usually get away with being asleep or pretending to be asleep when he arrived home.

Needless to say, Thursday was my favorite day of the week.

It was after eleven already. I wondered whether I should pretend to be asleep and put the whole thing off until tomorrow night. But I didn't want to. I wanted to get it over with. I was as ready as I'd ever be.

I had gone to CVS in the morning to purchase a test. I hadn't agonized over the different varieties the way I had last time I purchased a pregnancy test. It didn't matter this time. I knew what the result would be. I grabbed one at random and tossed it into my basket.

The cashier had swiped the test across the sensor, taken in my three-carat emerald-cut solitaire—she clearly needed to ascertain that I was married before deciding that purchasing a pregnancy test was a happy occasion—and smiled at me. "Good luck," she'd said.

"Thanks," I had replied, smiling back at her, because I needed all the luck I could get. Just not for the reason she thought.

When I got home, I locked myself in the guest bathroom upstairs and practiced my reaction in the mirror over and over.

I furrowed my brows. I frowned. "I don't understand," I said. "What does this mean?" "How could it be negative?" "I need to take another one." I paced. I wailed. I even shed a few tears.

I had changed into my pajamas and was waiting for Zack in the family room. It was a warm evening, and I had pushed the windows in the family room and kitchen open earlier in the day. A tepid breeze was filtering through the screens, along with sounds of crickets and peeper frogs in the woods beyond our house.

He would find it strange that I wasn't in bed already, but it would also be strange if I leapt out of bed and prepared to take the test upon his arrival. And I didn't want to risk him suggesting we take the test in the morning. This had to end tonight.

When he emerged into the kitchen, he visibly startled to find me sitting on the sofa in the family room.

"What are you doing up?" he asked. He strode past me, to deposit his keys and briefcase in the kitchen. He didn't come over to greet me, which was unusual. I felt the hairs on my arms rise.

"I couldn't sleep," I replied.

I waited for him to ask if I was ready to take the test, but he didn't. He poured himself a glass of water and drank it in front of the sink, as though he'd run home, rather than driven in his luxury car.

"Did you eat?" I asked.

"I grabbed a sandwich in the city before I left," he said.

The box holding the pregnancy test was resting on the kitchen counter. He didn't bring it up.

Again, I waited.

Zack stood in the kitchen watching me.

"Well," I said, "did you still want me to take the pregnancy test? If not, I guess I'll try to go to sleep." I tried to sound breezy, casual.

"Let me just go change," he replied. "I'll be right back."

"Okay," I said. I watched him walk away and heard his footsteps climbing the stairs. I moved to the counter and opened the optimistically bright box. My hands were shaking.

Zack returned to the kitchen wearing his white undershirt and navy sweatpants. He stood in front of me, watching me silently.

My heartbeat quickened, because it was clear he knew something I didn't. I fingered the plastic wrapper holding the test, then smoothed the instructions down atop the counter, the crinkling paper the only sound in the room.

"Do you really need to take that, McKenna?" Zack asked, nodding his head toward the test.

I furrowed my brow in confusion, an expression I had practiced, though not in this situation. I was flying by the seat of my pants. He had the upper hand. Whatever was about to go down, it wouldn't be good for me. Now, it was all about minimize, mitigate. "I thought you wanted us to take a test together?" I asked.

Zack reached his right hand into the pocket of his sweatpants. "I did," he said, "but there's really no point, is there? You know that."

"Why?" I asked. I genuinely didn't understand. How could he know?

"Because of these," he said. His hand emerged from his pocket, holding my little envelope of birth control pills. He tossed it onto the counter. It skidded toward me, then fell to the floor.

I gripped the counter until my knuckles turned white. I felt like my head was spinning.

"You thought I wouldn't find out about this?" he asked. His eyes, which could be as warm and sweet as melted milk chocolate, had turned into treacherous pits. "I knew you were lying about being pregnant. I know you. I checked the insurance claims, and I was right."

I felt brutally foolish. My carefully thought-out plan. I'd thought I was in control, but he'd wrenched it away from me with the flick of his wrist. The shame of it. I practically melted to the floor in a puddle of shame. I was a doctor. Zack's tiny company had a health insurance policy through which his assistant was covered, as well as us. Of course he would find out about the prescription, as soon as he thought to look at the explanation of benefits forms. I couldn't believe that I had failed to cover that track.

It was six weeks after the doctor's appointment at which the miscarriage had been confirmed. Zack had asked me if I was ready to start trying again.

"Almost," I'd said. "I'll be ready soon."

By that point, I had known that we couldn't have a baby. I knew that I needed a plan to prevent that from happening.

I'd gone to my gynecologist for what I had told Zack was a follow-up doctor's appointment. While there, I had advised her that I wasn't ready to try having a baby again. I needed more time. I needed birth control. She had submitted a prescription to my pharmacy of choice.

I had been so focused on how I would pay for the prescription that it never occurred to me that there would be evidence of it by way of the explanation of benefits information the insurance company provided to the policyholder. I had been so busy worrying about whether I would be able to pay for the birth control with a credit or debit card. I didn't know if the statement would indicate something different, something revealing, for a purchase made at the pharmacy portion of CVS, rather than the retail store. I had been squirreling away a little bit of cash to pay for it, just in case.

As it turned out, insurance covered everything. The prescription was free. I had been so relieved, when I should have been more scared than ever. Zack had no reason to scrutinize the explanations of benefits, to review the insurance claims. But, as soon as he doubted me, he did so. And there it was. Evidence of my lies.

I had taken my pill this morning and concealed the pack within a compact mirror in my makeup bag, my chosen hiding place. He must have searched for the pills when I was asleep, left them there, and put them in his pocket when he went up to change his clothes. It was all so calculated.

"Zack," I said, almost a whisper.

"All this time," he said, "you were pretending that you were trying. You were acting as if you were so frustrated that it wasn't happening. And then, you pretended that it had."

His voice was quiet, but white hot. I'd never seen him so furious.

"Zack, please," I said. I released the counter and began to back away from it. I needed to get out. I knew that I needed to get out.

But he had never hit me. He wouldn't.

"This isn't my fault," he said. "You have done this to yourself. How could you do this to me?"

"I didn't have a choice," I said. I didn't know which would be worse for me—fighting back, or not. It probably didn't matter. "How could I bring a baby into this relationship?" I asked.

"I do everything for you," Zack spat. "I have given you everything."

"Because you wanted to," I said. "Because that's how you wanted things to be. So that you were in control. I didn't need you to do it. I used to be a doctor. I loved my job." Once I started, I couldn't stop. It was almost as if I was egging him on, but I wasn't sure why. "I worked so hard to get that job," I said.

"I didn't make you quit your job," Zack said, incredulous.

"Yes, you did," I told him.

There was a flicker in my mind. Was I wrong? Was he right? But then I felt a rush of shame, so familiar it was almost a comfort, because that was just what he did. He lied. He made me feel like I was going crazy.

"Why else would I have left my job?" I asked.

"Your job made us lose our baby," he said. "We didn't want that to happen again. At least, that was what you said. You said you wanted to have children. Apparently, it was all a lie."

"It wasn't because of my job," I told him. "You know that it wasn't. And I did want a baby with you. Not anymore. You changed after the miscarriage."

He took a step toward me, and with one sharp push, I was on the floor. My tailbone stung, and I sat blinking at the grain of the hardwood floors, linear and stretching away from me, as if suggesting a path out.

Almost immediately, I forced myself up. Because that had not just happened. My husband had not just pushed me.

My mind resisted. I refused to accept the obvious. I denied the undeniable.

But, just as I had risen to a standing position, he pushed me down again. I fell, sprawled on the floor, looking downward, but I could sense him looming over me.

Without warning, he kicked me. One fierce blow to my stomach, so forceful that my body rolled sideways. Pain rippled from the place where his foot had struck me.

I shifted onto my hands and knees and started to propel myself upward. The pain was still throbbing in my stomach.

As I began to stand, Zack's leg shot forward, his foot catching me just below my ribs. He had not seemed to have a response to my words, but this was the only response he needed. He was almost a full foot taller than me, and about eighty pounds heavier. I didn't stand a chance.

In a way, I was relieved. Because now there would be bruises, marks. There would be evidence. I could take pictures. I could leave him.

Assuming I made it through whatever was coming next.

I twisted to my side, so that I could look up at him. Whatever he was about to do, I wanted him to look me in the face as he did it.

I stared into his face. I could still see the anger flickering in his eyes like the flame of a candle. I wondered if he could see the hatred in mine.

It happened so fast.

There was a blast like a firework, and his head exploded. Blood and brain splattered, and he slumped to the floor beside me.

I stared at his body. The life had left it already; that much was clear.

I covered my head with my arms, as if that would stop a bullet, and I braced for the sound, the pain, of a shot. I braced, but it didn't come.

My breath huffed in short, quick bursts. I crawled away from him and pushed myself up to my hands and knees.

Stand. Run. Hide. The words were flashes of sound and light, like the bullet that had ripped through my husband's head.

I looked up, toward the window through which the bullet had torn, expecting to catch a glimpse of the person who was about to kill me, too.

"I won't hurt you."

A voice—faint and female—drifted through the window screen.

And when I peered through it, I wasn't staring down the barrel of a gun. Instead, it was held above the figure's head, in her right hand. Her left arm was raised parallel to her right, her palm facing out. Although she held a weapon, she was displaying the universal sign of surrender.

I stood. I moved closer. Was it a trap? Was the gesture a ploy to draw me near, to set up her shot?

"I won't hurt you. I swear," she said again.

I was compelled forward, desperate to see her more clearly.

She had blond hair, pulled back in a ponytail and darkened from the rain that had started to fall at some point without my noticing. She was wearing black clothes, and her face was familiar, whether because we had met before, or because it was just a common-looking face, I wasn't sure.

"He hurt you," she said.

She'd seen. But how?

"Who are you?" I asked. My mouth, my throat, parched from the hyperventilation, the fear, clicked as I forced the words out.

"I'm someone like you," she said.

I blinked. In that millisecond of darkness, I felt my body swaying.

"I saw him hurt you," she said, beseeching. "I was trying to help you. Please," she added. "I know you have to call the police. But, can you wait five minutes? Please."

I stared at her. Her hands were still raised. The gun was still pointed upward, but at any second, she could lower her arm. She could point it straight at me. She could pull the trigger.

He hurt you. I was trying to help you.

I felt paralyzed. Without deciding to, I felt myself nodding.

She turned, and she ran.

I looked at the clock above the stove. It was 11:32.

Five minutes, she'd said.

At 11:37, I would dial 911.

Or now? I'd nodded, agreeing to wait. But she was gone, and she was a killer.

My thoughts were like legs trudging through thigh-high snow. They pushed forward, but they got nowhere.

I didn't want to look at my husband's body, but I also didn't feel capable of leaving the room. I held my breath and moved to the other side of the counter. I sank to the floor and rested my arms on my knees, my head on my arms. I closed my eyes, and I listened to my heartbeat pounding in my ears. I counted the beats until it slowed, softened.

When I lifted my head, I checked the time. 11:36. I stood on trembling legs and reached for our cordless phone, resting in its docking station against the wall, beside the coffee maker.

I had never called 911 before. Doing so felt strange, like I was part of a scene in a movie. And I hadn't even needed to execute the scene I had rehearsed.

"Nine-one-one, what is your emergency?" answered the operator.

"My husband," I said. "He's been shot in my home. Someone shot him through the window in my kitchen."

The police. They would come. They would speak to me. They would want to know who had shot him. They would want to know what I had seen and heard.

I didn't have much time to decide what exactly to tell them. But it seemed clear. Even through the overwhelming shock still reverberating through my bones, it seemed clear they would think that I did this.

Leah

I shot him.

Oh my God, I shot him.

Did I actually shoot him?

I couldn't have really pulled the trigger.

But my right hand, white from the force with which I was gripping the steering wheel, was aching, throbbing.

I didn't think I'd really do it. But I did. I shot him.

McKenna

The operator offered to walk me through CPR. She told me to apply pressure to his wounds. I was a doctor, but I didn't have to be one to know that there was no point.

"His head," I told her. "His head exploded."

She asked me whether I was in danger. I told her I didn't know. I was hiding behind a kitchen counter. She told me not to move until police arrived, and she said she would stay on the line with me until they did.

"Can I call my brother?" I asked quietly.

"On the other line," she agreed.

I reached for my cell phone. Despite the hour, Aiden answered immediately. It was the nature of his work, I supposed. He was always ready for tragedy.

"What's wrong?" he asked.

"Zack," I said. "Zack was shot?" My voice lifted at the end, as if it was a question.

There was a stunned pause. "Where?" he asked. I could hear movement. He was getting out of bed. Monica was murmuring nearby, asking what was wrong.

"In the house," I said.

"Are you—"

"I'm not hurt," I interrupted. "The police are coming."

"I'm on my way."

I returned to the call with the operator, and we waited, the only sound my shallow breath.

Finally, she told me that police were combing the area around my house, looking for signs of danger. If the area was clear, they would ring the doorbell, and I would be free to let them in.

I sat on the floor and listened and waited.

I thought about the woman. She had asked for five minutes. To get home? Did she live that close? Was that why she looked familiar?

Had I seen her around my house before? Watching me? Watching Zack? Was she his lover? Her unkempt, un-primped appearance told me that she was not. I supposed she might clean up well, transform into a person he might find attractive, but I wasn't convinced. Was she a patient of his? Someone delusional and crazed? But that wouldn't explain her familiarity. I didn't know the names or faces of any of my husband's patients.

There was rain pattering at the roof and windows. Car doors slamming. Voices outside, getting louder and softer and then louder again.

The neighbors would be having fits. I was certain that if the gunshot hadn't awoken them, the commotion certainly had. They would be pulling their curtains to the side, peeking out.

The doorbell chimed. I cupped my hands around my eyes like blinders, so that I couldn't see Zack's body, and ducked around the counter. I pulled the front door open and found two officers standing on the porch. Their badges were splayed open. I'd never seen police badges in person before. I didn't know what to look for. They could have been fake, for all I knew.

"Mrs. Hawkins?" asked the female officer. She was tall and thin. Her skin was smooth and tan, and her dark hair was slicked back in a bun. "Officer Diaz," she said. "May we come in?"

I nodded numbly, pulled the door open wider, and stepped aside to invite them into the house.

I paused in the foyer, not wanting to return to the kitchen or Zack's body and the mess of blood.

"He's in the kitchen," I said. My hands fluttered around my face, pushing back my hair, then gripping my cheeks, like a portrait of dismay.

"Would you like to have a seat here?" Officer Diaz asked, gesturing toward the living room.

I nodded and settled onto the cream suede sofa, which was one of many expensive pieces of furniture in our home that had only ever been used a handful of times.

"As I said, I'm Officer Diaz, and this is my partner, Officer Pace. We cleared the outside of the house. You're safe now. We are going to head into your kitchen, okay? The detective will be here soon with the crime scene techs."

"Okay," I said.

After a number of minutes, I wasn't sure how many, had passed, the doorbell rang again. I stood to answer it, but Officer Diaz emerged from the kitchen and beat me to it.

"This is the detective," she said. She was tugging a pair of blue rubber gloves off her hands. "I'll just let him in."

I stood and watched as she opened my front door as if it were her own and a tall man entered the house. Unlike the officers, he wasn't wearing a uniform. His suit was charcoal, his shirt crisp and white, a contrast to his dark skin, and his tie was the same gray-blue as the Atlantic Ocean during a thunderstorm. He ran a hand across the top of his head, wiping the rain from his buzzed hair.

He held out his other hand. "Mrs. Hawkins, I'm Detective Jordan Harrison," he said.

I reached out to shake his hand, and I blushed, as if he could read my mind and knew that I was thinking how handsome he was, which was an undoubtedly abnormal thing to be thinking when one's husband had just been shot. But nothing about this situation was normal, and I wasn't thinking clearly.

"It's McKenna," I said automatically.

"First, I want to let you know that you're safe," the detective said. He looked straight into my eyes as he spoke. "We have secured the scene. Whoever shot your husband is gone, which is probably not what you want to hear. But I promise you I will do whatever I can to find that person. It just may not be tonight. So, is there someplace else you could go? Someone you could stay with?"

"My brother," I said. "He's on his way here. He can take me to his house."

"That's good," said Detective Harrison. "It's going to take some time to process the scene here. We're going to have to search the house, perform some tests. It will be a while before things quiet down."

"That's—that's fine, I guess. I can stay with my brother."

"Now," he said, but he became distracted and tucked his hand into his jacket pocket. "Excuse me," he said belatedly, extracting a vibrating cell phone. After a few seconds, he locked his phone and slid it back into his pocket. "The medical examiner and a team of technicians are here to process the scene in the kitchen and the backyard. We will chat for a bit, while we wait for your brother, then you can leave. We will let you know when we're finished."

"That's fine," I said again, although it hadn't been a question or suggestion. I didn't mind being told what to do. It was easier to not have options.

"I'll be right back," he said, and he moved to the front door and stepped outside. When he returned, it was with a trail of other people, whom I assumed must be the crime scene technicians and the medical examiner, to whom he had been referring. They moved past me in an indistinguishable blur of faces, rubber gloves, and blue paper booties. No one looked my way at all, and no one offered condolences.

After he had, I presumed, walked them to my kitchen, Detective Harrison returned to the living room. He pointed to one of the teal armchairs across from me, his brows raised, as if to say, *May I sit?* But he hadn't actually spoken.

"Please," I said.

"I know this is very difficult for you, Mrs. Hawkins," he said. He leaned toward me, his elbows resting on his knees. "But it would be very helpful if you could tell me what happened tonight."

"Please call me McKenna," I said. "When you say 'Mrs. Hawkins,' it makes me want to look over my shoulder for my mother-in-law."

Which was a stupid and highly overused joke, and why the hell was I telling jokes?

I slid my hands beneath my thighs, pinching the underside of them, like a physical admonishment. *Hold it together.*

"McKenna," he amended, and I felt myself blush again.

But I had started thinking about my mother-in-law, and I was suddenly unable to think of anything else. She would be devastated to learn about her perfect son's death. I hoped I wouldn't have to be the one to tell her.

She lived in a condo in Boston, having downsized from the sprawling suburban home in which Zack had been raised several years ago, after his father passed away. I wondered if Detective Harrison could be the one to tell her what had happened.

He was looking at me, waiting.

"Um," I said. "Sorry, where should I start?"

"Were you and your husband home all evening?" he asked.

"My husband works late on Thursdays. He got home around eleven. I was in the family room waiting for him. He went upstairs to change his clothes. He came back down. We were talking in the kitchen. Then, I heard the gunshot. He went down."

I covered my eyes with my hands, trying to block out the images of that which I was describing.

"The windows were open," he replied.

"I'd opened them earlier in the day. It was a nice evening and I hadn't closed them yet. We like the house to be cool at night. This is a safe neighborhood." I cleared my throat. "I thought this was a safe neighborhood."

"Before or after the gunshot, did you see or hear anything?" Detective Harrison was leaning back now, but not in a relaxed way. He was still extremely intense. It was radiating off him, almost visible, like smoke swirling from flickering flames.

I took a breath, buying time.

"No, I just—we were talking," I said. "I was just looking at and listening to my husband."

I couldn't tell him about the woman. Why hadn't I mentioned her immediately? Why hadn't I told the 911 operator?

I didn't know the answers to those questions.

He might already think I'd shot my husband, and if I told him the truth? He'd never believe me. He'd think that the woman and I were a team. Working together. Partners in crime.

The detective paused. I could tell he was deciding whether to press further.

"When the kitchen is clear, we would like you to show us where you both were standing," he said.

"Okay," I replied. I wouldn't be telling him that I was in fact not standing anywhere, but was lying on the floor, having been pushed down several times by the victim himself.

That, too, would only incriminate me.

"And after he went down," Detective Harrison said, "what did you do?"

"I—nothing," I said. "I picked up the phone. I called nine-one-one. I sat on the floor and waited for the police. For you."

"Like I said, we'll need to have a look around the house, take some samples from your hands and arms, to test for gunshot residue." He gestured around the room. "I'm sure you understand. You're the only one here." He studied my face. He wanted to know if that made me nervous.

"That's fine," I said. I knew they'd find nothing. So, maybe it was a good thing that they test my hands, poke around my house.

"What were you and your husband talking about?" he asked.

My pulse quickened. I reached for my stomach, still aching from Zack's kicks. "Nothing much. Just about our days."

He nodded. He had no reason to doubt me. Not yet, but maybe he would soon.

"I'm going to pop into the kitchen," he said, pushing to his feet. He towered over me and I tried not to flinch. "You okay here for a few minutes?"

"I'm fine," I said. I shook my head. "I mean, I'm not fine but it's okay. I can wait here alone."

He nodded once, then left the room.

As I watched his tall form heading down the hall to the kitchen, I felt caught in a tangle of emotions, through which I was attempting to weave. There was confusion, shock, alarm. There was a tickle of loss.

But, overwhelming, inappropriate, unseemly—something to be hidden—was the sense of relief.

FRIDAY, MAY 10

Leah

You're probably wondering where I got the gun.

Well, it isn't mine. It belongs to him, and for a long time, I didn't know he had it.

It was just another thing that could be used to exert control over me. Something to keep me in line.

When I returned home, I had pulled into the garage and closed the door behind me. My heart was still thudding wildly, but my breath, which had been as rapid as the pant of a dog, had slowed.

Pain was radiating from my right hand, the residual effect, I supposed, from the recoil of the gun. My right index finger, my trigger finger—because I had suddenly become a person who had a trigger finger—had felt hot and stung by a thousand bees. I'd pried my hands from the wheel.

I'd been aiming for his chest, his heart, but the bullet had torn through the upper portion of his head. I couldn't believe I'd hit him. That I'd done so, was that luck? Would it have been luckier to miss?

It was like I'd been looking down at myself, helpless, a heap on the floor in a beautiful house where peril pulsed, beneath a handsome and charming man who could kill me at any moment. It was like I'd known what he would do to her tonight. And maybe I had. After all, I'd been there before. I had known that it would be up to me to stop him.

I knew, too, that I had to get rid of the gun. Liam might kill me if I did. But he might kill me if I didn't.

I had to believe it was registered. If anything caused suspicion to fall upon me, the existence of that gun would be the nail in my coffin.

I'd carried it into the unfinished portion of our basement, which held Liam's workbench and tools. I unloaded the bullets from the gun, put a towel down on the concrete floor, then wrapped another around the gun.

I had slammed a sledgehammer onto the weapon, over and over, until my shoulders burned and my hands began to blister. It was surprisingly cathartic and productive. The gun had shattered. I'd collected the pieces, stuffed them into the zippered pockets of my pants, and headed to the lake ten minutes away from my house.

It had been months since I'd been there. I used to go often, to run along the path surrounding it.

I'd checked the mirrors of my car the entire way, making sure I wasn't being followed, although I suspected that if anyone had been in pursuit, they would have already pounced.

I'd stood at the edge of the water for a few minutes, staring at the surface of the lake, still and reflecting nothing but darkness. I slipped rubber gloves onto my hands and threw the pieces of the gun into the water, one by one, as hard as I could, then the towels, which quickly became waterlogged and disappeared.

I'd shoved the gloves into my empty pockets and gone home.

As the garage door had lifted, a strike of terror had plunged through my gut, as I'd seen Liam's car there. I'd forgotten for a second, in my panicked state, that he'd not taken his car to the airport. After all, I'd driven it earlier in the night. Still, what if he had arrived home? What if he returned any minute? I wasn't expecting him until the afternoon. But that meant very little. He liked to surprise me. He could have changed his flight.

What would I tell him, when he realized the gun was gone?

He would hurt me. I knew that he'd hurt me. But the first time I'd seen the gun, he'd held it to his own head, not mine.

I'd tell him I threw it out with the garbage. I'd tell him I got rid of it to protect him, that I couldn't bear for him to hurt himself. It would sicken me, but I'd say it anyway. How else could I explain its absence? And I needed it gone. The gun was, as far as I could think, the only thing tying me to Zackary Hawkins's death.

In the garage's privacy, I had used disinfecting wipes to clean the door handles, steering wheels, and the gear shifts of Liam's and my cars, as well as the knob on the door leading into the house. I untied the full trash bag inside the large can in the garage and shoved the rubber gloves, used wipes, and my sneakers inside it.

Inside the house, after ensuring that Liam was still not there, I had cleaned the floor in the basement—vacuuming, mopping, like a good little housewife. Then, I stepped into the laundry room and stripped in the dark, depositing my clothes into the washing machine with a generous pour of detergent. I set the machine spinning and sudsing and climbed the stairs. I showered in the master bathroom, where I used to shower every single morning, usually after a run through the neighborhood or on our basement treadmill. I had located a few of my old toiletries in the cabinet beneath the sink—things that had been left behind from before my move to the basement. I dried myself with Liam's thick, navy towels, which were not ideal but were proximate and therefore preferable to my other options, and dressed in shorts and a T-shirt I tugged from the drawers in my side of our closet—other items that had been left behind.

My mind was racing and firing. I drank a glass of water in the kitchen, then returned to the basement. It was nearly one in the morning, but I wasn't tired, whether from the night's events or my afternoon snooze, I didn't know.

I climbed into bed anyway, and closed my eyes, but the images, the memories, flashed. I saw Zackary's head erupt in blood. I saw McKenna's face. White with terror, hysteria wavering just below her surface. Had she waited five minutes, before calling the police? Or had she reached for the phone the second I turned away from her? Had she told the police what she'd seen when she had looked through the window? Had she told them what I said?

Had someone else seen me run away? Had they seen Liam's car?

The neighborhood had felt peacefully dormant and still as I'd torn through the sodden woods and driven down the rain-slicked streets.

But there seemed to be so many ways I could be tied in, tracked down. I feared it was inevitable that I would be a suspect. And what about McKenna? Would the police suspect her?

Surely, when they arrived, they'd search the house for a weapon. She couldn't have shot him. If she had, the gun would still be around.

Her husband had hurt her. It wasn't an isolated incident—it never was, but even if it had been, that would have mattered little. It occurred to me that I'd brought the gun with me for a reason. Had I been planning to shoot him all along?

McKenna had needed saving. But if she didn't see it that way? If she changed her mind, if she turned me in, the police would be looking for me.

She had been terrified. But so had I.

I still was.

I could only hope she understood that I'd saved her. I could only hope that she was grateful.

I lay in the darkness for a long time, thinking, wishing I could have saved myself.

Could I?

Liam would be home from Charlotte in the afternoon, and I was gripped by an unfamiliar sense of power. I had killed a man. Surely, I could handle my own escape.

I thought about packing up some clothes and snacks, getting in my car, and driving away. I thought I might have enough cash to fill up my gas tank and get myself to my mom's condo. I hadn't squandered all of it on alcohol this week.

My mom would be happy to see me. She would think that I had taken the day off work and driven up to surprise her. I would have to explain that I didn't have a job. I would have to tell her why I'd been fired and explain how it impacted my ability to find other employment. I would have to explain why I had fled the beautiful house I shared with my husband. I would have to help her understand why I could not use my credit or debit cards while I was with her. I would have to make her understand that I was in danger, and that by my being there, she was, too. It was those things that still stopped me. I needed another way out. There had to be another path. I just couldn't see it yet.

After several hours, as I was trying to figure out what that path might be, I drifted off.

The sinking of the bed pulled me from sleep. I could sense his presence before I opened my eyes. He wore a cloud of authority, control, like generously applied cologne.

He had let himself in.

I rolled over in bed and checked the time on my cell phone. It was only ten in the morning.

"What are you doing here?" I asked.

"I took an earlier flight home," he said. "Something has come up at work. I need to head into the office."

"Okay," I said. *Then go,* I was thinking. *Please just go.*

"Here," he said, and I looked over reluctantly. He was holding a bottle of water and a bottle of Excedrin. It was probably the same bottle he had taken from my nightstand earlier in the week, causing me to go out to buy another. It was yet another power move. I was so used to them.

I reached out and accepted the water and medicine, even though I didn't have a headache. I returned it to its rightful place on the nightstand.

It was time to play the game again. I knew that. This week had been a reprieve, but my husband was home now, and the game had resumed.

I wanted to tell him to get out, to leave me alone. But it was safer not to. Like most women, I understood that it was better to keep my enemies close to me. To keep my hatred under wraps, concealed beneath false smiles and superficial conversations. To pretend that we wanted the same things, were on the same page.

"How was your mom?" I asked.

"She was happy to see me," he said. "She's doing well. We took the boat out on the lake every day. It's beautiful there. I wish you had come with me."

I ignored that comment. "That's good," I said. "I'm glad you got to see her for Mother's Day."

I had nothing against the woman, aside from the fact that she had raised a monster. But, not being a mother myself, I was hard pressed to blame her. Growing up with a single mother, having no contact with our fathers, was something Liam and I had in common. It had drawn us closer together. But, while I had been raised by a teacher and had everything I needed growing up, but not everything I wanted, Liam's mother had worked for an accounting firm in Charlotte. He had grown up in a spacious Colonial in an affluent neighborhood. She had worked her way up to a partnership level, and was now semiretired, spending most of her time in a house on the coast of Lake Norman. She had never remarried since her divorce from Liam's father when Liam was a toddler, but she'd had a slew of fairly long-term, and some quite short, relationships with other men.

She was actually not very similar to my mother at all.

"How has your week been?" he asked. He shifted his weight, leaning a little closer to me. I inched away as subtly as I could.

"It's fine," I said. "Just, you know, kind of boring."

I imagined telling him what I had really been up to.

"I know you miss your job," he said. "I know it's hard on you to not be working like you used to."

I nodded. It was a flash of purported kindness, but I was not fooled.

"What are you going to do today?" Liam asked.

"I don't know," I told him.

"Exercise?" he suggested. "Head out for a run like you used to?"

"Maybe," I said. But I knew that I wouldn't.

"I think you should," he said. "Get you back on track, so you can return to our bedroom."

A spike of nausea sliced through my gut. I swallowed.

I didn't respond, so Liam sighed and pushed himself off the bed. He paused in the doorway. "I love you more than anything, Leah," he said quietly.

I felt a sob welling up inside of me, threatening to spill over the edges. That line might've worked in the past, but not anymore. I'd become wise to his tactics. Still, his words couldn't help but strike a familiar nerve, and I hated him for that. Because, who didn't want to be loved, especially by her husband? If only things were that simple.

Again, I did not respond, so again, Liam sighed and walked out of the room. I heard the door click closed gently, and I wished it was him I'd shot.

SEVEN MONTHS EARLIER
THURSDAY, OCTOBER 4

Leah

"Thank you so much for meeting me here, after business hours," said Emily Mayer. I estimated her to be in her midforties, but she wore her hair in a ponytail, which I liked about her. I was a proponent of ponytails myself.

She stood up from her desk, letting me know that the meeting was over, which was fine with me. I was exhausted. A telltale ache was forming behind my eyes.

While I'd anticipated it would be an unremarkable week, it had turned out to be extremely busy, and I had stayed at the office until nine the previous night, drafting a new employee handbook for an old client. It was a much shorter turnaround time than I was used to for such a project, and I'd been on the phone with the client for much of the day, making revisions in real time. The client wasn't interested in exchanging drafts back and forth. He had two new employees starting the following day, and he wanted to give them the handbook at their orientation.

I had left my office at six to meet Emily Mayer in the office of the accounting firm she owned, which was only fifteen minutes from my home. She had found someone who wanted to sublet an office she was leasing—her suite afforded more space than she needed, and it would be financially beneficial for her to rent the extra square footage. She was looking for an attorney to draft the sublease for her. She remembered meeting Claudia at a networking event, and when Claudia's schedule was too tight this week, she had landed on mine.

"No problem at all," I told her. "Your office is closer to my house than my own, so I've missed rush hour and cut down my commute. No complaints here."

"Never underestimate the mood-boosting power of a short commute home," Emily said. "That's why I chose this office location."

She handed me the check she had written for my firm's retainer and the retainer agreement she had signed. I had prepared it before leaving the office, with the hopes that she would be ready to sign after our meeting.

"Here," she said. "If you could email me a receipt or invoice for it tomorrow, that would be great."

I accepted the check and agreement and carefully paper-clipped them inside the file folder of notes I had brought with me to the meeting. "Of course," I said. I tucked my folder into my tote bag–sized purse and turned to leave her office. "Have a great night."

"Unfortunately, I have a few more hours of work to finish up before it's quitting time," she said, pushing her reading glasses to the top of her head. "But, thanks. You, too."

I waved and left the room, grateful that my work was complete for the day. The clock hanging on the wall opposite Emily's desk was wrong— the little hand was approaching the eleven—but it felt like it was right. I felt like I hadn't slept or eaten in days.

But I also felt a tiny rush of adrenaline and satisfaction because the meeting had gone well and I had secured a new client for the firm. I was hopeful that after this project, Emily would come to us for all of her legal needs.

As I descended the two flights of stairs to the lobby and parking lot beyond, I sent Liam a text message. *On my way home.*

Emily was right. The commute was mood boosting. I didn't have to get on the highway. I didn't have to sit in even a second of traffic. I pulled into my garage exactly sixteen minutes after I had left her office.

I had expected Liam to be home, but the other half of the garage was empty. I reviewed my text messages, but he had not responded to my last message letting him know that I was heading home.

ETA? I texted.

I left my phone on the kitchen counter, hung my purse on the back of a kitchen chair, and headed upstairs to change my clothes.

I kicked off my pumps and pulled off my blazer, dress pants, and shell, changing into a pair of yoga pants and a T-shirt. When I returned to the kitchen and checked my phone, there was a reply from Liam sent five minutes earlier. *Leaving.*

There had been no further discussion about his suggestion that I did not need to work if I didn't want to. If I thought about the conversation, it sent a flash of anger to my core. He'd made me feel like my career was just a hobby. *Look how cute, with her business suits and office and file folders. She thinks she's important, aww.* Like I was a child, playing make-believe. He made me feel that everything I did and everything I earned was superfluous.

Logically speaking, perhaps it was. Liam's practice had taken off. We could certainly pay all of our bills and sustain our standard of living on his income alone. But, to me, that was a fact without import or significance. If I didn't work, what would I *do* all day?

I chalked his point of view up to the way he'd been raised. He'd grown up with a single mother who had worked long hours to provide a privileged life for him, completely on her own. Maybe he wanted his wife to feel that she did not have to be like his mother. That she could live a life of leisure and luxury if she so chose.

I just hoped that he could accept that was not the type of life that I so chose.

Having grown up with a single mother myself, I had learned the importance of financial independence. Of not having to depend on someone else to be able to feed or clothe or shelter myself. I needed to be able to take care of myself, in the event the people around me let me down. If I was not employed, and Liam died or walked out the door one day, never to return, where would that leave me?

I was trying not to think about the whole discussion, or the evening at all. It had come out of nowhere, and I didn't understand it. It was an aberration to our new and idyllic marriage.

After he had exercised in the basement, he had made his way upstairs to shower, where he'd found me sitting in bed, trying to read, still shaking from anger. He had brought with him another glass of pino grigio, filled to the brim. He had placed it on my nightstand. "A peace offering," he'd said.

He had crouched down on the floor beside the bed and apologized profusely for the way he had reacted.

"I just work so hard for you, Leah," he had said. "I work so hard to give you everything. You're my everything."

What choice did I have, but to forgive him? I thought that, as long as he didn't push the issue again, we could move past it. But I still wasn't certain where things stood. On November 1, was I still expected to have a special meal waiting for him when he arrived home from work? And what would happen if I didn't?

I heated a drizzle of olive oil in the wok that had been a wedding gift and tossed in a few handfuls of precut, washed broccoli and squash. I was rinsing the shrimp that had been defrosting in the fridge since last night when the house began to rattle slightly as Liam's car pulled into the garage.

He had purchased a brand-new silver BMW sedan after we had returned from our honeymoon, replacing the more elderly version.

"I can't be seen rolling up to the courthouse in a four-year-old car," he'd told me. "It makes it seem like business isn't good, and then people won't want to hire me."

I couldn't imagine that to be the case, but I had kept my mouth shut.

He had suggested that we trade in my car as well—a sporty blue Honda I had been driving since I had started working at the firm where I had met Liam. I had declined his offer. I didn't need a new car, and I would not be seen by anyone "rolling up" to the courthouse because I never went to the courthouse.

I was microwaving a sleeve of brown rice when Liam walked through the door.

"Hey," I called.

"Hey," he replied. He approached to drop a kiss on my head as I stood in front of the stove. "Smells good. Let me just go change."

He disappeared upstairs. I finished assembling our stir-fry and was spooning it onto plates when he returned to the kitchen.

"How did your meeting go?" he asked as we sat down at the table.

"Good," I said. "She's hiring me. She wrote a retainer check on the spot. How was your day?"

As we ate, he told me about his motion hearing, which he had, of course, won, and that he'd spent the rest of the day negotiating a child access schedule in a highly contested custody dispute, and I felt myself relaxing. The adrenaline from the high-paced nature of my day was subsiding. My stomach was growing full. My pulse was slowing, my breathing becoming more even.

Liam cleared the dishes while we continued to talk. I was careful not to check my phone.

"I'm going to head downstairs to work out," Liam said.

I never understood how a person could exercise after eating dinner, or right before bed. If I didn't take care of it in the morning, I didn't do it at all, but Liam liked to head into the office as early as possible, saving his workout for the end of his day.

"Okay," I said. "I'm going to bed. I'm exhausted."

"I'll meet you up there," he told me, before turning and descending the stairs to the basement gym.

In the privacy of our bedroom, I reviewed my emails as I reclined in bed. My boss, Claudia, had clearly worked later than me. She had fired off several emails while I was eating dinner.

After fifteen minutes of Netflix in bed, my eyes were starting to close.

I didn't wake when Liam went to bed, nor when he got up and left for work. When I opened my eyes, there was sunlight streaming through the crack between our navy blackout curtains, and the place in the bed beside me was empty. A faint dent in his pillow and rumpled sheets on his side of the bed were the only indication that my husband had been there at all.

I had forgotten to set my alarm the previous night, and it was nearing six thirty in the morning—too late for me to exercise before work. As I showered and dressed, I tried to remember the last time I had failed to set an alarm before bed. I couldn't recall it ever happening.

I stirred peanut butter into a bowl of oatmeal and packed my lunch between bites, then slung my purse and lunch bag over my shoulder and rushed to my car. If I didn't get on the road by seven thirty, the length of my commute could double.

I pulled into the parking garage forty-five minutes after I had left the house. I peeked into Claudia's office on my way by, but she wasn't there.

After tucking my lunch bag into the communal fridge and brewing myself a cup of coffee, I headed into my office. The red light on my phone was flashing, so I entered my PIN and played my messages while I logged in to my computer. I had only one—a voicemail from Harry Miles, the client for whom I had drafted the employee handbook earlier in the week. He had requested a few more revisions, things that had just occurred to him the previous night.

I got to work revising the document and was so immersed in it that it took a few seconds for me to notice Claudia standing in the doorway of my office.

"Hey," she said when I looked up. She settled into the guest chair across from my desk, crossing her long legs. "What are you up to?"

"Revising Harry Miles's employee handbook," I said. I paused the timer in the software we used to track our billable time and swiveled my chair to face her. "He got the final draft Wednesday night, but he left me a message this morning requesting revisions."

She snorted. "Expect that to happen a few more times. He's always thinking of something he wants to add or change." She shrugged and rotated her neck from side to side, as if working out a kink. "Oh, well. Better for our billables."

"How are you?" I asked. Claudia looked tired, but I knew not to say as much. Doing so would be akin, in her mind, to telling her she looked bad, even though she didn't—just tired.

"Tired," she said. "Whatever. Nothing wrong with being tired. It means we're working hard. Business is good." She uncrossed her legs and recrossed them, throwing the left over the right this time. "Speaking of which, how did the meeting go last night with Emily?"

"Oh," I said, startling. "I completely forgot. She retained us. I have the check and agreement." I tugged my bag out from under my desk and pulled out the folder I had brought with me to Emily's office. I removed the papers clipped to the front of the folder and handed them to Claudia.

She took them from me and riffled through them. "You said there was a check?" she asked.

"It's there," I said, watching her. I knew that I had clipped the check with the retainer agreement.

She shook her head.

"Hang on," I said. I flipped through the remnants of the folder, and felt relief wash over me as I located the check, tucked between two sheets of yellow paper torn from a legal pad, on which I had scribbled notes during the meeting.

"Thanks," she said. She took it from me and pushed herself out of the chair. "I'll deposit this. You good with drafting the sublease for her?"

"Yep," I said. "It's next on my list."

"Great," Claudia said once she was almost out of the room. She was already moving on to the next thing.

I returned my attention to Harry Miles's revisions. Once I was finished, I fired off an email, attaching the new document, and moved onto Emily's sublease.

Again, I didn't notice Claudia entering my office until I heard the door closing behind her.

I felt my heart fluttering in my chest because she never closed my door when she spoke to me in my office. No one ever closed their doors at the firm.

But privacy didn't always mean bad news.

"What's up?" I asked. I turned to face her and tried to sound breezy.

"Leah," she said, sitting down across from me. She pushed a small piece of paper across the desk. "Can you explain this to me?"

I looked down. It was the check from Emily Mayer. Three thousand dollars was the amount. The memo line said *Legal Retainer Payment*. It was dated October 4.

"This is the check Emily gave me," I said. I didn't understand. "I just gave this to you."

"Okay," said Claudia. "And can you turn it over, please?"

I did. On the line for endorsements was a legible signature that looked nothing like the real thing: *Claudia Granderson.* It was missing its looping *G,* and each letter was written out neatly, rather than melding together in a squiggling trail. And below it, in slightly messy, though still readable handwriting that looked shockingly like my own, *Pay to the order of Leah Dawson.*

I furrowed my brow. "I—I don't understand," I said. "I didn't write this."

Claudia didn't say anything.

"Why would I have done that?" I asked. I wouldn't have signed her name. I wouldn't have endorsed the check to myself. I didn't.

"It's not just this," Claudia said. Her brows were low and stern. "The check bounced. I called Emily, who said it already cleared. Someone already deposited it."

"Not me," I said. I was shaking my head so hard it was making me dizzy. "I didn't deposit it."

"Leah," said Claudia. "What am I supposed to think? This check was for unearned retainer funds from a client. What am I supposed to tell her? I was mortified when she said on the phone she thought we had already deposited the check because it had cleared her account."

"I—I don't know." My head was spinning. I felt like I was in a bad dream. I pinched my thigh beneath my desk. But I didn't wake up.

Claudia was looking at me like she didn't know me. "I'm sorry," she said. "But there isn't any other explanation. This situation is a massive breach of the ethical rules. You know that. Not only that. It's criminal. Forgery. Theft."

"I swear," I pleaded. "I didn't sign that check and I didn't deposit it."

Claudia was shaking her head. "I don't have any other choice. You must understand that."

I closed my eyes. *No, no, no.*

"I have to let you go, Leah."

I tried to protest, but my voice died in my throat.

"I'll need to deduct the three thousand from your final paycheck for Emily's retainer. I'm sorry. You can gather your things."

"I didn't do this," I whispered.

"I wish I could believe you, Leah. I really do. There's just no other explanation for this. I have to protect my business. My reputation is everything. Without that, this firm won't survive."

What she didn't say hung in the air. *My reputation is everything, and you just ruined yours.*

My hand was shaking as I reached for my mouse to save my files and close them.

I lifted the singular picture frame from my desk. My and Liam's smiling faces looked out at me from within the turquoise frame, resplendent and filled with joy. Our wedding day. I dropped it into my purse.

Claudia paused in the doorway. "I really thought you were going to grow here," she said. "I can't tell you how disappointed this makes me."

I bit my lip and nodded. I wanted to plead my innocence again, but it felt pointless. She was right. What other explanation was there?

Claudia disappeared, closing the door behind her, so that no one could hear me cry.

She'd taken the check, left my office, returned with it. Had she signed it and endorsed it to me, during those few minutes that she was gone? Had she wanted to get rid of me, and fast? I paused to press the heels of my hands into my burning eyes. I couldn't imagine why she would have done that. We worked well together. She had never expressed any displeasure with me. Never.

I finished stuffing my personal belongings into my purse and I slipped out of my office and into the stairwell nearby. I would rather descend the seven flights down to the parking garage than walk past the other offices or receptionist.

I always hated the parking garage beneath my office. The turns were too tight. The spots were too small. It was always too crowded, and visibility was bad. But I was suddenly overwhelmed by the realization that, unless I could figure out a way to prove my innocence, unless I could figure out a way to explain what had happened with that check, it was the last time I would be here.

It wasn't until I had slammed my car door that I realized I had forgotten my lunch bag in the communal fridge. But there was no way I could go back in to retrieve it.

I wouldn't be needing it anyway. Not only had I lost my job, suddenly, shockingly, I had lost it in a way that essentially precluded me from being able to find another one. Every prospective employer would want to know why I had left my previous position before having something else lined up. Everyone would want to know why I wasn't using my most recent boss as a reference.

As I corkscrewed my way around the garage, I began to sob. How, I wondered, would I explain this to my mom? How would I tell my husband? Or, I asked myself as I reached up to blot the tears from my cheeks, would he secretly be happy?

You don't even have to work. Wasn't that what he'd said on Monday night?

I didn't have to work. Four days later, my job was gone.

THE SAME DAY
FRIDAY, OCTOBER 5

Leah

I was sitting on the family room sofa, waves of disbelief still shaking me, like aftershocks from an earthquake.

I had no memory of signing Claudia's name or depositing Emily Mayer's check, but I must have. It wasn't Claudia. I knew it wasn't Claudia. And, beyond that, there was no other explanation.

Well, there was one other possible explanation. The only one I could think of. But it wasn't preferable in any way.

I had called Liam from the car as soon as I had pulled out of the parking garage, sobbing so hard I could barely get the words out.

"Did you forge her name? Did you deposit the check?" he had asked incredulously.

"Of course not," I had insisted. "Why would I do that?"

"Maybe you did it by accident." It sounded absurd.

"Check the account," I told him, suddenly feeling hopeful. "See if there's a new deposit."

"Okay," he said, and I waited for him to do so.

Immediately after our wedding, per Liam's suggestion, I had transferred the entirety of my bank accounts into Liam's, and he had added my name to them. I had signed up for online access to the accounts, although I never actually checked them. Liam took care of all bill paying. That was just one of his chores in our division of labor at home.

I had no reason to doubt his ability to handle our funds. Besides, I was a lawyer. I knew that the money earned during our marriage was marital property, and I had an interest in it, regardless of the way it was titled or moved around or used.

"No," he'd said. "I don't see it."

I had slammed my hand on the steering wheel. "See? That proves my innocence. I can show the statement to Claudia. Print that for me. Or send it in an email."

"Leah," he had said cautiously. "You aren't thinking clearly. She will just think you altered the statements. Or, she'll think you have another account where you did deposit it. I mean," he added, "you could have accounts that even I don't know about."

"How could you say that?" I'd said. "Are you saying you think I am hiding money from you? That I did take the money?"

"No, no," he'd replied, placating. "Look, everything is going to be fine. Just go home. Try to relax. I will see you later tonight, okay?"

I had gone home, but I couldn't relax.

I had left my work laptop in my office—it was no longer mine—but my personal laptop was resting on the coffee table. I grabbed it, opened it, and logged in. I navigated to the website for Charles Schwab, with whom we had our bank accounts. My log-in information was saved. I clicked the Sign In button and waited, watching the cursor turn into a little wheel and begin to spin.

My heart was pounding as I scrolled through the recent transactions in our checking account. There was no deposit for $3,000. Emily Mayer's check wasn't there.

I needed to speak with my husband.

The minutes, the hours, ticked by more slowly than I'd thought possible, as I waited for Liam to get home.

Although it was Friday, and most people stopped work for the day a little earlier than they did Monday through Thursday, it wasn't until seven that I received a text message from Liam letting me know that he was leaving the office.

I knew that I should be preparing dinner, but I simply couldn't do it. My mind was racing. I felt betrayed. By my boss. By my husband. Something was going on.

When he flung the door from the garage open and entered the kitchen, I practically pounced.

His face was filled with concern. He stepped toward me and pulled me into a hug.

"You okay?" he asked.

"No," I said. I stepped away from him. I began to pace. "What is going on, Liam? What happened with that check?"

"Maybe Claudia did it. Someone else at your firm. Maybe she needed to lay you off without having to spring for severance or benefits."

I shook my head. "No." I was adamant. "It wasn't her." How could I be so sure? Why did I trust her more than I trusted my husband?

The concern had drained from his face. It was replaced by anger.

"What," he asked, "are you suggesting?"

"I checked the accounts. It wasn't there. I didn't deposit it anywhere else. I didn't go anywhere after work, after Emily Mayer gave it to me. How could it have been deposited?" I stopped pacing. I spun around to face him and planted my feet on our family room rug, as if preparing for a sword fight.

"What are you suggesting?" Liam asked again, behaving as though he was affronted, but there was something mocking about it.

"Are you seriously suggesting that I went into your purse and stole a check from a client? Leah, you sound crazy right now." He spread his hands out. He was no longer mock-affronted. He was becoming mock-afraid, of me, his crazy wife.

But that was exactly what I was suggesting, was I not?

"Why would you have done that?" I demanded. "Where did you put it? Do you have other accounts I don't know about?"

It reminded me of a snake. Very still, frozen in time, watching his prey. It happened in the blink of an eye, my eye. He lashed out and slapped me across the face, his right hand coming into contact with my left cheek.

Automatically, my hand rose, to cradle my stinging face. My mouth dropped open, but I couldn't speak. Tears were leaking from my left eye.

"You're insane," he said, jabbing a finger toward me. He turned on his heels, and he disappeared.

I sank to the floor. I rested my forehead on my arms, and I sobbed. The day had held a year's worth of tears. When I awoke this morning, I'd had no idea that I was about to lose my job. I'd had no idea that my husband was about to slide a mask over his face and turn into a monster.

Yet I was the crazy one?

I don't know how long I sat there on the floor, my head down. I felt more alone than I'd thought it possible for a person to feel.

Eventually, I heard footsteps approaching. The rattle of ice in a glass. I lifted my head. Liam crouched down beside me. He was holding two drinks. He handed one to me. I hesitated, then accepted it, took a sip. A vodka soda. It was strong.

He took a sip as well, then put his drink down on the rug. I felt his hand rest on my back, and I flinched.

"Everything's going to be okay, Leah," he told me. "Don't worry about your job. I will take care of you. I will take care of everything."

I didn't respond. I took a long pull at my drink, watched the level of liquid in the glass drop down.

I still had so many questions, so many things that I didn't under-stand. But I didn't ask. Because my cheek still stung from the feeling of his hand against it. The hand that was now, still, rubbing small circles on my back.

There was a welcome numbness washing over me. I didn't want to fight or to cry anymore. I did want everything to be okay, just as Liam had said. I did want to trust him. So, I didn't say anything. I didn't ask any of the questions looping through my mind. I stayed there, on the floor beside my husband, and I finished my drink. But, I knew that something had shifted. Nothing would be the same ever again.

NOW
FRIDAY, MAY 10

Detective Jordan Harrison

It was my second time visiting the house. I parked in the driveway as if it were my own. It was midday on a Friday, a workday, but the woman across the street was home, standing in her front yard. She was aiming a watering can over the pots of begonias lining her front steps. A looky-loo. That's what my mom would say.

I held up my hand in a wave, and she had the self-awareness to look embarrassed and turn away. She crouched down in her front garden and began tugging at a weed.

Her name was Yesenia Traynor, and Officers Diaz and Pace had already interviewed her earlier this morning. They'd sent me the CliffsNotes of their neighbor interviews and I had read through them before leaving the station.

While a handful of neighbors had alarm systems installed in their homes, none of them had cameras, aside from the doorbell variety, which captured nothing more than the front porch, and did nothing more than keep an eye on delivered packages. It was a safe neighborhood.

The only neighbor who had heard anything was Faith Gardiner. She had been my previous stop.

I had parked in her driveway, as well.

She and her husband had sent the kids to school as usual, but they had stayed home from work, so shaken were they by the murder of their next-door neighbor last night.

"It could have happened to us," Faith had said, wide eyed.

"Mrs. Gardiner," I said, "there's no reason to believe that what hap-

pened to Dr. Hawkins could have happened to you or your husband.
We have no indication that it was a random incident. We believe he was
targeted, and we are doing everything we can to determine why."

Faith Gardiner had gasped, her right hand to her throat.

"Please have a seat, Detective," said Roger Gardiner, not acknowl-
edging his wife's histrionics. He gestured to the family room sofa. The
cushions were lumpy and misshapen. It was clearly oft used, and well
loved. Unlike the Hawkinses' house, this was a home.

Faith snapped out of her daze. "Tea?" she asked. "Coffee? I could
bring out some scones or bagels or something."

I shook my head. "No, thank you. I'm fine."

I actually did want a cup of coffee. It had been a late night. This
woman struck me as the type of person who made a mean scone, and
I was quite comfortable enough with myself to thoroughly enjoy one.
But sipping from the same mug they used and dropping buttery crumbs
down the front of my suit would upset the professionalism of the interview.

"I understand from my colleague, Officer Diaz, that you heard something unusual last night," I said. I propped my right ankle atop my left
knee. "Why don't you tell me about that?"

"Well," said Faith, worrying the hem of her shirt in her hands, "I
heard a loud sound when the clock beside my bed said 11:32. That
meant it was 11:31 because I keep the clock set a minute fast. It helps me
stay on top of things."

"I see," I replied. Faith Gardiner reminded me of my mother. "What
sort of loud sound did you hear?"

"It—it was my neighbor Zack, being shot." She looked at me like I
had grown a second head.

"That's what you know now," I said. "But what did you think at the
time?"

"I've never heard a gunshot before," she said. She released the hem of
her shirt. "To be honest with you, I thought it was a firework. I thought
it was some kids setting off a firework. Never did I imagine someone
would be shot in my neighborhood. I looked at the clock, then rolled
over and went back to sleep." Faith bit her lip. She looked embarrassed.

"What about you, Mr. Gardiner? Did you hear anything?" I turned slightly toward him. Sunlight trickling through the windows behind him reflected off the bald spot on the top of his head.

"I didn't wake up," he said. "Not until there was all the activity outside, with the police and everything."

"How well do you know your neighbors, Drs. Zackary and McKenna Hawkins?" I asked.

"We were friendly. We always waved to each other. We'd chat for a minute or two if we were getting the mail at the same time. But we didn't hang out or anything. We're very different." Faith looked embarrassed again, as though not being close with her neighbors was a petty crime from her youth.

"Different how?" I asked.

"We're, what, ten or so years older than them?" She looked to her husband for support and he provided it in the form of a nod. "More importantly, we have children and they don't. We just don't have a lot in common with them."

"And how old are your children?" I asked. I was wondering whether I should talk to them about what they had seen and heard last night.

"They're seven and five," said Mr. Gardiner. "Kindergarten and second grade."

Or not.

I'd have Officer Diaz check in with the Gardiners this evening, under the pretense of seeing how they were doing. She could talk to the kids, too. She was a mother herself, and she'd gain far more traction with them than me.

I had assured the Gardiners that I would do everything I could to find the person who had shot their neighbor, and stood up from their sofa, which was very soft and comfortable and into which I had sunk deeper and deeper during our conversation. It felt like pushing myself out of a pit of mud.

"Do you think," Faith Gardiner had asked as they walked me to the door, "that the person will come back?" Her husband placed a hand on her back.

"I've no reason to think that," I had told them. I didn't say that I couldn't rule it out. Not yet. "I'll send an officer to check on you later," I'd added, laying the groundwork for Diaz's visit.

I'd left them standing in their foyer, Mr. Gardiner's hand still resting on Mrs. Gardiner's back, and climbed into my car, moving it to the driveway next door. The looky-loo had been looking the whole time. Why couldn't she have been looking last night around eleven thirty?

I locked my car and loped toward the Hawkinses' front door. Hawkins, singular now, I reminded myself.

Mrs. Hawkins. *McKenna,* she'd said.

I knocked twice on the front door and rang the doorbell once, letting her know that my presence wasn't optional, my visit wasn't a friendly one. I was coming in.

For the tenth time of the day, at least, I missed my partner. I missed her discerning gaze. Her quiet and calming presence. Her hair was as orange and crimson and wild as fire. Her eyes were as gold and luminous as a cat's. She was nearly as tall as I was. She was whip smart. She was a thousand times stronger than she looked.

But Detective Mallory Cole was not standing on the porch step beside me where she belonged, and there wasn't anything I could do about that. She was recovering. It was early, still, and it would take time. Excruciating time. I wished it would pass in a blink.

But the show went on without her.

McKenna Hawkins's front door swung open.

"Detective," she said. "Come in." She stepped aside and permitted me to enter.

We walked into the living room, staying away from the kitchen and what had happened there the previous night. I knew that the scene had been processed and cleaned. I knew that the sight of it would no longer reveal the violence that had happened there. But the remnants of it would be suspended in the air. You'd be able to smell it, to feel it. I didn't know if McKenna was truly incapable of returning to the room, or if she just wanted me to believe that she wasn't capable of doing so.

I watched her perch on the edge of her sofa like it was white hot and she was trying not to get burned. She was objectively attractive, although she wore no makeup today. Her hair was long, hanging to her breasts, and it was brushed but un-styled.

I tried to picture her shooting her husband.

Granted, there was not a speck of evidence that she had.

The only physical evidence that anyone else had been at the house last night was three footprints on the stone patio outside the kitchen windows. They could have been McKenna's. Not particularly large. But we'd confiscated all of her flat-bottomed shoes from the house, with her consent. None of them had been wet. Still, the techs were checking to see if any of them matched, to see if McKenna's shoes were the same size as the prints.

Neither McKenna's yard, nor the sparse woods behind it, had yielded anything useful. The Hawkinses' grass was lush, well cared for, coaxed into a verdant and springy comforter. The woods were too slick with vegetation to reveal fresh prints. It was the sort of woods residents might ramble through with dogs, letting them shit and not bothering to clean it up. Or to which neighborhood teenagers might sneak off, with skinny joints or half-full bottles of liquor. In fact, we'd also found two empty beer cans and an empty fifth of Smirnoff. These, too, were being tested, though I was confident that was a waste of time. Upon responding to the house, handfuls of officers had combed the entire area by foot—finding the shooter had been the priority, in that moment, over preserving his or her prints in the ground.

I was still awaiting the results of the fingerprints we had pulled from the windowsills. I could only hope they'd give me something more.

"How are you holding up?" I asked. I sat on the edge of the chair across from her, mimicking her posture. "I wasn't sure you'd be here."

"Okay," she said. "I mean, considering." She shrugged. "My brother dropped me off this morning."

"Are you planning to stay here, or head back to your brother's?" I asked.

"I'm staying with my brother again tonight," she said. "I'll be there before it gets dark."

I had looked into the brother already. He worked in law enforcement and had been issued a handgun—a nine-millimeter Glock 17—as part of his employment. I was waiting for the ballistics results to come back. They would tell me if Aiden Lyons's gun could have been used to shoot Zackary Hawkins. If so, I would get a warrant. I would get my hands on it.

I'd buzz Diaz and Pace from the car, have them track down Aiden and Monica Lyons by the afternoon. I wanted to speak with them before McKenna got to their house. I wanted to find out where they'd been last night, before Aiden had—allegedly—left there to pick up his sister.

"Do you have any leads in the investigation?" McKenna asked. She picked at a cuticle. Her nails were short and dark navy. They looked freshly painted. I had never seen Mallory with paint on her nails. She used to chew them when she was deep in thought, while she sat in the front seat of my county-issued, unmarked sedan.

"We are waiting for fingerprints to come back. So far, all we've uncovered in terms of physical evidence about the person who was outside your window are three footprints on your patio. One going toward it, two away. The rain didn't help."

She folded her hands together in her lap, as if in a conscious effort to stop ruining her cuticles. They were pressed together tightly, as if she was trying to stop them from shaking. I waited for her to ask me something more about these prints—Male or female? Large or small? She didn't.

"We spoke with your neighbors," I continued. "Only your next-door neighbor, Faith Gardiner, heard anything. She heard the gunshot at 11:31 p.m."

"Did she look outside? Did she see something?" McKenna asked. Her shoulders lifted half an inch.

"She assumed the sound was from a neighborhood kid setting off a firework. She went back to sleep."

McKenna visibly relaxed. "Kids do sometimes set off fireworks in this neighborhood. Not in May, though."

"What's interesting," I continued, "is that your nine-one-one call did not come in until 11:36."

McKenna watched me. She didn't speak. Her eyes were inscrutable cobalt orbs.

"Five minutes," I said.

McKenna blinked twice.

"What happened to those five minutes?"

"I'm not sure," she said. "I heard the shot. Zack went down, and so did I. I was terrified and shocked. I'm not sure how long I laid on the floor. It could have been five minutes."

Again, I tried to picture her shooting her husband in the head. I pictured her standing outside on the patio, waiting for her husband to get home from work. As he moved around the kitchen, she had shot him through the open window. She then concealed the gun—where she got it or where she put it, I didn't yet know—her shoes, too, and entered the house. She washed her hands. She called the police. That explained those five minutes between the gunshot and the call. It was the only theory I had.

And it was full of holes.

McKenna Hawkins had been subjected to a test for gunshot residue while the techs had processed the scene in the kitchen. It would have been impossible for her to remove all of the residue from her hands and arms between the 11:31 gunshot heard by Faith Gardiner and the arrival of the police at 11:48 p.m., even if she'd jumped in the shower and changed her clothes.

She'd been fully cooperative with the test. She knew she was clean.

And what had she done with the gun?

She couldn't have shot him. Not without help, whether from her brother, or someone she had paid.

I moved on for now.

"There was another nine-one-one call about your house the previous night," I said. "Someone called to report a domestic disturbance."

She swallowed. "I know."

"Can you tell me what happened?"

I could see her thinking, calculating. It was a lost cause. She knew what Zackary had told the police about the incident. She wasn't going to alter that story. She was protecting him, or she was protecting herself. I wasn't sure which.

"We were having an argument, but we weren't very loud. I'm not sure how someone heard us or why they called the police." She tucked her hair behind her ears. "Who was it?" she asked. "Who called? It's a little troubling, to be honest. Someone must have been very close to our house to hear us."

"We don't know," I said. I recognized she was trying to turn the incident around, to distract me from what mattered. "It was a female caller. She reported hearing raised voices. She said she was concerned for your safety. She called from a blocked phone number and hung up before leaving her name."

"Isn't that strange?" McKenna asked. "I mean, she involved herself by calling, but she was trying to conceal her identity?"

"Not particularly," I said. "She might have felt compelled to do something but didn't want to be interviewed. She didn't want her name in a police report."

McKenna bit her lip. She looked around the room. She was becoming antsy, and she wanted this conversation to be over.

"What were you arguing about?" I asked.

"It actually wasn't an argument, per se," she said. "I was upset and frustrated. I had a miscarriage in January. We have been trying to get pregnant again ever since. It's not working out, and I sort of lost it. I was just feeling very emotional."

Zackary had greeted the officers at the door. He'd smoothed things over, told them he was a psychiatrist, that his wife had been having an episode, and he had calmed her down. McKenna had then made a brief appearance, confirming his explanation.

Her story sounded plausible. Except for the little envelope of birth control pills my team had found on the floor at the edge of a kitchen cabinet. The techs had bagged and tagged the pills. I assumed she would notice their absence soon.

McKenna was lying. But again, I moved on for now.

"Let me ask you this," I said. "Who do you think could have killed your husband? Who were his enemies?" I didn't ask whether he had any enemies. I knew better than to ask that. Everyone had enemies.

"My husband was a psychiatrist," she said. "He worked with many mentally ill people. A lot of his patients have been in and out of psychiatric hospitals. Is it possible it could have been one of them?"

"It's possible," I said. "We will look into it, but HIPAA is going to protect his patient records. Absent specific evidence, we are not going to be able to get access to his files. But if that's where our investigation leads, we can get a court order."

"I understand," she said. "I'm a doctor, too."

"Are you?" I said, even though I already knew. "What kind?"

"I was," she corrected. "I used to be a pediatrician. I stopped working in January."

"Any particular reason?" I asked.

Her expression hardened. "Health reasons," she said.

She knew I couldn't pry any further than that.

"That's all I have for you for now, McKenna." I leaned forward, preparing to push myself upward.

"One thing," she said, looking self-deprecating and sheepish.

"Yes?"

"Could you, I mean, is it something you would do to notify my husband's mother about what happened? I don't think I can bear it." She wrung her hands together in her lap.

She was a decent actress.

"Of course," I said. "We can perform notifications to the family." I pulled a card and pen from my pocket and handed them to her. "Write down her number for me. I'll give her a call." I wanted to talk to the mother, anyway.

She did so, looking grateful.

I stood up, and my knees cracked. Thirty-five, and my body was already failing me. Too much running. That's what Mallory would say. "Why do you run so much?" she always asked. "What are you running from?"

"This job," I'd tell her. I ran from the things I saw. The things that kept me up at night. I couldn't escape them, but I tried.

I moved into the foyer. "I'll be in touch soon."

"Thank you," she said again. She flipped the dead bolt on the front door and pulled it open for me.

My hand gripping the door, I looked into her eyes one final time, preparing to reassure her that I'd be working day in and out to discover who had killed her husband. But I recognized something familiar, something unexpected, in them.

McKenna Hawkins was relieved, and I was determined to find out why.

McKenna

Friday afternoon, and I was making my usual trip to Pine View Liquors. This time, I had no order from my husband. I didn't need to comb the shelves, searching for the specific type of craft beer he wanted. I was picking something out for myself, and only myself. It was refreshing and sweet, like the crisp glass of pinot grigio that I was craving.

Upon my insistence, Aiden had dropped me off at my house before he headed to work. I planned to spend the rest of the day going through the house, cleaning up the mess the police had made last night, and drinking some wine. Not too much. Not enough that I wouldn't be able to drive back to Aiden's house later.

At some point, as I'd lain in Aiden's guest room, staring at the ceiling, listening to the peeper frogs and crickets in the woods around his house, it had sunk in.

I could drink and eat whatever I wanted. I could wear sweatpants and an old T-shirt, stained and threadbare. I could dye my hair pink if I chose. I could gain ten pounds. I no longer had to look the part of the perfect wife. I could taste the freedom. It was exhilarating and intoxicating and I wanted to gulp it down and bathe in it and melt into it until it was indistinguishable from every other part of me.

My husband's death. Was that not what I'd fantasized about many times before? A car accident. His head smashing into the windshield. Blood filling the car.

The manner had been shocking and implausible. Not like anything I could have or would have imagined. It had happened when I was only feet away from him. But it had happened nonetheless, and I was free.

I no longer felt scared to be in the house. If the woman had wanted to kill me, I realized, she would have done so last night. But I acknowledged that it was possible I was being watched by the police, and I knew that I should be scared, considering what had happened there. I needed to behave as though I was still scared. And I did want to see my brother. I could visit him as often as I liked now. I could move in with him permanently, or for as long as I wanted. He'd said as much after he'd picked me up, and we'd raced up I-95. In fact, he had pleaded with me to stay with him for at least a few weeks. He was just being my protective little brother. He was worried about me.

He didn't understand that, actually, I was now the safest I'd ever been in the house. I couldn't tell him that. To pacify him, and to make Detective Harrison believe that I was afraid to be alone, I had agreed to sleep at his house "for now."

But I didn't want to stay there all the time. There was much to be done at my house. I was going to sell it and move into something smaller. I had decided that, too, as I'd lain awake until the early morning hours, trying, and failing, to fall asleep.

While I had waited for Aiden to arrive, the police had combed through our things, looking, I assumed, for a gun. They had tested me for gunshot residue, pressing sticky rounds to my hands and arms before bagging them up. Aiden had given me a hug and had the conscientiousness to tell me that he was sorry. He walked me to his car, where his true feelings about Zack, left unsaid, hung in the air: *I never liked your husband.* My reply did, too: *You were right about him.* My stomach was still stinging from his kicks, almost as shocking as the moment the bullet had sliced through his head.

Oddly, I wasn't exhausted, although I'd only managed a few hours of sleep. My head and limbs were buzzing with disbelief about everything that had happened. I felt an energy and hopefulness that I hadn't felt in a long time. I understood that this mystery woman had done for me what I had been unable to do for myself. She had freed me. Hadn't she said as much? *He hurt you. I was trying to help you.*

I didn't know whether she was a person from Zack's life with a vendetta against him, or whether she had been motivated by a desire to save me.

Either way, she had escaped the patio undetected. I was pleased that she hadn't been caught, but I'd seen the suspicion in Detective Harrison's eyes earlier in the day. Even though I hadn't told him about the woman, even though he hadn't found a gun, he thought I was involved in my husband's death. I couldn't blame him. It was the convenient, the obvious, explanation. I didn't think he would be able to prove it—I wasn't involved, after all, but I knew he would spend a long time trying.

In the meantime, I was desperate to understand why the woman had shot Zack. While I continued cleaning up the house, erasing the evidence of the police officers' search and packing away Zack's things, I would comb through them, looking for some clue as to the woman's identity. If the police had come across anything interesting, they would have taken it with them. But I knew more than they did. I knew my husband, and I had seen who had shot him. Perhaps the house would hold some hint as to who she was.

I grabbed a bottle of pinot grigio around the neck and headed for the register. Just like last Friday, I selected a bag of chips, as well as a dark chocolate bar stuffed with cookie butter, simply because I wanted them, and I could have them.

It felt unbelievable that a week ago today, I'd been in this same store, purchasing Zack's beer and the wine and snacks for Alyssa and Mina's visit. Zack had come home early. He'd surprised me. He'd thrown the basket of chips against the wall. I had knelt to the floor and picked them up, one by one.

There would be no more incidents like that.

I paid for my items with a credit card, relishing the fact that there'd be no one checking the purchase history and asking me questions. It raised an issue, though. I'd have to gain access to our credit card and bank accounts. Zack had handled all of the finances. He had paid all the bills. We had merged our bank accounts when we got married, and I never set up online access to the accounts. Occasionally, I would ask him how much money we had in our savings, checking, and investment accounts. He would open the accounts in the apps on his phone and tell me. I didn't have a reason to distrust him. Now, I would need access to everything—the mortgage and utilities accounts as well. I would need to stay on top of the bills.

The only funds to which I had access were those in my 401(k), into which a portion of my paycheck had been deposited twice a month. That account had remained relatively steady ever since I stopped working.

Which raised another issue. It was time to find a job. I wondered if my old medical practice would rehire me.

I wasn't sure if I wanted to ask. My former coworkers would all have questions for me and about me. They knew too much. They'd speak in hushed voices, stopping when I entered the communal kitchen. *Her husband was murdered. Are the police investigating her? Do you think she was involved?*

It was probably best to have a fresh start somewhere new.

I wrapped my arms around my brown paper bag and carried it to my car. I nestled it onto the floor in front of the back seat, and climbed into the driver's seat, pushing my sunglasses onto my face.

I was about to back out of my parking spot, but I paused. A woman was approaching the front door of the store. I didn't know her, but I'd know her anywhere.

My first instinct was to turn away, to flee.

But curiosity prevailed, and I watched her through my windshield.

She was average height and weight. Her hair was long and dirty blond at the roots, lighter toward the ends, as if she was growing out a dye job. Her posture was slumped—she practically slunk into the store. Her face was aimed downward, but I could still see her features. They were the same features that had looked in at me through the window screen in my kitchen last night.

If a week or so had passed, I might not have recognized her. She was pretty, but in a rather generic, blond-haired, blue-eyed, not especially memorable way. But mere hours had passed since she had stood on my patio and shot my husband.

That I would come across her here, today, felt intentional and predestined, rather than coincidental.

After she disappeared inside, I pulled out of my parking spot and drove around the side of the store. I performed a three-point turn, and backed into another spot, where I idled, waiting for her to emerge. Who was she? I was desperate to know everything about her. What connection did she have to Zack, and why had she shot him?

A few minutes passed, and she sidled out of the store. I was struck by how alike we looked, aside from the extra fifteen or twenty pounds she was carrying. We could have been sisters. If she was my husband's lover, his secret girlfriend, she seemed an odd choice. If he was going to have an affair, I'd think he would have sought a bit of variety. Someone tall or curvy. Someone who looked entirely different from me, with tan skin and dark hair.

I was quite sure she was not Zack's girlfriend. She was too casually dressed. Her hair was loose and sleep tousled. Her posture was too dejected, her body too soft. She wasn't up to Zack's standards. She had potential, but she wasn't there.

Maybe she had been, in the past. She could be someone who had been in his life before I entered it and became his wife.

Obviously, Zack had girlfriends before me, but we'd never discussed our past relationships. Whenever I had asked, and whenever I had casually brought up something about an old boyfriend of mine, he had become angry, so I'd let it go.

When the woman climbed into a Lexus SUV almost exactly like my own, except that it was black and a touch newer, I almost laughed out loud. I eased onto my gas pedal as she did the same. I paused at the edge of the parking lot until she had made a right and then another right. I accelerated through a yellow light so that I wouldn't lose her. I had never followed someone before. Not by car, not on foot, not while trying not to be seen. The thrill of it was an indication of how boring my life had become.

Not anymore, I supposed. My husband had been murdered. I was a suspect, at least a person of interest, in the investigation into his death. That part was unwanted excitement.

I had not shot him. I knew that. I wanted to believe that, because I was innocent, I could not be arrested for—certainly not convicted of—his murder. I didn't have a gun, nor any residue from a shot on my body last night. I didn't know how the police would be able to find any evidence against me. That many, many innocent people had been arrested and convicted, even executed, for crimes they did not commit, made me nervous. At the same time, I didn't want this woman to be implicated. But I did want to understand her.

I was grateful to the detective for agreeing to notify Zack's mother. He must have done so shortly after he'd left my house earlier, and she had called me immediately after, sobbing uncontrollably.

"I'm coming down there," she'd said.

"No," I'd told her. "There's no reason. It will be too painful. Stay put."

I think I convinced her. I'd suggested she call her sister, have her pick her up. I hoped she would listen.

I felt genuine sympathy for his mother. She didn't know her son.

I'd successfully staved off my parents' plans to visit, too. My brother and I had called them together, that morning, dread billowing in my stomach. I was already tired of talking about what had happened, and it was only the beginning. "I have Aiden," I'd told them. "I'm fine. We'll see each other soon." They were shocked by my coolness, I thought, as much as by my husband's murder.

It seemed as if the woman was heading to my house. I followed her down River Road, a red Mazda between us, until her turn signal flashed and she made a left into a neighborhood a mile or so ahead of my own. The neighborhood was similar to mine, featuring large Colonial-style homes and third- to half-acre yards. I recalled touring a house here with Zack before we had found what had become our home.

The black SUV hung a right onto a cul-de-sac called Silver Star Lane. I pulled to a stop at the curb of the street off which several cul-de-sacs sprouted. If I followed her onto her cul-de-sac, I was sure to be noticed. She turned into the garage of a charming white house with dark green shutters, a matching door, and a wraparound front porch. The houses here were slightly smaller than my own, but the yards were larger and more secluded. The driveways were long. The hedges were tall and bountiful. People who lived here valued their privacy.

The garage door closed behind the car, and I could see no more. I waited a few minutes, but there was no further activity at her house.

I eased away from the curb and cruised around the neighborhood. I turned onto the cul-de-sac that ran parallel to Silver Star Lane.

I peered between the houses toward the place where the back of the woman's house would be. There were woods between the cul-de-sacs, and I could only catch glimpses of the white siding, black iron fence, a spacious deck, and a dark green pool cover. I couldn't see anything of interest, nor could I sit on this street. Although I wouldn't look out of place as a blond woman in a Lexus, it still wasn't a good idea, so I headed back to River Road.

I would go home. I would sip my wine, letting the cool sweetness run down my throat. I would comb through my husband's possessions, searching for an explanation for the events of last night. Then, I would go to Aiden's. But I would be back to Silver Star Lane. Now that I knew where to find her, I would return until I knew why she had shot my husband.

THREE MONTHS EARLIER
THURSDAY, FEBRUARY 21

Leah

Something awoke me from a deep sleep, and for a few seconds, I wasn't sure where I was, what day it was, or what lay ahead of me. I blinked, waiting for the gears to click into place.

Where am I? *In bed in my house.*

What day is it? *Thursday. Maybe Friday by now.*

What lies ahead of me? *Nothing.*

Because it didn't matter what day of the week it was. There were no longer workdays and non-workdays. Every day was a non-workday. Every day was the same. Every day I could have as much wine or as many mixed drinks as I wanted. I could sleep as late as I wanted to sleep. I could do whatever I wanted to do, except for the one thing I actually wanted to do, which was go to work.

I peered at my nightstand, looking for my cell phone, but it wasn't there. The room was lit by a faint blue glow, and I could see the plug for my charger, lying exposed on top of the table, not plugged into my phone like it should have been.

I rolled over. Liam was awake. The faint blue glow was covering him like a light summer blanket.

"What time is it?" I asked. I tried to swallow and my throat felt like it was coated in glue. I desperately needed water.

"Eleven thirty."

Still Thursday.

"Is that my phone?" I asked. The fog was clearing from my mind. I pushed myself to a sitting position and my head spun.

Liam pressed the button on the side to lock it and handed the phone to me.

"You were sleeping," he said. "You got a notification. I was just checking to see who was contacting you so late."

I took the phone from him and returned it to my nightstand. I tried to shake the feeling of unease that was burgeoning within me. I couldn't help feeling violated.

But it wasn't like he hacked into my phone. He had my passcode. A few weeks ago, when I had been looking at my phone while we were sitting on the family room sofa, he had told me that married people shared their passcodes with each other. Doing so was normal, he said. It showed we had complete trust in each other.

Numbly, I had recited my PIN. It had taken some time for me to realize that he had not shared his own.

"And?" I asked.

"It was just an advertisement about a sale at Ann Taylor," he said.

"Oh." I rolled away from him and slid to the edge of the bed. I stared out into the blackness of the room. The only light now was the tiny red speck on my phone, indicating that it was charging.

I no longer had any need for sales at Ann Taylor. I had no need for the beautiful suits or silky blouses or suede pumps that filled my side of the closet. I hadn't slid a leg into any of those pants, stuck an arm through any of those tops, in months, and I was virtually certain none of it would fit me anymore.

"Leah?" Liam asked.

"What?"

"You've been applying for jobs," he said. "I saw the confirmations in your email."

"So?" I asked. I felt belligerent.

"Why?" Liam asked, with a *we've been through this* tone.

"Because I want one. Because I want to have a job and to have purpose in my life again. I want to have somewhere to go and something to do when I wake up every morning." It had been four months, but I was still struggling to process the abrupt demise of my career.

Liam reached over and placed a hand on my back. "I know, Leah. I know," he said. He was using his exaggeratedly kind and patient voice. "But how can you get another job? You know that any new employer will find out about what happened. The legal community is small and tight. They will speak to Claudia."

He was right, but I still wanted to try. "What do I have to lose?" I asked. "I already lost everything. I might as well try to apply for things."

"Everything? How can you say you have lost everything? You have me. You have this beautiful house. You have your brand-new car."

I did have a brand-new car. My Christmas gift. A shiny black Lexus SUV that had shown up in our driveway on Christmas Eve, complete with an ostentatious red bow, like something out of a television commercial.

"Let's go for a drive," Liam had suggested after our dinner for two of take-out Chinese food, eaten while sitting cross-legged on the family room floor, while multicolored lights twinkled on the tree behind us and Alexa played holiday music. "Let's check out some Christmas lights in the neighborhood."

Liam had been adamant that we have our own, private Christmas together our first year as a married couple.

"What about our moms?" I had asked. We were both only children. I couldn't imagine celebrating Christmas without my mom. She had other family members she could be with—her brother, his wife, and their two children, one of whom had two children of her own, as well as her cousins. But I had never been away from my mom on Christmas Day.

"We can have our moms come to visit after Christmas," Liam had said. "I just really want our first Christmas here to be about us. I want us to start our own traditions." He had leaned toward me and taken my hand in his.

What was I supposed to say to my new husband? *No, thanks, I'd rather spend it with my mom?*

I was too close with my mother. I was probably too attached to her. Maybe it was time, as I approached my thirtieth birthday, to focus more on the family I was creating, the one I had chosen, rather than the one into which I'd been born.

Despite that we were so close, I hadn't told her about the loss of my job. It was far too shameful. She had worked so hard for me to be able to pursue my dreams and have a successful career, and I had completely, utterly failed her.

She would never believe that I had stolen the check. Outraged on my behalf, she would tirelessly search for an alternative explanation—the truth.

I didn't want her looking too closely. The truth, I thought, was even more shameful.

So, when our mothers flew into town after Christmas, we maintained a charade that I was still working at the same firm. We pretended that I had just taken the week off.

I know my mom suspected something was off. I could feel it when she hugged me. I could hear it in her voice and see it in her eyes. But when we got a minute alone and she asked, I had assured her that everything was fine.

Lying got easier. And I reminded myself that my intentions were pure. I was trying to protect her. By hiding what was happening, by staying, I was maintaining her ignorant bliss.

When I had stepped in the garage Christmas Eve night, reaching my hand toward the passenger-side door of Liam's car, I had noticed that the garage door was already open and there was another car in our driveway.

"Is someone here?" I had asked Liam, confused by the presence of the strange car.

"Let's check it out," he had said. He'd taken my arm and led me to the driveway.

The red bow had explained it all.

I hadn't been lying when I had told Liam that I didn't want a new car. I was perfectly happy with my little Honda. And without my job, I didn't have many things to do or places to go.

But the gesture of it. He would be so disappointed if I didn't seem thrilled. He must have spent a fortune on the car.

"Is—is this mine?" I had asked, my hands to my chest.

"Merry Christmas, Leah," said Liam. He had pulled me close to him. "I love you so much."

"Love you, too," I had said, which may have been the first time I wasn't sure if it was the truth.

I'd quite impressed myself with the little show I'd put on, remarking about the smooth leather interior, fancy technology, and slick, sporty shape.

I shifted in bed and his hand fell away from me. "Okay," I conceded. "Maybe I haven't lost everything. But I'm bored. Imagine if you lost your job and couldn't find a new one. Imagine how you'd feel."

He didn't respond.

"Hey," I said. "Why can't I join your firm? I don't want to litigate but I could help you with drafting." I couldn't believe I hadn't thought of it before.

"Leah," he said softly, and I knew he was refusing. "We're lucky Claudia didn't report you to the Attorney Grievance Commission. You could have lost your license. If she finds out you're practicing again, or if she spreads the word about what happened, it could hurt my reputation, and that of my firm. Where would that leave us?"

"Fine," I said. "Forget it. Forget I asked." I felt like a bratty child. I wanted to get my way. Why did it feel so impossible?

Liam turned toward me and draped an arm over my side. "Don't worry about anything," he said. He pulled my body close to his and I felt so trapped I almost cried out. "You can do anything you want, all day. I will take care of you. I will give you anything you need and want."

He thought he was reassuring me. But, didn't he know? That was what scared me.

"It would be good," he whispered, "if you started running again. The way you used to."

He was right. Before I lost my job, I used to run five or six times a week. I had raced in several half-marathons and had been contemplating training for a full one. I used to drink smoothies and lie down on the floor with my foam roller, working the kinks out of my sore legs. I used to soak in hot baths full of Epsom salt, speeding the recovery of my muscles, so that I could wake up the next morning and challenge them all over again.

Now that I had time to train as much as I wanted, I no longer had the desire. Although I occasionally went out for ambling walks, feeling the cold and punishing air burn my lungs and the inside of my nose, I had stopped running completely. As a result, my weight had creeped higher and higher, but I couldn't bring myself to care.

"I don't feel like running anymore," I told him.

"You've gained quite a bit of weight, Leah," Liam said softly, gently, as if he was trying not to offend me. But he couldn't feign concern. His disgust was clear.

"Why does it matter?" I asked. "Who cares?"

His arm dropped away from my body, and I could sense his tensing. "I care," he said, as if that were the only thing in the world that mattered.

I scooted to the very edge of the bed, as far away from him as I could. I didn't respond.

I felt the mattress shift as he climbed out of bed. He left the room. I could tell he was angry. I was just glad he had walked away. He would, I hoped, gain his composure, calm himself down, and not bring it up again.

As I waited for him to return to bed, I drifted off to sleep, and when I awoke, he was still gone. I'd slept deeply and dreamlessly. I knew that alcohol made many people sleep very poorly, but it made me sleep like the dead.

I sat up and checked my phone. It was only a few minutes past seven, but the house was silent. I could tell Liam had already left for work.

I climbed out of bed and went into the bathroom. I splashed cold water on my face, and reached for my toothbrush, but it was missing from the chrome cup perched on our swirling marble vanity. Odd.

I checked the drawers and cabinets, thinking that I might have placed it elsewhere by mistake, but I couldn't find it. Also missing was my makeup. My face wash. My lotion. All of my toiletries.

I checked the shower. My body wash, my shampoo, my conditioner, even my razor and loofah, were gone.

I moved into our walk-in closet, outfitted with custom drawers and hanging rods. My suits and blouses were all intact, as were my high heels and flats. But my casual clothing—my sweatshirts, T-shirts, yoga pants, and leggings, the only clothing into which I could fit these days—was missing.

It was as if my things had been removed from our master suite, my presence cleaned out, as I slept.

I returned to my side of our bed, grabbed my cell phone, and called my husband.

"Good morning," he said, answering on the first ring. "How did you sleep?"

"Could you explain to me," I said coldly, "what happened to my things? My toothbrush? My clothes?"

Liam sighed. "I have to admit," he said, "you quite upset me last night, when you said that you don't care about your weight gain. You no longer care about exercising."

"And it quite upset me," I said, "when you essentially told me I was getting fat."

"Leah," he said, sounding appalled. "I am coming from a place of love. I care about you. I want you to be healthy."

I pressed my lips together. "Where are my things?"

"I think it's best that you stay in the basement guest room for a while," Liam said. "You've let yourself go, Leah. I think it makes sense for both of us if you sleep there until you get yourself together. So I took the liberty of taking your things down there for you."

Was I supposed to thank him?

I lowered my phone, preparing to hang up.

"I just want my wife back, Leah. I miss my perfect wife," he said.

I tapped the button to end the call.

But the thing was, he had a point. I missed her, too.

I reached behind my nightstand to unplug my phone charger. I left our bedroom—Liam's bedroom—and I made my way downstairs, to my new home, to get ready for my day full of nothingness.

NOW
FRIDAY, MAY 10

Detective Jordan Harrison

The image of McKenna Hawkins's face was still lingering on my mind as I lifted my arm to rap on the chipped red front door of the row home in Georgetown. It was the middle house, in a line of only three, not twenty yards behind a gas station—the only one I'd seen within the limits of the District. Its specialness, self-importance, was revealed in the posted prices of the fuel it sold. The Watergate building loomed in the distance, and beyond it, the rippling, odorous Potomac River.

I pushed my thoughts of McKenna aside, closed my mind to the obvious relief in her eyes, to the secrets behind them, because Dr. Zackary Hawkins had been a psychiatrist with a busy private practice. He treated many patients who were mentally ill, and I needed to know more about them—as much as the law would allow me to know. I couldn't peruse his patient files without a court order, and I couldn't get a court order without good cause.

I was wondering whether, hoping that, Erica Dern could provide it.

A tall, thin woman with an abundance of artificially dark hair answered my knock. I placed her in her early thirties but would have gone younger if not for the faint wrinkles crossing her forehead, the divots between her brows, drawn low with concern, fear.

"Ms. Dern?" I asked, flashing her my badge.

She nodded, stepped aside. She was expecting me.

I followed her into the front room of the house, a sitting room. Behind it was the dining room, then a galley kitchen at the back. She sat down on a sofa, without suggesting that I take her lead, but I did so anyway, perching on an ottoman that had seen better days. She watched me, and began to wring her hands, with nerves, I assumed. I'd called her that morning, notifying her about the death of her boss, that she wouldn't be needed at work that day. She had agreed that I could stop by to speak with her in person later in the day, and I sensed that she'd been quite anxious about our prospective meeting ever since—after all, her boss had just been murdered. She had wanted to know what any person, in her situation, would be wondering. Did I think she was in danger?

As with Faith Gardiner, I'd assured her that I didn't have any reason to believe she would be targeted as Zackary Hawkins had.

"Do you live here alone?" I asked, glancing around the room. It rang of a disjointed energy. There was a whiteboard hanging on the wall by the door, half covered with a grocery list. The sofa on which Erica sat had two throw blankets, one crumpled, partially spilling onto the floor, the other neatly folded on an armrest. There was a bong and a stale, smoky odor in the far corner, to the right of a television stand. I would continue to pretend I hadn't noticed it unless I needed to encourage further cooperation from her.

"I have two roommates," she said, with a blush of embarrassment. "I'm kind of old for roommates, I guess, but I'm single, and it's expensive to live in this area."

"And you're close to the office where you work," I said. *Worked*. The practice would be shut down without its namesake. I'd cruised by it on my way to the house. It occupied another row home in a more desirable, upscale area of the neighborhood, closer to the hospital and university. I'd return there next, poke around to the bounds of the law. I wouldn't have much leeway unless Erica Dern gave me something to work with.

"I walk to work," she said. "Walked," she added, clearly sharing my thoughts. "I have some personal items in my desk. Will I be able to retrieve those?"

"Soon," I said. "You'll be able to get your things soon. Anything you need urgently?"

She shook her head. "I can't believe it," she said. "I just can't believe he was killed." And she did look shocked, but she didn't look sad. But was it due to dislike, or simply distance, coolness, between assistant and boss?

"How long did you work for Dr. Hawkins?" I asked.

"Only a year," she said. "I started with him last April. I was working in the customer service and scheduling department of the medical center before that. I wanted more regular hours, no more overnight shifts, so I applied for the position with him. It was advertised on a website. I can't remember which." She chewed her bottom lip.

"What was your role with his office?" I asked.

"I did the patient scheduling and billing. I sent claims to insurance." Her right shoulder lifted in half a shrug. "Boring stuff, I guess, but it was much less stressful than my last job."

"What was Dr. Hawkins like?"

"He was very smart," she said fervently. "Very calm. That's why he was so good with his patients, I think. He was fine to work for. I mean, we weren't friends, or anything. But we had a fine professional relationship."

"And what did you think when you found out that he'd been killed?" I asked. "Are there any patients that have given you any issues recently?"

"I mean, not really," she said. "Like I said, I worked in a hospital setting before starting the job with Dr. Hawkins. That's why he wanted to hire me, I think," she added primly. "Managing patients in a hospital setting is much more difficult. His patients were largely controlled, visiting for medication management, check-ins. If there were severe, psychiatric concerns, they would be in inpatient treatment or more intensive outpatient treatment."

"Right," I said. I couldn't fault her logic. "But can you think of anyone who might have wanted to hurt him?"

She looked upward as she thought, gathering her hair in her hands. She piled it on top of her head in a swirling, looping bun as, I had noticed, young women her age seemed apt to do. "Not that I know of," she said after a long pause.

"What about his wife?" I asked. "Have you ever met her?"

Erica shook her head and the bun wobbled precariously. "I was aware of her. There are pictures on his desk. But I never met her in person. She's busy, I suppose, being a doctor, too. I don't think she works around here."

"Did Dr. Hawkins speak about her?" I was considering the apparent fact that he had not informed his employee that his wife was not, in fact, working as a doctor any longer.

"Sure, he mentioned her." Erica laughed abruptly, almost unbidden, then covered her mouth delicately, as though she'd burped. "He called her quite a bit, actually. I would hear him calling her between patients. Just checking in. They were very close, I suppose."

"How often did he call her? How many times a day, would you say?"

"Um." Erica adjusted the bun and shrugged. "I don't know. At least a few. Say, three. That I could hear. But it wasn't as if I was keeping tabs on phone calls he was making," she added rather defensively.

"Did that seem odd to you?" I asked. "How often he called his wife?"

"Odd?" Erica seemed perplexed by the direction in which the interview had turned. I was anything but. "I don't know, maybe a little odd considering they were both so busy working. And, if you're speaking on the phone all day, what's there to talk about when you get home at night? Would've driven me nuts, if he was my husband, but to each their own, I guess."

"Right," I said, pushing myself up from the ottoman. I fished a card from my pocket and handed it to her. "Well, I appreciate your time, Ms. Dern. Please feel free to call if you think of anything else that might be important."

I averted my eyes from the bong as I moved past, bursting through her front door, feeling quite eager to get to Dr. Hawkins's office, but only to check that box, to get it done, to move on.

Because the image was back. The exhalation, the dip of her shoulders, the absence of fear in her eyes. I was wasting my time with Erica Dern, with Dr. Hawkins's office. I had to go anyway, look around, but my gut was pulling me elsewhere, and I'd learned long ago to let myself be pulled.

McKenna Hawkins was hiding something. She was glad her husband was gone, relieved he was dead. She had what I needed. Buried, but there. It was just a matter of digging it up, of prying it from her grip. It was just a matter of getting her to give it up.

ONE MONTH EARLIER
THURSDAY, APRIL 11

Leah

I was waiting for him in the kitchen. A pot of minestrone was simmering on the stove. I had no excuse but to make dinner for him every night. Not anymore. Our life together had become some sort of predictable and stereotypical tableau from the 1950s. My husband worked all day. I waited for him at home, or else I engaged in various approved activities aimed toward improving and maintaining my physical experience. Shopping, exercising, attending hair or nail or spa appointments. At least, those were the activities he suggested. Mostly, I just drank. I had dinner waiting for him when he arrived home. We ate together, then we went to bed, separately. Me to my basement prison, and Liam to the master suite. I snuck an extra cocktail or two from my secret stash beneath my mattress, so that he wouldn't know exactly how much I was drinking. I slipped into oblivion.

From the outside, it seemed nice. Idyllic, even. The closer you got, the better you could see—all of it was fraudulent, counterfeit.

Liam was working late and had sent me a text message around eight. *You can eat without me. Trying to finish something.*

"Thank you," I'd said out loud. "Thank you so much for giving me permission to eat."

I had done so, toasting a thick slice of Italian bread to dip in my soup and pouring a stiff drink to wash everything down.

I'd given up on wine. Wine required too much volume. Vodka was my drink of choice of late. I would start early, after Liam had left for work. I'd sleep it off in the afternoon, and then start again while I prepared dinner and waited for him to get home. If necessary, after my nap, I'd run out to the nearest liquor store to replenish my supply. I paid with cash as often as I could, cash withdrawn when I made purchases with my debit card at grocery stores, pharmacies, or Target.

After dinner, I had refilled my drink—vodka with a splash of Perrier and lemonade—and settled down at the kitchen table to wait for my husband, like every perfect wife.

My cell phone vibrated on the table in front of me.

Be home soon.

I swallowed the rest of the cocktail like it was a dose of medicine, washed the glass in the sink, and went downstairs to brush my teeth.

I was back in my spot at the kitchen table, this time with a glass of ice water, when Liam walked in the door.

He waltzed into the kitchen and bent down to drop a kiss on my cheek. "Hello," he said. "It smells good. What did you make?"

He wandered over to the pot on the stove.

"Minestrone," I said. "You're in a good mood." Said bitterly. Enviously. I remembered the feeling of walking in the door after a long day at work, feeling mentally exhausted but satisfied. I missed that feeling.

He turned. "I just settled a huge case," he said. "Couldn't have asked for better terms for my client. He's getting everything he wants. You know how rare that is in a divorce settlement."

"How'd you do that?" I asked.

He shrugged rather smugly, then began to spoon soup into a bowl.

"My private investigator caught her fucking their son's soccer coach."

"Lovely," I replied. I was certain the facts were far from that simple.

"That alone wouldn't have been damning enough," he said. He joined me at the table with his dinner. "But she was also pissing away marital funds on him. She told my client she was taking her sister to Mexico. Her sister would pay for the flights, she'd pay for everything else. She took her boy toy. They stayed at the Four Seasons for a week while my guy was at home with their kid, footing the bill for everything."

"Hm," I said. I wasn't interested in the details of his latest victory.

But he shared them nevertheless. He prattled on and on while he ate. When he was finished, I stored the leftover soup in a glass container for him to take for lunch the following day and loaded the dishes into the dishwasher.

"I'm going to go change and then lift some weights," Liam said, standing up from the table.

"Okay," I said. I waited a minute, then followed him upstairs.

I found him in the walk-in closet, lacing up his sneakers.

"What?" he asked upon seeing me in the doorway.

"I need to talk to you about something," I said. My heart felt like a wild animal, my chest a cage.

"Okay," he said. He stood and crossed his arms.

"I'm not happy."

"You—why not?" His face collapsed.

"I miss my job. I feel worthless. And—" I paused. This was the harder part. "I don't like being your perfect housewife. You've banished me to the basement, because I no longer look the part. It's not fair."

"I don't understand," Liam said. "You can do whatever you want, Leah. Most women would be thrilled to have your life."

Maybe you should have married one of them.

That's what I wanted to say, but I didn't dare.

"You have the ability to change things," Liam said. "You are in control."

But we both knew that couldn't be further from the truth.

"All you need to do," he continued, "is get some exercise. Drop the weight. Spend some time in the salon. And, you can come back to our room. You can sit here all day with your feet up. When the weather gets nice, you can relax by the pool. You can shop, you can go to the spa." His hands swept through the air, as if fanning out my many options in the space between us.

"I don't want that," I told him. "I want my old life back. My job. That's what I want."

"All right," Liam said. "And what exactly do you want me to do about that?"

He was starting to get angry, which wasn't what I wanted. I was hoping for reason and contrition, not anger.

"I need some space," I said. I leaned back against the wall of the closet, accepting the support it provided. "I need some time to myself, to figure things out. I want to go stay with my mom for a while."

I hadn't asked her yet, but I knew she'd welcome me. I planned to leave in the morning, to call her from the road. The part I didn't know was how much to tell her. I wasn't sure if I would divulge everything that had happened since we had returned from our honeymoon—the check, being let go from my job, losing control of my life, bit by bit, to Liam. I was leaning toward telling her that I had been laid off for some benign reason. I would say nothing about my marital nightmare. I didn't want to upset her.

And I didn't want her judgment. Because there would be judgment, as to how someone as intelligent as myself had found herself in the situation in which I had become quite stuck.

And what if, when I'd had some time and some space, I wanted to return to Liam? We had been together for four years. I had married him for a reason. For many reasons. I longed for those reasons to become clear once again. I honestly wasn't sure what had happened. Was this just a phase, this anger and control and sometimes violence? I didn't know whether he had hidden his true colors, or I had refused to see them. Regardless, I missed what I had thought we had.

Liam was shaking his head. "I don't understand. Are you leaving me?" He spat out the word like it had left a foul taste in his mouth. *Leaving.*

"I don't know," I said. "I just need some time to myself to figure out what I want."

"No," he said. His eyes were hard and determined.

"You can't tell me 'no,'" I said. "You cannot control me."

"I can," he said. "You cannot leave me, do you understand? I am the most sought-after divorce attorney in the Baltimore-Washington area. I cannot get divorced myself. That would ruin my career."

A jolt of surprise struck my core. "That's why you care? It all goes back to your career, doesn't it?" I was shouting now.

His eyes softened. "No, Leah. That's not why I care."

"Then let me go!" I yelled. "I need time and space. I miss my mom. Let me go."

He turned away from me and pushed a section of suits to the end of the rack. Beeps rang out as he entered the code into the wall safe, which he'd had installed when we had our closet remodeled. We would use it, he had said, to store my jewelry, our important documents. I'd no idea what was actually in there. It was yet another thing in our house, our lives, to which I did not have access. He reached inside, taking something out. When he turned around, he was holding a gun.

I had never seen a gun in person before. It looked glimmering and black and fake.

He lifted it to the side of his head.

"Liam," I said. I could feel my body shaking. I pressed myself harder against the wall.

"I will shoot myself," he said, his voice dripping like melting ice. "I will shoot us both if you leave me."

"What the hell is that? Where did you get that?" I asked.

He didn't respond.

"Tell me," he said, "you won't leave. Tell me you'll never leave me."

"Liam," I pleaded.

"Say it."

"I won't leave you," I said, because I didn't know what else to do.

He lowered the gun. He turned and returned it to the safe. I was astonished. I had no idea when he had bought it, or why. I sank to the floor, my legs bent beneath me, my hands to my face.

He walked toward me, paused. I thought he was about to bend down, to pull me close, to hug me against him and tell me he was sorry and that he'd never hurt me.

"You know, Leah," he said, looming over me, "if you were to leave me, I'd know where you'd gone."

I gripped the carpet, trying to catch my breath.

"I'd find you, and that wouldn't be good for you, or your mother."

I squeezed my eyes closed, shook my head.

"I wouldn't hesitate to hurt her, Leah," he said.

He walked past me as if nothing unusual had happened.

He paused in the doorway, looked over his shoulder. His face had softened. His eyes were crinkled and wet looking. "I can't live without you, Leah. You know that. I love you more than anything."

He disappeared. I started to cry as his footsteps quieted, as the distance between us grew. I sobbed because I was scared, for myself and for my mom. And I sobbed because the urge to somehow get my hands on that gun and chase him downstairs and shoot him while he reclined on his weight bench was almost too strong to resist. Finally, my hands still shaking, I pushed myself up.

I tiptoed down to the basement and into my bedroom. I closed the door behind me, wishing that I could lock him out. I slid a bottle of vodka out from beneath my mattress and poured a dose into the glass on the nightstand. I swallowed it down and placed my hand over my heart. It was still thundering. My mind was still racing.

I hadn't even told my husband what I really wanted to say, and that was the scariest part. What would have happened if I had? If I told him that he had become controlling? If I told him that he was violent, that the very sight of him terrified me? That he needed help, and so did I? That I thought I knew what had really happened with that check from Emily Mayer and the loss of my job?

He might've turned the gun. He might've pulled the trigger.

I gulped down another drink, then returned to the first floor. I wanted to put more distance between us.

Liam found me there, an hour later. I was still drinking. This time, it was a vodka soda, prepared from the provisions in the dining room cabinet. It was doing its job, dulling my thoughts, anesthetizing the horrors of the evening. Already, they felt fuzzy and distant.

"Leah," he said. "Are you okay? You look tired. Are you tired?"

I nodded meekly. I didn't look up.

"Here," he said, taking my elbow. "Let me walk you downstairs to bed."

I left my drink on the counter and let him lead me down the basement stairs, gripping the railing as we went.

"Be careful," he whispered. "I wouldn't want you to fall."

My breath caught in my throat. Because it wasn't a remark of concern. I knew better. I recognized it for the threat it was.

He walked me into the bedroom. I staggered to the bed and sank onto it, dragging myself across the top of the comforter, letting my head fall to the pillow. Even with my eyes closed, when all I could see was blackness, somehow, everything was still spinning.

"Good night, Leah," Liam called.

I didn't reply. He closed the door behind him, and as I drifted out of consciousness, I was aware, as I always was, of the click of the lock and the jingling of the key as he carried it with him.

NOW
MONDAY, MAY 13

Detective Jordan Harrison

The key was to catch them by surprise. It's why I never called first. Not
before I stopped by McKenna's house on Saturday, to let her know that
the autopsy of her husband's body had been completed. The cause of
death was a gunshot wound to the head. The manner of death a homicide. No surprises there.

I hadn't called first yesterday, either. Mostly, I'd wanted to catch her
in action. I'd wanted to see if she was still home. What would a woman
whose husband had been murdered be doing in the house where it had
happened? Neither her appearance, nor that of the house, had afforded
any clues.

She had assured me, as we sat down in her living room on Saturday
afternoon, that, just like the night her husband was killed, she had spent
the previous night at her brother's house and intended to return that
evening.

"Why come back here at all?" I had asked. "Why not just stay at his
place the whole weekend?"

"I don't want to impose on them twenty-four hours a day," she had
replied. "Besides, it's good for me to be here. I'm getting used to my
husband being gone. I'm processing." Her blue eyes had flashed, daring
me to question her further on that topic.

I chose to let it go for the time being.

On Sunday morning, I'd shown up with an update on the results of
the fingerprint tests and footprint analysis, which had been expedited
and came back in record time.

A prominent and successful psychiatrist is gunned down inside his home in an affluent suburb mere feet away from his pretty, white, blond wife? If that didn't garner the most expedient processing and analysis of the evidence, or lack thereof, collected at the scene, I didn't know what would.

McKenna had taken the news about the lack of physical evidence well. Too well? I wasn't sure. Her manner was stilted and cold. I had a talent for reading people. I had to. It was part of the job. But she was a challenge.

I'd felt the same way when I had stopped by on Saturday. I had told her that the autopsy had been completed—again, the case was a priority, especially in a county that usually only saw one or two murders a year— and the death had been formally ruled a homicide. It was only May, and already the county had met its murder total from last year, before the weather had even heated up.

The first had been a domestic disturbance turned deadly. A murder-suicide late last month. A husband had shot his wife and himself in their five-thousand-square-foot house with a circular driveway and a pool, while their two kids were away at college. It had shocked the community.

The wife had managed to call the police before she had been killed. Detective Mallory Cole and I had responded to the house. I would never forget what had happened there. My partner was still in the hospital. She was yet to wake up.

Zackary Hawkins was murder number two.

In a relatively law-abiding suburb such as this one, violence tended to be of a domestic nature. Based on what I'd seen, and not seen, thus far, I was thinking the Hawkins killing was going to fall into that same category.

His body would be released to McKenna as soon as possible, I'd told her, so that she could make arrangements for his funeral. She'd looked surprised, as if that was the first time it had occurred to her that she would need to plan a service for her husband.

I'd told her that I had spoken with her husband's employee, Erica Dern, that we had not yet uncovered any evidence indicating his profession had anything to do with his death. She'd been accepting of this development, or lack thereof. Accepting, and something else—disappointed?

Her phone records had arrived last night. I'd forwarded them to Officer Diaz and asked her to send me the highlights. I wanted to know the names and addresses of everyone McKenna Hawkins had been speaking with recently.

I'd been nervous when I had requested the court order for her phone and financial records. I'd taken it to Judge Souder on Friday evening, on my way back from DC. She was the duty judge that day, meaning she was on call to sign warrants and court orders, and that was just fine with me. She was tough, and I knew that she would invite me into her house, offer me a cup of coffee and a couple homemade cookies, and then cross-examine me at length about my reasons for requesting the records. I appreciated it, because I wasn't sure if what I was doing was right. Judge Souder wouldn't sign the order as a favor. She wouldn't sign it unless I truly had probable cause sufficient to entitle me to the records.

I had nothing specific on McKenna Hawkins. All I had was a lack of evidence that anyone besides her had been on her property on Thursday night when Dr. Hawkins was shot. I had no means—as far as I knew, she didn't have access to a weapon. There was the brother's gun, but according to the ballistics, which had come in early this morning, Zackary Hawkins was shot with a thirty-eight-caliber bullet, which couldn't have come from Aiden Lyons's service weapon.

I had no motive—there wasn't anything besides a gut feeling telling me that she and her husband had anything other than a happy marriage. All I had was opportunity—she was there, and as far as we knew, she was the only one there. There were no fingerprints on the outside of the window through which the bullet had torn—it had been opened through the inside. The footprints on the patio had not matched any of the shoes confiscated from McKenna's home, but they were the same size—8.5. It was, I discovered, the most common women's shoe size.

Still, Judge Souder had thought it was enough.

"You're on a short leash with this," she'd told me, pushing the signed court order toward me. "Don't come back to me for anything else unless you have more."

I was grateful, because without the records, I was stuck. If McKenna hadn't shot Zackary Hawkins herself, she had hired someone to do it. If she had hired someone to do it, she had had contact with that person, and she had paid that person. I couldn't look into that possibility without her phone and financial records.

I wanted the phone records for another reason as well. I needed to learn more about McKenna and Zackary's relationship. I wanted to speak with her friends and family members. I needed to both clear them as suspects and find out what they could tell me about the victim and his wife.

Officer Diaz had sent me a shockingly short list.

Gene and Kathleen Lyons of West Palm Beach, Florida. They were in their late sixties. McKenna's parents. I'd put them to the side for now.

Aiden and Monica Lyons of Monkton, Maryland. I'd already cleared them on Friday. Aiden's registered firearm, as part of his work as a federal law enforcement officer, couldn't have been the murder weapon. Anyway, Aiden and Monica had alibied each other. They had been at home in their cottage in the woods, sound asleep, while their brother-in-law had been murdered. It wasn't airtight, but I had no reason to doubt them.

Aside from the fact that Aiden didn't like his brother-in-law. This, too, was interesting to me. But Aiden couldn't or wouldn't provide a concrete explanation as to why he felt the way that he did.

Zack was controlling, he'd told me. McKenna had suffered a miscarriage in January and abruptly quit her job as a pediatrician, a job she had worked very hard to obtain. Aiden blamed Zack for this. Again, he couldn't or wouldn't tell me why. After his sister had married the psychiatrist, he had seen less and less of her. When they did spend time together, Zack was always present as well, cold and anxious to leave.

Also on the list were Mina Lee and Alyssa Vercarro, both of Clarkstown. They had addresses within fifteen-minute drives of McKenna's house. I assumed they were her friends.

That was it. Aside from her husband, McKenna Hawkins had only communicated with six people during the previous six months: her parents, her brother, his wife, and two friends. She had no social media accounts. She had no job. She had no children. All of this, to me, was strange.

Mina's house was a large brick box, not dissimilar to McKenna's. The yard was smaller, and it was closer to the neighbors' homes. A *McMansion* my mother would call it, with a disapproving air.

I rang the doorbell, listened to it chiming through the house, and waited.

A petite woman with black hair that cupped her chin answered the door, a baby draped over her shoulder. She held the door open with her right hand, her left rubbing the baby's back, encased in blue striped pajamas.

"Mrs. Lee?" I asked.

She looked scared. I wasn't in uniform, and my unmarked sedan was parked in the driveway. But she knew immediately I was a cop. "Yes?" she said.

"Detective Jordan Harrison." I showed her my badge. "I wanted to speak to you about your friend McKenna Hawkins and the murder of her husband. May I come in?"

She exhaled, but I could still sense her tension. "All right," she said. She stepped aside and reluctantly welcomed me into the house.

I followed her through the foyer, down a hallway, and into the kitchen. She sat down in a chair in front of the kitchen table, her left hand still resting on the baby's back. I could see the rise and fall from his breath. He had fine black hair and his face was turned toward his mother's neck, but I could see one silky smooth, plush-looking cheek.

"Can I get you something to drink?" Mina Lee asked. She looked exhausted. Dark circles beneath her eyes stood out from her fair skin. The baby probably wasn't letting her get much sleep.

"No, thank you," I said.

"Sorry, can he stay here?" she asked, gesturing to her infant. "If I put him down, he will wake up and scream."

"Of course," I told her. "How old is he?"

"Three months," she replied, rubbing little circles on his back.

"He's beautiful."

She preened.

"I suppose you heard," I told her, leaning back against her kitchen chair, "about the murder of your friend's husband on Thursday night."

She pressed her lips together for a second. "I did," she said cautiously, "just like everyone else in the county. I heard it on the news on Saturday."

I sensed she was bitter that her friend hadn't told her directly.

"You didn't hear from Mrs. Hawkins?" I asked.

"I called her. Once I heard it on the news, I called her. I was shocked. I wanted to make sure she was okay. I told her she was welcome to come stay with my family. She said she didn't want to. She said she was sleeping at her brother's, but she was fine in the house." Mina shuddered. "I can't imagine how she could be okay there, after what happened."

"Why do you think she didn't want to leave?" I asked.

Mina's mouth twisted to the side as she thought. "McKenna had become increasingly reclusive over the course of the year. I'm not sure why. She always seemed to want to stay home."

"You're not sure why. Any ideas?" I asked. I wanted to know her thoughts.

"Well, maybe after what happened in January. I think that's why she didn't want to stay here. It might have been too painful for her, being around William." She patted the baby, who, I gathered, was William.

"And why is that?"

"McKenna had a miscarriage in January. I understand it was very hard on her and Zack. She's been trying to get pregnant again. It hasn't happened. I think she's been withdrawing from Alyssa and me because we have children, and it's hard for her when we talk about our kids."

This information was consistent with what McKenna had told me on Friday, but it didn't jibe with the little packet of birth control pills my team had found on her kitchen floor.

Not only had McKenna lied to me, saying that she had been trying to get pregnant, she had also lied to her friend.

I ran through another scenario in my mind. Zackary wanted to have a baby. McKenna did not. She wasn't ready. Maybe she never would be. Rather than tell her husband the truth, she had pretended she was trying. Meanwhile, she was secretly taking birth control pills. Zackary found out about the pills. He confronted her after returning home from work on Thursday night. McKenna shot him. To protect herself?

But where did she get the gun? And why did she shoot from outside, while standing on the patio? If she had left the house and taken aim from outside the kitchen window, it hadn't happened in the heat of the moment. It hadn't been self-defense. It had been calculated.

And how to explain the absence of gunshot residue?

Like the Hawkinses' kitchen window screen, the theory had holes. I needed to fill them.

"When was the last time you saw McKenna?" I asked.

Mina looked around, as if the answer to my question were hanging on the wall somewhere. "You'll have to forgive me," she said. "Maternity leave has been an adjustment for me. Every day is the same. They all run together. But, I'm pretty sure I saw her last Friday afternoon. I remember my in-laws were visiting. I left William with them and our other friend, Alyssa Vercarro, and I went to McKenna's house in the afternoon."

"What time was that?" I asked.

"Umm." Mina shook her head. "Maybe around three? We made the plans by text message. I could check if you wanted."

"That's okay," I said. I didn't think it mattered, and I didn't want to stifle the flow of our conversation. "What did you do while at her house?"

"Well, we drank some wine and chatted. She and Zack had a new patio put in. It was a nice day. We sat outside for a while. Then Zack came home, and we wrapped things up."

I leaned forward just a hair. "Any particular reason you wrapped things up when he got home?"

She shrugged. "McKenna seemed a little anxious. It seemed early for him to be home from work. I always thought he worked long hours. He came out to say hello, then said he was going to do some work in the home office. It was strange. Like, if you have to work, why come home to do it? Why not just stay at work until you're finished, then leave?"

"Maybe he wanted to beat traffic," I suggested. I'd done the drive myself, from the station to Dr. Hawkins's office and back. It took forty-five minutes without traffic. But there was always traffic. The travel time could easily double during rush hour.

"Maybe," Mina said. She shrugged again. She didn't seem convinced.

"What would your thoughts be," I said, "if I told you that your friend had been taking birth control pills?"

"McKenna?" she asked, her eyes widening.

Who else? I nodded.

Mina shook her head emphatically. "No," she said. "McKenna wasn't taking birth control. She was trying to get pregnant."

She wasn't willing to believe that her friend had lied to her. This was not unusual.

"Can you think of a reason we would have found birth control pills in the Hawkinses' kitchen on Thursday night?"

Mina blinked. "They were old?"

"The pack seemed up to date," I said. "All pills were missing, up to Friday's pill."

"Maybe they weren't McKenna's." Mina tried again. "Maybe she found them. Maybe they belonged to Zack's girlfriend."

That caught my attention.

"He had a girlfriend?"

Mina slumped in her chair. "No," she admitted. "I mean, not that I know of. It was just a thought."

"Is there any reason you would think Dr. Hawkins was having an affair?"

"No," Mina said again. She looked disappointed. "In fact, he always seemed very obsessed with McKenna. I always thought that."

"What made you think that?" I asked quickly. The baby was beginning to stir. I didn't know how much time I had left.

"She was just so rarely available to spend time with us. She always had plans with Zack. She stopped working in January, to focus on getting pregnant, she said. That was strange. McKenna loved her job. Then she canceled her gym membership. She used to love taking group classes at the gym. That's where I met her and Alyssa. It seemed like everything was disappearing from her life. Except him."

"And you think that was his doing?" I asked. I wanted her to tell me why.

"I guess it could have been her way of dealing with the miscarriage. That was really when everything started to change. Maybe she was just depressed." She tapped her chin absently. "But the pills," she said. "The birth control. Maybe there never was a miscarriage at all."

Which was my thought exactly.

"Zack always seemed to be jealous of everything in McKenna's life. It was only a handful of times that we all hung out as couples. But I always got the feeling that Zack didn't like it when she talked about anything other than him or their life together." The baby started to wriggle and whine. "If she talked about work, or the gym, he would pout or change the subject."

"Any other examples?" I asked over the baby's wails, growing more powerful by the second. Its tiny face was scrunched and red. "Can you think of anything else?"

Mina shook her head. "No," she said. "That's it." Her attention was captivated by the baby now. I wasn't going to get anything else out of her.

I stood and pulled a card from my pocket. "Thank you for your time, Mrs. Lee. Please feel free to call me anytime if you think of anything else worth sharing."

She was bouncing and rocking the baby. "You're welcome," she called over its screeching cries.

"I'll show myself out," I said, but she followed me to the door.

"McKenna," she said. With the motion, the baby had quieted down and was gurgling softly. "Is she a suspect?"

I shoved my hands into my pants pockets. "To be honest with you, Mrs. Lee, I don't know."

I left her there, standing in her foyer, hugging her baby against her chest. I don't know what she had expected me to say, but it wasn't that.

I climbed into my car and plugged Alyssa Vercarro's address into the GPS app on my phone. What would she have to say, I wondered, about the good doctor and his picture-perfect wife?

A curtain in Mina Lee's living room was pushed to the side. She was standing there, watching me go. She was probably cradling the baby in one arm, holding her cell phone to her ear with the other. She was probably warning Alyssa Vercarro about my visit. I wouldn't be able to catch her by surprise.

As with Erica Dern, her perspective on the relationship between McKenna and Zackary Hawkins had been helpful. But she had raised more questions than she had answered. I knew that there was only one person alive who knew the truth. I also knew she wasn't about to offer it up on a silver platter.

I'd get there eventually. My investigation was a road, and it was only the beginning of the journey. It was like unwrapping a present. I'd only torn back one tiny corner of the paper.

But, like on Christmas morning, soon enough, the paper would be ripped away and discarded, and all would be revealed.

TUESDAY, MAY 14

McKenna

It was too early to call a Realtor. That would make me seem callous, like I couldn't wait to capitalize on Zack's death by unloading our most valuable possession.

Instead, I had decided to do everything I could so that when it was safe to list the house, it would be ready to sell, and I could move out almost effortlessly. I was tugging his expensive dress pants and crisp button-downs from hangers and pulling sweaters and ties from his drawers and shoving them into trash bags, which was highly satisfying. I pictured the way his face would look if he could see what I was doing. The horror in his eyes made me smile. But then, a jolt of sadness caught me by surprise and almost knocked me off my feet. I knew I didn't miss him. I missed the person I thought he was. I was sad for myself because I had accidentally married a monster. And I was sad for his mother because she had accidentally raised one.

I didn't blame her. I was a doctor, but I didn't understand whether it was nature or nurture that had caused my husband to be the way he was. It could have had to do with his father, whom I'd known only briefly and superficially. He had died of pancreatic cancer three years ago, and two years after we'd met. He'd been ten years older than Zack's mother and he had never accompanied his wife when she traveled to visit us. He didn't like to fly—he said he was too old to squeeze himself into a cramped and stiff airplane seat, even though Zack always offered to spring for first class. I had only met him a handful of times when we had traveled to Boston for holidays over the course of our five total years together.

His mother had called me each day since she had been notified of Zack's death. It was the most we had ever spoken without him being present. I didn't know whether she was calling to check on me, or whether speaking with me made her feel better, or whether she was hoping, waiting, for me to tell her it had all been a cruel joke and, here, let me just get Zack on the phone.

"I'm holding up fine," I'd told her each time she had asked, which was the truth, and I felt very bad about that because she didn't seem fine at all.

We did not know when Zack's body would be released by the police. An autopsy had been performed—a formality, since the cause of death was apparent. I'd seen it happen with my own eyes. It had been ruled a homicide, which came as a surprise to no one. Detective Harrison had stopped by on Saturday afternoon to share the results with me, but he'd not been able to provide any indication as to when Zack's family would be able to take possession of his body.

"We will keep it safe," he'd said.

I didn't care what he did with it. I just wanted to know for his mother's sake. She was making arrangements for a funeral in Massachusetts, where all of Zack's extended family resided. When she had asked me if I minded if she planned the service, and if it would be held up there, I could tell she was nervous that I'd tell her that I wanted to take care of it myself, and I wanted it to be held in Maryland, near our home. Really, she'd been giving me a gift. I could not think of anything I wanted to do less than plan my husband's funeral.

"It gives me something to do," she'd said. "It's something for me to focus on. Being productive helps a little."

"I think it should be up there," I had assured her. "It should be where Zack grew up, where his family lives."

"You'll stay with me, won't you?" his mother had asked. "When you come up for the funeral, will you stay with me?"

"Of course," I'd told her, already filled with dread. If there was a way to get out of attending my husband's funeral, I'd do so. But I knew there was not.

Unless his murder hadn't been solved by then. Unless I was considered a suspect and was not permitted to travel outside the state.

"I just can't believe this is happening," his mother had said on the phone this morning. "This is like a bad dream."

It was clear she, at least, did not suspect my involvement at all. She had no idea. For me, the nightmare had just ended, while for her, it was only beginning.

I pulled the drawstrings of the trash bag and tied them in a knot. I had spent the weekend, beginning Friday afternoon, moving through the house, room by room, studying Zack's possessions, trying to tease out his secrets. Our bedroom, and his clothes, was all that was left. Finding nothing there, I was packing up his things, for donation, so that they could be put to use by someone else.

He had saved all of his textbooks from college and medical school, and they'd lined the shelves of our home office, but I knew that neither of us had cracked the spine of one since moving in. They were merely decorative for him. I'd opened each one anyway, shaking them so that the pages fluttered, feeling ridiculous, yielding nothing.

I'd been hopeful that the office, a room I had never used, would have offered some information of interest, some hint as to something Zack had been hiding from me, something that had led to his death. I had tried to log into his computer, but after three incorrect attempts to guess his password, I had been locked out for twenty-four hours. I would continue to try, but it was possible that his password was a random string of letters and numbers that I'd never be able to guess.

I'd found personal documents in the desk drawers—information about our mortgage, investment accounts I'd never seen and which, I'd discovered with alarm, were not titled in my name, and tax returns from years past. There'd been nothing scandalous or earth shattering. Nothing elucidating as to the identity of the woman in the window, the woman from Pine View Liquors, who lived on Silver Star Lane, who had shot my husband.

I was conscious of the expansiveness of the house as I moved from room to room. It was an outlandish amount of space for one woman.

I had started browsing other options on Zillow and Redfin, but I couldn't determine where I wanted to live without determining where I would be working. Money wouldn't be an issue. I could afford something much bigger than I would ever want. Over the weekend, I had received paperwork documenting Zack's death, and I had contacted the banks. For the first time since we got married, I had unfettered access to our money. Also, there'd be life insurance proceeds of two million dollars. I wasn't sure when that would come through—perhaps not until, or unless, I was cleared from all wrongdoing. If they thought I had killed my husband, I wouldn't get the money. I didn't need or want it. I thought about trying to transfer it to his mother. Otherwise, I'd donate it to charity. Maybe an organization that helped victims of domestic violence.

Because that's what I'd been. It was difficult to put that label on my situation. I'd been in denial for so long. I'd been paralyzed. Right or wrong, it was an embarrassing label to have. It came with a measure of shame and assumption of fault and weakness. Unfairly. But I felt it nevertheless.

I'd learned about all forms of domestic abuse in medical school. We'd been taught how to spot the signs, how to screen patients for issues so that we could refer them to the appropriate services. How would a person get herself into such a situation? I'd wondered. When it started, why wouldn't she just leave? Why wouldn't she just call the police after the first time? It'd not made any sense until it had happened to me.

It had snuck up on me, disguised as something else. Love, obsession, devotion? It had been visible only to me, and I'd refused to see it for what it was. It had taken some time for the violence to start. The coercion, the control, the isolation were the first manifestations of the abuse. I didn't know how much further it would have gone, how much worse things would have become, had the stranger from the window not shot my husband.

It was still early, and the day stretched ahead of me. I'd not a clue how to fill it. I was used to that. The difference was that I could now fill it however I pleased. I could search for jobs and houses. I could rejoin my gym. I could call my friends.

I'd heard from Mina and Alyssa over the weekend as well. The press had learned of the death of Dr. Zackary Hawkins—a young and handsome, prominent DC psychiatrist—and several articles had been printed. One of the articles mentioned that Dr. Hawkins's wife, McKenna Hawkins, had been home at the time of the murder. None of them identified me as a suspect in the crime.

Both Alyssa and Mina had suggested that I was welcome to stay with them if I wanted. *Anything you need,* they'd said. *Please say if there's anything you need.*

I'd heard from them again yesterday. They had both called, about an hour apart, to let me know that a detective had visited them—Mina in her home, and Alyssa at work, after he had shown up at her house and been informed by her nanny that she wasn't there. My stomach had dropped.

"What did he ask?" I had wanted to know.

They said he had just asked questions about Zack, what he was like, what they thought of him, how often we got together. My mind had raced. Nerves had burned in my gut. What was the detective getting at? What was he trying to prove?

And, most importantly to me, how had he found Mina and Alyssa, my only two remaining friends? What else did he know about my life?

There'd been something they weren't telling me. Both of them. I could tell they were holding back. They were anxious, and they thought I was fragile. They were trying to protect me. I'd wanted to demand more information, but I'd let it go. I didn't want to rouse suspicion from them, in the off chance it wasn't already there.

I moved into the kitchen and sipped from a glass of ice water. My eyes were drawn to the cabinet above the fridge. It almost glowed with the secret of what lay behind the door.

I hadn't known where to put it. I hadn't wanted to take it at all. But Aiden wouldn't let me return to the house unless I did.

"Don't you need it?" I'd asked. "I mean, don't you need this for work?" I'd eyed it, shiny and black and reflective, feeling uncomfortable.

He'd laughed. "Mac, I wouldn't give you my service weapon. This is my personal weapon."

"Oh." I hadn't known that he had a *personal weapon.*

He had walked me into the woods behind his house on Saturday night, and showed me how to use it. He'd taped two sheets of paper to a tree. One represented the head, and the other represented the center body mass. As I'd fired round after round at the papers hanging ahead of me, I had pretended it was Zack, even though I didn't need to do that because someone else had taken care of it for me.

"You're a natural," he'd said, as the bullets had sliced through the paper, cutting into the tree trunks, as my hand ached from the recoil, and the deafening shots enveloped me.

Once Aiden was satisfied with my abilities, we had picked our way across his acres of land, returning to his house. "Listen," he'd said, glancing at me briefly, "don't mention this to anyone, all right?"

"Mention what?" I'd said. "Practicing with the gun?"

"The gun," he'd told me. "Anything about the gun. It's not registered."

I had stopped dead in my tracks. "What are you talking about? It's an illegal weapon? Was it stolen?"

My brother worked in law enforcement. I didn't understand what he would be doing with an unregistered firearm, not when he possessed a perfectly legal weapon that he used for work.

"Look," he had said, turning to face me. "A lot of the people I work with have an extra gun, okay? It's better if you don't know any more than that. Don't tell anyone about it, but please, please, use it if you have to."

I had stared at him. I wanted him to elaborate, but I knew that he wouldn't. And he was deadly serious about keeping me safe.

The whole thing felt ridiculous because I knew that I would not need the weapon. I did not need protection. The woman was no threat to me. But if it made my brother feel better, I told myself it wouldn't hurt to take it and put it away in a cabinet or drawer and forget it was there. I had already let the police search my house. I didn't think they'd be back to do it again.

I sat down at the kitchen table with my laptop and browsed the job search websites I had bookmarked, looking for new openings. But nothing had popped up since yesterday afternoon, so I shut it down, grabbed my purse, and headed out to the garage.

I glanced at Zack's Audi as I climbed into my car. His things were everywhere. That would be yet another thing I would have to sell or donate.

I backed out of the garage and turned out of my neighborhood, onto River Road. I made the short drive to Silver Star Lane, just as I had on Saturday morning, on Sunday afternoon, and twice yesterday. I had not seen her once. I hoped I'd have better luck today.

My phone sat silent in my cup holder. It was nice to not feel like I needed to check it every few minutes. Zack had frequently called and texted me throughout the day, between his appointments. Where was I? What was I doing? Was I being a good little girl, a perfect little wife?

I parked my car on the road from which the woman's cul-de-sac sprouted. I could see the front and right side of her house.

As if she had been waiting for me to arrive before doing so, she emerged from behind the house. Her hair was pulled back in a low ponytail and she wore black athletic capris and a black Orioles T-shirt. She was holding something at her side, but I couldn't tell what it was.

She pushed the gate open and made her way across the grass of her front yard and down the driveway. There was a large blue county-issued recycling bin parked at the curb of the house next door. She looked around her, as if making sure no one was watching, didn't see that I was, lifted the lid, and tossed something inside. Then, she turned and went back the way she'd come, through the gate and around the back of the house.

It was strange that she hadn't exited or entered through the garage or the front door. She had clearly come from her house's walk-out basement. I wondered whether that was where she slept. Maybe the house had a basement apartment, and she was a tenant.

A woman stepped onto the front porch of the house across the street.

She was holding a leash, the end of which was clipped to the collar of a beagle-looking dog. There was a baby in a carrier attached to her front. Her other hand was cupping its head, as if shielding it from the late morning sun. I picked up my phone and pretended to be typing on it furiously as she walked by my car.

But the woman didn't even glance my way as she passed. She tickled the head of her baby, then tilted her own head forward to plant a kiss on its silken hair. She inhaled deeply and smiled. I knew she was enjoying the spectacularly sweet scent of warmth and milk and innocence, only possessed by new babies. Of all my patients, I'd loved seeing babies the most. I would always sneak a sniff when I examined them.

I was struck by a blow of sadness, like a punch to the gut, because I did still want to be a mother. Not with Zack. Not that that was an option any longer anyway. But I still wanted it to happen at some point.

I wondered whether the woman whose house I was currently watching was a mother. I'd now seen her out and about during typical working hours twice, so it seemed that she wasn't employed. Although, she could work unusual hours, or she might work from home. I hadn't seen her with a baby or child. I'd only seen her alone. She seemed like me.

I wished I knew her name.

Was she married? Did she plan to have children? Had she ever been pregnant before? Had she come as close as I had to becoming a mother? Had she suffered a miscarriage? Did she feel the pain of the loss, but realize soon after that it was for the best that the little bundle of cells inside of her had failed to thrive, had failed to become a baby?

There'd been little things before the miscarriage. Zack had a temper. When he got angry, it was like the flick of a switch. It was emphatic and volcanic, but when it was over, so were his apologies. When he wasn't angry, he was sweet and affectionate and charming.

There were other things, too. A preoccupation with my weight and physical appearance. He wanted me to be thin and blond and primped. There was the sense that he wanted to be the only thing in my life— him and our baby. He'd discouraged my relationships with my friends and my family. He assumed control of our finances and foreclosed my involvement. He was isolating me. I could see all of that now. He'd liked that I was—*was*—a doctor. I was intelligent and accomplished. Perhaps that made it more of a challenge, more thrilling, for him to enter my life and level everything I had, as though he'd detonated a nuclear bomb. I'd done a little research at some point, as things had begun to click into place, even as I was fighting to dig my head in the sand. Coercive control. Professional abusers—meaning professional men who were abusive, who sought out relationships with women who could become subservient, who could fit into an external image of "perfection." But, *no, no, no.* I'd not wanted that to be me, so I'd simply told myself that it wasn't. Not me. I was too smart and educated. I was not weak. How ardently I had lied to myself.

And I wasn't weak, but it had become me, nevertheless. It was so clear, so obvious, so undeniable now. But at the time? Most of the time? It felt like love.

Until we lost the pregnancy. After that, his irrational, angry outbursts increased in frequency and power. He had all but coerced me to give up my career.

He had blamed me for the loss. It had been months since I had thought of it, but I could remember the time he had shaken me awake in the middle of the night.

"What?" I'd asked. "What happened?" I'd thought there was a fire or bad news. I'd thought he was trying to help me, or that he had needed help.

"I talked to my friend Chris Winter from med school today," Zack had said. "Remember him?"

I'd nodded, reaching for my phone, checking the time. 2:32 a.m. My mind was still foggy with sleep.

"He called me to catch up. He and his wife had a baby last month," he said. "A girl. Hadley Rose."

I had blinked into the darkness while he turned roughly onto his side, dragging most of the covers with him. He'd not said another word.

There'd been no reason for him to wake me up. No reason for him to tell me that in the middle of the night. No reason, but to torment me. The message had been clear. *See? Some people aren't broken like you.*

Some people don't get stomach viruses and lose the most important thing in the world.

Afterward, I'd lain in bed, thinking, wanting to leave him, to get away. I knew that I could have climbed out of bed, gotten in my car, and driven to Aiden's. I knew that Aiden would protect me.

But I also knew that wouldn't be the end. It would only be the beginning, and even Aiden wouldn't have been able to protect me from the various horrors that followed as I worked to extricate my life from Zack's.

I watched the woman across the street return to her house with her baby and dog. She pushed the front door open with ease. She hadn't locked it before setting out.

I waited until she'd had enough time to move into the depths of her home before I climbed out of my car. I looked around me, but there was no one outside. The kids were at school. The adults were at work.

I hurried over to the recycling bin and lifted the lid. I let it fall closed and walked away, back to my car, as quickly as I could without quite breaking into a jog. I started my car, glancing at the woman's house one final time before driving away.

As I made my way home, I wondered why she was hiding empty bottles of vodka with her neighbor's recycling.

More importantly, from whom was she hiding them?

Leah

After the plate of food had ricocheted off my lap, after the slap, after the violence, the threats in the closet, there had been apologies. Sometimes, there had been tears. Sometimes flowers. Apology flowers. Other times, flowers for no reason. Bags of takeout from my favorite restaurant. Little robin's-egg-blue-colored boxes with platinum, diamonds, amethysts, or peridots.

Evidence, objectively speaking, that he loved me. Or so he would say. The redness from the slap had faded in an hour. The bruise on my stomach was gone in days. The diamonds? Those lasted forever.

The morning after the incident in the closet, Liam had visited me in my bedroom. My cell?

"You know I love you more than anything, don't you?" he had said, sitting on the edge of the bed while I crouched at the top, my knees bent, my back to the headboard.

I had nodded once, almost imperceptibly. All of it was calculated. My every word, breath, and movement. Holding him at arm's length was safer than pushing him away entirely.

"Why do you have a gun?" I had asked him, even though I knew he wouldn't tell me the truth, and I knew the real reason. We weren't gun people. At least, I hadn't thought so. I was opposed entirely to anyone possessing one. Turns out, one had been living beneath my roof all along.

"It's for protection," said Liam. "I'll get rid of it. I just keep it for our protection."

"In this neighborhood? Protection from what? Raccoons?" I had replied, my skepticism obvious. The nonexistent crime level had been one of the factors that had drawn us to our neighborhood.

The gun, and the threat it carried with it, the fear that he'd use it on me, on my mom, were tools, weapons, to keep me where he wanted me to be.

"I've had it since I lived in the city," Liam said, and I was struck by the reality that I hadn't a clue how many secrets my husband kept.

Ever since he had brandished the gun, threatened my mother and me, he'd been on his best behavior. But it wouldn't last.

I didn't know how much time I had left.

I had finished another bottle of vodka last night and had accumulated quite a little collection of empty bottles. It was Tuesday, so it was time to dispose of them. I gathered the empties from beneath my mattress and let myself out the basement door. I unlatched the gate and made my way across the grass and down the driveway.

Wednesday was recycling day, and the Biedermans always brought their bin out to the curb on Tuesday morning before they left for work. In accordance with the homeowners' association, recycling and trash bins weren't supposed to be put out until after 6 p.m. the evening before collection day. I don't know why the Biedermans put theirs out so early, but I wasn't about to complain.

I looked around me to ensure no one was watching before lifting the lid to their bin and dropping my bottles inside. They clattered together emphatically. I turned and hurried back toward the gate. I hoped no one had seen me, but it didn't matter. It only mattered that Liam hadn't.

He didn't mind the alcohol. In some ways, he even encouraged it. It made me more pliable, less likely to fight back. Less likely to escape. It numbed my feelings and dulled my thoughts. And that was why it was so important that he wasn't able to keep track of how much I had consumed. I didn't want him to use it against me. I needed to drink, but not too much. It was a matter of life and death that I retained some modicum of control.

I reentered the house through the basement door. It was quiet. Liam was at work. So, I went upstairs and into the kitchen. I retrieved a fresh glass with ice and returned to the basement to pour myself a drink. Back upstairs, I began to pace the first floor as I sipped.

I knew that time was running out. I knew that Liam's patience was running thin. There would be another episode, and soon. At what point would he take it just a little too far? Which episode would kill me? I needed to prove who he was, and the things he had done to me.

I considered instigating another fight, which I could somehow record. I knew what to say to do so—I could tell him I was leaving him. But I was genuinely afraid that plan wouldn't help me escape, it would get me killed.

It might not be much longer before he realized that the gun was gone. He would know it was me who'd gotten rid of it. He would make me pay, probably in a way that was far worse than ever before.

There was another problem—one I'd thought about while tossing and turning in my basement bed after I'd awakened this morning, trying, unsuccessfully, to fall back asleep, to pass some more time.

The night I had called 911 about McKenna, I'd had my cell phone with me near her house. Liam saw my location—I knew he had. He had sent me the text message.

I hope you're being good.

I'd told him I was out for a walk. But if he realized the gun was missing, thought about the widely reported murder of Dr. Zackary Hawkins in his home on Apple Blossom Lane, recalled the location of my cell phone, and therefore myself, the night before the murder, he might put it all together. He wouldn't know why I'd done it, but he might know what I'd done.

It would be yet another thing he could hold over me.

It was yet another reason I needed to get out.

I was no longer worried about McKenna telling the police about what she'd seen through the window that night. In the news stories about the murder of Dr. Zackary Hawkins, there'd been not one mention of a suspect. If McKenna had told police about me, there would be a widespread woman hunt. There would be descriptions, possibly a sketch artist rendering of my face, circulating widely.

McKenna wasn't a risk to my freedom. There remained only one risk, the one there'd always been.

Unsure what I was doing or what I was hoping to find, I made my way to Liam's office on the first floor of our house. Using an unfolded hairpin and a credit card, I picked the lock to the door, and entered the room.

It was a place I was typically forbidden from entering. Liam claimed attorney-client privilege to keep me out. He said that he kept private client files in there, and if I was snooping around inside, I could gain access to privileged information. It was ridiculous because I was an attorney myself. I wasn't about to shout information protected by attorney-client privilege from the rooftop of our house. Besides, Liam rarely worked in his home office. His office on the ground floor of the old Victorian house was only fifteen minutes away. Even when he worked on weekends or late into the night, he would do so in that office, not our house.

Like the door to the basement bedroom, Liam had installed a doorknob that locked from outside the room, with the use of a key. There was only one key for each door, and both of them were in Liam's possession.

I had broken in only once before. It had been my project on a late April day, when I knew he would be gone the entire day, working late into the night, preparing for a trial. I had gained access to the room with the assistance of the same hairpin and credit card, a technique I had learned from a YouTube video. I had methodically combed through the shelves, cabinets, and drawers. I had found, in one folder tucked toward the back of a file cabinet, a packet of information about the wall safe Liam had paid to have installed in the master closet. I had read it, front to back, and in the bottom corner of one page was a list of codes. Liam appeared to change it once a month or so. The numbers were meaningless, seemingly random, and he kept track of them there.

He must have believed that the codes would be safe, behind the locked door, in the forbidden room.

He had been wrong.

I had committed the most recent code to memory, headed upstairs, and tried the safe, which had slid open smoothly and easily, revealing the gun.

I'd had no use for it, not that day, but it had been nice to know I could get to it if I needed to.

After returning to the office, I had cleaned up all traces of my visit, and turned the lock on the door before closing it behind me.

I had left his computer untouched, assuming I would try to get into that another day.

Today seemed like as good a day as any other.

The room was darkened by heavy cream drapes, which I left closed. I turned on his desk lamp and sat down in his high-backed leather chair. There was a coaster beside his mouse pad, on which I placed my drink.

I began to open his desk drawers, looking for something new, or something I had missed on my last visit. There wasn't much in them, mostly personal documents, like our social security cards and passports. Our marriage license. The titles to our cars. There was a folder with mortgage statements. Another with information about the plat on which our house sat, a copy of our deed, and information regarding our homeowners' association. We had bought the house the month before our marriage, before I had changed my name. It was still titled to Liam Dawson and Leah Bailey. Liam and Leah—I had thought our names sounded so adorable when said together. Liam and Leah Dawson.

Now, I longed to be Leah Bailey again. I only wished I could go back in time and warn her of what was to come.

A folder had slipped down in one of the drawers and was lying flat across the bottom of it. I pushed the others aside and slid it out.

Inside was beneficiary paperwork for two life insurance policies. One on Liam's life, of which I was the beneficiary, and one on mine, which would benefit Liam. Both were in the amount of two million dollars.

It was quite a lot of money for him to gain when I died.

I returned the folder to its resting place in the bottom of the drawer.

With a gentle press to the Power button, the screen of Liam's computer came to life. A password box appeared on the screen, asking for a four-digit PIN. I typed 0-7-0-1, and the screen flashed, giving way to the spinning wheel of the cursor, and the desktop. I felt a modicum of comfort that I knew my husband well enough to hack into his computer, in addition to the wall safe. What else, I wondered, could I hack?

I opened the internet browser. He had various websites bookmarked across the bar at the top of the screen. Pages for Charles Schwab, our bank accounts, and Chase and Marriott, our credit cards, and Vanguard, our investment accounts. But there was also a bookmark for Bank of America, and I wasn't sure why. As far as I knew, we didn't have any accounts there. I clicked on the button and was led to a log-in page. The username and password were already filled in. I clicked the Log In button and prayed for the lack of a two-factor authentication.

Apparently, Liam had selected an option to allow this computer to be recognized, and I was in. It had been a risk, but I had to take certain risks, calculated risks. If I didn't, the status quo would remain forever. Taking risks could kill me, but not taking them could, too.

Liam had one checking account with Bank of America.

I navigated to the images of checks deposited into the account on October 4 or October 5 of last year.

There was only one, but it was the one that mattered—a $3,000 check from Emily Mayer. *Legal Retainer Payment,* said the memo.

It was the check that had ruined my career, and I hadn't seen it for seven months.

Except, the check had not ruined my career. That had been my husband. The evidence was staring me in the face.

He had suggested that my job was superfluous, a hobby. He had complained about my failure to prepare a special three-month wedding anniversary dinner. I had protested, objected, and three days later, he had eliminated my job from my life.

Was it jealousy? Control? I wasn't sure. But the loss of my job had spurred the loss of so much else in my life. My friends. A level of closeness with my mother.

And when I had said that I needed a break, had said that I wanted to leave him, he'd threatened to kill us both. He'd told me he would hurt my mother if I tried to flee to Connecticut.

I opened a statement from last October and found the corresponding $3,000 deposit into the account. It was titled to us both back then. Later statements revealed it had been converted to an account in Liam's sole name. He'd opened it, then taken me off, all without my knowing.

I needed to capture it. I was afraid that if I printed the documents, Liam would be able to see evidence that I'd done so. If I took photos of the screen with my cell phone, he would see that as well. He had never had an issue with unlocking and perusing my cell phone whenever he felt like it.

I closed my eyes, trying to focus.

I downloaded the October statement and printed it, along with the check image, deciding that was best. I would hide the papers inside the sheets on my bed in the basement.

I concealed my actions by deleting the browser history and downloads. I had a feeling Liam would somehow find out anyway.

I swiped my papers from the printer tray and grabbed my drink. A ring of wetness remained on the coaster, which I wiped away with my sleeve. I left the office, making my way back to the basement to conceal the fruits of my investigation.

The evidence of the deposit into the account was meaningful to me, but it wouldn't prove anything to anyone else. If confronted, Liam would still maintain that I had somehow made the deposit into that account myself. That, in reality, I had no access to it, that I didn't open it, that it became his sole account, didn't matter. He would deny, deny, deny, all tall, dark haired, and charming, innocence radiating from his handsome face.

It wasn't enough. What I had uncovered this afternoon was just a start. I would need to compile more to escape my husband.

But how could I possibly escape him, when he had everything, unlimited resources, and I had nothing?

The answer—all that came to mind—wasn't really an answer. It was a solution that would only create more problems for me.

Still, the only thing I could think of was to kill him.

WEDNESDAY, MAY 15

McKenna

I hadn't noticed them before.

My neighborhood has paved walking paths, winding between the houses, through the surrounding woods and county-owned property, connecting the various roads. They're shaded by trees, decorated with forsythia, wildflowers, and shrubbery. They're dotted with trash cans and canisters full of complimentary, biodegradable dog waste bags. I should have considered that this neighborhood might have them, too.

I had cruised past her house this morning, but there'd not been any movement. I drove around the cul-de-sac, planning to turn around and head home, when I caught sight of what I had thought was a narrow driveway. Except, it was too narrow, and it didn't lead to a house. I realized it was a path like those in my neighborhood.

I left Silver Star Lane and turned onto the parallel cul-de-sac. There was a path attached to this one as well. I parked my car at the curb in front of a house that looked empty, hoped the residents wouldn't be home anytime soon, and set off down the path.

I had a black Baltimore Ravens cap covering my head and sneakers on my feet. I could have been any other housewife, out for a walk in my neighborhood, working off that glass of red wine or those chicken nuggets, left uneaten by the kids, from the night before. I moved quickly and purposefully, as if I belonged.

I looked around me as I walked. A woman approached me. She was jogging, her hair held away from her face with an elastic headband, earbuds peeking from her ears. We smiled at each other as we passed but didn't stop to chat. She didn't call me out as an interloper like I'd feared. There were no rules, no laws, against nonresidents going for walks on these paths and streets. I just knew from my own neighborhood that it was generally frowned upon in a supercilious way by those who did live there.

The path curved toward the woman's house but didn't run exactly behind it, although there was a wooded swath of county land that did. I glanced around me before stepping off the path and positioning myself at the edge of the woman's fence.

The woman. Leah Dawson.

I'd learned her name yesterday afternoon. I wanted to know who she was and whom she lived with. I had tried typing her address into a search engine, which hadn't yielded any results. But with a little research, I had realized that property records were public record, a fact I'd known all along but had forgotten. All I'd had to do was sign up for a free account on the Maryland Land Records website, and I was able to locate a copy of the most recent deed and promissory note for 6206 Silver Star Lane. The property had been purchased by Liam Dawson and Leah Bailey last summer.

I had searched for Leah Bailey and Leah Dawson but hadn't come up with any results that seemed to pertain to the blond woman I had seen outside my kitchen window.

I'd typed *Liam Dawson* into the search bar next. This had yielded many results. The first was a website for Dawson Law, LLC. The law firm was located in a nearby suburban city. I navigated to the *About Me* page and read that Liam had attended Duke University and Duke Law School before moving to Washington, DC, to work at a prominent firm. He had opened his own law firm several years later and focused on representing individuals in high-conflict divorce and child custody cases. There was a photo of him on the right side of the webpage. He had dark hair parted to the side and shiny with the product used to keep it that way. His eyes were green and his features were handsome, though he wasn't smiling in the picture. Based on the years in which he had graduated from law school and college, respectively, I calculated him to be thirty-four.

When he's not practicing law, Liam enjoys spending time with his beau-

tiful wife, Leah, read the final sentence of his biography. The descriptor—beautiful—felt like a command.

Leah Dawson.

I supposed she could still be Leah Bailey, but I didn't think so. Not if she was anything like me, and it seemed that she was.

She'd said as much, that night.

I'm someone like you.

I hadn't wanted to take Zack's last name. By the time we got married, I'd been working at the doctor's office for a year. My patients called me Dr. Lyons. I was profiled on the practice's website as Dr. Lyons. People knew me, and I didn't want to start over.

Zack didn't agree. "Do you really think the whole county knows Dr. McKenna Lyons, with your year of experience?"

He'd made me feel foolish. So, I changed my name. I got a new driver's license, social security card, and passport. My practice had updated the website with my new name, *Dr. McKenna Hawkins.* A year later, they removed me from the website. I had all but disappeared entirely.

The Dawsons didn't have a privacy fence. It was wrought iron and I could see straight through it to the dark green pool cover, the stone patio, the lounge chairs with navy cushions, and the white siding of the house beyond. But I couldn't see inside, not with the sunlight reflecting off the windows.

I turned away and returned to the path, then to my car. There wasn't any point in hanging around now, but I was hopeful I'd be able to learn more later, once darkness had started to fall and the windows were alight with artificial light and movement.

I drove home and into my garage, closing it behind me. There were no neighbors out to see me, and I was grateful to avoid their knowing gazes, their exaggerated pity. I knew they were thinking about how many secrets my house held.

People in glass houses . . .

That's what I wanted to remind them.

I spent the rest of the afternoon in the manner that had become routine for me. I sat down with my laptop for a few minutes, searching for jobs. I wasn't discerning. I was looking all over the country. I then moved on to continue my work organizing and packing the house. I'd purchased another stack of cardboard boxes the previous day. As soon as I found employment, I would be ready to move out. I would list the house when I left. I'd price it to sell and allow unlimited showings, any time of day.

I wondered whether Detective Harrison would stop by today. I didn't like the unpredictability. He didn't call first.

I hoped that he wasn't watching me, following me. I always kept an eye on my rearview mirror. I didn't want to lead him straight to Leah. At the same time, I wasn't willing to stay away from her. I still had so many questions.

I ate dinner alone on the patio, glancing, every few seconds, over to the kitchen window through which the bullet had come. The police had removed the screen from the window and taken it with them as evidence. I hadn't yet installed a new one.

A small glass of wine washed my dinner down, the last few swallows from the bottle I had purchased on Friday. The weather had turned over the last few days. It was breezy and in the low seventies. Spring was here, and summer was approaching soon.

I cleaned my dishes and perused my job search websites again. Finally, as the sun dipped lower and lower, I headed into the garage and slid into my car. I made the short trip to Silver Star Lane and drove through the neighborhood. There were a few people taking evening walks, enjoying the last hour of daylight before it was time to prepare for tomorrow's workday, watch mindless television, and head to bed.

I parked my car, and I joined them, exploring the paths, winding through the neighborhood, smiling and nodding as though I knew the people I passed. My phone was attached to my arm with the armband I used to wear when I went for runs outside or went to the gym. There were earbuds in my ears, but I was not listening to anything aside from the chirping of birds and bugs, the conversations of people who passed, and my own footsteps.

Once it was sufficiently dark, I made my way to the swath of grass and trees behind Leah's house. My heart leapt because I could see her in the kitchen. She was moving around the room. She appeared to be making dinner.

I didn't have a complete view of the room. Unlike my own house, the Dawsons' kitchen was not on the ground level. There were sliding glass doors against the back wall, which led to a deck. Leah moved in and out of my view as she worked. She appeared sluggish, listless. Something was off.

After a few minutes, another figure entered the room. Liam Dawson was back from work. I shrank down, as did Leah. My shoulders slumped. I remembered all too vividly how it felt when my husband returned home.

I checked the time on my phone. It was 8:33.

He was tall and he moved with authority. If his hair had been shorter and sandy rather than dark and combed to the side, from a distance, he could've been Zack. He wore a black suit and a pale blue button-down shirt. I watched him unknot his yellow tie as he stood in the kitchen.

He disappeared from the room for several moments. When he returned, he was wearing a T-shirt. Leah startled. She hadn't heard him coming.

I glanced around me, to make sure no one was approaching on the nearby paths.

Dinner was ready, but Leah and Liam didn't fill their plates or sit down to eat. They were talking, he was angry, and she was scared. They were standing in front of the island in the kitchen, a couple feet apart. Finally, Leah had enough. She tried to move past her husband, but she stumbled. He reached out an arm to push her, and she collapsed, disappearing from my view.

I felt as though I was back in my own kitchen, the night she had shot Zack. The surprise, the shock, when Zack had thrown me to the ground, had shaken me to my core. He'd done what I'd thought he'd never do. *At least he doesn't hit me.* That excuse had fizzled and died, no longer available for use.

My breath caught in my throat as Liam grabbed her hair and pulled her down again. He used the hand gripping her hair to manipulate her. He turned her body and pushed her forward, facedown, toward the stove. I couldn't hear them, but I could sense her fear and panic, fluttering, rising, taking flight.

He let go, and she slid downward.

Liam moved toward the stove, serving himself dinner, as if nothing had happened, as if he hadn't just pushed his wife down against it.

A second later, Leah appeared again, her face defeated, but not surprised. It wasn't the first time he'd hurt her. It wouldn't be the last. She slunk out of the kitchen.

I watched Liam sit down on a barstool at the island. His back was to the windows and sliding door. Meanwhile, a light flickered to life a floor below the kitchen—a walk-out basement. Leah, I presumed.

I pictured her shut away in a room in the basement, emptying more bottles of vodka, to be tossed into her neighbor's bin next Tuesday. I couldn't blame her.

There was nothing more to see. Not tonight.

As I returned to the paths and found my way back to my car, I hoped that she had locked the door. I hoped that she was safe.

Leah

I was reeling, spinning. My mind. The room. I'd had too much. Yesterday and today, I'd had too much.

After finding the proof that Liam had deposited Emily Mayer's check into a bank account about which I hadn't known, and caused me to lose my job, I'd been determined to cut back. The alcohol was preventing me from thinking clearly. It was eating up my cash, which provided my only ability to work toward funding an escape. Instead of saving the money toward gaining my independence, I was drinking it down every week. It made my mind fuzzy. With the alcohol, everything was all blurred edges and warmth and numbness, so preferable to the blinding terror of sobriety. But it wasn't exactly conducive to critical thinking, to problem-solving.

I'd been moderating it, but not enough. If only I could stop, maybe I would be able to figure a way out.

But I'd felt like I couldn't face Liam after what I had found yesterday. While I was admonishing myself to stop, I was having an extra drink in the afternoon, and two before bed, after I had retreated to my living quarters in the basement.

I awoke with a throbbing head, chasing away the images I saw when my eyes were closed—blood, brain exploding from Zackary Hawkins's head. His back was to me. His hair was sandy blond, not a dark and shiny helmet, but I fantasized, anyway, that it was really Liam I had shot.

The pounding was so powerful that I'd felt waves of nausea washing over me as I had sucked down handfuls of water and three Excedrin while standing in front of the bathroom sink. Should it have been guilt twisting my stomach? Perhaps. But it wasn't. I had taken a life, but I didn't feel guilty. I felt selfless. I felt trapped.

I'd lain in bed for another hour, with the curtains drawn—the sunlight sent a sharp pain through my head when I'd tried to allow the natural light into the room—and then had given up. I'd poured myself a glass of vodka and orange juice, over ice. The acid from the juice had burned the inside of my stomach, until the vodka had coated everything and the numbness, familiar and welcome, had set in.

Once I'd started, I had no choice but to continue. I'd dozed off on the sofa in the family room for a couple hours in the early afternoon, which was risky. I was getting sloppy, when I should've been more careful than ever. Liam could have arrived home early and found me there. He could have used the opportunity to go downstairs and snoop through my room. He could've found my copy of the bank statement and check or my stash of alcohol and empty bottles.

Fortunately, I'd awoken to a text message that he'd be working until eight or so, and I was glad. The later he worked, the fewer hours I would have to spend interacting with him.

A month had passed, and I was no closer to leaving him than I was the night he held the gun to his head.

I needed a deadline. I needed to ignite a fire in my belly. I needed a burn from something other than vodka.

Friday.

It would have to be on Friday. By Friday, I would have a plan. That would give me enough time to pack up the things I needed. I wouldn't be able to transfer any money. Not when my name was no longer tied to the accounts. But I would get in my car anyway, and I'd be gone before Liam got home from work. I would pack the food I needed, for the drive up to my mom's condo. I could use a credit card locally to fill up my gas tank. I could save the little cash I had left for a refill. Or I could fill a gas can when I filled up my car, and use that to replenish the tank once I was on the road.

I'd leave my cell phone at the house. It was tied to Liam's account and he would use it to track my location. Maybe I could purchase a burner phone, for peace of mind during the long drive.

I knew that Liam couldn't prevent me from divorcing him. I knew that I had grounds. But he would make it extremely difficult for me.

I didn't want anything from him. I understood that, even though I hadn't earned any income for most of our marriage, everything we had acquired during that time was marital property, and I was entitled to an equitable portion of it. But I didn't care about getting my equitable portion. I didn't care about any portion.

I would find a new job. Once I had escaped, I would reach out to Claudia. I would tell her everything. If she would give me a reference, I would be a thousand times more likely to find employment.

I'd tell my mom everything, too. I didn't have a choice. I'd have to tell her how dangerous it was for her that I was there at all. I knew she wouldn't care.

I could no longer just wait for something to change. I couldn't keep waiting for a solution to fall into my lap. I would be waiting forever.

I would die waiting.

I drank two glasses of water, ate a slice of toast, and sat down on the family room sofa, waiting anyway, for time to pass, for the room to stop spinning.

I was supposed to go to the grocery store today—we'd nothing left for dinner tonight, nothing left for Liam's lunch tomorrow. He would be expecting me to prepare dinner for him, and I knew it was dangerous not to. Until I could leave, I needed to maintain the charade.

Two more days. Two more dinners. Then, I'd be gone.

Going to the grocery store would serve another purpose as well. I could pay with my debit card and withdraw a bit of cash at the same time. I could hide it and pack it away, use it toward my prepaid cell phone, or some gas or food for my trip.

By five thirty, I felt like I was okay to drive, so I pushed myself off the sofa and headed into the garage. It wasn't an ideal time to go—the stores would be crowded with shoppers stopping by on their way home from work. But I wouldn't stay long. I'd grab only a few items that we'd need until Friday. After Friday, Liam's meals would no longer be my responsibility.

I drove to Whole Foods and parked as far from the store as possible, away from the rest of the cars clustered toward the storefront. I couldn't risk grazing someone's vehicle as I tried to slide my SUV into a spot.

I took a basket from the doorway and moved through the aisles quickly, grabbing several trays of precut vegetables, a few packaged sandwiches and salads, and four pieces of fresh fish. Things that Liam liked, but were easy to get and easy to make.

I loaded my items onto the conveyor belt as I greeted the cashier.

"How are you today?" she asked, smiling robotically.

"Great. How are you?" My reply was automatic.

My total came to $54.32, and I slid my debit card into the reader and entered my PIN. My finger hovered over the keypad, as I waited to direct it to withdraw twenty dollars of cash. I wanted to take more but was too afraid.

Card declined flashed across the screen.

I wrinkled my brow and tried again, with the same result. I handed my card to the cashier.

"This isn't working," I told her. "Would you try it for me?"

I could feel the fluorescent lights beating down on me, like I was in the middle of the desert at high noon. I could sense her impatience, and that of the person behind me in line, as she shook her head and handed the card back to me.

"I'm sorry," she said. "It's coming back as declined. Do you have another card you can use?" she asked with exaggerated kindness, thinly concealing her irritation with me, with my inoperable debit card.

I slid a credit card into the machine, hearing nothing but the blood rushing in my ears, feeling nothing but the burn of a blush on my cheeks. Mercifully, the card was accepted, the transaction went through, and the cashier's genuine smile was back.

"That one worked," she said, tossing my receipt into my brown paper bag. "Have a great day."

"You, too," I murmured blindly. I took my bag and returned to my car. I sat there for a few minutes, with the engine running, letting the blasting air-conditioning cool my still red-hot face.

Why had my card been declined? What had he done? What did he know?

I opened the browser on my smartphone and navigated to Charles Schwab. I tried to log in, to check the account, looking for an explanation.

Authorization denied.

I couldn't get access.

Something was happening, and I was already a few steps behind him. I needed to catch up. I needed to get out.

Should I leave now? Never return to that house? Drive straight to my mom's condo and never look back?

But I needed my small stash of money and the bank statement and check image I had printed out. I needed to leave my phone at home. Besides, I was tired. There was still alcohol coursing through my veins. I didn't feel up to the five-hour drive.

I drove home and unpacked my groceries, then made myself a strong drink and sat down on the family room sofa once again, the cushion still dented and drooping from the many hours I'd spent upon it earlier in the day. I sipped my drink and I waited, because I'd no idea what else to do.

At seven forty-five, I received a text from Liam.

Be home at 8:30.

I pushed myself off the sofa, went downstairs to brush my teeth, and then headed into the kitchen. I was thinking about McKenna. I wondered whether she was enjoying no longer having to make home-cooked meals for her husband. Was she enjoying her freedom?

I wanted very badly to go check on her, but I knew it wasn't a good idea. I couldn't be seen by the police at or around her house.

I tossed precut zucchini with olive oil and herbs, arranged it on a pan, and slid it into the oven, while I rinsed the tilapia fillets.

While I waited for the squash to cook, I went into the basement. I couldn't help myself. While the room was no longer spinning, and the buzzing numbness had diminished, I found that I missed it. I wanted the blurriness back. My mind was racing, thinking about my debit card not working, and not being able to log into our accounts. I wanted it to stop.

I removed my bottle of vodka from underneath my mattress and unscrewed the top. I took a sip, and then another, cringing as it set my throat on fire. I brushed my teeth again and returned to the kitchen.

As I heard Liam's car pulling into the garage, I slid the tray of vegetables out of the oven, turned off the burner beneath the pan of fish, and moved it to the cool back burner.

He waltzed into the kitchen in his expensive suit, and I wished I was doing the same. I missed my pointy-toed pumps and pencil skirts and candy-colored blouses. I missed the relief of taking them off and changing into lounge clothes after a long day of sitting behind a desk.

"Hey," said Liam. He began to unknot his tie.

"Hey," I replied. He knew better than to hug or kiss me. He knew I would recoil, and that would only make him angry.

"Smells good," he said. "I'm just going to change."

I removed two plates from the cabinet and pulled silverware from the drawer while I waited for him to return.

Liam appeared beside me. He was too close, and reflexively, I took a step back. He didn't take his plate.

"Leah," he said. "I noticed a log-in to my Bank of America account from Tuesday. It wasn't me. Was that you?"

I blinked at him. Should I deny, deny, deny?

"Whenever you log in, it reminds you of the last time you did so. I logged in this morning to pay a bill, and the screen said my last log-in was Tuesday at 2:34 p.m." His voice was casual, as if he didn't care, was merely curious, but I knew better. "Was that you?"

"Um," I said, "maybe you logged in and forgot. I didn't even know you had an account with Bank of America." I dodged the question.

"No," he said. "I was in trial on Tuesday. I know I didn't check the accounts."

I shrugged. "I'm not sure what to tell you," I said. I turned toward the counter and reached for my plate, but I was becoming filled with rage. It was threatening to brim over and spill out. "Why would it matter?" I asked. "It's our money. It's marital money. You're hiding it. You have an account you never even told me about."

"Leah," he said, almost pityingly, mock offended, "I'm not hiding it from you. We are married. I take care of the money. You don't need to worry about it."

"What if I want to? What if I want to worry about it? Why can't I?" My voice was rising. I was already in trouble. I was going to get hurt anyway. I might as well stand up for myself. Perhaps it might hurt less if I did. "I tried to use my debit card at the store today. The card was declined, and I can't log into the accounts. Why? What did you do?"

"Leah, I think it's better if you don't have access to them." His voice was still calm. "After you secretly logged into my account on Tuesday, and after what happened to you at work, I think it's better if I manage our money. You shouldn't have access. Once you're able to be more responsible, you can earn your access back."

My pulse quickened. "What do you mean, 'what happened at work'?"

"I mean," he said, still pitying, patronizing, "with the check. You clearly deposited a check without even realizing it. There's no other explanation for that. Then, on Tuesday, you hacked into my account. You can't be trusted, Leah. Not with money."

I balled up my hands. I was resisting the urge to take my plate and smash it over his head. I couldn't let this go. "How dare you say that?" I told him. "You know what happened. We both know what happened."

"What happened, Leah?" he asked, his voice dripping with condescension.

"You took that check," I said. "I mentioned it to you. You took it out of my purse. You forged my boss's name and endorsed it to me. You deposited it into an account I didn't know about. You put it back. You got me fired, so that I would ruin my career and stay home every day. So that I could be your perfect little wife."

He laughed. "Of course I didn't deposit that check. It was probably your boss. Her signature was on it, yet you blame me? Don't be ridiculous."

"I don't care if you don't admit it," I said. "I know the truth."

He was standing in front of me, almost a foot taller. It was time to get away. Before things escalated further, it was time to get away.

I tried to dart past him, but he reached out an arm and pushed me down. The vodka, the dizziness. I lost my balance and collapsed to the floor.

"You pushed me," I said. I sat on the floor, blinking. My elbow was throbbing. I needed him to hear it, to admit what he'd done, instead of just moving forward with an apology and a drink.

"I didn't push you," he said. "You fell. You're drunk, Leah. You think I can't tell? You're drunk and you fell down because you're a mess."

I stared at the floorboards, willing my eyes to focus. I could feel him looking down at me.

I didn't deposit that check. I didn't push you.

He was denying it, even to the one person besides him who knew the truth.

I pushed myself up, holding on to the edge of the counter. His hand shot out, grabbing a fistful of my hair. I cried out as he yanked downward, and I fell. Hairs tore from my scalp. My eyes were streaming so badly I couldn't see.

"Stop it," I cried. "Stop."

He reached toward me again, gripping my hair. He had always told me he liked it long. Was this why?

He pulled me upward, spun me around, and pushed me down, against the stove. The front burner, still hot from cooking the fish, pressed into my chest. My face was inches from the hot pan, still sizzling with oil.

I screamed, even though he was the only one there to hear me. "You're hurting me." As if he didn't know. As if that wasn't exactly what he wanted to do.

A half a second passed, just long enough to let me know that he wasn't letting go because I'd told him to, before he released me. I slid to the floor.

"I don't know what you're talking about, Leah," he said. "I've not done anything to you."

He held out a hand, as if checking a nail that he'd broken while throwing me around, pushing me into the stove.

"You're drunk, and you fell. It's sad, really," Liam said, looking down at me. "You just can't be trusted. It's why you don't have access to the money. It's why I keep the gun locked away from you."

Cold terror washed over me.

Because the gun wasn't locked away. The last thing I needed was for him to go check on the gun, to discover that it wasn't there.

I dragged myself away, across the kitchen floor, pulling myself forward with my hands. This time, he let me go. I stood and hurried down the basement stairs and into my bedroom, my head still throbbing, a piercing pain pounding against my chest.

I closed the door behind me, but I couldn't lock it. I pulled my shirt away from me, stinging and hot, and looked in the mirror hanging above the dresser. The imprint from the stove was burned into my skin. I had nothing down here to put on it, no gel or ointment. But I wouldn't go back upstairs.

It would be hidden beneath my clothes, and if I lifted them up, to show anyone, to tell anyone what had happened, they'd look to my handsome, charming husband. They'd hear his vehement denials, as he spoke about his pathetic wife, crazy and drunk. Look how patient and kind he was, for sticking by my side. No one would believe me. Not even with my printouts from the bank account. It didn't matter.

I sat down on the floor, my back against the closed door, and I cried. It wouldn't stop him. If he wanted to come in, he would throw the door open, tossing me aside like I was weightless.

I needed more distance between us. I needed to leave. Before he opened the safe and realized that the gun was gone, I needed to be several states away. He might come for me, and for my mom, but what choice did I have? I would die here.

Friday. Friday. Friday.

But leaving, it didn't feel like enough.

I still wanted him dead.

THURSDAY, MAY 16

McKenna

The sun was creeping, slowly, steadily, upward. It had rained last night, and a faint fog hung in the air.

I watched the house for movement. I wanted to see her. I wanted to make sure she was okay.

But there was nothing. The house, the neighborhood, remained still and quiet.

Until. The light rumble of a car engine. A garage door creaking open.

A silver BMW backed out of the garage at 6206 Silver Star Lane. I sank lower in my seat, watched him drive by. I could see his dark hair combed perfectly into place. His blazer was navy today. He passed without tossing a glance my way. Heading into work, as if nothing unusual had happened the night before. Maybe it hadn't. How often did he hurt her?

I returned to my house, feeling a frenetic sort of buzz in my limbs. I hung my purse on a kitchen chair, then changed into my running clothes quickly. I laced up my sneakers, downloaded a podcast, and slid my iPhone into my armband. As I stepped onto the front porch, a familiar gray sedan pulled into my driveway. I watched it come to a stop.

It looked like my run was going to be delayed.

I watched Detective Harrison unfold his long frame from the car. He removed his sunglasses and tucked them into the chest pocket of his blazer as he approached me.

"Going out for a run?" he asked.

"I was," I replied. Every time he came here, I wondered if he was going to arrest me.

"Could we talk inside?" he asked.

I nodded, turned, and led him into the house. To the kitchen this time. I figured enough time had passed since the murder. We could sit there without the scene feeling so vivid and fresh.

"Drink?" I asked.

"No, thanks." He sat down on a chair in front of the kitchen table. It was Zack's chair. Our kitchen table had four chairs around it, four different options, yet Zack and I had always sat in the same spots.

I sat in the chair across from him, which wasn't my usual spot, to Zack's left. I wanted a little extra space between us.

"I wish I was here to tell you we'd found the person who murdered your husband. I wish I could tell you that we had an update. Unfortunately, I'm sort of here to share no news." He was studying my face as he spoke, looking for a reaction.

"Okay." I shrugged. "I mean, I'm disappointed of course. But what can I do?"

"I'm hoping you can think of something," he said. "Anything you haven't thought of before. Anything that might provide a hint as to who might've wanted your husband dead."

"I can't think of anything," I said. I forced myself to look straight into his eyes.

"Like I said before, we didn't recover any useful physical evidence from the scene," he continued. "We've no indication that one of his patients was involved. Without ideas about specific people we should look into, we're a bit stuck."

"I understand," I said. I didn't know what he wanted from me.

Detective Harrison leaned back in the chair. He looked up to the ceiling, as if he was deep in thought. It felt like a gimmick. "What can you tell me," he asked, "about your relationship with your husband?"

"What do you want to know?" I asked. I wasn't about to walk right into a trap. I felt it in my bones that his true motivation for these questions was to trick me into implicating myself in the murder. I wasn't going to fall for it.

"Was yours a happy marriage?" he asked.

"Of course." And it actually pained me to say it.

"Did you ever feel like your husband was jealous or controlling?"

"Why would you ask that?" I felt my heartbeat begin to race.

"I spoke with Mina Lee and Alyssa Vercarro earlier this week," he replied. He picked at the cuticle on his left thumb.

"You talked to my friends," I said. I hadn't meant to sound accusatory, but I did. "Why?"

I already knew that he had spoken to Mina and Alyssa. I'd just forgotten, so consumed had I been with watching Leah Dawson, and trying to understand who she was and why she had done what she'd done.

Detective Harrison didn't answer my question. "Your friends both believed that your husband was jealous. They were surprised when you left your job. They believed that it was due to your husband's influence."

I shook my head. I tried to look emphatic. "I told you that I had a miscarriage in January. It was very hard on me. I contracted a virus at work, and we weren't sure if that had something to do with the miscarriage. My job put me in contact with a lot of sick, contagious kids on a daily basis. It made sense for me to stop working and focus on having a healthy baby. That was what we both wanted."

"But did you want to leave your job?" he asked.

Clearly, he already knew that I hadn't wanted to leave my job. I'd never said that to my friends. Apparently, they had picked up on it anyway. I didn't know why he needed me to admit it.

"Why does any of this matter?" I asked. It was my turn to not answer his question. "What does this have to do with someone murdering my husband?"

Detective Harrison folded his hands together. He struck me as a person who was not easily rattled. In fact, he seemed like a person who never got rattled.

"Just trying to understand your relationship," he said.

"But why?" I asked. "Is that the key to finding out who killed him?" There wasn't any other reason for it, unless he believed I had killed Zack and he was trying to prove it.

"Information is key," Detective Harrison said. "I gather as much information as I can."

"Am I a suspect?" Best to come right out and say it. "Should I have a lawyer with me every time you come over?"

"I haven't read you your rights," he replied. "This isn't an interrogation. You are not being held. If you ask me to leave, I will do so immediately." He stretched his arms out in front of him, as if loosening his upper back. Getting comfortable. Making himself at home. He wasn't going anywhere.

I said nothing. He waited.

"Well," he said finally, once the silence had stretched thin and brittle, pushing himself up from the chair, "that's all I have. Please call me anytime, McKenna, if you think of anything, anything at all, that might be helpful."

"Of course." I stood and walked him to the door. "I'm the only person who wants to find his killer more than you do."

I said it while his back was turned, as he pulled my front door open. I hoped that he couldn't tell I was lying.

I closed and locked the door behind him, then moved into the living room to watch him drive away. I no longer felt like going for a run, but I didn't feel like sitting in my house and waiting for time to pass, either. Once the detective's car had disappeared, I stuffed my earbuds into my ears and headed outside.

I wound around the paths and through the streets. When I reached Pear Tree Circle, I glanced to my right to look at the back of my house, which was visible from the curve of the road, as I always did. But I looked at it differently than I had before, not admiring its stateliness, the neat stone patio, or the abundant windows and gleaming French doors. Not admiring, but analyzing.

This section of the street abutted county property—the neighborhood was dotted with it, and it surrounded the paths. It was one of the appealing aspects of the community. It made the yards look bigger than they were. Beyond the county property was my backyard. We didn't have a fence, so it wasn't clear where the county land ended, and our property began.

I could see our flagstone patio and the white cushions of our furniture, which I had stopped bringing into the house each night for protection. I would allow the furniture to convey with the house, or I'd sell it separately, or donate it. The sunlight bounced off the windows and French doors lining the back of my house. I couldn't see inside. I'd never been at this spot in the evening once darkness had fallen, or in the morning before it had lifted. It was possible that anyone on this road could see straight into our house. I knew that from inside the kitchen and family room, I could see cars riding down the street, but they felt far away, and it wasn't a busy road.

Was this where she had parked her car that night? Had she crossed the county land and made her way through my yard? When had she decided to pull the trigger, and why?

Instead of continuing down the street, I picked my way through the county property to my backyard. I traveled the same route as her. It didn't take long.

The French doors were locked, so I made my way around the house and entered through the front door again.

After a shower, lunch, and an hour browsing job postings and submitting applications, I climbed in my car and headed to the address I'd seen in my search earlier in the week, on a street near the county courthouse. What was Liam Dawson up to while his wife was at home, recovering from the violence of the previous evening?

The street was lined with rows of Victorian homes that had been converted to offices, mostly law firms, by the looks of the signs hanging out front. I drove slowly past a yellow Victorian with a wraparound front porch and a sign in the front yard, advertising offices for DAWSON LAW, LLC on the first floor and COMPASSIONATE COUNSELING, PC and the LAW OFFICE OF JACQUELINE PRENTICE on the second floor. I continued down the street, turned around in a driveway a few houses down from the yellow Victorian, and headed back toward my house.

As I cruised down River Road, I flicked my turn signal on. But a black Lexus SUV rushed past me and I caught a glimpse of a dirty blond head behind the wheel. It was her.

I made a U-turn at the entrance to her neighborhood and followed her. She led me to a different liquor store, one I had never visited. It didn't seem particularly convenient and it took us twenty minutes to get there. I parked at the opposite end of the parking lot from her and looked into my rearview mirror, waiting for her to emerge from the store. Four minutes after entering, she did so, swinging a bottle wrapped in a brown paper bag from her right hand. It made me sad, how much she drank. I wanted to think that she simply sipped an evening cocktail, that her husband did, too, but she definitely seemed to be concealing the alcohol. Otherwise, she wouldn't have tossed the empty bottles into her neighbor's recycling bin.

Leah climbed into her own Lexus. She didn't even look at her sur- roundings. She was oblivious to me following her. If she was anything like me, she let her guard down, her level of alert declined, when her husband was at work. It was the closest she ever got to freedom.

After longer than seemed necessary to deposit her bag and purse on the seat or floor and start her car, the SUV purred to life and she backed out of her parking spot. I did the same, and we headed back in the direction from which we'd come, toward our neighborhoods off River Road. But Leah wasn't going home. She zipped past the exit that would have taken us there and continued a mile farther, taking the next one. We arrived at a strip mall. It looked vaguely familiar, but I wasn't sure whether that was because I had driven past it before, or because it looked like any other strip mall.

Leah parked her car in an open spot between an eye doctor's office and a Verizon store. I didn't know where she was going at first, and she didn't seem sure herself. She hesitated on the sidewalk for a second, before pulling the door of the Verizon store open and heading inside.

Ten minutes later, she emerged with a small bag dangling from her right hand. She climbed into her car. After three minutes, she climbed back out with the same bag. She walked to a trash can in the corner of the sidewalk and tossed the bag inside, before returning to her car.

When she drove away, I did, too. We headed to her house, where she disappeared inside the garage. The door lowered behind her car. None of it made sense. Had she bought a new phone, then thrown it away? I supposed she could have been simply tossing the packaging. She could have extracted her purchase in the car, then thrown away the trash. But, like with the bottles in her neighbor's recycling bin, the evidence of her new purchase in the public trash can told me she was hiding something.

I left her neighborhood and returned to the strip mall. I looked into the trash can. Someone had tossed an empty soda cup on top, but Leah's bag from the Verizon store was still visible. Inside, I could see a little box from a prepaid cell phone. I recognized it because I had contemplated buying one several times before.

A prepaid cell phone was always part of a plan to leave. You couldn't take your own smartphone, tied to your husband's account. He could use location services to find you. He could track your calls, your messages.

This told me that Leah was planning to leave, and soon. I was scared for her. Leaving might be more dangerous than staying.

I drove home slowly, deep in thought. Tackling the house's most daunting organization project—the basement storage area, to which many items that were unwanted but not quite trash had been relegated—consumed a few hours of my day. After eating dinner, I returned to my car, and to Leah's street. I parked on the main road and walked to the paths.

The sunlight was beginning to diminish. I stood behind Leah's house. The windows were bright with light spilling from the stylish pendant lights that hung above the kitchen island. Even after the events of the previous evening, Leah and Liam moved around the room. He must have arrived home earlier tonight. I had missed dinner. They appeared to be cleaning up.

Their body language was stilted. Their mannerisms cordial but distant. He was on his best behavior, kind and apologetic. I knew.

I'm someone like you.

Meanwhile, Leah was plotting her escape.

It could get her killed.

I stepped onto the paths, found my way back to my car, and returned to my dark and empty house. Pieces clicked into place. It all made sense to me now.

I understood that Leah Dawson had saved me because she was too scared, or didn't know how, to save herself.

It was my turn to save her.

FRIDAY, MAY 17

Detective Jordan Harrison

My job isn't the only reason I turn the volume on my phone up at night. Every time that grating sound drags me from sleep, my stomach drops. Not because I'm afraid of being called to the scene of a murder, burglary, or assault. That's what I do. That's who I am.

I'm afraid it's going to be someone calling me about Mallory. Someone from the hospital, or a relative, telling me there's been a complication. Someone telling me it's worse than they thought. Someone telling me it doesn't seem as if my partner is going to make it. Someone calling to break my heart.

I don't even know if I'm important enough to her to get that kind of call.

I reached for my phone and switched off the ringer. I looked at the number on the screen, and my heart lifted a fraction.

It was dispatch.

I swiped across the screen to answer the call, holding it to my ear. "Harrison," I said, scrubbing at my face, rubbing the sleep away.

I looked at my alarm clock with one eye closed, which was never a reliable way to see something. It was 5:16 in the morning.

I listened to the call. Another murder. The third this year. We were on pace for a record-setting year for murders.

Who would this third victim be?

Would Detective Mallory Cole pull through? Would she be victim number four?

I shook my head, tried to focus on the dispatcher's words. I committed the address to memory. When I hung up the phone, I typed it into my GPS app so it would be waiting when I was ready to leave.

I set a pot of coffee brewing while I brushed my teeth and changed. It was early. It was Friday. Still, I dressed in a suit with a crisp blue button-down and a green patterned tie. No casual Friday for me.

After pouring a generous helping of hot black coffee into a tall travel mug, I was out the door, hustling toward my sedan, parked in its designated spot in the parking lot for my condo community, then rushing toward the scene. I didn't bother with breakfast. I knew that if I ate, I would regret it. The roads were almost empty, and I was the police, so I sped.

The address led me to a street with which I was quite familiar, near the county's wheezing, old courthouse. I had driven down it many times to get to court, so that I could testify in various criminal trials and motion hearings. It was lined with old houses, mostly Victorians with wraparound porches, which had been converted to offices. It was a prime location for lawyers—walking distance to the courthouse—but there were other offices, too—therapists, dentists, CPAs, even a psychic, who apparently managed enough business to afford the rent. She'd been there as long as I could remember.

There was a marked police car blocking the road. I parked in front of it and waved to the officer sitting in the front seat as I passed.

I approached the yellow Victorian house surrounded by yellow caution tape. There was another marked police vehicle on the opposite side of the house. No one would be able to access it. There were two young and uniformed officers stationed outside. They were working the late show, and this was probably the most exciting shift of their short careers. I could practically smell the adrenaline on their breath, like it was mouthwash that they'd gargled.

"Medical examiner and techs on their way?" I asked.

"Yes, sir," said the redhead. His skin was so fair he was practically glowing. I didn't know if that was how he always looked, or if the scene inside the house had drained his color.

"What do we got?" I asked. I read the sign in the front yard, which told me that it held three different offices. Two law firms and one counselor.

"White male, early to midthirties." This time, it was the Black officer who spoke. I'd met him before but couldn't recall his name. "Single gunshot wound to the back of the head. He was sitting at his desk. He slumped forward."

"Who found him?" I asked.

"Cleaning lady," he replied. "She arrived at the house for her five o'clock shift to clean the office. She found the body, ran outside, called nine-one-one."

"She ID him?"

"Yep," he said, shifting from foot to foot.

"Where is she?" I asked.

The redhead pointed to an elderly beige Jetta parked at the curb. "Waiting in her car. She's pretty shook."

No shit.

"I'm going to talk to her first," I said. "When I'm done, I want you two to take her fingerprints, get a formal statement, and send her home. Then, I'm gonna go inside, check things out," I continued, pointing to the front door of the house.

"Ten-four." They were standing taller now. They had direction, something on which they could focus.

I walked over to the beige car and tapped on the window. I placed the woman sitting inside in her early fifties. Her hair was long, dark, and braided, and was draped over her right shoulder. She jumped in surprise, her hand rising to her chest.

"Detective Jordan Harrison," I said, showing her my badge. "Can I speak with you?"

She nodded, then climbed out of her car. She wrapped her arms around herself.

"What's your name, ma'am?"

"Maria Vasquez," she said, her voice only a whisper.

"Do you want to sit down?" I asked.

She shook her head. "I'm not going inside."

"In your car?" I asked. "Or mine?"

She shook her head again.

"Tell me what happened," I said.

She inhaled, then let out a deep and shuddering breath.

"I clean these offices every morning," she said. "I empty the trash. I vacuum and dust, clean the bathrooms. I'm supposed to arrive at five o'clock, so that I finish before the people get to work."

"And what time did you arrive today?" I asked.

"Five o'clock." She looked at me like I was slow.

"What happened when you arrived?"

"The door was unlocked, the alarm was disabled," she said. "That was strange, but also there was a car out front." She pointed to the silver BMW parked in the driveway beside the house. "I thought maybe he arrived to work very early, and left the front door unlocked. Maybe he was working all night. He works a lot." She closed her eyes.

"So you opened the door," I said. "Then what?"

"I called out, 'It's Maria.' I didn't want to startle him. No answer, but the lights were on in his office. I pushed the door open. I peeked inside." She lifted her hands and covered her eyes with them.

"What did you see?" I asked.

"Blood. He was slumped over his desk." Her shoulders shook.

I thought about placing an arm on her back, but I didn't know if that would make her feel better or worse.

"I screamed," she continued. "I ran out to my car. I called nine-one-one."

"This man," I said, gesturing to the house, "did you know him?"

She nodded. "I met him a couple of times. The other people who work here, I never met them, but he was working a couple of times when I arrived at five."

"What was his name?" I asked her.

"Liam Dawson," she said. Her eyes fell to the ground.

"Did you ever speak with him? Did you know anything about him?"

She shook her head. "I said hello, he said hello. He asked my name and he told me his. That was it." Her voice was stronger now. She was emphatic. She did not want to be involved any further. I couldn't blame her.

"His office is on the ground floor?" I asked and she nodded. I looked again at the sign in the front yard. Dawson Law, LLC was one of the businesses inside.

"Thank you for your help, Mrs. Vasquez," I said, glancing at the thin gold band on her left ring finger. "These two officers are going to speak with you briefly and get your contact information, then I want you to go home. Is that okay?"

"Okay," she said. "But I need to clean the office. I need to finish this house and then get to my next one."

I almost laughed. "Mrs. Vasquez, you aren't going to be cleaning this house for quite some time. This is an active crime scene."

"Okay," she said, looking uncertain. "My boss. Will you tell my boss?"

"We will be in touch with the landlord," I told her. "Is that your boss?"

She nodded, fingering the end of her braid.

"Take care," I told her. I handed her a card. "You should feel free to reach out to me for any reason."

She took the card and slid it into the pocket of her jeans.

I left her standing in the yard, then nodded to the officers before ducking around them, where they were still positioned at attention in front of the house. I removed blue rubber gloves from my pants pocket, pulled them onto my hands, then climbed the three stairs to the house's porch.

I looked up first, scanning the ceiling. It was in the corner where the roof of the porch met the wall, to the right of the front door. It was large and conspicuous. I snapped at the two officers, then pointed at the camera.

"Hey," I said. "Can you guys get on this? Who owns the camera? We need the footage from the last twenty-four hours, to start."

I turned away as they nodded, and I opened the front door to the house. I stepped inside.

The foyer opened up to a grand staircase, which led to the offices on the second floor. To the left of the stairs was a sitting area. I stepped inside and could see that behind it was a kitchen, which was probably shared by all the offices in the building. To the right of the stairs was a wall of modern glass doors. DAWSON LAW, LLC was printed across the top. The office seemed to have two rooms. The front room had a love seat, coffee table, and two armchairs. There was a tall desk, which I assumed belonged to an assistant.

I stepped behind the desk to find a desktop computer, a phone, and several stacks of files. There was a framed photo in front of the monitor, featuring a young and thin Black couple smiling into each other's faces. She wore an ivory lace wedding gown. Her hair was twisted away from her face elaborately. His head was shaved, and his suit was light gray. A to-do list scrawled on a yellow legal pad rested on the desk to the left of the keyboard. To the right was a mouse pad and wireless mouse. I jiggled the mouse with my thumb and a log-in screen appeared. *Morgan Jones* said the username, and there was a box for her to enter her password.

I would be speaking with Morgan Jones later today. I'd have one of the officers track her down, tell her not to bother heading into work today.

Beyond Morgan's desk was a door, standing open. Dim light was emanating from it. I pushed it open wider with my index finger and stepped inside. It was an L-shaped room, and the portion farthest from the door held a U-shaped desk, over which the dead man was slumped. There was a hole, cavernous and red, in the back of his head. He had fallen forward, his face resting on his keyboard.

I would be telling my mother about this one. It would be a cheap shot.

The plan had been for me to go to law school. I'd wanted to become a prosecutor. I had joined the police academy straight out of college. I thought I'd work as a cop for a couple years, save up some money, then start law school. Maybe I'd keep working and go part-time.

My parents had been devastated. They had wanted to have a lawyer in the family. Besides, being a lawyer was safer, said my mom. Lawyers didn't get shot at work.

But that was exactly what had happened to Liam Dawson.

The walls of the room were lined with shelves full of jewel-toned, pedantic-looking books, extravagant and authoritative. Two guest chairs were perched in front of the desk.

I moved closer to the body. His computer screen was dark, but there was a tiny blue light blinking at the base of the screen, telling me that the machine was merely sleeping. The man was not. Cause of death was apparent.

An iPhone in a black case was on the desk beside his head. Aside from one file folder with a paper peeking out, the desk was immaculate.

Behind the desk was a credenza decorated with several framed pictures. All three showed the same couple, tall and dark-haired Liam Dawson with a petite and pretty blond woman. Them standing in front of the Eiffel Tower. Them on a white sand beach, with a backdrop of clear aquamarine water and a sky shot with orange, pink, and purple. Them on their wedding day. Her dress was one shouldered. Braids framed her face.

My stomach dropped, as I looked into the face of the woman whose heart I'd be breaking in a few hours.

Unless, of course, she'd killed him.

I returned to the center of the office and made one final scan of the room.

There were two windows on the wall to the right of the man's head, and one window behind him. All three were open, letting in a breeze that was gently rustling the long and heavy-looking burgundy drapes. I stepped toward the window behind Liam Dawson's head, then stepped closer still. I bent down and peered through the rounded but jagged hole that had been torn into the window screen as the bullet had propelled through it, meeting its target in the back of the head.

Abruptly, I thought of McKenna Hawkins.

Leah

I became aware of myself waking up. My eyes remained closed while I tried to answer the questions running through my mind and chase away the echoing gunshot and curtain of blood. It was my usual routine when I felt disoriented.

Where am I? I gripped the silky sheets in my hands. *In bed. In the basement.*

What day is it? *Friday. The day I leave.*

Am I safe? *For now.*

What happened last night?

I drew a blank.

I opened my eyes.

Light was flickering beneath the curtains. I could tell, without checking the time on my phone, that it was late morning.

I remembered sneaking a drink before dinner last night. After Wednesday evening's incident, there had been nothing I wanted less than to make dinner for my husband, let alone sit in the same room as him and eat it.

After ignoring his text messages all day, I had been in the basement when he arrived home from work. He had shown up earlier than usual and crept down the stairs to my bedroom. He tapped on the door.

It was a formality because I couldn't keep him out. If he wanted to enter, he could, and he would.

"You pushed me," I'd said. "You pulled my hair and you burned me." I wanted to lift my shirt and show him the marks across my chest, but I also didn't want him to see me unclothed and vulnerable.

"It upset me that you said I took that check from you," Liam said. He neither admitted, nor denied, what he'd done. But, when it mattered, he would refute my description of last night's events.

I pressed my lips together. I knew I needed to let it go. I had purchased a prepaid cell phone earlier in the day. If I'd been having any doubts about escaping, the events of Wednesday night had shown me that I didn't have a choice. He would continue to escalate. With every week, every month, that went by, it would only get worse. I was scared to leave, but I had to ask myself: Should I be even more scared to stay?

But I needed to keep him close until I could get away. There couldn't be another incident. He couldn't go to the safe, looking for the gun. I had to pacify him, for one more night.

So, I'd gone upstairs with him. We had prepared dinner together. We had made small talk. He hadn't tried to touch me. He'd kept his distance.

After our meal, I'd told him that I wanted to be alone for the rest of the night, knowing he would let me be, and returned to my basement bedroom to drink.

I hadn't just purchased the phone earlier in the day. I had stopped at my Thursday store as well for another bottle of vodka. I'd told myself that Wednesday would be my last day, but after what happened on Wednesday, and with the anxiety that was coursing through my veins as I prepared to leave my house for a final time on Friday, that was impossible.

Thursday. Thursday would be the final day. It would have to be. Because Friday I would be free.

Friday. Today.

I would turn off my cell phone and leave it in the house. I would get in my car. I would purchase a gas can. I would drive to my usual gas station and fill up my car and the can, and then head to my mother's condo.

I was both dreading, and looking forward to, my arrival. She would be so happy to see me. She'd think everything was fine. She'd think I had just come up to surprise her. When I told her the truth, it would break her heart.

I'd have to tell her that we weren't safe, and I'd have to tell her why. Liam might be on his way. Would we go to the police? I didn't like that idea, but I didn't see any other option.

I'd think about it on the road. With the distance between us growing, I hoped I'd be able to think more clearly.

I heaved myself out of bed and staggered into the bathroom. My mouth was so dry, I practically had to pry it open. I brushed my teeth, then drank several mouthfuls of water and splashed cold water on my face. I swallowed four Excedrin, one by one. My stomach roiled. I needed some toast or crackers or something.

After dressing, pulling a T-shirt gingerly over my chest, I made the bed and went upstairs, locating an old backpack I'd had since I was in law school. In the master bathroom, I winced as I rubbed aloe across my burns. I returned to the basement and began to collect my toiletries and my clothes, shoving them into the backpack. There wasn't much there. It didn't take long to clean up the room. I moved slowly, my head still pounding.

I folded up the bank statement and check image I had printed out in Liam's office and shoved them into the bottom of the backpack. I collected my empty vodka bottles and carried them up to the garage, tossing them into our recycling bin. Liam might see them there, but it didn't matter. By the time he found them, I would be long gone.

I carried my backpack upstairs and dropped it to the floor by the door to the garage, just as the doorbell chimed through the house. I rolled my eyes.

"Fuck off," I said to no one. "I have a horrendous hangover."

I moved into the kitchen, opened the fridge, and looked inside, trying to decide what I could bring with me for my journey.

The doorbell rang again.

I went into the living room, pulled the curtains back a few inches, and peeked out.

A very tall Black man was standing on the porch. He was wearing a black suit and a blue button-down shirt, with a green tie. He was either a cop, a salesman, or someone trying to foist his religion on me.

Whoever he was, I didn't want to answer the door. But he'd seen the curtain move and was looking directly at the window. He waved.

I moved to the front door, flipped the dead bolt, and pulled it open.

"Hello," I said hesitantly. "Can I help you?"

"Mrs. Dawson?" asked the man. He reached into his pocket and pulled out a badge, which he held out to me.

Cop.

My pulse quickened.

"Yes," I said. "Can—can I help you?" I asked again.

"Detective Jordan Harrison. May I come in?" he asked.

I hesitated, but I stepped aside and let him enter. I led him into the kitchen and stood by the island while he hovered several feet away. I knew I should offer him a drink and tell him to sit. But all I could think about was McKenna Hawkins, on the floor in her home. Zackary Hawkins standing over her. The way it felt when I pulled the trigger. The way his head exploded. Was this how it would end?

The detective rubbed the stubble on his chin. "I'm afraid—can you sit down?" he interrupted himself. "Please, have a seat." As if I was a guest in his house.

I moved to the kitchen table and sank onto a chair.

"I'm afraid I have some bad and shocking news," he said. He sat down in the chair across from me. "It's about your husband. I'm afraid he was killed last night."

I blinked. Once. Twice. Three times. I could almost hear it, my eyelids meeting. Time stopped. I didn't breathe.

"I'm very sorry to have to tell you," he continued.

"Killed," I said, trying out the word for size. "Killed. In a car accident?"

"No, ma'am," the detective said. "I'm afraid he was shot. In his office."

"Shot," I repeated. "Shot with a gun?"

My mind felt stuck. Wheels were spinning, but I was going nowhere. I couldn't comprehend what this man was saying to me.

"Yes," said the detective. I'd already forgotten his name. "He was shot from behind in his office."

I sat quietly at the kitchen table like I had countless times before. But this wasn't like any other time. It was like I was being electrocuted every few seconds as I turned the news over in my mind. I should probably be crying. I should be collapsing to the floor, sobbing and wailing. That's what a wife should be doing after being informed that her husband was murdered. I just couldn't muster the energy to act. I wasn't sad. But the shock—the shock was real. It was as paralyzing as the shame, the fear, that had kept me frozen for the last seven months.

"Do you need something?" the detective asked. "Some water?"

I nodded, then watched him open cabinets in my kitchen, looking for a glass. He finally found one and moved toward the sink.

"There's a pitcher in the fridge," I said, even though it was quite customary for me to drink water out of the sink. I'd done it just this morning. But that was my secret life. Secret Leah drank two-thirds of a bottle of vodka in a day, swallowed tap water from her cupped hands, popped Excedrin like candy, and plotted an escape from her husband. I couldn't let this man see Secret Leah. He needed to see the perfect wife, the grieving wife, who was devastated. Who did not kill her husband. Because I couldn't help but wonder whether Secret Leah had done just that.

The detective removed the pitcher from the fridge and poured some into the glass before handing it to me. I sipped it. "This doesn't feel real," I said. I stared at the kitchen table in front of me. "I can't believe this is happening. What happened to him?"

"We don't know what happened," the detective replied. "Not yet. Are you up to answering some questions about last night and this morning? Anything you could tell us could be helpful."

"Okay," I said. "But it was just a normal evening." I placed my glass down and watched condensation run down the side.

"Your husband worked yesterday?" he asked.

"He worked. He came home around six. We made dinner together and ate. That was it. Nothing strange happened." I was flying blind. I didn't know what he knew.

"What time did he leave for work this morning? Or did he return to the office last night?"

"He did," I said. It was coming back to me. "He had come home earlier than usual to have dinner with me. During dinner he told me he had to go back to the office. He was prepping for a big trial. Starting Monday."

"What time did he leave for the office?" he asked.

"I'm honestly not sure," I said. I had retreated to my basement bedroom after dinner. I knew that. I had been granted space, time, after the events of the previous evening. After that? This detective knew as much as me. Probably more. "I think he left around seven thirty. I had a headache. I went to bed pretty early."

"Did he return to the house and go to bed?"

"I'm sorry," I said, shaking my head. "I don't know."

"So," said the detective, "he could have come back to the house, slept for a few hours, and then headed into the office. Or, he could have been there all night."

"What time was he shot?" I asked.

"We are waiting for an estimate from the autopsy," he said. "All we know is that he left here around seven thirty, you think, and he was found by the woman who cleans his office shortly after five this morning."

An autopsy. I thought about them cutting into Liam's body. Sawing through his bones. Removing his organs.

Abruptly, I started to cry, and I was glad. Because the detective would expect me to cry. It was the right thing to do. But I wasn't crying because I had lost my husband last night. I had already lost the person I thought he was. I had come to terms with that loss. It was a combination of sadness that I'd never get that back, not that I'd expected to, and relief, because it was over, and fear, because what had I done?

But I couldn't have shot him. I took a shuddering breath and folded my hands together. I reminded myself that Liam's gun was gone, disposed of. I couldn't have gotten my hands on another one. I might have wanted to shoot my husband, but I couldn't have. I waited for the detective to ask me about the gun. Surely, he knew that Liam owned one. Of course he would want to confiscate it, to examine and test it. What could I say about its absence?

The detective looked around. "Tissues?" he asked.

I shook my head and wiped my face with the hem of my T-shirt.

"Would you like me to come back another time?" The detective scooted forward to the edge of his chair, as if preparing to launch himself upward and flee the house. "We can continue this conversation when you feel more up to it. Unfortunately, though, there will be a few officers arriving to search through the house. Someone will sit with you while they do that."

It wasn't a request. They would be searching the house, whether I liked it or not. Did they have a warrant? I didn't want to ask. I didn't want to raise suspicion. I took an inventory in my mind. What might they find? Nothing that would implicate me. Not the gun. The absence of the gun, though, would be troubling to them, assuming it had been registered. My eyes flicked to the backpack by the door. That, I would have to explain.

I waved a hand through the air. "That's fine," I said. Might as well get it over with.

"What did you do last night?" he asked.

"Like I said, I just went to bed early. I had a migraine, and I slept straight through until this morning." I shrugged. "I'm sorry, but I didn't have any more interactions with my husband."

"How are you feeling this morning?" the detective asked. "How's your head?"

"Getting better," I told him.

"What were your plans for the day? Going to work?"

For the first time, I glanced at the clock. It was 9:36.

"I don't work right now. I was let go in October," I admitted, but only because I felt like I had to. Any story I told would be too easily checked out. I hoped he wouldn't think that commandeering $3,000 of unearned client money was evidence that tended to prove I was a criminal by all accounts and had somehow killed my husband, or arranged to have him killed. He didn't press the issue. For now.

"I was actually planning to go visit my mom today," I said, rather abruptly, thinking of the backpack in the hall. "In Connecticut. I was about to leave. I suppose I won't go, though."

He was watching me closely. "That would be best."

"Of course." I looked away, pressed the tips of my fingers against my glass.

"We're going to speak with the people who work in your husband's office building and the other offices on that street," the detective said. "Maybe someone else saw him between the time he left the house and when the cleaning woman found him this morning."

"I hope so," I agreed. I took a sip of my water and waited.

"The cleaning woman who found him said your husband worked a lot. What was his typical schedule?"

"He didn't really have one," I said. "It depended on his workload in any given week. He usually went to the office at six or seven. He worked until seven, sometimes eight, at night. Sometimes he went in as early as four. Sometimes he worked until one or two in the morning, if he was getting ready for a big trial. It wasn't unusual for him to do some work on the weekends, too." I rubbed my eyes. The medicine was kicking in, but a dull ache was still pulsing behind them. I knew from experience that it would last all day. "I'm sorry," I added. "I know that's not very helpful."

"It is what it is. Let me ask you this," the detective said, leaning forward, his elbows on the table, "did your husband have any enemies?"

Besides me?

"No," I said. "Not that I know of. My husband was a very charming man. People liked him."

The detective nodded, and I thought it was likely he might find something in Liam's life. He might find other people who wouldn't have minded if he died. People did like Liam. Then, they got to know him, and realized that the charm was there on purpose. It was wrapping paper and a bow around a venomous snake. But that wasn't revealed until it was too late: he'd already lashed out; he bit you; the poison spread.

"Do you have any suspects?" I asked, wondering whether he was going to say, *You!* in a *gotcha* sort of way.

"Unfortunately, we don't have any leads right now. I promise you, we are working on it."

I nodded, wishing he would just let it go—*Don't work too hard*—knowing I could never say that.

"There is one thing," the detective added, his hand to his chin, like *The Thinker,* "that's sort of interesting."

"What's that?" I asked.

"Did you hear about the murder of Dr. Zackary Hawkins, a week ago from yesterday?"

My heart hammered in my chest. I was certain he could hear it. "Yes," I said. "Terrible," I lied.

"Maybe you saw in the news," he continued, "that Dr. Hawkins was shot in his home through an open window. The bullet tore through the screen."

I'd done more than see it in the news.

"Yes," I whispered. "How awful."

"Well," said the detective, "the same thing happened to your husband."

"The same thing?"

"He was shot through an open window in his office."

He watched me. He was looking for a reaction. I stared stonily back at him, while my vision swam, and my heart beat a staccato number against my ribs.

"It seems likely," he continued, "that the same person killed both Dr. Hawkins and your husband."

"Oh," was all I could manage. My heart was still thundering. I knew he was wrong.

"Did you know Dr. Hawkins?" he asked.

"No."

"Did your husband?"

"Not that I know of."

The doorbell rang yet again.

"That'll be my backup, to look through the house." He stood up. "That's all I have for you at the moment, Mrs. Dawson."

I left my water glass sweating on the table and followed him to the front door.

The detective reached into his pocket and pulled out a card. *Detective Jordan Harrison,* it said, with two phone numbers and an email address.

"Keep this," he said. "And please call me anytime if you think of anything that might be helpful. I will keep you updated, as well."

"Thank you," I said, taking the card.

He pointed to the living room, which, despite its name, was the least-used room in our house. "You'll wait here, while we have a look around?" he suggested.

But, again, it wasn't truly a suggestion. I nodded numbly and sat down on an armchair. I watched as he opened my front door, allowing three uniformed officers to enter. They had rubber gloves in their hands.

I sat, powerless, as they dispersed throughout the house. They'd note the locked office, the safe upstairs. They'd pore through my backpack, resting by the door. My mind raced, as I tried to concoct explanations for the things they would find, and the thing they wouldn't—the gun. Why hadn't he asked me about it? With Liam shot, it should have been the first thing the police wanted.

It seemed inevitable that there'd be evidence that I hated, feared my husband. It seemed written on the walls. I could see it in every room. I wondered whether they could, too. If they did, they would surely suspect me. They probably already did.

And I hadn't killed him. I couldn't have. But that didn't mean I was innocent.

Detective Jordan Harrison

Morgan Jones lived in a brick town house with a cherry-red door and gray-blue shutters. I rang the doorbell, and her husband—I recognized him from the wedding picture on her desk—answered the door.

"Detective?" he said.

I flashed my badge. The officers had already caught the Joneses before Morgan left for work and told her what had happened to her boss. They had advised her to stay home and wait for a visit from the detective leading the investigation. Evidently, her husband had decided to stay home, too.

"Jordan Harrison," I said.

We shook hands. "Elijah Jones," he replied. "Please come in."

Morgan was sitting on a gray sectional in her family room, waiting for me to arrive and provide answers I didn't have. Her hair was long and braided, her face was tear streaked, and a balled-up tissue was clutched between her fingers.

"Mrs. Jones," I said, "I'm Detective Jordan Harrison. Would it be okay if I asked you some questions about your boss, Liam Dawson?"

She nodded and twisted the tissue in her hands.

"What can you tell me about him as a person?" I asked. I sat down on the footrest portion of the sectional, and her husband sat down beside her. He draped an arm across the sofa behind her head.

"He was intense," she said, then swallowed. "He was a very good lawyer. He was aggressive. An advocate for his clients. In those ways, I wanted to be like him. I'm taking night classes at the University of Maryland's law school," she explained. "I was hoping he would hire me as an associate after I graduated. Now—" She shrugged, didn't finish the sentence.

"I'm sure you'll find another position," I said.

"She will," Elijah chimed in, his dimples flashing briefly. "She's in the top ten percent of her class." Despite the circumstances, he was unable to pass up the opportunity to brag about his wife.

"You said those are the ways in which you wanted to be like him," I said. "Are there any ways in which you didn't want to be like him?"

"He's a workaholic," she said, echoing Maria Vasquez. "My hours were set, eight thirty to five, then I would drive up to the city for class. Unless he was in court, he was always in the office when I arrived, and he was always there when I left. I know he worked a lot of late nights and weekends. I always felt sort of bad for his wife."

"Why is that?" I asked, my gut buzzing.

"Because he was always working. She must have been lonely."

"Do you know his wife?" I asked.

"Not really," Morgan said. "I mean, I have met her a few times, but it wasn't like we hung out or anything. She's a lawyer, too," she added.

I filed away the fact that Liam Dawson had not informed his assistant that his wife had been let go from her job in October and hadn't been employed since. Just like Zackary Hawkins hadn't told Erica Dern that McKenna had left her job.

"How long have you worked for him?" I asked.

"Two years this past February," she said. "I can't believe it's been that long."

"How was he to work for?"

"Like I said, he's intense." She wasn't yet comfortable referring to her boss in the past tense. "He likes things done a certain way. When I first started working for him, I thought he was a little mean, to be honest." She looked surprised by her own revelation. "But once I got the hang of things, and I proved myself, he respected me. We got along fine. As long as I got my work done and I answered the phones when they rang and stayed on top of my email, he didn't care if I sat at my desk and did my reading for class." She started to cry again. "I'm going to have to find another job. I don't know if my new boss will let me do that. It's hard to work full-time and go to school."

Her husband rubbed her back.

"I'm very impressed," I said. "I wanted to go to law school, too. But I was intimidated by working my way through it."

I wasn't sure if that was the truth, but it had felt like the right thing to say. I should have been intimidated by the prospect of working and attending law school at the same time, but that was more than a decade ago. I was cocky and I felt invincible back then. The truth was, I'd decided against school because I had wanted to focus on the job I loved and hated, the job to which I had become addicted. Since then, that job had shown me enough to knock me down a few notches. I wasn't cocky anymore, and I knew I wasn't invincible. I'd seen too much to think like that.

That I was impressed by people who did take the plunge, to work themselves into the ground with the hope of rising up much higher than before? That part was true.

Morgan sniffed and held up her shredded tissue, then decided against using it.

"When was the last time you saw Mr. Dawson?" I asked.

"Yesterday," Morgan replied. "Five thirty. The spring semester is over. I don't start my summer classes for a few more weeks, and we have a big trial starting on Monday, so I stayed a little later to help out." She placed her hands on her cheeks. "Oh my God," she said. "That poor client. It's supposed to be a seven-day trial. What's going to happen to her?"

"I'm sure she will get a postponement," I assured her.

It would be a messy process, postponing deadlines and hearings in all of Liam Dawson's cases. Based on what we'd seen, he had a busy practice, probably thirty or so active cases. The clients would all need new lawyers. The state would step in to make arrangements for the clients, their files. This situation was exactly the reason it seemed so risky to truly operate as a sole practitioner. I was surprised Liam didn't have another attorney working for his firm.

"Mr. Dawson never had an associate attorney?" I asked.

Morgan shook her head. "Not while I worked with him. Like I said before, he liked things done a certain way. He mentioned he'd had one in the past, but it didn't work out."

"Do you know when that was? Or the person's name?" That would be a person to look into, although I had no idea how that person might be connected to Zackary Hawkins, and I was certain the two murders were connected in some way.

Morgan shook her head again. "He never said."

"Who was his assistant before you?" I asked.

"Her name was Christina something? She trained me. She was seven months pregnant and she was planning to stay home with her baby. We overlapped for a month, and then she left. She was his first assistant, I think."

"So you left the office at five thirty," I said. "Mr. Dawson was still there? Did you speak to each other?"

"I peeked my head into his office to say goodbye. He told me to have a good night. Actually, he said, 'I'm right behind you,' which was strange because it was my understanding he usually stayed much later. He said he was going home to have dinner with his wife."

"And that was unusual?" I asked.

"Like I said, I always left before him, so I suppose he could have walked out the door behind me every day. But it didn't seem like that was the case. There were offhand remarks about him working very late or very early and on the weekends. Sometimes I would flat-out ask him how late he had worked. I teased him a little."

"Is it your belief that it was strange for him to leave in order to have dinner with his wife?"

"Not necessarily. I mean, maybe she eats whenever he does, at eight, or ten, or midnight. Maybe it was a special occasion. I don't know. He just hadn't specifically mentioned it before."

This seemed to be a significant piece of information, but I wasn't sure why. It coincided with Leah Dawson's version of events.

"Are you aware," I asked, "of whether he returned to the office last night after having dinner with his wife?"

She wrinkled her brow. "No. Is that what he did? I wouldn't know."

"It appears so," I told her.

"So, is that when he was shot? He ate dinner, returned to the office, and got shot?" I could hear the panic rising in her voice.

"We don't know," I said. "Not yet."

Morgan was staring at a spot above my head. Her eyes were glazed. I'd lost her.

I pushed myself up and handed her husband a card. "That's all I have for you, Mrs. Jones. Please feel free to reach out to me if you think of any other information that might be important."

Morgan didn't respond, but her husband stood up and walked me to the door. "She's very upset," he said. There was concern etched in his face. "Do you think it was random?" he asked.

"I don't know for sure," I said. "But no, I don't."

He nodded, we shook hands again, and I left him there, staring at a closed door and worrying about his wife.

I returned to my car and turned it on, backing out of whatever resident's designated parking spot I had temporarily commandeered.

It was time to pay another visit to Mrs. Hawkins.

As I made my way to her house, I suddenly and very badly wanted to talk to Mallory. I wanted to tell her everything about the case. I wanted to see her cock her head to the side as she listened and twirl a lock of crimson hair around her finger as she thought. I wanted to bounce my ideas, my theories, off her, and wilt when she told me they were dumb.

But Mallory wasn't available. I could have requested another partner, in her absence. That would have felt wrong. Whoever it was, I would've treated him or her terribly for not being Mallory.

I pulled into the driveway and climbed out, slamming my car door behind me.

When McKenna met me at the door, I was struck by how similar she looked to the other victim's wife, Leah Dawson. They were roughly the same height, with pretty features, blue eyes, and long blond hair, although McKenna's was lighter and appeared to me to be chemically enhanced, and Leah Dawson was heavier, though not overweight by any means. They were around the same age. They were highly educated, but no longer employed. They both had handsome and successful husbands, who had been murdered in exactly the same manner.

By the same gun? That, I didn't yet know.

I needed to find out whether they knew each other. There had to be a connection.

I knew I couldn't count on McKenna Hawkins to tell me the truth. But I had to ask her anyway.

She looked nervous to find me standing on her front porch. She sighed. "Come in," she said.

We stayed in the living room this time, which was fine with me. I sat on my usual teal chair.

"I'm wondering," I said, "if you've seen the news today."

The news of the murder had broken, sometime after I had spoken with Leah Dawson and stopped at the station, and sometime before I had interviewed Morgan Jones.

With the proximity to the courthouse, the placement of the police cars and yellow crime scene tape, and the morning rush of people flocking to their offices in the yellow Victorian and the surrounding houses, reporters had been circling within hours after Maria Vasquez had discovered Liam Dawson's body. Apparently, by interviewing the bystanders hoping to get to work, the reporters had discovered who was missing. One of them probably had a source inside the department who had confirmed the identification. Or, maybe one of them had found and spoken with Maria Vasquez. Either way, Liam Dawson's murder had been revealed on the eleven o'clock news. Thankfully, the information that he'd been shot through the open window behind his desk had not been leaked.

I wanted to drop that particular bombshell on McKenna myself.

McKenna crossed her legs. She wore athletic shorts and a GEORGE WASHINGTON UNIVERSITY SCHOOL OF MEDICINE T-shirt, highly incongruous to my suit and long-sleeved button-down. Her affect was wary. "I did watch some of the news this morning," she said.

"I'm assuming you heard, then, about the murder of a man named Liam Dawson."

She stiffened, then recovered. She folded her hands in her lap. "The man who was shot in his office? I did see the story about that. It's terrible."

"Is it?" I asked.

Her eyebrows, a handful of shades darker than her hair, lowered. "What do you mean?"

"Is it terrible?" I shrugged. "Maybe he deserved it."

"I don't know," she said. Her voice was firm. "I didn't know him."

"You never met him?"

"No."

"What about his wife, Leah Dawson? She used to work as an attorney."

Again, McKenna stiffened for half a second. "No, I don't know her, either. Can I ask—what does this have to do with my husband's death?" She was losing her patience.

"Maybe nothing," I said. "Maybe everything."

"In what way?"

"It's interesting, because your husband was shot through an open window. The bullet tore through the screen."

"Right," she said. "I was there." She was really losing her patience.

"Well, Liam Dawson was shot through an open window as well. Through the screen."

This time, she didn't stiffen, but she should have. She was too cool. Any reaction she had was imperceptible.

"What—" She paused. "What does that mean?"

"It would seem to indicate," I explained, "that the same person who killed your husband killed Liam Dawson last night. It would seem to indicate that if we could determine the connection between your husband and Mr. Dawson, we would have a better shot at figuring out who killed them."

"I didn't know him," she said again. "And, as far as I know, neither did my husband. I'm sorry."

"He was a lawyer," I said. "A divorce lawyer."

"Okay," she said. "I still didn't know him."

"Is it possible he and your husband had a professional relationship? Could they have met at a networking event? Served as a source of referrals for each other?"

"It's possible," she said, tapping her fingers on her thigh. "I guess that is possible. My husband did attend networking events pretty regularly."

I would have a few officers look into their professional circles. Try to determine whether they might have crossed paths.

"That's all I have for you, McKenna. Unfortunately, I don't have any other updates about the case." I paused before standing, letting the silence linger, waiting to see if she was going to fill it.

She didn't, so I stood up and we walked to her front door.

"If anything comes to you, give me a shout," I said.

"I will," she replied.

But I was positive that she wouldn't. I nodded anyway, then hopped off her porch.

Add it to the pile, I thought as I climbed into my car. It was just one of many lies I'd been told by McKenna Hawkins.

SATURDAY, MAY 18

Detective Jordan Harrison

The analysis of the fingerprints lifted from Liam Dawson's office had come in early this morning. There had been a rush on the Dawson case ballistics and fingerprints, due to the similarities between the cases. The public was growing antsy. Successful white men in their thirties were growing scared. Who would be next?

I remained convinced that the murders had not been random, but I hadn't yet found anything connecting the two men.

I was still waiting on the ballistics on the bullet that had torn through Liam Dawson's head. Would it be a match for the bullet that had killed Zackary Hawkins?

I was paying Leah Dawson a surprise Saturday morning visit to discuss the status of the case with her. I was certain she'd be thrilled to see me.

When she grudgingly invited me inside and told me to have a seat in the living room, not ten feet from the front door, I could tell that I was right.

"I wanted to give you some updates," I told her. "Let you know where things stand."

"Okay," she said. "What's going on?"

Her shock had thawed but I felt that something was missing. Grief and loss manifested itself in all forms. I knew not to judge a person for his or her behavior after suffering the tragic loss of a loved one. But something seemed off about her reaction. I had to wonder whether he had been a loved one at all.

True, she had cried yesterday. But that wasn't dispositive. People cried when shocked. They cried when happy. They cried when relieved.

"The technicians searched the scene for physical evidence," I told her. "Unfortunately, nothing was recovered. It seems that the person who shot your husband did not enter his office at any point. He or she never got closer than the porch or yard."

Leah twirled the end of her ponytail. "Okay," she said. "I understand."

If anything, she seemed a little too understanding.

"There was a camera, on the porch of the office building," I said.

Leah nodded. She was waiting, eager. I could tell she didn't know what I was about to say.

"It was fake. A deterrent only."

"Oh," she said. "That's too bad."

She was right. I'd been so hopeful when I'd seen that camera. But it was a safe area, on a street near the suburban courthouse, around which there was often a heavy police and sheriff presence. The landlords and building owners weren't yet with the times in terms of security measures, relying upon locked doors and alarm systems. It simply wasn't necessary to have more. Perhaps, now, it would be.

"Did you or your husband own a gun?" I asked. I rested my left ankle across my right thigh. There was no weapon registered under either of their names in the state, but I knew enough to know that wasn't conclusive.

She stared at me, her eyes flicking back and forth. "No," she said, firmly, definitively. She was sure, or else she was sure that she needed to lie.

No gun had turned up in Liam Dawson's office, nor in the Dawsons' house yesterday, or their cars. Just like no gun had turned up in the Hawkines' house, or in Zackary's office.

With a warrant, we could search more thoroughly. We could tear the houses apart, looking for the gun. I was clinging to the hope that there'd be only one.

"Your relationship with your husband," I said, switching gears. "How was it?"

Confusion flickered across Leah's face before she shrugged and said, "It was fine. Good."

Whether she killed him or not, she didn't want me to suspect her. I knew that she would not admit it if they fought every day. There were no records of any 911 calls from or about the house. No police reports. But that meant very little to me. What went on behind closed doors often stayed there, even, or especially, when it was dangerous and violent and should not have been a private matter at all.

"You don't seem convinced," I said.

Leah looked away, opened her mouth, closed it again, then said, "I am."

I didn't believe her, but what was I supposed to do with that?

When searching the house on Friday, we had found a backpack on the floor near the door to the garage. It held some clothes and toiletries, a prepaid cell phone, as well as an old printout of a bank statement and a copy of a check from someone named Emily Mayer to the law firm of Granderson & King for a "Legal Retainer Payment."

When asked about the backpack, Leah had said that she'd been planning to take it with her when she left for Connecticut, to visit her mom for the weekend. The phone was a backup she had purchased, to store in her car, which I didn't buy for a second. When shown the bank statement and check image, she had wrinkled her brow.

"Those must have been in the backpack already when I packed up," she'd said. "I'm not sure why they were in there."

Again, I didn't believe her. But I couldn't prove she was lying. Not yet.

"I'm wondering if your husband's death could be in any way related to his cases," I said. "Can you think of anything he mentioned to you that might have raised red flags?"

"He specialized in high-conflict divorce and custody cases. Every case was messy. Even if he did discuss a case with me, he was careful to not mention names or too many details. He wouldn't breach attorney-client privilege."

I'd been expecting her to say as much. As with Zackary Hawkins, we weren't going to get access to Liam Dawson's files. Not without reason.

Leah stared at me, her lips pressed together, as if preventing truths from spilling out. I knew there was a lot more she could share. I also knew she wasn't going to.

I again asked her to contact me if she thought of any other information that might be important to the investigation and I bid her goodbye.

In the car, I checked the time on my dashboard clock. I plugged the address for the county hospital into my GPS—I knew where it was, just not the best way to get there from here—and backed out of Leah Dawson's driveway.

I had paid another visit to Judge Souder last night. She had agreed with me that there seemed to be a connection between the two murders and had approved a court order granting me access to Leah's phone and financial records. Just like the ballistics results, I was waiting for them to arrive.

In the meantime, I was not sure where to go, what to do. I had no helpful physical evidence in either case. No one had seen Zackary Hawkins's shooter. No one had seen Liam Dawson's, either. The medical examiner had estimated that his death had occurred sometime between ten at night and two in the morning. No one had reported seeing him between the time he left his house at approximately seven thirty in the evening and when Maria Vasquez arrived to clean the office at five in the morning. My team had tracked down every single employee of every single office on the same street as Liam Dawson's office, and every single one of them had headed home by seven at night and had not returned until at least seven in the morning, at which time we had already been on the scene. We didn't have any camera footage of anyone approaching the Hawkinses' house or Liam Dawson's office.

Officers Pace and Diaz were searching for evidence of some link between Zackary Hawkins and Liam Dawson. That they knew each other, that they'd met, anything. So far, their searches had yielded nothing helpful. All I could think to do now was wait for the financial and phone records I had requested and hope that they would reveal a literal smoking gun. Or two.

I had to believe that if McKenna Hawkins had killed her husband, and Leah Dawson had killed hers, they had not pulled the triggers themselves. Women like that would pay someone to take care of something so messy for them. It was my understanding that they paid people to file the calluses off their feet and paint their toenails, they paid people to pull the weeds from their yards, and they paid people to clean their toilets. If the need arose, they would pay people to kill their husbands, too.

But, how to explain the similarities between the murders? Had

McKenna shot Zackary through the kitchen window—or, more likely, hired someone to do so—and then Leah had heard about the manner of death on the news? What a good idea, she'd thought. When her husband had returned to the office, and worked long into the night, had she deployed her hit man, or woman, to shoot him through the window?

I liked the theory, but I'd no evidence of any of it.

I was stuck. The only thing I could think to do next was pay a visit to my sounding board, my better half.

I wanted to see her anyway, of course. It had been a week since I'd seen her.

If not for the two murders I was working, I would have been thinking about her constantly, every minute of every day.

I received a VISITOR badge at the information desk and rode the elevator to the third floor, following the signs to room 312. My breath caught in my throat as I pushed the door open.

Her face was pale, but her hair—what was left of it—was like a firework, bright and alive and the grand finale of the display. She wore a hospital gown, beneath a scratchy-looking hospital sheet.

She looked beautiful, albeit listless and weak. But I knew that she was not. She was the strongest person I had ever met.

Part of her scalp had been shaved before the surgery to remove the bullet that had ricocheted into her head that April night.

We had been called to a domestic disturbance in an affluent neighborhood. The woman in the house had managed to call the police. She'd been as terrified as I'd ever heard anyone sound. Her husband had a gun, she'd said, and he was threatening to kill her. I listened to the recording of the call later, I didn't know why. It was during the time I was torturing myself, going over everything, trying to figure out how I could have prevented all of it from happening.

Detective Mallory Cole and I had been nearby, so we had arrived on the scene first. We had approached the house and waited for backup. We couldn't go in alone. We knew that. It was late and dark. The street was quiet.

We had parked our car in the house's expansive, circular driveway, and stood on its grand front porch, our guns drawn, waiting, when a shot rang out. Mallory's face lifted. Her eyes met mine, and she pushed the front door open—it wasn't locked, it was a safe neighborhood—and disappeared into the house.

It had been her instinct to save the woman inside. Against all of our training, everything we knew to be logical and true, she had rushed inside to help. There'd been more shots, as I'd run to catch up with her, and by the time I made my way through the spacious house, to the family room at the back, there were three bodies on the ground. The woman had been shot in the chest, and the man had eaten his gun, but not before he shot my partner in the head.

I'd knelt at her side and not left until they'd forced me to, at the hospital, when she had been rushed into surgery.

She'd made it through the operation, but there was swelling in her brain, and the doctors had placed her into a medically induced coma, in which she'd remain while we waited for the swelling to go down.

The full extent of the damage to her brain, her mind, would remain to be seen.

I sat down in the chair beside her bed. There were tubes and wires all around her. I hesitated, then reached for her hand.

"Hey, Cole," I said. "It's me, your partner."

I always called her by her last name to her face. That's how all the men on the squad referred to each other, and she didn't want to be treated any differently. In my head, though, we were on a first-name basis.

"I'm sorry I haven't been here in a while," I told her. "I'm working two murders."

I filled her in on the two cases. I told her about my interviews, the lack of physical evidence, and the absence of helpful witnesses. I told her that we had not been able to find any connection between the two victims—as far as we knew, they had never met. And I told her that both men had been shot through open windows.

"That can't be a coincidence," I said. "But it doesn't necessarily mean Liam Dawson and Zackary Hawkins knew each other, or that their wives knew each other. Maybe McKenna Hawkins offed her husband, then Leah Dawson copied her. But I can't prove it. Not yet."

She looked dead, but her hand was warm in mine.

"My question is, of course, why did they do it? There was one previous nine-one-one call from an anonymous person about a domestic disturbance at the Hawkinses' residence. That was it. No proof of domestic violence and the wives haven't told me about it."

I could picture Mallory snorting, rolling her eyes. "That means nothing," she would say, and she would be right. If she could speak with the women, I suspected she would get a lot further than me.

"Am I looking for something that doesn't exist?" I asked. "Maybe these were truly random crimes. Maybe it was just some weirdo who cruises around the suburbs looking for white men he can shoot through open windows. Maybe there's going to be a third victim."

The machines surrounding my partner were softly beeping and whirring. I found it comforting, to see and hear the evidence that her heart was still beating.

"I hope not." I stated the obvious. I had enough pressure to solve these cases.

Interestingly, though, it was pressure from the public. From the neighborhoods. From the mothers. I wasn't feeling pressure from the wives. None at all. They weren't calling me, tearfully asking for updates. And when I showed up, they startled like deer in the woods.

"I'm still waiting on the ballistics," I said. "If there's a match between the guns that killed them, I will get my hands on that weapon somehow. I'll get a warrant for their houses. We didn't find one before. But I'll get another shot at it."

Mallory's fair face was very still. I squeezed her hand, then stood up from the chair.

"Oh well," I said. "You'll help me solve them. When you get back."

It was wishful thinking. I knew it would be a long time before my partner returned to work.

"I'll see you in a few days, Cole," I said from the doorway. I turned and left the room.

It was wishful thinking, too, that I would get anywhere in these cases. I needed something to break.

SUNDAY, MAY 19

Leah

To wake up with no headache, no fog in my mind, no nausea spinning my intestines, felt foreign and remarkable.

Two days in a row, Friday and Saturday, I had consumed no alcohol.

Although I had studiously avoided the topic in my mind, if I acknowledged the thoughts, I understood that I had developed something of a drinking problem.

Even though I had tried to hide the extent of my drinking from Liam, he must have known. He must have smelled it on me, seen it in the droop of my eyes, and heard it in the slowness of my speech.

I had made excuses. As long as I was beneath his fingertip, a puppet, with him controlling the strings, I needed to drink. But not too much.

Turns out, I hadn't needed meetings in a circle of folding chairs, sponsors, or a rehab program. I had just needed to escape my husband.

I had moved my things back to the basement bedroom, although I was no longer being locked inside. I had no desire to return to the master, even with Liam gone. There were too many memories there. I couldn't set foot in the closet without picturing my charming husband, the gun to his head, as he told me he would kill us both if I left.

But the memories were everywhere.

I brushed my teeth, and as I washed my face, I pictured the dark green scrub oozing from the bottle, after it had slammed into the bathroom wall. After it had been thrown by my charming husband.

It was early November, last year, almost a full month after I had been let go. I felt lost. My sense of purpose, my hope for getting it back, was gone. I had already been withdrawing from my friends. To some, I had admitted that I wasn't working, but had said that I was laid off, implying that it was not fault related. Or, rather, not *my* fault. The more time that passed, the more suspicious it was that I hadn't found another job.

But a friend from college was planning to get married in February. Liam and I had been invited to the wedding. Her family was wealthy, and so was the man she was marrying. She was planning a large bachelorette party in Key West for the weekend after New Year's. I hadn't been especially close with her in college, but we had lived on the same floor of our dorm freshman and sophomore years, and she seemed to be including all the women from our floor in her plans.

It would have been a chance for me to get away for a bit. To forget about my employment woes. To have a reason to leave the house, aside from the grocery store or other menial errands.

I had received the invitation via email and had skimmed the list of invitees and the itinerary for the long weekend. The group was planning to rent a mansion on the water. There would be dinners out, trips to the beach, hours spent relaxing at the pool, shopping trips, and wine tastings.

I'd brought it up to Liam one night. I had just finished washing my face and was preparing to brush my teeth before heading to bed. Liam had just finished showering after his evening workout and was smearing shaving cream across his stubbled chin and cheeks. He always shaved at night, after a hot shower.

"What friend is this?" he had asked, looking skeptical, as if I had invented her existence.

"Carly DiFiore," I said. "We went to college together."

"I've never heard about her before." He rubbed the white foam onto his face.

"Okay," I'd told him. "Well, like I said, we went to college together."

"Are you saying you want to go to this *bachelorette party*?" He said it like I'd suggested the event was being held in the public restroom of a fast food restaurant. "With this friend you haven't spoken to in years?"

"It hasn't been years since I've spoken to her." It had been months, but so what? "Besides, I know other people going. Tess is going."

"Tess is single," Liam said, thinking, I assumed, of her city life filled with expensive cocktails and bad dates with guys she'd met on the latest app.

"What does that have to do with anything?" I asked.

He didn't speak again until he had finished drawing his razor across his face and had rinsed away the remnants of the cream.

"A bachelorette trip is a little better suited for someone like her," he said, admiring his handiwork.

"It's just a trip with friends," I said. "It's not like we would get strippers or male prostitutes or anything."

"Whatever, Leah," he said as he patted his face with a towel. "Do whatever you want."

"Okay," I said. I squirted a blob of toothpaste onto my brush. "I want to go."

It happened as fast as a flash of lightning. Liam reached for my tube of face wash resting on the vanity and hurled it across the bathroom. It flew inches from my face and slammed into the wall. The cap broke. Scrub oozed out of the tube lying on the floor and dripped down the wall, clashing with the dove-gray paint.

Liam ducked past me and left the room. I had stood there for at least five minutes, my hands shaking too badly to brush my teeth. I'd been shocked. That had been the first incident since the slap after I had suggested that he had been the one to deposit the client check.

It was only the beginning.

Of course, afterward, there had been apologies, like all the other times. There had been assurances that he had just been upset because he loved me so much. He didn't want me to go away without him. He was worried about what might go on at the bachelorette weekend.

Of course, I hadn't gone.

There would be no more incidents like that.

But the feeling of relief and freedom was tempered by the fear that my freedom would be taken away if I was implicated in the murders of Zackary Hawkins and my husband. Or was it *when* I was implicated?

I still didn't know what had happened Thursday night. I didn't know what I'd done. I could remember speaking with Liam at dinner. I could remember him telling me he had more work to do. After that? Just blackness.

I assumed I had retreated to the basement to drink. But there was no way to be sure.

I couldn't have shot him. I knew that. But I'd been trained, for almost ten months, to doubt myself. That's what my charming husband had done to me.

My charming husband, and his secret gun. The police didn't seem to know that Liam used to have one. The detective had asked me if he did, but didn't press me when I'd told him no. I'd decided that was what I'd have to do—pretend that I never knew a thing about the gun. At this point, I could only assume it was unregistered. Perhaps he'd bought it in another, more gun-friendly state. Maybe in North Carolina, or somewhere nearby, during a trip to visit his mom. Knowing that it hadn't been registered in the state made it seem all the more sinister. Though he'd only ever held the secret gun to his own head, I was certain that he could have, would have, used it to kill me. I was relieved it was gone. That Liam was, too.

But that didn't mean I was free or safe. I had the feeling the detective knew more than he was letting on. He was probably compiling evidence against me, evidence I didn't even know existed, and he was going to keep it in his pocket. He would continue to visit me and ask me questions. He would catch me in a lie I didn't know I was telling.

I acknowledged that if I believed I was being considered a suspect, I should retain an attorney to represent my interests and be present for any conversations with Detective Harrison. But he had not yet read me my Miranda rights. I had not been brought to the station for questioning. Every time he came to my house, I invited him in.

I didn't want to raise his suspicions any further by bringing legal counsel into the mix. I would wait until I was Mirandized.

I also didn't want to raise his suspicions by telling the truth about my relationship with Liam. Like the faded red burns on my chest, I hid that away from him.

I changed into a fresh T-shirt and pair of athletic shorts and slid my feet into my sneakers. I double knotted them and went upstairs.

It felt good to not have to swallow Excedrin and cups full of water just to feel halfway human in the morning.

Yesterday had been my first time going for a run in months. I'd had to take a few walking breaks, but I had done better than I thought I would. My lungs had felt like they were full of fire and my legs had ached, my stomach and shoulders had been sliced through with cramps, as I followed the paths through my neighborhood. I knew, from experience, that if I kept it up, it would get easier.

With Liam gone, no longer encouraging me to get myself together and drop the weight I'd gained, my desire to be active had returned.

I was preparing to head out the door, sliding my phone into my armband, when it started to ring.

I had the urge to ignore the call, but I knew that I couldn't.

"Hi, Mom," I said.

"Sweetie. How are you doing?"

I'd spent almost the entire day on Saturday on the phone with my mom. I had told her everything.

At least, everything I knew to be true.

I had thought that telling her about what was happening with Liam would break her heart. I hadn't realized that hiding it would, too.

She had been shocked. "I had no idea," she'd said.

"That was the point," I'd told her. "No one had any idea. Not even me."

"I'm fine," I said now, as I walked into the living room and bent over, stretching out my hamstrings. "I promise."

"I still think I should come down there," she said. "You shouldn't be alone."

"Mom, it's okay," I insisted. "The kids need you for the rest of the school year. You can come down when it's over. Or I can go up there."

"All right. Have the police been by to see you?" she asked. "Any updates on the case?"

"Not today," I said. "Not yet." I didn't know when to next expect Detective Jordan Harrison at my door. I was virtually certain that was purposeful.

"What are your plans for the day?" my mom asked, trying to steer the conversation toward something normal.

"Nothing really," I told her. "I was just about to go out for a run."

"Oh, I won't keep you, then," she said. "I just wanted to check in. I'll call you later. Love you."

"Love you," I replied. Although she had initiated the call, she seemed in a rush to get off the phone.

I couldn't help but think that she, too, might be wondering whether I had killed my husband.

I decided to leave my phone behind, like I'd been conditioned to— silence was no longer so unwelcome, so filled with shameful thoughts— then stepped onto my porch. I walked to the end of my street, loosening up, before I broke into a jog. My muscles were sore from yesterday, but they hurt in a comforting and familiar way. It felt like reconnecting with an old friend. Which was something else I planned to do. I would take my life back from Liam, piece by piece. My family. My friends. My job.

I looped through the streets, cutting onto the paths that connected them. I was remembering all my usual routes. My three-mile loop, for when I wanted something short and sweet. My five-mile loop, on a normal day. My eight-mile loop, when I wanted to get out of the house a little longer than usual. And my ten-mile loop, when I wanted something punishing.

As I ran down the path near the back of my house, I saw a familiar-looking blond head. It belonged to a woman standing on the grass near the paths. She was dressed casually and was looking up toward my house. I stopped in my tracks.

It was strange. The second our eyes met, I knew what she'd done.

"What are you doing here?" I hissed. I looked around to make sure we were alone before stepping off the path. I stood to the side of a tree, realizing belatedly that we would likely only look more suspicious there.

"I just," she whispered, "was checking on you. I wanted to see how you were doing."

"I'm being investigated," I told her. "That's how I'm doing."

"So am I," she said.

I shook my head. "Don't you get it?"

McKenna Hawkins looked surprised. "I was trying to help you," she said.

"Your 'help' is going to get us both arrested," I told her.

I stepped away from her, returning to the path.

"This doesn't work unless we're strangers," I said. "You have to go. And don't come here again."

She opened her mouth, but all that came out was a sharp exhale, in dismay, in understanding. She nodded once, then turned and walked away from me, down the path.

Run, I wanted to shout.

I watched until McKenna Hawkins had disappeared from view.

I wondered whether I'd been too harsh. And I felt bad, because I hadn't said what I truly wanted to say. *Thank you.*

I turned and ran back toward my house.

I needed to get inside. I needed to put distance between us. I needed her to never come back to my neighborhood. Because they could be following us. They could be watching.

We'd escaped our husbands, but now it was the police in pursuit. And if she came here, she would be telling them, showing them, exactly what we'd done.

THREE DAYS EARLIER
THURSDAY, MAY 16

McKenna

They had finished dinner, and Leah had disappeared to her hideaway in the basement. I could tell, because she was no longer visible in the kitchen, and a light on the floor below it had flickered to life.

I had waited as long as I could, but there had been no other movement in the house. I assumed there would be no further action for the night, so I returned to my car. I was disappointed, because there was anticipation humming in my body and a feeling of intrigue sparking in the air. I'd thought something more was going to happen tonight than just another stilted meal.

I turned on my car and slid my sunglasses off my face. The sun was dipping low, preparing to set completely within the next hour. I gripped the wheel and was about to ease away from the curb when the door to the Dawsons' garage began to rise. The silver BMW emerged. I was so surprised to see it that I sat frozen for a few seconds before I regained the presence of mind to follow him. This was different, for him to leave the house after dinner. I wanted to know where he was going. Then, I would check on Leah one final time and return home.

I followed him along the same route as I had traveled earlier in the day. He was returning to his office. All of the houses seemed to be deserted. There was one navy pickup truck parked at the curb, near the end of the street. I pulled up behind it and watched Liam Dawson park in the driveway and enter the front door of the yellow Victorian that housed his office.

I waited for a few more minutes, but he didn't reemerge, so I returned to the Dawsons' house.

The front was dark, aside from the light on the front porch. I parked on the street and headed to the paths. Darkness had descended, but not so much that I couldn't see where I was going. There was no one else out walking. Kids had gone to bed. The parents were packing lunches and cleaning dishes and finishing up little things for work they hadn't had a chance to do before rushing out of the office to pick up their children and shuffle them to soccer practice or piano lessons.

I watched the back of the Dawsons' house. The light in the basement remained on, and everything was still.

I was about to give up when Leah appeared in the kitchen. Her movements were jolted and staggering. I assumed, from the vodka. She moved to the fridge and stood in front of it, doing something, I couldn't tell what. Then she moved to the island in the middle of the room and covered her face with her hands. She was crying.

After a few minutes, she disappeared from view. I drove home.

Back in my bathroom, I brushed my teeth and washed my face. I was preparing to lie in bed with a book or some Netflix, but something was niggling at me. I reclined on top of the covers. I felt feverish and antsy, like my body wanted to be in motion, but my mind wasn't sure what it should be doing. I tried to fall asleep, but hours passed, and I wasn't successful.

I felt like I was being drawn toward something, like a bug to a streetlamp on a hot summer night. What, I didn't yet know. For the first time in a long time, I felt that there was something that I needed to accomplish. Something helpful and important and selfless.

Leaving my phone behind on my nightstand, I descended the stairs and got back into my car. I followed the now somewhat familiar route to Liam Dawson's office. Light rain had just started to fall, and I switched on my wipers, peering through their intermittent slashing.

I pulled my car to the side of the main road, prior to reaching the courthouse and the streets of homes-turned-offices. I didn't want to be captured on any cameras. I looked at the clock on my dashboard, watched the numbers change from 11:59 to 12:00. And the clock struck twelve. It felt strangely meaningful.

I climbed out and moved through the woods by foot, toward the row of Victorians, approaching them from behind.

In the gaps between the houses, I could see his BMW was still parked out front, the light from a streetlamp reflecting off the silky silver exterior. Literally burning the midnight oil. Probably getting ready for a big trial while his wife slept off the vodka in hiding, or laid awake, tossing and turning, trying to come up with a way out. How many hours had I spent doing just that?

Her attempted escape was imminent, I thought, based upon her purchase of the prepaid phone.

All of the houses on the street were dark, except for the yellow Victorian. I moved along the tree line, then ducked toward the house, walking through the grass. It needed cutting, and it brushed my ankles as I moved through it. I held my hand above my eyes, to shield them from the rain.

The porch wrapped around the entire ground floor of the house, and light spilled onto it from one of the office windows. I could see Liam Dawson sitting inside, typing away at his computer. A green desk lamp and the glow from his monitors lit the room. It was the closest I'd ever been to him. He was a handsome man, but I knew better.

I paused for a second before slipping off my sneakers, letting them rest at the edge of the walkway, at the base of the stairs, knowing that I was making a decision. It sent a shiver of fear, of horror, down my spine. Would I trade my fear for hers?

She'd done it for me.

I climbed the porch steps carefully, as quietly as I could. A floorboard creaked and I winced, freezing in place, but Liam didn't react. His face remained trained forward, staring at his screen.

When I saw that the windows were pushed up, letting the cool breeze into the old Victorian through the screens, it felt like destiny.

Afterward, I slid into my shoes, then ran back to my car, as light and quick and cautious on my feet as a little woodland creature, feeling twice as weightless.

I drove home and pulled into the garage, directing it to close behind me. I couldn't bring the gun in the house. It couldn't go back into the kitchen cabinet, as if it were as innocent as a little-used hand mixer or waffle maker. I knew that.

I carried it out back, to the patio, lifting the loose stone. I dug into the earth beneath it with my fingers, pushing it aside, clearing enough space to bury the gun. I replaced the stone on top. I shifted the furniture, cringing as it scraped against the stones, though it only echoed into the still and empty night. I pushed the sofa so that its back-right leg rested atop the loose stone. Would it be enough?

I thought of her again, lying in bed.

You're safe now, I wanted to tell her. *It's over.*

I slipped into the house to clean away the evidence of my favor.

NOW
MONDAY, MAY 20

Detective Jordan Harrison

I brought the records home with me last night. I wanted to be able to look at them in peace, without the hustle and bustle of the station: calls coming in, my lieutenant asking me how the cases were going. All the records were provided electronically these days, but I had printed them out. I hated staring at computer screens. That was one of the reasons I had decided to become a cop. It was one of the reasons I had decided that law school wasn't for me.

I stood at the whirring printer in the station copy room, as it belched hot air, as the pages shot out and landed in a growing pile in the tray. I put them in a banker's box with a couple highlighters and drove home.

I had started with Leah Dawson's phone records. We had the records through Saturday, May 18, the day after the murder. There were two calls that day. Each for several hours. This was very interesting to me, but when I looked up the number, it belonged to Karen Bailey of Stamford, Connecticut. A quick search revealed that she was the mother of Leah Dawson, née Bailey. I was no longer interested in those calls. It made sense to me that Leah Dawson would spend hours on the phone with her mother the day after she found out that her husband had been killed. Her mom was probably concerned, and being several states away, she wanted to be assured that her daughter was safe. Perhaps they had stayed on the phone with each other as they went about their days, so that Leah felt less alone than she was.

What was interesting, though, was that only two phone numbers showed up in Leah's phone records for the past three months—that of her mother, and that of her husband. I had intended to use her phone records to locate, without telling her, additional people with whom I could speak to, to learn more about the Dawsons. What had been happening in their lives, their relationship, over the past few months? But it appeared that no such people existed.

I was confident that whatever had happened that had led to Liam's untimely demise had happened in the past few months. The older records would not be informative as to who had killed Liam Dawson.

But they were informative of something.

The activity on her phone account remained relatively constant until early October of last year. I knew that Leah Dawson had stopped working as an attorney around that time, so a decrease in phone use made sense to some extent. There would be no more phone calls or emails with clients, no more text messages with coworkers. But her phone activity had decreased much more than I would have expected, and it continued to decrease until she was in contact with only two people: Karen Bailey and Liam Dawson.

Immediately, I had wanted to call my partner. What did it mean? I was certain she would know. But of course I would have to figure it out for myself.

Since Liam Dawson had been killed at his office, I had requested Leah's phone location data as well. According to the data, she had not left her house the night her husband was killed.

Rather, her phone hadn't left her house. I couldn't be certain of anything more than that.

Anyway, the location information was not comprehensive. It didn't allow the phone's location to be tracked constantly. Only when the phone was pinged, by way of incoming or outgoing messages or calls, would it send or receive signals from a tower and provide an approximation of where it was at that time. With the relatively low volume of use Leah Dawson's phone saw, there hadn't been much pinging.

Liam's phone had provided more information about his wife's whereabouts than her own.

We had gained access to both victims' cell phones. We'd recovered Liam's from the scene of his murder, and McKenna had voluntarily turned over Zackary's phone to us. Zackary Hawkins's phone had not provided any information of note.

But installed on Liam Dawson's phone was a program that tracked the whereabouts of his wife's phone. It recorded everywhere the phone, and she, went, storing the data for a week's time. By the time we had obtained the phone, on May 17, we had data about her whereabouts for the preceding seven days.

Our tech team had tried to recover the past data, which had been erased, but they'd had no luck and weren't optimistic that we'd get it.

That Liam Dawson had been tracking his wife was interesting. The data itself was not. Between May 11 and May 17, Leah hadn't left her neighborhood except to run a few errands.

According to Liam's app, Leah, or her phone, hadn't done anything interesting since the day her husband had been killed. She hadn't left her house at all on Friday or Saturday.

If I wanted earlier or later records, I would need another court order.

I had pushed the phone records to one corner of my dining room table and reached for Leah's financial records next. But my eyes were losing focus, and I knew it was time to quit. Better to get some rest and start fresh in the morning, than have to redo everything I pushed myself to do at night.

I had awoken at four in the morning, after only a few hours' sleep, something pressing, needling, my mind like hands punching a mound of dough. But it was yielding no results.

I brewed a pot of coffee and returned to my seat at the table, in front of several months' worth of the Dawsons' bank statements. My first observation was that Leah did not have her own account. The couple previously had two joint accounts—one checking and one savings, both with Charles Schwab—but they had been recently converted to individual accounts, in Liam's name only. There was a third account, with Bank of America, titled to Liam only. There were no accounts in Leah's name.

This told me it was very unlikely that she had hired and paid someone to kill her husband. If she had hired someone good, and clearly, she had, that would be expensive. Even assuming she was able to access the accounts in Liam's name, he would have seen and questioned the sudden disappearance of a large amount of money. I reviewed the cash withdrawals, but their frequency and volume raised no alarm. It seemed unlikely, even impossible, that she had saved up enough cash to pay a killer. I looked over the images of checks deposited into and written from the account. Every single check had been written by Liam Dawson.

I moved on to the Bank of America account in Liam's name only. This account had relatively little activity. As far as I could tell, only one check had ever been deposited. At 12:14 a.m., on October 5, Liam had deposited a check into the account. The recipient was Granderson & King, the amount was for $3,000, and the image of its back bore an endorsement by Claudia Granderson, to be paid to the order of Leah Dawson. At that time, the account had been jointly titled. The statement for the following month showed that it no longer was.

It was strange, and I knew that it was meaningful. If Leah was given a bonus, designated additional funds from her firm, why would she have been given this check, signed over to her by a named partner of her firm? The check also matched up with the bank statement and check image that had been folded up and stuffed into the bottom of the backpack near Leah Dawson's door. I just didn't yet know why.

I flipped back to the first pages of the Charles Schwab records, which contained information about the accounts, and over which I had previously glossed. As of May 18, the accounts were titled to one person alone and online access was set up for only one user—Liam Dawson. The accounts had previously been jointly titled, and online access had been arranged for Leah Dawson on July 12 of last year, but it had been canceled on May 15, at 7:28 a.m., Eastern Standard Time. He had been killed only a couple days after removing her from the final two accounts.

I continued to flip through the pages.

Later that morning, at 8:52 a.m., Liam Dawson had faxed paperwork to Charles Schwab removing his wife's name from the accounts. This had been accomplished in short order. By 9:14 a.m., the accounts had been retitled. I assumed Liam had called the bank to ensure it was taken care of.

The paperwork included several signatures of Leah Dawson.

Why had she signed documents removing her name from their joint accounts? Why had she left herself without a bank account?

Those were questions I would pose to Leah, next time I stopped by for a visit.

I stacked the Dawsons' financial records and placed the pile next to Leah's phone records. I moved on to the Hawkinses' financials. They had only two bank accounts—one checking and one savings, both with Wells Fargo, both jointly titled. They, too, revealed no evidence that McKenna had hired or paid someone to kill her husband. There were regular cash withdrawals in nominal amounts. There were no large transfers, no suspicious checks. In fact, each check had been written and signed by Zackary Hawkins.

Again, I flipped to the first few pages of the documents. There was, and had only ever been, online access set up for one person: Zackary Hawkins.

I had brought McKenna's phone records home with me as well. Even though I had already reviewed them, I wanted to have them available in case something from her financials looked interesting and needed cross-checking.

I went backward in time. The most recent months, I already knew, revealed that McKenna Hawkins regularly communicated only with Gene and Kathleen Lyons, Aiden Lyons, Alyssa Vercarro, and Mina Lee. As I flipped backward, more phone numbers were involved. The further back I flipped, the more there were. In January, the number of people with whom she was in contact had dropped off significantly and had decreased ever since.

January of this year to McKenna Hawkins was like last October to Leah Dawson. McKenna had stopped working in January, she had suffered a miscarriage. Wasn't that what she had told me?

I leaned back in my chair and rubbed my chin. I didn't know what any of it meant. Not yet.

I glanced at my phone, which lay silent and still and dark on the table beside me. I checked the time, then stood, stacking the records on the table. If I didn't leave soon, I would be late for my next interview.

Claudia Granderson had asked me to meet her at her office, early, before her workday started, which meant driving downtown. At least it was, I hoped, too early to get caught in morning rush hour.

The law firm of Granderson & King was located on the seventh floor of a high-rise office building in Baltimore City, two blocks from Camden Yards and three blocks from M&T Bank Stadium, where the Ravens played. Those were my only points of reference. I wasn't a city guy.

I pulled into the parking garage and tucked my car into a narrow spot. It was only seven thirty when I arrived in the entryway of the law firm, and the receptionist wasn't sitting behind her desk. I looked around and shifted from foot to foot. No one emerged from the depths of the office, so I rang the little silver bell resting on the top of the desk.

Seconds later, a woman, tall and polished, swept in. Her hair was blown out straight so that it hung to her shoulders. She wore a bright green wrap dress and a navy blazer. There was no makeup on her face, but her appearance was tidy and professional, elegant and put-together.

"Detective Harrison?" she asked, extending her hand. "Claudia Granderson."

We shook hands firmly and she led me down the hallway to her office, which was decorated with Baltimore Orioles memorabilia and diplomas from the University of Maryland and Yale Law School.

Upon her invitation, I sat down in the chair across from her desk.

"I have to say," Claudia said, settling into her ergonomic-looking swivel chair, "I was surprised to hear from you. I haven't spoken to Leah Dawson since the day she was let go, almost eight months ago."

"I'm working to gain an understanding of Mrs. Dawson and her husband, trying to figure out why he was killed," I said.

"How very shocking that was," Claudia said. "She must be devastated." She took a sip from the coffee mug resting on her desk. It read CAFFEINATED AF.

"Can I get you a cup of coffee?" she asked.

"I'm fine," I said. "Thanks. How long did Leah Dawson work for you?"

Claudia's eyes tipped upward as she thought. "I believe she started with my firm in November, the year before last, and she was let go in October, so just under a year."

"What was she like?" I asked. "A good employee?"

"She was a model employee, until she wasn't. She was a hard worker. I never had to worry about her, or her work, being late. She was very smart, but she knew what she didn't know, which is important. I was disappointed when I had to let her go. I had hoped she would work for me for a long time and grow with the firm."

"And did you ever meet her husband?"

"Once," Claudia said. "But I knew him by reputation, of course. He was a very successful and well-known divorce attorney in this area."

"What was his reputation?" I asked. I had a general idea, based on my research, but I wanted to know how other local lawyers saw him.

"His reputation was that he was a young gun. Aggressive, sometimes overly and unnecessarily so. But it worked for him. And he could turn on the charm and schmooze with the best of them when he needed to." She shrugged.

"Got it. And you said you met him once. Under what circumstances?"

"We have a Christmas party for our employees and their significant others every year. Leah brought Liam to the party the first year she joined the firm. I think she was uncomfortable because she was relatively new. I remember Liam was very quiet, and they didn't stay long."

"He was quiet?" I asked. "That's not really what you would expect out of an aggressive guy like him, is it?"

Claudia tipped her head to the side. "I had the sense," she said, "that he didn't like being the arm candy, so to speak, accompanying his wife to her firm's holiday party. He preferred to be the center of attention."

"I see." It was interesting information. Had Leah killed him because she was tired of living in his shadow? Did she want her turn in the spotlight?

"When and under what circumstances did Mrs. Dawson stop working for your firm?" I asked.

"I remember the date very well," she said. "It was very upsetting to me. I've never had to fire anyone before. It was Friday, October fifth."

A tingle switched to life in my gut, because I had just seen that date in Liam Dawson's Bank of America account records. I'd seen it on the bank statement Leah Dawson had packed up and planned to take with her when she escaped the house.

"What happened?"

"Leah met with a potential new client after hours in the client's office. We usually conduct all meetings in our office, but this client worked close to Leah's house, so it made sense for them to meet there instead. The client signed the retainer agreement at the meeting and gave Leah a check for the retainer. Leah then took that money."

"How much was the check for?" I asked.

"It was three thousand dollars."

Not an insignificant amount of money for many people, but for Leah Dawson, it would seem to be pretty insignificant. Based on the amounts in their accounts, it would have been a tiny drop in the bucket.

"How do you know that Mrs. Dawson took the money?"

"The morning after the meeting, I stopped by Leah's office, asked her how it went. She said it went great, the client had retained the firm. I asked her for the signed agreement and check. She looked for it in her purse, and I remember very distinctly that she couldn't locate the check at first. Once she did, she gave it to me. I returned to my office to deposit it into our trust account via mobile deposit. When I turned it over, I saw what purported to be my signature, and it was endorsed to Leah. It was alarming, and the check wouldn't deposit. I called the client immediately to tell her to cancel the check, there had been an issue. She was very upset because the funds had already cleared her account. It was extremely embarrassing for our firm. I had to let Leah go. I had no other choice."

As she spoke, the tingle in my gut became more intense.

"And you didn't sign the check."

"It was signed when I received it," she replied.

"Why would Mrs. Dawson have done that?" I asked. "That wouldn't have been a substantial amount of money to her, I assume."

Claudia shook her head. "I have never stopped wondering why she did it. It has never made sense to me, but there also was no other possible explanation for how my signature ended up on that check, how it was signed over to her, and how it was already deposited. It went straight from the client, to her, to me. I wondered if she was suffering from some sort of addiction, drugs or gambling. Shopping. She was struggling to hide it and needed money. I don't know. It didn't seem like she was, but people can be pretty good at hiding those sorts of things."

"But why would she have given the check to you?" I asked. "She could have just said she had lost it, or it had been stolen. If she knew she had forged your signature and deposited the money, she was guaranteed to be caught by giving the check to you."

Claudia was looking at me, but her wide brown eyes were focused on something else. She was wondering whether she had rushed to judgment and made a mistake. "I have no idea," she said. "Like I said, it never made any sense to me, but I never had an explanation that did. I had no choice. I needed to protect my reputation, my business."

"What if I told you"—I leaned toward her—"that Leah Dawson previously had three joint bank accounts? Two were converted to individual accounts very recently, titled to her husband only. She'd been removed from the third account already, on October fifth. It was that account into which the client check was deposited. What would you think?"

Claudia placed her hands together and held them below her chin. She looked like she was praying.

"I would think," she said, "that Liam Dawson had signed my name and deposited that check. That he hid it from Leah."

I nodded. "That's what I would think, too. And why," I continued, "would he have done that?"

Claudia frowned and two caverns appeared between her brows. "The only thing I can think of is that he wanted her to get fired."

"Bingo," I said. I stood up from the too-short chair and my knees cracked. "Thank you for your time, Ms. Granderson. That's all I have for you."

Claudia nodded, but she wasn't looking at me, and she didn't speak. It wasn't until I had stepped out of her office that I heard her say something. It sounded like, "Poor thing."

And she was right. But she was also wrong. Because it was starting to look like Leah Dawson was a killer.

WEDNESDAY, MAY 22

Detective Jordan Harrison

It was time to pay a final visit to McKenna Hawkins, to show my cards, to push her a little further than I had before. If it got me nowhere, I truly wasn't sure where to go next.

I noticed her hesitation in the doorway. She wasn't sure if she should let me in. She was growing weary. It was about time.

This time, I accepted her offer of a drink, if only to inconvenience her further.

I followed her into the kitchen. I sat at the table facing the window through which the bullet that had killed Dr. Zackary Hawkins had ripped. The other windows in the room were open. Not that window. Maybe she hadn't yet replaced the screen.

"Looks like you're packing up," I said, glancing around the room. There were two cardboard boxes in one corner, stacked on top of each other. The house was looking decidedly emptier, less lived in, than it had before.

McKenna placed a glass of ice water on the table in front of me. She seemed nervous. "I would like to sell the house," she said. "Too much space. Too many memories." She clamped her lips together as if she'd said too much.

"Bad memories?" I asked. I took a sip of my drink.

"Some good. Some bad. Like with every marriage." She tried to recover. I watched her. A silence settled over us like an overnight frost.

I cracked it. "I have a confession," I told her.

"Oh?" Surprise shot through her face. She thought she was supposed to be the one confessing. She was tapping her fingernails on the table. The navy polish was still there, chipped away to little slivers.

"I got your phone records."

She stopped tapping. "Why?"

"The obvious solution in this case is that you killed your husband. You had opportunity. It seems you were the only person who had opportunity. We had to look for evidence that you had done it. Or, maybe you hired someone to do it for you."

She watched me. "And what did you find?"

"You used to have a much wider circle of contacts," I said. "That changed in January. After that, you only communicated with your parents, your brother, your two friends, and your husband. Mostly, though, it was just your husband. He was the only person you were talking to every day. Every week. He checked in on you quite often. He was the only one."

"Okay," she said.

"Why was that?"

"January was a difficult time for me. I mentioned to you that I suffered from a miscarriage. Maybe I haven't been as sociable since then. We were focusing on starting a family."

"January was also when you stopped working."

"Right." She shifted in her chair. "That was related. I left my job so that we could focus on having a baby, and to reduce my chances of getting sick during my pregnancy."

"You loved your job," I told her. "Your friends, Mina Lee and Alyssa Vercarro, both said that you loved your job."

Her right shoulder lifted in the fraction of a shrug. "I wanted a baby very badly."

"Do you really think that working would have prevented you from having a baby?" I asked. "Working women have babies all the time. Doctors have babies. They sometimes work late into their pregnancies."

"Not everyone suffers a miscarriage," she said, and I could tell that the miscarriage had genuinely devastated her. She had wanted a baby at that point. What had changed?

"You said you were still trying to get pregnant when your husband was killed?" I asked.

McKenna looked uncomfortable. My question was too personal. "We were," she said. She crossed her arms in front of her chest. The room chilled a couple degrees.

I reached into my pocket and removed a small item, wrapped in a plastic evidence bag.

"How do you explain, then, why those were found on your kitchen floor?"

Her eyes widened. Her pupils dilated. Somehow, she had forgotten about the birth control pills. Or she'd assumed they'd been collected from the kitchen floor that night, that their significance would be lost on me. That much was clear.

She didn't respond, just continued to stare at the little envelope of pills.

"I have another confession," I said.

She met my eyes. Two blinks. She didn't say a word.

"I got your financial records, too. Your bank statements." I swirled the water in my glass like it was a fine wine. "I thought, maybe you paid someone to off your husband."

"I didn't," she said. Her voice was a whisper, innocent, soft, the faint breath of a newborn.

"I know," I told her. "I couldn't find any evidence that you had paid a hit man. In fact, I don't think you could have, even if you wanted to."

"What do you mean by that?"

She knew, of course, but she wanted to hear my explanation.

"You didn't have access to the money," I told her. "Not really. Your name is on the accounts, but you didn't pay bills, or transfer money. You weren't registered for online access."

McKenna's shoulders lifted and fell again in the hint of a shrug. "What do you want me to say?"

"Do you want to know what I think?" I asked.

Her nod was almost imperceptible.

"I think that your husband was controlling. It was textbook coercive control. He was charming, handsome, and successful. He wanted the perfect life with the perfect wife. An important part of that? A baby. You got pregnant, just like you were supposed to. But then, you lost the baby. And he blamed you. That was when he really started taking control."

I could see tears forming in the corners of McKenna's eyes.

"He made you quit your job. He wanted you to focus only on him and on starting a family. There was no place in his plans for your career or friends, or your other family members. Maybe before he was a little bit possessive. A little bit jealous. But it was taken to an extreme. He was powerful. He was a psychiatrist. Who would believe you?"

I took a long pull of water. I was on a roll.

"You realized that you no longer wanted to have a baby. Not with him. Not with the person you now realized that he was. You started taking birth control pills in secret. Meanwhile, you were pretending that you were trying."

The look on her face, I could tell I was dead right.

"He found the pills. He confronted you. Maybe he got violent."

Her eyes were wide. She was scared by how much I knew.

"You escaped him. You snuck outside, and you shot him."

Her face relaxed. She exhaled. I wasn't right anymore. Somewhere, somehow, I had gone wrong.

There was no gun, no residue, no confession. The footprints didn't match.

"No," she said. "I didn't shoot my husband." She dabbed at her eyes with the back of her hand. "Look, I might have wished he was dead. But I swear I didn't kill him."

I tried again. "But you know who did."

Vigorous shake of the head. Tight lips, ice-cold stare.

I felt like she was lying, but there wasn't a damn thing I could do about it.

I stood up. I tossed another business card onto the table. "Call me when you're ready to tell the truth," I said, and I left the house.

McKenna

But you know who did.

I'd denied it. I doubted he believed me. He probably wouldn't stop until he knew what had happened. I pressed my index fingers into the corners of my eyes and willed myself to take deep breaths.

I still wondered what exactly Mina and Alyssa had told him. What did they really think of Zack? Why was I the last to know? Perhaps they might tell me one day. I was free to rejoin our gym now, to take classes beside my friends, under the suspicious and knowing (when they didn't know anything) gazes of the other patrons, noses tipped upward, Lululemon leggings fighting to remain in control as they raced past me to claim the last set of ten-pound dumbbells.

My phone vibrated from its resting place on the kitchen table and I jumped.

I'm not sure if you remember me, the text message read, *but this is Amelia Brown from residency. I recall you were planning to stay in the D.C. area to work, not sure if you still are. There's something I wanted to chat with you about.*

I did remember Amelia, of course. We had worked many exhausting shifts together during our residency program, which we'd completed three years previously. I hadn't heard from her since. Zack had come into my life by then, and I made no effort to stay in touch with any of my friends from med school or residency.

Hi, I wrote back. *I'm still in the area. Feel free to give me a call. I'd love to catch up.*

To write the words filled me with warmth, a welcome distraction. I could have friends again. I could catch up with the people with whom I'd lost touch. I could have a life.

No sooner had I put my phone down on the counter when it started to ring.

Amelia was calling.

"Hello?" I said, wondering what she could possibly want to speak to me about so urgently, after three years apart. I prayed it didn't have anything to do with something she'd seen in the news about Dr. Zackary Hawkins.

"McKenna, it's Amelia," she said. "I'm sorry to bombard you like this. I just—there's something I wanted to throw out there. Are you still working in the area?"

"I'm living in Maryland, but not working right now," I admitted. "I took some time off. I'm actually looking for jobs now, though. I'd like to get back to work soon."

"Really?" she asked. Her enthusiasm was palpable. "As a pediatrician?"

"That's the plan," I told her. "Why? What's up?"

"Well, this might actually be sort of perfect," she said. "I'm working for a practice in Gaithersville, and one of my coworkers and I were talking about leaving and opening our own practice. We started working on the plans, then she decided she wanted to stay. I'd still like to go out on my own, so I'm looking for a partner."

"For a pediatrics practice?" I asked.

"Right," she said. "Do you think you might be interested?"

I closed my eyes for a second, pictured her calling me clandestinely, on a break between appointments, pacing in the parking lot outside her office. Was she still rail thin, with long black braids, held back loosely with a rubber band? Was she married? Did she have kids? It had been so long since I'd thought of her, and I felt an abrupt, irrational longing to jump back in time to our residency, when we'd hurried through the hospital halls together, drinking coffee, laughing about the fact that it wasn't enough, wishing we could inject it straight into our veins. I was so tired, so optimistic then. Could I ever get that promise back?

"Honestly, I have never considered starting my own practice," I said. I had never thought of myself as an entrepreneurial person. "But it might be sort of cool."

"We could have a lot of flexibility," she said. "My current practice, I absolutely hate their on-call policy. We could come up with something much better. Much fairer. We could hire more doctors, as well, besides just the two of us. But I was really hoping to partner with someone I know."

As she spoke, the idea was growing on me quickly. My job applications hadn't yet yielded even an interview, despite what I'd thought were fairly impressive credentials. Perhaps my time out of work made me unappealing to prospective employers. Amelia didn't seem to share that concern.

"It sounds like you're on board," Amelia said. "We should meet up and chat some more. And catch up on each other's lives."

Catch up on each other's lives. Did I ever have a tragic story for her.

"Sure," I told her. "I'm free this week."

But a pang in my chest gave me pause. I thought of Leah, and her anger at catching me behind her house. For how long would I be free?

Amelia asked me to text her my email address so that she could send me some information she had put together about the steps we would need to take to get the process started.

"Start trying to brainstorm some names for the practice," she said. "And I'll do the same. This is so exciting!" she gushed. "I'm so glad I thought to reach out to you."

"Me, too," I told her. To feel hopeful was so unfamiliar, so welcome.

I wondered if she remembered Zack from residency as well. He hadn't worked in the pediatrics department, but he was well known around the hospital. I thought she'd been aware that we started dating back then. I would have to tell her that he had become my husband, and that he'd been killed, assuming she didn't already know. If that wasn't a secret that would start a partnership off on the wrong foot, I didn't know what was.

I hoped she would still want to work with me.

Leah was right.

My favor had tied us, and our husbands, together, in a way that previously had not been apparent. The police wouldn't just be investigating the murder of Zack and the murder of Liam. They'd be trying to link the crimes together. They'd be looking for a connection.

Detective Harrison had already asked me whether Zack or I knew the Dawsons. I'd denied it, but it was foolish of me to think he'd let it go so easily.

I couldn't go back to see her again. It was too dangerous.

And the gun. It suddenly felt very obvious under the loose patio stone, beneath the leg of the outdoor sofa. It couldn't stay there forever. Would the police return? Would they search again? I felt, with a sickening certainty, that they would. Were they watching me now?

How could I get rid of the gun? I couldn't.

But, it couldn't stay there, either. Damned if I do, damned if I don't.

I was trapped. When I'd only just been freed.

THURSDAY, MAY 23

Detective Jordan Harrison

I'd been going over yesterday's conversation with McKenna Hawkins in my mind, again and again, ever since I left her house.

The interview had been like riding a roller coaster. The anticipation built as we creaked slowly up the rails, higher and higher. The car reached the peak. It paused. But, instead of hurtling down, it had simply fallen off the tracks, plummeting to the ground below.

I was hoping that today's visit to Leah Dawson would yield better results.

I had intended to stop by to see her yesterday, after my visit to McKenna, but I had needed a break, to lick my wounds, to recharge my battery, to gather my thoughts.

I had just left the station when Julian Klein, the ballistics tech working the cases, had called me.

"Harrison," I'd said, lifting the phone to my ear. "Please tell me you have something good."

By good, I meant something connecting the two murders—proof that the same gun had been used to kill both Zackary Hawkins and Liam Dawson. That there was only one gun wouldn't make it easy. Not by any means. But one was better than two.

"I don't," Julian had said. "No match."

"Shit. Really?"

"Really. The gun that shot Hawkins was different from the gun that shot Dawson. You're looking for two different guns. A thirty-five-caliber bullet killed Liam Dawson, and a thirty-eight killed Hawkins."

I'd hung up, feeling like a pouting toddler, denied a packet of candy while grocery shopping with his mom. I'd wanted to get my way.

If the guns weren't a match, that meant there wasn't a judge in the county who'd sign off on a warrant for me to search the houses again, more thoroughly. I'd been holding out hope that a match between the guns would push what I had into probable-cause territory, that a warrant would allow me to find something that would lead me to the murder weapon and trace its history and close these cases.

I parked in Leah Dawson's driveway, rang the doorbell, and knocked on the door. After a few minutes passed and no one had answered, I moved my car to the curb to wait for her to get home.

After twenty minutes, a black Lexus SUV rolled past me and pulled into the driveway, and then the garage. I hopped out of my car and approached.

She was unloading reusable grocery bags from her trunk.

"Need help?" I asked.

She startled, turned. She wasn't relieved it was me. She was still scared. "I guess," she said.

When she passed two bags to me, our hands touched. Despite the warm day, hers were ice cold.

"Lot of stuff for just one person," I said as I followed her into the house.

"My friend is coming to stay with me for a few days," she said. "So I don't have to be alone."

"A friend?" I asked.

"My best friend of more than ten years. My former college roommate."

We dropped the bags on the floor of the kitchen. "You can sit down," Leah said. "I'll just put this stuff away."

I perched on the edge of a barstool in front of her kitchen island.

"You haven't spoken with your best friend in months," I said. "Isn't that right?"

Leah turned to stare at me, a bag of frozen strawberries sweating in her hand. "How would you know that?"

"It shouldn't surprise you to hear that we requested your phone records as part of the investigation," I said.

"Oh," she said, sounding quite surprised. She tossed the bag of fruit into the freezer.

"It's interesting that you had not communicated with anyone over the past couple months. No one aside from your husband and mom."

Leah didn't respond, just continued unpacking her groceries.

"In fact, there was much more activity on your phone account before October. It steadily declined ever since."

"Well, I lost my job in October, so I was definitely using my phone less after that." She turned to load a canister of oats and a jar of peanut butter into the pantry.

"October fifth," I said. "It seems that was something of a turning point for you."

"The day I lost my job?" she asked. "Why do you say that?"

"Your integrity was called into question that day," I said. "Your reputation was damaged."

Leah had finished putting her purchases away and was staring intently at the reusable totes as she folded them up.

"I think we all know what happened," I said. "Why the charade? He's dead."

Leah tucked the bags into a cabinet.

"I spoke with your former boss." Her head snapped up. Hope filled her eyes. "I should have mentioned—we requested your financial records, too. You previously had a joint account with Bank of America. A check written to your former law firm was deposited there at 12:14 a.m. on October fifth of last year. The same day, you were taken off the account."

She stood at the island across from me, waiting for me to continue. She knew this information already. She had printed out the statement, the check image, and packed them in the backpack. She'd been planning to take them with her when she escaped.

"Your boss's signature was on the back of that check," I said. " 'Pay to the Order of Leah Dawson,' it said."

She shook her head. "I didn't write that."

"Someone forged her signature and signed it over to you."

She didn't reply.

"It's interesting," I said, and she waited. "Last week, paperwork was submitted to the bank to remove your name from the other joint accounts. Paperwork you had signed."

Again, she shook her head.

"Paperwork your husband signed for you," I said. "Just another way he was taking away your independence."

Leah Dawson shrugged.

"You knew your husband deposited that check," I said.

"I knew it wasn't me. I thought I was losing my mind."

"Why did he do it?" I asked.

"He didn't want me to work," she said. She leaned forward, her hands on the smooth marble of the island. "We had an argument about it earlier that week. He made a nice dinner for me, and he got mad that I checked my email during it. He made me feel like my job was just a hobby. It was unnecessary because he was doing so well."

"That must have been offensive," I told her. "You went to law school, just like him. You worked just as hard."

"I wasn't making as much money. Not even close."

"Who cares?"

"Well, that was how I felt about it, too. He seemed to think that just because I could have afforded to quit my job and sit at home all day, or spend the day shopping and going to salons, that's what I should have wanted to do. But I didn't. When I lost my job, I lost my identity."

"He wanted you to be a stay-at-home wife. You didn't want that. So, he forced it upon you."

"Pretty much." She looked down. She was embarrassed.

"Why didn't you confront him? Why didn't you leave?" I felt bad asking.

Just like I expected, irritation flickered across her face. "I was with Liam for four years before we got married. He was always a big personality. He filled every room he entered. He dominated every conversation. After we got married, he wanted to be the star of our relationship. He wanted to make me fit a certain role. He became controlling. He started to isolate me. I didn't see it coming. It shocked me. I didn't know what to do."

"He wasn't just controlling," I said. "He wasn't just isolating. He was violent."

It had been a guess, but understanding flashed between us.

"You needed a way out," I continued.

"I did," she agreed. "But I didn't kill him."

"You had a copy of the bank statement and the check image in your backpack," I said. "Evidence of what he'd done. You were going to leave, finally. You weren't going to visit your mom. You were going there to escape him. You weren't coming back."

"That was the plan," she replied.

"But then someone killed him, and you didn't have to."

"Right. But that someone wasn't me."

"We got your location records from your cell phone, as well," I said, watching her face for a reaction, but there was none. "The night your husband was killed."

"I couldn't have left," she interjected.

"Couldn't have left?" I demanded. She'd provided no alibi before. "How do you know? What were you doing?"

"I don't remember," she blurted. She lifted her hands to her mouth a fraction too late. Her secret had already tumbled out, and there was no putting it back.

"What do you mean?" I hadn't expected that.

"Since October," she said, "I've been drinking more and more. It was the only way I could get by. The night before, I confronted him about taking the check and getting me fired, about taking me off the accounts. He hurt me. I was scared. I drank too much that night, and I blacked out. I don't remember what happened."

I slumped on my stool. She had been blackout drunk in the house. She hadn't been driving to her husband's office and shooting him in the back of the head.

"Your phone didn't leave the house," I told her.

"I couldn't have left," she said again. It made sense to me now. "I know I didn't leave. I was in no state. I just can't remember."

"How are you doing now?" I asked.

"I haven't had a drink since he died," she said. "He was the problem."

She was feeling more comfortable around me. She was opening up. How long had it been since she'd had someone with whom she could speak freely? She was desperate for it.

"One other thing," I told her. I slid my cell phone out of my pocket. I pulled up the recording and pressed Play. A voice filled the room.

"I think my neighbors are fighting. I can hear them. Three-two-two-four Apple Blossom Lane in Clarkstown. It sounds like it's escalating and I'm afraid the woman is in danger."

She was staring at the phone.

"What is that?" she asked.

"Sounds an awful lot like you," I said.

She shook her head. "No. That's not me. I don't know what that is." She was finished opening up to me.

"That," I said, "was a recording from an anonymous nine-one-one call made about the home of Zackary and McKenna Hawkins."

"Okay," she said. "Well, I have never met them, like I told you before."

"Remember," I said, "I have your phone records. You made this call. You were there."

It was the only call that had jumped out at me. Any call to 911 would have been of interest, but I knew there were no police reports regarding the Dawsons or their home. It rang familiar, though, and I realized that it matched the time and date of the call made to report a domestic disturbance at the Hawkinses' house.

Most days, Leah's phone had stayed in and around her house. But that day, she had been in the Hawkinses' neighborhood. It was the only time I could place her there.

She knew she had to admit it. "Fine. I was out for a walk. I walk in other neighborhoods sometimes. I heard them fighting. The woman sounded scared. With what was going on in my own life? I couldn't not call. But I didn't want to get involved."

"And the next night, Zackary Hawkins ended up dead."

She shrugged. "A coincidence, I guess."

"Was it?" I asked.

She didn't reply. She tapped her nails along the countertop. They were short and unpainted. She stared straight back at me.

"Your husband was tracking your location. We combed through his phone, looking for evidence as to who might have killed him. He had an app that tracked the location of your phone."

"That was what I always suspected," she said.

"Unlike with the records we received directly from the phone provider, your husband's app tracked your phone constantly, not just when it sent or received calls or texts. It collected data continuously."

Her face was unreadable.

"It seems," I continued, "that you were in the habit of leaving your phone behind. It rarely left your house. You suspected your husband was using it to track you, so you didn't bring it with you." I cleared my throat. "So, the location of your phone isn't really a reliable indicator of your location, is it?"

She pressed her lips together, didn't reply.

I rubbed my hand over my chin, as if thinking. "Mrs. Dawson," I said.

"Bailey," she said, sharp and cutting as a Wüsthof fresh from a bridal shower gift bag. "It's going to be Leah Bailey now. Again."

"Ms. Bailey," I said, letting her contemplate the correction she'd made, and why she'd made it, and whether it had been a mistake. "What size shoe do you wear?"

Her eyes narrowed, so cold and swirling gray blue that a chill ran down my spine.

"I'm beginning to feel uncomfortable with all this questioning," she said after two beats. "I'm going to have to ask you to leave. And, if you want to come back, I'm going to have to insist that I have an attorney with me."

She had slipped into lawyer mode. She knew her rights. I hadn't Mirandized her. Still, once she asked for her attorney, I couldn't ask her a single question until her lawyer was present. I'd pressed her enough. She wasn't willing to be pressed any more.

I stood up. "Fair enough," I said.

I walked to her front door, and she trailed behind. I paused in the doorway. "I'm sorry for what you went through," I said. It was the least I could do. I knew why people like her, people like McKenna Hawkins felt trapped. I understood why they felt like they couldn't tell anyone, even the police, about the private hell in which they were stuck.

Leah Dawson had tried to warn the police about Zackary Hawkins, and what had happened? Nothing. The psychiatrist had talked his way out of it, like he would have every time.

Leah nodded, but she knew better than to say anything more. She had invoked her right to counsel. She wasn't about to walk that back by reopening the conversation.

I jogged down the driveway and climbed into my car.

I sat for a few minutes, looking at her house and thinking.

It was becoming clearer and clearer that Leah Dawson hadn't killed her husband, and McKenna Hawkins hadn't killed hers. Both might've wanted their husbands dead, but neither had pulled the trigger.

Unless.

I grabbed my phone and dialed Officer Diaz.

"I'm on my way to the station now," I said. "But I need you to get started on something for me. You available?"

"I'm here," she said. "What do you need?"

"I need more recent cell phone records for McKenna Hawkins," I said. "I need those ASAP. I need those yesterday." I was speaking quickly.

We had previously received the records through Saturday, May 11. I'd thought that was sufficient. I'd had no reason to be interested in McKenna's communications or whereabouts past the date her husband was murdered. That was no longer the case.

"And I need you to get started on three warrants," I continued. "One for Leah Dawson's house. One for McKenna Hawkins's house. And one for her brother's house. Aiden Lyons."

A second of hesitation. "Okay," she said. "What are we looking for?"

"We are looking," I said, "for the guns that were used to shoot Liam Dawson and Zackary Hawkins. A bullet. Something. We are looking for a thirty-five caliber at the Dawson house, and a thirty-eight caliber at McKenna's. And we are taking Leah Dawson's shoes. Every single one. I'll be there soon."

I dropped my phone onto the seat, and I jammed my foot onto the gas.

FRIDAY, MAY 24

Leah

The surface of the lake was a cloudy and opaque gray blue, and I was glad, because it held one of my deepest secrets.

Or, more accurately, several of them, shattered to pieces and dispersed throughout.

"It's so pretty," Tess said, looking out at the water.

It had been her idea to come here. She had arrived late morning. I had picked her up from the airport and we'd had brunch before returning to my house.

"Let's go out for a walk somewhere," she'd suggested. "I've done nothing but sit still all day. I need to stretch out my legs a little."

I had assumed we would just walk around my neighborhood, but Tess had thought of the lake, where we had gone when she had visited me last June, shortly after Liam and I had moved into our house.

Liam had been salty and lurking around everywhere we went during her visit. We wanted to go someplace private where we could speak to each other freely in the way of best friends. I'd thought of the lake, ten minutes from the new house. I had already been there a handful of times to run along the path surrounding it.

Tess and I had walked slowly on the path, stopping now and then to sit on a bench. It was suburban living at its finest, and I understood why Tess, who lived in a high-rise apartment building in the midst of a bustling city, had wanted to return.

That time, her visit had only lasted a night. She had flown down Saturday morning and left Sunday evening. I saw her again at my wedding in July. She had been one of the very few people on my side to make the guest list.

I hadn't seen her since.

When I thought about how much had changed since I'd last spent time with my friend, it was unbelievable. Liam had transformed from my handsome, charming fiancé into my handsome, charming husband. Then, just a few months later, he'd become my abuser.

Now, he was gone, and I was relieved about that. But I still wasn't free. I was living beneath a cloud of suspicion.

I had saved McKenna and she, in return, had saved me. But she'd also implicated me in a way I hadn't been implicated before.

"Is this making you rethink your urban life?" I asked Tess.

"Oh, no way," she said. "I like being able to walk to the grocery store and work and mostly anywhere else I need to go, thank you very much. But this is nice, once in a while."

We sat down on a bench and looked out at the water.

I had called her on Sunday, and I'd told her everything about my relationship with Liam. It had been long overdue, and, like when I'd shared all the details with my mom, it had been both painful and embarrassing to relive them.

Tess had been quiet for a long time after I'd finished.

"Did you kill him?" she had asked finally. "I wouldn't blame you if you did."

"I didn't kill him," I had answered honestly. After seeing McKenna, I'd understood what had really happened.

"I always wondered," Tess had said. "Something was always off with him, Leah. I feel so bad. I wish I could have done something."

"You couldn't," I told her. But I wished she could have, too.

She had insisted on flying down to visit me at the end of the week. She would take a day off work and spend the weekend with me, she'd said.

"Are you excited to be starting your job soon?" Tess asked. We watched a gaggle of geese fly low across the water.

"Definitely," I said. "It's a relief that the truth came out."

I had, at least, managed to clear my name of that crime.

My former boss, Claudia, had called me on Wednesday, a couple days after she had been interviewed by Detective Jordan Harrison.

I still had her number saved in my phone, and apparently she had saved mine.

"Let me first say that I'm so sorry for what you're going through, with the loss of your husband." She swallowed audibly. "But, from what I understand, perhaps it's no worse than what you were going through before he died."

"Right," I said. "You're right."

"I owe you an apology, too, for the way I handled things last October. I was too quick to assume the worst of you, and I was wrong. The detective I met with, he told me Liam must have been the one who forged my signature and deposited that check."

"He did. I didn't know at the time. I thought I was going crazy. But that was the sort of thing he did."

"Listen, if you'd like your job back, we'd be delighted to have you. If you need some more time off, I understand. Or if you'd like to go elsewhere, I understand that, too. I will write the recommendation letter you deserve."

The truth was, I wasn't sure what I wanted.

Things I knew: I wanted to sell the house. It had only ever been my house with Liam, and I wanted something that was new and my own. Besides, it was an obscene amount of space for one person alone. Also, I knew that I wanted to work, and soon. I wanted to practice law again. I wanted to fill my days with writing and negotiations.

But, things I didn't know: where I wanted to live. I felt like I was ready to return to Connecticut to be near my mom, although I was only licensed to practice law in Maryland and Washington, DC, so starting over in a new state would mean a lot of paperwork, possibly studying for and taking another bar exam. I also didn't want the detective to think I was fleeing the state. Not when Liam's case was still open.

I thought I should probably hang around for a year or so. Next May, I hoped it would be okay for me to move away.

I had accepted Claudia's apology, and her invitation, and we had agreed that I would resume my old job on the third of June.

"I'll be honest with you," I'd told her. "I'm not sure how long I will want to stay. I'm thinking about returning home, to live closer to my mom."

"I hope you'll change your mind," said Claudia. "But I understand. You're not locked into anything."

It was cooler today than it had been earlier in the week. A breeze was tickling my arms, and the sun was dipping in and out from behind the clouds.

"Should we keep walking?" I asked Tess.

"Sure," she said, and we stood up from the bench and continued to wind along the lakeside path.

We didn't need to speak. It had been so long since I'd had comfortable, companionable silence with anyone.

I was grateful for the company, and the gesture behind her visit. Even though I had spent almost ten months pushing her away, she had never stopped being my best friend.

I was grateful, too, that she hadn't arrived last night, while my house was being torn apart by the police.

Detective Harrison hadn't been present, but I knew he was behind the search.

The police had hammered at my front door, only a few hours after the detective had left, and I'd had no choice but to open it and let them in. I was served with a warrant, which I read while sitting in my living room. One officer babysat me, while the others ripped through my house, looking, according to the paperwork, for a handgun, or any other evidence relating to the murders of either Liam Dawson or Zackary Hawkins.

The search had gone on for hours, and I'm sure they'd found much that was of interest. They'd unscrewed the hinges of the door to Liam's office, gaining entry to the secrets he kept inside. They had rummaged around in the basement, observing, I was sure, that some of my things were there in the bedroom and bathroom. They had broken into Liam's safe.

But they hadn't found a gun, nor any documentation related to one. They had filed out of the house, looking dejected, and leaving behind a mess I had spent five hours trying to clean. All they'd taken with them were my shoes. My sneakers. My Toms. Even my flats. I could only assume

I must have left a footprint or two outside McKenna's house. I was worried, but perhaps not as much as I should have been. The shoes I'd worn that night were long gone.

There was a dirt path that sprouted from the paved walkway around the lake. It led to a scenic lookout. Tess and I continued past it, which was fine with me.

It was there that I'd stood the night I had shot Zackary Hawkins. I'd walked around the lake, wearing my jogger pants with the zippered pockets and a baggy sweatshirt, peering wildly into the darkness.

There'd been a hint of relief as the pieces of the gun had plunked into the water, but I hadn't known if that would be enough to protect my freedom.

I still didn't know.

Clearly, Detective Harrison suspected me of something, or he wouldn't have obtained the warrant. He had my phone location data, but I knew that wasn't enough to link me to Zackary Hawkins's murder. He could only put me in that neighborhood the evening I'd made the call to 911. Not any of the other times I'd been by the Hawkinses' house. Not the night Zackary had died. I'd been trained, by Liam's control, to leave my phone at home.

If the detective had anything on me, I would be arrested, sitting in a cell, not strolling around a lake in the middle of the day.

I hadn't been lying to him yesterday when I'd insisted on having a lawyer present if he had any further questions for me. I didn't plan on speaking with him voluntarily anymore.

He could continue digging as much as he wanted. But I wasn't going to make it easy for him.

I wasn't weak, and I wasn't going to give up. Not again.

I had been through enough.

Detective Jordan Harrison

"How ya feeling?" I asked. I felt silly, because Detective Mallory Cole didn't acknowledge me in any way, and I knew that she couldn't.

Yesterday had been a rough day. It had been a rough week. Hell, it had been a rough month.

Every day since my partner was shot in the head had been rough.

Worse for her, though, than for me. I had to remind myself of that.

"I'm really struggling without you, Cole," I said.

I could picture her grinning at me. "I'm sure you are," she'd say.

I'd been certain that the warrants would get me somewhere. Judge Dorsey had signed off on the orders that would allow us to search Leah's house and McKenna's house, but not Aiden's.

"A law enforcement officer?" he'd said. "There's no probable cause to believe he, or his gun, was involved in either murder."

I'd pleaded my case, but that had done nothing but piss him off.

So, when a team of officers had been sent to Leah Dawson's house and another team to McKenna Hawkins's house to execute the warrants, I had driven straight up to Aiden Lyons's house in northern Baltimore County. If I couldn't search his house, at least I could speak with him again, while there were cops at his sister's.

He had invited me in, and we'd sat down at his dining room table while his wife lurked nervously in the kitchen.

"You own a firearm, isn't that right?" I'd asked.

"Of course," he'd said. "As part of my employment, with law enforcement, I have a Glock 17."

"And what caliber bullet does that take?" I'd asked, leaning back in my chair.

"That would be a thirty-five," he'd said.

"So, nine-millimeter?"

"That's right."

"And where is the gun?" I asked.

"Well, I'm not on duty right now, obviously," Aiden Lyons said. "It's locked in the gun safe in our basement. I'll grab it before heading into work tomorrow morning." He'd scratched his cheek, squinted at me. "Why do you want to know about my gun?"

"I assume," I said, "that you heard about the murder of a man named Liam Dawson. He was shot in his office in a very similar manner to the way your brother-in-law was killed."

"I did hear that," Aiden said. "I keep up with the news."

"Your brother-in-law was shot with a thirty-eight-caliber bullet. Liam Dawson was shot with a thirty-five-caliber bullet. You have access to a thirty-five-caliber gun. It couldn't be a match for the weapon used to kill your brother-in-law, but it could match the weapon used to kill Dawson. A stranger, supposedly. It's interesting," I'd said, rubbing my chin, "that's all."

Aiden had watched me for a long time. He knew exactly what I was suggesting.

"I can't give you my gun," he said. "I'm sure you understand. It's government property. But what I can do is follow you to your station. I can wait while your tech takes a look at it, sees if it fired the bullet that killed Liam Dawson."

He either had no idea what his sister had done, he was throwing her under the bus, or he knew that she hadn't used his gun.

But I needed to dot my i's and cross my t's, so I agreed with the plan.

He followed my government-issued car in his own government-issued car. I called Julian Klein from the road. "If I bring you a gun right now," I'd said, "can you take a look and tell me if it could have fired the bullet that killed Liam Dawson?"

"I can take some measurements, run some tests," he'd said. "I'll see what I can do."

Aiden Lyons had waited out front, until what he'd probably known all along was confirmed.

His gun hadn't been used to kill Liam Dawson.

By that point, I'd heard from the officers executing the search warrants that no gun had been retrieved from either Leah's house or McKenna's house.

Early this morning, the results of the footprint analysis had come back. The prints on McKenna's patio didn't match any of Leah Dawson's shoes, which were, incidentally, also size 8.5. The most common shoe size, of course.

These felt like the final nails in the coffins of these cases, and I had never missed my partner more.

"I talked to the wives again on Wednesday and Thursday," I told

Mallory. "I got a lot more out of them." I undid the buttons at the wrists of my sleeves and started to roll them up.

"There was domestic violence there. There was coercive control. Call it what you want, both of them were suffering. Zackary Hawkins made his wife quit her job. Liam Dawson got his wife fired. These women were forced to look a certain way, act a certain way. Liam was tracking Leah's cell phone. It seems that she was living in a basement bedroom that locked from the outside. We found some of her things there. He was violent toward her, she admitted that. She was planning to leave, the day he was killed. She had packed a bag. She was ready to go."

There was a commotion in the hall. Someone shouting. Someone running. I waited for it to die down.

"The obvious answer is that each woman shot her husband," I said. "But I couldn't prove it. I've got no physical evidence of that. I've got no witnesses. Leah Dawson's cell phone didn't leave her house the night Liam Dawson was shot in his office. I've got nothing tying Leah to a nine-millimeter handgun, and I've got nothing indicating McKenna had access to a thirty-eight caliber.

"What's interesting, though," I continued, "is that McKenna Hawkins's brother owns the type of gun that was used to kill Liam Dawson. But it wasn't a match. It seemed promising, but it was a dead end. Two different guns were used to kill the men, and we can't find either of them."

I pushed myself up from the chair and began to pace back and forth beside Mallory's bed.

"What's also interesting is that, while the women deny that they know each other, Leah Dawson had been in McKenna's neighborhood before. She made an anonymous call to nine-one-one about a domestic disturbance at the Hawkinses' house, the night before Zackary Hawkins was killed. She told me she was walking through the neighborhood and heard a fight. She said the woman sounded scared and she felt bad for her, considering her own situation."

I paused at the end of Mallory's bed, planted my feet, and rolled my neck from side to side. I couldn't remember the last time I'd gotten more than a few hours of sleep.

"It's not just that," I added. "McKenna has been in Leah's neighborhood, too. After Liam's murder, she was there."

I'd received the additional phone records the previous night. They'd been my last hope, after the warrants had been a bust. I'd combed through them quickly, noticing that McKenna's phone had pinged in Leah's neighborhood a single time, the afternoon after Liam Dawson was shot. It wasn't exact enough to place her at Leah's house. But it was close. And, it still didn't mean it was the only time she'd been in the neighborhood. It was just the only time her phone had accessed a tower while she was there. Location services hadn't been enabled on McKenna's cell phone. She had likely turned them off, trying to take back a modicum of control and maintain a little privacy from a spouse who was always watching.

Would it be enough?

My heart pounding, at half past ten, I'd abused the privilege of possessing the cell phone number of Assistant State's Attorney Marcia Cohen.

"Tell me it's enough," I'd told her, after I'd filled her in on my theory, on the evidence I had. "At least we can get this before a grand jury."

Sometimes a silence, a pause full of nothingness, said more than words.

"Sorry, Harrison," Cohen had told me. "If you had the guns, if the footprints matched, maybe . . ."

I studied Mallory's face. She looked listless and faded, and it hurt my heart. I pictured her the way she used to be, vibrant and alive as a sparkler. I thought about what she would say to me. What would she say about these cases?

I continued to pace.

"This is what I think," I told her. "Picture this. Leah is out for a walk, just like she said. She sees or hears a domestic disturbance at McKenna's house. She calls the cops for her. The next day, Zackary Hawkins is at work, and Leah pays a visit to the house. She wants to check on the woman. She wants to make sure she's okay. They get to talking. They make a pact. Leah agrees to kill McKenna's husband, and McKenna agrees to kill Leah's. That night, Leah shoots Zackary. Then, it's McKenna's turn.

She scopes out the house, waits for her opportunity. She follows Liam to work, and she shoots him."

I chewed my lip. "The question is, why? Why do two perfect strangers do that for each other?"

I glanced out the window across from Mallory's bed. The siren of an ambulance screamed as it swung into the hospital's parking lot.

"Maybe it's the only way they can think to get rid of their husbands, without being so obvious. Hard to say for certain."

I knew they would never tell me.

It was also looking like there was no way for me to prove it. Not without the guns.

I knew it was time to talk to my lieutenant about closing the cases. He wouldn't want to. Not yet. But it looked like that was where things were headed, and I wanted him to know.

I returned to my chair. I reached for Mallory's hand, and I gave it a squeeze. I thought about what had gone on in that house last month, when Mallory had rushed in, trying to save that woman from her husband. We'd been too late to help her, another victim of domestic abuse, and my partner had nearly died in the process.

Perhaps these women had committed the perfect crimes. Perhaps these men were better off dead.

When we didn't know who did it? We kept looking. We never gave up. When we knew who did it, but we knew we couldn't prove it? To keep trying was pointless. On to the next case.

Besides, was it not justice this way? I felt it in my core that Mallory Cole would tell me it was.

I gave her hand one final squeeze and stood up.

"See you later, Cole," I said, standing beside her bed. "Next big case, you'll be out there with me."

I ducked out of the room.

TWO WEEKS LATER
THURSDAY, JUNE 6

McKenna

Amelia, my old friend from residency, and I sat in the reception area of the law firm of Granderson & King, waiting for our appointment.

We had met for coffee last week, to catch up, and to discuss the possibility of starting a pediatrics practice, and I'd told her about what had happened with Zack. I had left out many of the details but had given her the general idea. I'd married Zack after residency. He had become controlling and abusive. He had been shot from outside our house. As far as I knew, the case remained open and the police didn't know who had killed him.

Amelia had apologized profusely for what I'd been through.

"I know it's a lot of baggage," I'd told her. "I understand if you don't want to partner with me anymore."

"Oh, that's okay," she'd said. "As long as you didn't kill him." She'd laughed, then looked embarrassed.

I had assured her that I hadn't shot my husband, and our plans to open our practice had continued.

Neither of us was familiar with the process to form a business, and a friend of Amelia had referred her to an attorney named Claudia Granderson, whose office was in downtown Baltimore. Amelia had called to schedule a consultation for us.

"The conference room is available now," the receptionist said, standing up from her desk. "Sorry about the wait. I can walk you there, and Claudia will be in shortly."

"No worries," I said, standing up from the ivory armchair near the office's front door.

We followed the receptionist down the hall, declined her offers of coffee or water, and sat down in front of the conference table.

Amelia's leg bounced beneath the table, shaking it gently. "I'm so nervous," she said. "I don't even know why. I've never needed a lawyer before, for anything."

"I'm sure there's nothing to worry about," I told her. "I bet there will just be a lot of paperwork for us to complete. No big deal."

I wasn't sharing Amelia's nerves. After what I'd been through, a meeting with a lawyer, even launching my own medical practice, wasn't enough to cause a blip in my pulse.

Things had quieted down in the investigation into Zack's death, and I could only assume the same was true for that of Liam as well. When the group of police officers showed up at my house the Thursday before last, with a warrant to search for a gun or any other evidence that might link me to the death of my husband or Liam Dawson, I'd been understandably upset. I had been fairly confident that they wouldn't find anything, but watching them tear through my house, opening up and tossing aside the contents of all the boxes I had carefully packed up for donation or in preparation for my planned move had not been fun.

I didn't know what had spurred the sudden search of my home. They had already looked through it, with my permission, after Zack was shot. Why did they think they would find something now, when they had not been able to immediately after his death?

After speaking with Aiden, it had made sense. He had called me from the car, on his way home from the police station, he'd said. Detective Harrison had been to see him. The detective had been intrigued that Aiden owned a gun of the type that had been used to kill Liam Dawson. That meant that my—and Leah's—fears were confirmed. The detective was no longer just looking at me for Zack's death. He was considering whether I'd been involved in Liam's murder. Which meant, I could only assume, he was considering Leah for Zack's.

Aiden had turned over his service weapon voluntarily and let them test it to ensure that it wasn't a match. He'd not asked me any questions. He was smart enough to understand that some things were better left unsaid.

The police hadn't found the other gun, the one that mattered. It was still resting snugly beneath the soft earth, tucked below the loose patio stone that was no longer loose. I'd secured it with a dollop of instant concrete, from a fortuitous tub I'd located in the garage, drying around the edges, cracked and dusty. It was left over from some house project Zack had undertaken shortly after we'd moved in. He'd stalked through the house, muttering and sweaty, in an undershirt and jeans, *working through home inspection items,* he'd said, referring to the report of recommended repairs we'd received after our offer was accepted. It had been strictly for show—he'd ended up calling in contractors to fix everything. Zack wasn't handy. But I was. I was impressed with the way the stone rested flat and flush with the others. I still pushed the outdoor sofa on top. Eventually, I'd have to dispose of the gun completely, I supposed. Perhaps I'd ask Aiden to take care of that for me, to make it disappear without a trace, in the same mysterious manner in which he had obtained it.

I was aware that what lay beneath the stone would keep me at the house. My impending move was no longer impending. As long as that gun was there, I would be, too.

Leah Dawson had been right. I'd been foolish not to realize how quickly the police would see the similarities, the connection, between us.

I had not heard from the detective since the search of my house had come up empty. I hoped that they would be closing both cases soon. But I knew that they might not. Detective Harrison might let the suspicion linger over us, like a foul odor, for the rest of our lives.

Which, I supposed he had a right to do. We were guilty. But we were also victims.

We were survivors.

I should have felt badly about what I'd done. But, when I awakened gasping in the middle of the night, it wasn't from nightmares about putting a bullet through Liam Dawson's head. I'd been feeling Zack shoving me to the ground. Seeing Liam grab Leah's hair, push her toward the stove in their bright and pretty kitchen. The fear, the helplessness, the shame that I felt, that Leah must have felt tenfold, was stronger than the guilt. Pulling the trigger had scrubbed that away. I'd only done what needed to be done. I'd done what she had done for me.

There was a tap at the conference room door before it swung open with authority. A tall Black woman swept in. We stood to shake her hand.

"Hi, Amelia. Hi, McKenna. Claudia Granderson," she said. "So, I understand you ladies are looking to open a medical practice?" She was not a person who had time for pleasantries.

"We need to lease space. We need to form a corporation. We need articles of organization." Amelia laughed. "Well, you tell us what we need. We've no idea, actually."

"My pleasure," said Claudia.

She spent the next hour going over all the steps we would need to take to launch our medical practice. Amelia furiously scribbled notes in a notebook she'd brought with her.

"We want to move forward as quickly as possible," said Amelia, glancing at me. "How do we get started?"

Claudia stood up from the table. "I can have a retainer agreement sent to you today. As soon as you sign and pay the fee, we can begin drafting everything."

"That would be great," I said. I could feel my excitement rising. Just a few weeks ago, I was hopeless and unemployed. It was hard to believe I might soon be a partner in my own medical practice.

"Let me walk you out," said Claudia.

We followed her out of the conference room, back to the reception area. A woman was pushing the glass office doors open, the key to the women's bathroom dangling from her right hand. Her dirty blond hair was tucked back in a bun. She wore navy ankle pants, a floral blouse, and tortoiseshell glasses I'd not seen on her before. She froze for several seconds at the sight of me before she recovered and dragged her eyes away from mine.

"How perfect," said Claudia, gesturing toward her. "This is Leah Bailey. She works closely with me and could be assisting with drafting some of your documents."

So, she had changed her last name back, just like me.

It had been the final vestige of Zack's control.

"This is Amelia and McKenna. They are retaining us to start their own pediatrician's office," Claudia was saying, but I could barely hear her.

"Nice to meet you," Leah said. She stepped forward to shake Amelia's hand, then mine. To touch her, it was like waving a hand through a ghost, her palm and fingers icy from the office's aggressive air-conditioning. She was inching away, trying to escape. She didn't want to speak to me.

I wondered whether she would tell her boss she couldn't work with me. She wouldn't be able to tell her why.

I could see it in her face before she moved past us, into the depths of the office. She was still anxious being around me. I'd shined the light of suspicion upon her, which had otherwise not been there. She was still nervous.

I was, too. But, even with the suspicion, wasn't this preferable? Maybe we would be arrested. Maybe we would end up in prison. But hadn't we been there all along?

At least, for now, we were free.

As time passed, as suspicion dwindled, as it seemed less likely that either of us would be arrested, I hoped she would see what I'd done the way it was intended to be seen. I hoped she would see I had returned the favor.

I had never fired a gun before. There'd been no practice round. But there wasn't time for practice. It had to be now. It was kill, or be killed. Kill, or watch her be killed.

I focused on his center body mass—the largest part of his body. That was where, I'd learned in criminal procedure class in law school, police aimed when trying to eliminate a danger.

I couldn't help myself, but perhaps I could help her.

It seemed almost deafening, the sound when the gun fired. I watched the bullet meet its target. Though, instead of his chest, it ripped through his head.

I wasn't good with blood. Not my own. Not anyone else's. It always made me feel faint, but I couldn't faint now, so I didn't, even though there was quite a lot of blood. The man's head had burst in an eruption of blood and brain.

I stood, frozen in place, watching him fall. Rain streamed down my face. My breath caught. My heart was a bass drum, announcing a rapid beat, steady and reverberating.

I lifted my arms, as if I'd been directed to do so by the police, as she came into view, letting her know that I wasn't going to hurt her.

The police weren't here, but they might be soon. It was time to go. It was time to escape.

I had helped her do just that. I felt that in my core. I had ended something that was sinister and dangerous. Something that was becoming violent, that might have become deadly one day soon.

272 | NORA MURPHY

I knew, because I was living it.
It was her turn.
I spun, and I ran.
I hoped that one day, it might be mine.

ACKNOWLEDGMENTS

This book would not be a book at all if not for the help and support of many people.

Thank you, first, to my brilliant agent, Helen Heller. I have been honored and thrilled to work with her. Her unending brilliance and thoughtful suggestions have continued to astonish me. Without her vision and experience, this book would be a barely recognizable shadow of itself, and I'm eternally grateful.

Thank you to my talented editors, Catherine Richards and Trisha Jackson, and to their respective colleagues at Minotaur Books at the St. Martin's Publishing Group and Pan Macmillan. Thank you to Nettie Finn for her continual support. Thank you to my sensitivity reader, Johanie Martinez-Cools. In addition to being incredibly visionary, encouraging, and astute, my editors and their colleagues have been simply lovely people to work with. I couldn't have asked for a better team.

Thank you to my law professors and mentors for the important work that they do, and who helped broaden my understanding of the issues on which *The Favor* just barely touches.

Thank you to my parents. Thank you for all of the things you've given me—the list is never ending—including my (very expensive) education, and instilling in me a love of reading, to which, really, I owe everything, and which continues to inspire some of life's greatest joys.

To my sister, Amy, and my best friend, Theresa, for their support, distraction, and listening ears as I reached for my dreams and complained more than was fair, while navigating life as a new and working mom.

Of course, thanks to you, Reader. I'm so honored that you chose this book.

Finally, thank you to my husband for your encouragement and unconditional support, for believing in me more than I believed in myself. And, at last, to our son. I will never forget, as I was writing *The Favor* on my phone—the only way you let me write—while observing you pull yourself around the room, just beginning to learn to crawl, you touched the screen and highlighted and deleted the entirety of the text, replacing it with the letters, "aq." Thank you for everything except that. And thank you to the Undo button, which for several panicked and breathless seconds, I forgot existed. Everything that we do is for you, Brooks. I love you more than a person should be able to love another. May you always be empathetic and kind. May you love to read as much as I do. It will take you places. I promise.

AUTHOR'S NOTE

Dear Reader,

The abusive relationships in which Leah and McKenna found themselves are unfortunately all too common. In fact, my experience with the practice of family law and my legal studies have made clear to me that domestic abuse is not just common, but endemic, to the point that many women we know and encounter on a daily basis have suffered or are suffering from such abuse. Statistics from the Centers for Disease Control and Prevention (CDC) show that one in four women have experienced sexual violence, physical violence, and/or stalking by a current or former partner or spouse.[1] It carries many different labels—domestic violence, domestic abuse, intimate partner violence—and the physical toll from such violence can be enormous and irrevocable. Data suggests that approximately one in five homicide victims are killed by an intimate partner.[2] Women of color are killed by men they know at even higher rates than white women, yet their deaths often receive less attention by the media.[3] The mental effects of intimate partner violence are immense and long lasting.

Factors like low income, low self-esteem, and low academic achievement are linked to a greater likelihood of intimate partner violence,

---

1. "Preventing Intimate Partner Violence," CDC, https://www.cdc.gov/violenceprevention/intimatepartnerviolence/fastfact.html.

2. Ibid.

3. "When Men Murder Women: An Analysis of 2018 Homicide Data," Violence Policy Center (September 2020).

but abuse also occurs in many relationships marked by high levels of education and affluence. Professional individuals possess specific skills and expertise, which may afford them special access or credibility. Such professionals may be able to professionalize abuse—to carry out abuse that is unique and dangerous, through the use of skills and access provided to them through their careers and training. For these types of relationships, financial and psychological abuse may be more common than physical abuse, sexual abuse, or stalking.[4] Thus, it may be more hidden, more difficult to prove.

While Leah's and McKenna's situations are not unique, perhaps the manner in which they finally escape is. Many people looking at their situation, and at those of women like them, might think: Why don't they just leave? But even when it is viable, even when a woman has the support and resources to leave, abusers tend to take extreme measures to prevent their victim from leaving.[5] They cling to control at all costs. Often, it is a threat of separation that precipitates a murder.[6] Even if a survivor shares her truths with others, she may fear not being believed. This fear may be intensified if her abuser is a professional individual, a pillar of the community, highly educated, and highly credible. If she is married to her abuser, and must seek a divorce, she is likely to be revictimized through the judicial process. She'll have to file a complaint for divorce, have her abuser served, and, if he does not cooperate, if the case is not resolved outside of litigation, she may have to face him in a courtroom. She may have to testify about what she's been through while he sits feet away, watching, listening.

Intimate partner violence can debilitate us. Our friends. Our sisters. Our mothers. Our daughters. Our neighbors. Or, a stranger, just as Leah was to McKenna, and McKenna to Leah. We must work to understand them. We must support them. We must support each other. We must support ourselves.

---

4. Kara Bellew, "Silent Suffering: Uncovering and Understanding Domestic Violence in Affluent Communities," *Women's Rights Law Reporter* 26, no. 1 (Winter, 2005).

5. "Why Do Victims Stay?" National Coalition Against Domestic Violence (NCADV), https://ncadv.org/why-do-victims-stay.

6. Ibid.

If you believe that you or someone you know is struggling with intimate partner violence, please consider the following resources:

United States
National Domestic Violence Hotline
National Dating Abuse Helpline
National Sexual Assault Hotline
National Suicide Prevention Lifeline
National Resource Center on Domestic Violence
Futures Without Violence: National Health Resource Center on Domestic Violence
National Center on Domestic Violence, Trauma & Mental Health

Canada
Shelter Safe
Ending Violence Association of Canada (EVA CAN)
Families Canada

United Kingdom
Refuge
AARDVARC

Australia
1800RESPECT
Family Relationship Advice Line